Ghostly Protector

(Ghostly Encounters #3)

Stacy McKitrick

Mythical Press * Dayton, Ohio

MYTHICAL PRESS * DAYTON, OHIO
www.mythicalpress.com

Cover designed by Maria Zannini of Book Cover Diva
http://bookcoverdiva.blogspot.com/
Edited by Michele Stegman and Stephanie McKitrick
Formatted by Enterprise Book Services
http://www.EnterpriseBookServices.com/

Published in the United States of America
Print ISBN 978-1-7331762-2-4
First Edition

For Dr. Matthew Rendo

Thanks for thinking I'm a big-time author!

Chapter 1

Her name reverberated with the swish of the wipers as Adam drove through the darkened Chicago streets.

Ev-ie. Ev-ie. Ev-ie.

He hadn't thought of her in years, but now she was all he could think about.

Ev-ie. Ev-ie. Ev-ie.

All because of those stupid pictures. Pictures of *her.* Pictures he'd buried. Not deep enough for a two-year-old it seemed.

Of course, if he'd thrown the damn pictures away, he wouldn't be in this position. His head would be clear and focused on the job ahead. But just the thought of tossing the photos had felt like tossing a piece of his heart, so he'd kept them. In his wallet. Where they couldn't remind him of the best and worst day of his life. And it had worked. Until tonight.

Ev-ie. Ev-ie. Ev-ie.

He pounded his forehead with the heel of his palm. *Get out of my head!* Someone was counting on his help tonight and a muddled brain only made things difficult. If not risky.

Adam parked in front of the apartment building, behind the medical examiner's van. Oh great. In every case he'd been assigned, he'd never arrived after the M.E. It figured he would tonight. After a deep breath, he turned off the wipers and killed the engine. Right on cue, the skies opened up and what had been a light rain became a downpour. Drops pounded on the roof and quickly turned the view through the windshield into some kind of abstract painting as the street lights blurred into one another. He wouldn't be able to make it to the entrance without getting soaked.

Because Heaven forbid something go right this weekend.

He reached inside the center console for a pair of gloves and found an empty box instead. Shit. Had he grabbed a replacement back at the station? He tossed the empty to the passenger footwell, leaned over to the glove compartment, and prayed as he pushed the button. Hey, lookee there, a fresh box of gloves. Maybe his luck was turning.

As he straightened holding the box, a spasm sliced across his back. Damn it. He stretched out the kink. Should he be happy he'd been woken with the call of another dead body at one a.m.? If he hadn't, he'd still be sleeping—or trying to sleep—on his couch, where he'd be warm and dry, but not exactly comfortable. But when his sister had called earlier from the Chicago bus stop—instead of her home in Springfield—announcing she was getting a divorce when he didn't even know she was having marital problems, what was a big brother supposed to do? Make her sleep on the couch? And what about her daughter? Yeah, it was only reasonable to give them the bed. If they were going to stay for any length of time—and it appeared they would—he would need a decent couch. Preferably one that turned into a bed. Otherwise, he might end up in traction.

He placed the full box into the console, punched his hand through the perforated top, and grabbed a pair of gloves. Bracing for the cold September rain, he quickly exited the car and dashed to the covered entrance. Lightning lit up the sky and thunder crashed barely a moment later. He flinched as the ear-shattering boom echoed off the buildings. Lights inside the foyer flickered.

Although the crime scene was in a public space, he didn't need to go inside dripping. Adam shook the rain from his trench coat and ruffled a hand through his wet hair. That should be good enough. He snapped on his gloves, opened the door to the foyer, and greeted the current occupants. "Boy, that's some storm, isn't it?"

The two officers inside—most likely waiting to be released—merely nodded, but Detective Celia Delavau, his partner, or rather mentee, looked up from her smartphone and strolled over to him.

The petite Jamaican had been an outstanding officer. Her compact size was no impediment to the havoc she could wreak if pushed. But now she wanted to be a detective. And he'd been the lucky one assigned to mentor her.

He fisted his hands. This mentoring job was more than inconvenient. It was a pain in his ass. Oh, he liked her well enough, but before he was saddled with mentoring a new detective, he'd been a solo act. For good reason. Now his captain thought he'd be a good teacher. Him. A teacher. Wouldn't that require being a good detective first? Just because he solved all his cases didn't mean jack shit. He'd never solved one on his own and he probably never would. But it wasn't like he could share *how* he solved his cases. They'd stick him in the loony bin.

And now he arrived on the scene not only after the M.E. but after *her*, too. All because his two-year-old niece had emptied his wallet.

"What took you so long?" Celia gave him that look. A look she'd used numerous times whenever she was frustrated. A look she must have perfected to appear fearsome. A look he needed a name for. The whites around her eyes practically glowed as they were a stark contrast to her dark skin. Yeah, sure, he should have made it here before her. He lived in the city, she did not. But they weren't exactly best buds and he didn't feel the need to explain himself. Especially since he was in charge.

That's right. He was in charge. Not her. He relaxed his hands.

"I'm here now. What do you have?"

"Spencer Elliott, a white male in his early thirties, was found by the mailboxes. M.E. is inspecting the body, but suspects the vic was hit with something heavy, like a crowbar or tire iron, so he contacted Forensic Services. No murder weapon on the scene, though. Do you think I can take lead on this one?"

This was the first time she'd asked. Were four cases enough to set her loose? Hell if he should know. He couldn't exactly use his experience as a base, although the sooner he got rid of her, the sooner he'd be on his own again. But would that be fair to her if he set her loose too early? Or let her have a case he could probably solve without the extra help? "Now how would it look if I gave you the easiest case to solve?"

She scrunched her forehead. "How is this easy?"

No way she hadn't noticed the cameras. He pointed to the ceiling.

Celia glanced at the small black globe. "Oh. That. Fake. Meant as a deterrent only."

"What?" Adam glanced at the entrance and the elevators. "How about security?" Although, he should know the answer to that. Hadn't he just walked in without any assistance? He opened the door to the garage. There wasn't any kind of keypad or lock on the door, either. Shit. He could have parked in there and avoided the rain.

"Zilch," she said. "There's nothing to stop anyone from entering or going up to the apartments. And apparently, not everyone knows they're fake. If I lived here and I found out, I'd be pissed."

Adam had nothing in his apartment building to keep people from coming inside, either, but then his building didn't have a view of Lake Michigan and his apartment rented for maybe a tenth of what these went for. "Is that what happened here? A disgruntled tenant? You got witnesses?"

"Not really. According to the officers on the scene…" She tapped her smartphone and read from it, "The building manager, Mr. Tony Fiori, heard an argument. When he came out later, he found the vic like that. He called 9-1-1."

"So no video and no witnesses." What did she know that he didn't? "And you think you can solve this case on your own?"

"I'll admit, I don't use voodoo like you do, but I can do this."

Adam stepped back. "Voodoo?" In all the years he'd been solving murders, no one had ever claimed he used voodoo. A crystal ball, sure, but voodoo?

"Or witchcraft. I haven't figured you out yet."

Okay, she was just guessing. Still… He smirked and headed toward the body.

Elliott was wearing blue flannel pants and a blue T-shirt so bloody it obliterated whatever band or saying was printed on the front. His slippers had come off during a scuffle or push, but the blood splatter on the mailboxes and the puddle on the floor suggested his head had been bludgeoned with something substantial. The medical examiner was snapping pictures of the gruesome head injury.

"I take it he's a resident of this building?" Adam asked.

Celia nodded. "He lives, or well, lived on the top floor."

He pulled out his pen and notebook from his coat pocket. She might be comfortable taking notes on her smartphone, but he preferred doing it the old-fashioned way. A way that didn't depend on a battery. "Where does the building manager live?"

"Over there." She pointed across the foyer to a door marked with the numbers 101, which was to the right of a door marked MANAGER.

"Anyone else live on this floor?"

"No. The garage takes up the south wing, and the north wing consists of the building manager's apartment, an apartment that the owners can reserve for guests, which is currently empty, and a huge rec room that leads to the pool and picnic area between the wings."

"Owners?" He stopped writing in mid-stride and looked up from his notebook. "So this is a condominium, not an apartment building."

Celia scrunched her eyebrows. "What difference does that make?"

"Maybe nothing. Maybe everything. It means everyone who lives here is part owner." And why no security? Anyone who could afford these units certainly wouldn't balk at the price. Adam turned back to the body. "Why does he look familiar?"

The M.E. stood with his arms wide. "Watch out. Detective Fox's gut is getting ready to tell us who did it."

The two officers chuckled. Adam waved them off and played along. "Will you stop? I need at least an hour."

That turned the chuckles into laughs.

Better to have them think was just freakishly good than learn the real reason. He liked his job and wanted to keep it because it gave him the best opportunity to help.

"You probably recognize him from the television ads or billboards," Celia said. "He's a lawyer with the ACE Team. Ashe, Callahan, and Elliott."

Oh, *those* ads. Yeah, he'd seen them and joked with his fellow detectives about the name. Just a bunch of lawyers who thought high about themselves. Except Elliott's face was the only one shown in the ads. "Is he married?"

"Not according to the building manager. But he has a roommate," she said.

A roommate? Why would a successful lawyer need a roommate? Or was it more like a girlfriend? Guess he'd find out soon enough. "Anyone check his condo yet?"

She grinned, but there was no joy behind it. "Just waiting on you."

Was that another dig on his tardiness? Gah! He couldn't wait to be a solo act again. Of course, if he did a good job with her, he'd probably get another mentee. And if he did a bad job he'd look like a schmuck. So, good job it was. He could only hope for a break between mentees. A nice, long break.

Two large elevators, the kind that could hold furniture, sat back in the foyer and faced the entrance. He punched the up button. Two doors marked as stairwells flanked each side of the elevator cars. While waiting for a car to arrive, Adam opened the north stairwell. Stairs led up only. He opened the south stairwell. Stairs led up and down.

"Anyone check the basement?"

"Officers did. It's clear. There is access to the lower level of the garage from there. And access to the utilities. Although, that's the only door that's locked. Building manager opened it up for the officers. It was also clear."

Lightning and thunder struck again. And the foyer lights flickered…again.

"How old is this building?" he muttered as he shut the stairwell door.

"I don't know. Why? Does it matter?"

Of course she'd heard him. The woman had exceptional hearing. Another reason he'd like to be free of her. "No, but should the lights flicker like that? The street lights didn't flicker."

A bell announced the arrival of an elevator car. The doors opened slowly, squeaking in protest.

"Oh my God. It sounds like a Wookiee."

"Like a what?" she asked.

"A Wookiee. You know, Chewbacca from *Star Wars*?"

"Never watched them."

That figured. Did they have anything in common? He held the doors open for Celia out of habit, really, but one she apparently didn't appreciate as she remained locked in place. Instead of apologizing, he entered the car, but Celia still didn't budge. "What's wrong?"

"Do you think we should ride it?"

Oh for Pete's sake. He removed his hand from the opening. "If you want to take the stairs to the…"—he glanced at the panel—"twentieth floor, be my guest. I'll wait for you."

She stepped inside before the squeaky doors closed. He nearly laughed at the sound. All he could hear was Chewbacca.

Adam pushed the button marked 20. "I've never seen you afraid of an elevator before."

"It's not the elevator I'm afraid of. But if the power goes out…"

He hadn't thought of it like that. And it was a valid fear. "You don't relish being stuck in one with me? Is that it?"

"I don't relish being stuck. Period. So what's with the suit? It's not usually this messed up. Did you sleep in it?"

He looked down at his pants. Sure, he'd wear his suits for a few days before changing. He couldn't afford a whole closetful of the things. And surprise! He was a tad more wrinkled than usual. But then his niece had decided to use his coat and trousers as a blanket, after she'd dumped the contents of his wallet all over the living room floor.

Including Evie's pictures. Damn it.

If he'd had a clean suit to wear, he would have changed, but he'd turned his dirty laundry in too late to pick up on Friday or even Saturday. If he admitted any of that, Celia would only ask more questions. "Didn't make it to the cleaners."

She snorted. "You actually have them cleaned? Where at? Wrinkles Are Us?"

"Ha-ha," he dead panned. "You should try out at the comedy club. There's more to the job than wearing a pressed suit."

"Like owning a crystal ball?"

Ahhh, that explained the voodoo and witchcraft remark. Some of the guys had joked about Adam's success rate and implied he was some kind of psychic. "You heard that, huh?"

"You're the talk of the department."

"They're just jealous of my gut feeling." He patted his stomach for effect.

"Gut feeling? Sure. One of these days you're gonna have to tell me what you do when you go wandering off on your own."

"You mean my job?" Another fine example of why he needed to be a solo act. How many more excuses could he come up with to be alone? And how many would Celia believe? If only he could tell her what he could do. But telling her would mean telling others and, well…that wasn't happening.

Before Celia could question him more, the Wookiee doors opened to two condo units across a hallway that connected the wings. Dull, brown carpet showed minor tread wear. He followed Celia down the north wing. Elliott's condo was at the end.

She rang the doorbell and lightly knocked on the door.

"It's after two in the morning. No one's going to hear that." Adam pounded on the door. "Hello! Police! Anyone home?"

"Hold on! I'm coming," a woman said from inside the condo.

He turned toward Celia. "What do you think? Girlfriend? Wife?"

"Building manager said Elliott wasn't married but has a roommate."

"Maybe she's his girlfriend." Lover's spat? That could get messy, not to mention dangerous, which was all the more reason to solve this case quickly.

"Maybe. Or maybe she's just a roommate."

The door opened and all thought vanished from Adam's mind. The woman standing in the doorway was a vision. An angel with the darkest hair, darkest eyes, and brown skin to compliment it all. Just like Evie had, all those years ago.

Damn it! Those stupid pictures were messing with his head. But still…she sure looked like Evie. What were the odds that he'd finally found her?

Zip. Zilch. It was the pictures. It had to be the pictures. They were stuck in his head.

"May I help you?" The woman, wearing what appeared to be an overcoat over a pair of leggings and a T-shirt, turned those heart-warming eyes his way. Her face squinted in confusion.

He pointed to the coat. "You going somewhere?"

"No. What's this about?"

He unclipped his badge. "I'm Detective Adam Fox with the Chicago—"

"Adam?" Her face smoothed out and she smiled. "Oh my God! It is you. It's me. Evie."

No way. No. Way.

Maybe he was psychic after all.

Chapter 2

This was a dream. It had to be a dream.

Adam pinched his leg. He was still standing in the hallway. Still staring at Evie.

He'd never gotten her last name so he wasn't able to track her down and find out why she'd left him high and dry. Or rather, beg her to give him another chance, because he'd been needy like that back then. At eighteen, he'd been sure she was the one.

But holy shit. Evie. His Evie. In person and more beautiful than he thought possible.

"You two know each other?" Celia asked, giving him that white-eye look again. Yeah, that's what he should call it. White-eye.

Shit. He wasn't giving up this case. Not now. So he played it cool, when everything in him wanted to grill Evie on what the hell happened that night. "Sort of. Six Flags Grad Night. Right?"

"I didn't think I'd ever see you again." Evie placed her hand over her heart. "How did you find me?"

Her smile transported him back to that amusement park. *Get a grip, Fox!* She'd soon be grieving, or fake-grieving if she was guilty of murder. He straightened, focusing on his job. But damn, was she wearing pig slippers? How adorable was that?

Celia held up her badge. "I'm Detective Delavau. We're here about Spencer Elliott. Are you his girlfriend?"

Adam's stomach clenched. Sure, he'd thought the roommate might be Elliott's girlfriend, but now that thought worried him.

Evie's smile evaporated as she stared at Celia's badge. "Girlfriend? No, we're not involved that way. I'm just his friend. His roommate. Evelyn Harper. I'll go get him."

All right-y. Not the girlfriend. Although that shouldn't matter. Shouldn't matter at all. She could still be guilty. "Sorry for the late hour. If you don't mind, may we come in?"

Evie nodded and stepped aside. She shivered and hugged the coat around her curvy body as she led them to the couch.

Even Celia shivered. The condo was far from being cold, which meant only one thing. A good thing, too. Once he got some privacy, he'd get his answers and close the case. And if Evie was innocent, maybe he could find out what happened that night eleven years ago. There had to be a good reason she left the way she had. Unless it was because he was white and she wasn't. Although, she had a white roommate, so that couldn't be it. Had he said something inappropriate? Shit. This was going to drive him nuts until he got some answers.

"Make yourselves comfortable. I'll go get Spence."

"That won't be necessary," he said before anyone had a chance to sit. "I'm sorry to have to inform you, but he's dead. We found his body downstairs."

"Dead? What? No. There has to be some kind of mistake. He's—" Evie rushed down the hall, calling out Spencer's name.

Her confusion seemed real enough. He'd know her involvement in a few minutes, though.

After she didn't get a response, she stumbled back into the room and dropped into one of the two, blue, over-sized chairs.

And what a room. Adam hadn't even noticed it until now. The building might be in need of maintenance, but this condo didn't. The wood floors shone and the colorful throw rug in front of the seating arrangement complemented the blue in the chairs and matching couch. The whole ensemble faced two huge windows, as if they were the focal point or works of art. Neither was covered. And if it wasn't the middle of the night with the indoor lights on, he might have been able to see the lake or part of the city. Right now the windows reflected like two huge mirrors.

"How?" Her voice soft, she hung her head.

Celia sprang into action. She sat on the couch, taking the side closest to Evie. "That's what we're trying to determine. Do you know what he was doing downstairs?"

He joined his partner and sank into the softest couch his butt had ever encountered. Whoa. If he had a couch like this at home, he wouldn't mind sleeping on it.

"Downstairs?" Evie looked up and shook her head. "No. I woke up when you knocked. Oh God." She covered her face as the sobs racked her body.

Her pain reached out to him and he stood. What the hell was he doing? He'd nearly given her a hug.

Celia grabbed some tissues off the side table and handed them to Evie.

Now was his chance to be alone. He mimicked drinking to Celia and she nodded. Thankfully, the kitchen was out of sight of the women.

Time to get his answers and solve this case.

"Spencer," he whispered as he opened a cupboard that contained canned goods. "Are you here?"

"Did you just call me?"

Adam spun around. Ahhh, Elliott in the flesh—so to speak. Long and lanky, wearing the same pajama bottoms and a non-bloody T-shirt. Metallica—that's what was on front. No matter how grisly someone was killed, their spirit appeared unharmed. Thank goodness for small, ghostly favors. "There you are. Where are the glasses?"

"By the fridge," Spencer whispered back and his eyes widened. "Wait. You can hear me?"

Adam almost chuckled. No matter how many ghosts he'd encountered, their expressions at being seen and heard bordered on the comical. Spencer was no different. Adam opened the cupboard by the refrigerator and found the glasses. "Yes. And see you, too. As long as no one else is in sight. And you don't need to whisper. No one else can hear you." He pulled out a glass. "Let's get you moved on, okay? Who killed you? A disgruntled client?"

"Killed?" Spencer nearly screamed the outburst. "What makes you think someone killed me?"

Adam nearly dropped the glass. If the ghost didn't know he'd been murdered, why was he still sticking around? Then Adam nearly slapped his head. How the hell was he going to solve this case? And did that mean Evie was a possible suspect?

Shit, shit, and triple-shit.

* * * *

Spencer hovered in the kitchen. His feet should be cold since he was no longer wearing his slippers and the tile floor always made his feet cold. But since he wasn't actually touching the floor—or anything for that matter—there was no chill. No warmth, either, now that he thought about it. He wasn't feeling…anything.

Nothing externally. His heart was still giving him pain. Pain at wondering if Evie would be okay without him. Oh, she'd be fine financially—he'd made sure of that—but mentally? She had no friends. Just him. And now he was gone.

Sort of.

But killed? The detective had to be smoking something. That might explain why he was wearing a wrinkled mess. Even his blond hair was going every which way, like he hadn't bothered to use a comb. Who left their house looking like that?

Fox turned on the tap and filled the glass. "Come on. You can't seriously believe your death was an accident. The evidence clearly shows that someone hit you."

"What evidence? My head wound? No one killed me. It was an accident." Couldn't the detective see he'd been pushed against the mailboxes? Sure, there was more blood than Spencer would have guessed, but head wounds tended to be bloody. Didn't they?

Fox took a deep breath and smiled. "Then you tell me who accidentally hit you with a crowbar or tire iron, took the weapon, and left you to die?"

A tire iron? Connor didn't have a tire iron on him. He didn't have anything on him. "No, that doesn't make sense."

"Then tell me what would make sense. You apparently argued with someone. Who?"

How did Fox know Spencer had argued? Had Tony heard? The building manager was more than just nosey, but if he had heard, he never checked it out, so he could have heard anyone. Anything. Hell, Tony could have killed him. But why would he? Something wasn't right. But until Spencer learned more, he wasn't about to get anyone into trouble. "I didn't fight with anyone. I went down to get my mail and accidentally bumped into some guy as he was leaving. He shoved me. But he didn't have any kind of weapon on him. Certainly nothing large like a crowbar or tire iron. It was an accident. He was mad and pushed me. That's all."

Which wasn't a total lie. Connor was mad and had pushed him. That was the last thing Spencer remembered before leaving his body as a ghost.

A damn ghost. Hell, he'd never believed they existed. Did everyone who died turn into a ghost or had he just been lucky?

Fox scrunched his forehead. "If you were certain it was an accident, how come you're still hanging around here? Why didn't you move on? It's been my experience only spirits with unresolved issues stay behind. Murder is usually at the top of the list."

Move on? To Heaven? How could he move on without knowing if Evie was going to be okay? Was that why he was a ghost? Maybe that was a good thing. If Connor was actually responsible, had committed murder against his own brother, what would stop him from coming after her next? Spencer eyed the glass. He couldn't leave Evie now. He just couldn't.

Fox looked at the glass of water as if he'd gotten a revelation. "Ohhh, your roommate. But you can see she's fine. So why haven't you moved on?"

"You just said I was killed? Why would I move on?"

Fox frowned. "So you think she did it?"

"No, I don't think she did it!"

Glasses rattled in the cupboard. Damn. Were they having an earthquake? Or had the detective bumped against the counter? It had to be the latter. Since when did Chicago have earthquakes?

Fox raised his free palm. "Take it easy. I'm here to help. But if she didn't kill you, who else could have?"

Spencer shook his head. He would not throw his brother under the bus, no matter how much he hated the guy. Not until he had some proof. But where would he get that? At the murder scene?

He wished to be in the foyer and found himself there. Wow. It worked. The only other time he moved like that was after he'd died and wished to be back in his condo. Well, more like wished to see Evie. And presto, he'd appeared in her bedroom.

An officer entered the lobby through the front door holding a large zippered bag. "Is this what you want, Doc?"

A body bag? Holy shit. Spencer turned around. He had to inspect that head wound before they bagged him up. He hadn't bothered to examine his body before. The blood alone had kind of freaked him out.

Was *still* freaking him out. So much blood. On his shirt, the mailboxes, the floor. But could a tire iron have done that damage? He moved in for a closer look. There was a hole just above his ear. And was that brain matter? Ugh. He gagged, backed away, and felt behind his ear.

There was no hole there now. No pain, either. And his hand didn't come away bloody—thank God. Guess that detective was right. Someone *had* hit him. No way could one of the mailboxes create that kind of damage. But Connor didn't have any kind of weapon on him. So who hit him? And why?

* * * *

Evie took the tissue from Detective Delavau and wiped her eyes. "Thank you."

First the shock of seeing Adam after all these years, and then finding out Spencer had died, her body didn't know how to react. Light one moment, heavy the next. It was like riding a roller coaster without the fun parts.

Her cell was on the coffee table. When did it get there? She'd taken it to her room when she went to bed. Oh, probably because Spence didn't want her to hear the notification when he left the condo. But why would he leave?

"This is quite a home," the detective said, gazing at the reflective windows.

"It is, isn't it? Spence loves…loved it here." And he would never be able to see out those windows again. She dabbed at her leaky eyes.

"How did you manage to become his roommate?"

Evie froze. Manage? Like she couldn't afford to live here on her own? Well, she couldn't, that was true, but why did the detective have to infer that? "Spence and my brother, Lee, were best friends. After Lee died, Spence offered me a place to stay. I think Lee's death affected him just as much as it affected me. So I agreed, as long as I paid him rent. And I do. Every month." Which had caused an argument. One she'd won. She lowered her head. *Oh, Spence.* "Guess I'm going to have to find my own place now, huh?"

"I'm sure you'll have some time. His estate won't be settled until his murder is solved."

Evie jerked upright. "Murder? Someone *killed* Spence?" And here she'd thought he'd just died from some freak accident. "Who? Why?"

"That's what we're trying to determine."

It didn't make sense. Everyone loved Spencer. He was a great guy and would help anyone in need. And he'd been downstairs? With his killer? Why?

Adam returned with a glass of water and handed it to her.

As she took the glass, her fingers brushed against his. That familiar spark rushed up her arms and she reveled in it. He must have felt something, too, since he held onto the glass. "Thank you?"

"Sorry." He released his hold and returned to the couch.

Eleven years later and he still affected her. Eleven years later and he was here. In person. Investigating a murder. Spencer's murder. Gosh, they didn't think she killed him, did they? She took a sip to wet her suddenly dry mouth.

Detective Delavau pulled out her cellphone and started typing. "Did you leave the apartment any time tonight?"

It *was* an interrogation. And why wouldn't they look at her? She was the roommate. Once they realized she couldn't possibly have any reason to kill Spencer, they'd leave her alone and concentrate on someone else. The person who had killed Spence. Evie shook her head. "I was inside all day. Went to bed at ten. You two woke me up. You can check the recording if you want."

"What recording?" The detective glanced back at Adam, who only shrugged.

"From the camera." As the two detectives just stared at her, the "d'oh" moment passed. "Sorry. Beside my door. There's a camera on my door frame." She picked up her cell and opened the app. "I get notifications whenever there is movement in the vicinity."

"Like the Ring doorbell?" Detective Delavau leaned over. "You said it records?"

"Yeah. Whenever there's movement and for about ten seconds after." Evie pointed at the display. "You can see all the notifications. Press on any that has a movie camera icon next to it."

The detective took the phone and accessed the videos from Saturday. At 11:37 a.m. it showed Spencer leaving the condo. At 11:51 a.m. he returned holding the mail. The 4:58 p.m. video showed the pizza delivery man. Spencer had opened the door and accepted it. At 12:17 a.m., the video showed Spencer leaving the condo in a rush. No robe, just his pajamas. The next video was of the two detectives.

"You didn't leave the condo all day?" Detective Delavau asked.

"That's me. Homebody. I haven't gone out since…" Evie thought for a minute. "Thursday?" Yeah, that was right. She'd gone to the library that day.

"I don't recognize the name brand of your system," the detective said.

"It's not well-known. The owner was a client of Spence's. He liked that it was small enough not to be noticeable, so he had it installed."

"Can the system be rigged?" Adam asked.

"Rigged?" Oh God. Evie took a deep breath. Panicking would do no good. She was innocent. She had nothing to worry about. Right?

"You know, disabled. So it wouldn't record anything."

"I know what you meant." But why did he have to ask? He didn't think she was guilty, did he? "The system reports any malfunctions, like when it loses the connection. That isn't controlled here or on the app. That's wherever the data is being processed. So yeah, I, or Spence, could have disabled the camera, but the system would have sent out a notification that it lost the signal. And as you can see, there's no such notification. I can't delete the notifications, either."

Adam smiled. Like he was relieved. That she was in the clear. *Thank you, Spence!*

"Do you know of anyone who had problems with Spencer?" he asked. "Did he argue with anyone in the building?"

"Not that I know of. He really wasn't the arguing type."

"But he was a lawyer," Adam said.

His confused expression caused her to chuckle. "A paperwork lawyer. You know, wills and contracts? He rarely went to court."

"How about family? Any bad blood there?"

"Spencer has no close relatives. His father died years ago and his mother this past spring. He has some cousins in Ohio, but that's all I know." It was one of the reasons their friendship worked so well. She was his only family and he was hers. Now? Now she had no one.

"I am sorry for your loss." Detective Delavau handed over a business card. "If you can think of anything that can help us, please call."

Evie took the card and escorted them out. Disappointment settled in her chest as Adam didn't hand over his own card. Although, if she really needed to contact him, she could just call the police station. And maybe when this was all over, she would do just that. So she could explain what happened that night.

To think she'd been this close to him all these years and not once had they run into each other. Of course, that meant she'd have to leave the condo more often than she did.

But Spencer was dead. Murdered. Whatever was she going to do now?

* * * *

Adam slipped his notebook inside his pocket as Evie shut the door. She had an alibi, that much was clear, and he couldn't be happier. But other than that? This case was not going the way he'd thought it would.

Had his luck finally run out? With every case he'd been assigned, the ghost knew their killer. Elliott was hiding something. Adam was sure of it.

Like guessing would do any good. Could he handle not having a perfect record at the precinct? Maybe. He certainly didn't have a perfect record of helping a ghost move on. Some of them were rather stubborn. But could he actually solve a case without a ghost's help? That was the question.

"So who did it?" Celia asked.

Adam almost laughed. She'd never been so bold to ask outright before. "What makes you think I know? We got nothing from her."

"Because you were in the kitchen a long time. What did you find out?"

He was surprised she hadn't told him what he'd whispered while in there. Maybe her hearing wasn't as exceptional as he'd first thought. "Nothing. It just took me awhile to find the glasses."

"Uh huh." She reached the elevators first and pushed the down button. Thankfully, the car was waiting on their floor and the Wookiee doors opened right away. He followed her inside and pushed the button for the lobby.

Since it appeared he'd have to use his non-existent experience to solve this case, maybe it would be a good one to give Celia. "You really want this case?"

Her eyes widened. "What? Why? Because you know her and think she's guilty?"

"Whoa. I don't think she's guilty. You saw the evidence. She never left the condo."

"True, but that doesn't mean she's not involved."

He didn't like the sound of that. But then they were trained to not discount anyone. Not until the proof said otherwise. "So, you don't want it?"

She practically snapped to attention. "I want it."

He prayed he wouldn't regret this decision. "Okay. Then you're in charge."

"Just like that?"

"Just like that."

"Because you know her."

He fisted his hands. "Eight hours over eleven years ago doesn't make one person know another that well." Although, at eighteen, he'd felt he'd known her forever. Until she'd left him without any warning. "Just consider it a test. I need to know how much I've taught you. Or haven't taught you."

Hell, if Celia could solve this murder, then she was definitely ready to be on her own. And if it took her awhile—and why wouldn't it—he would be in the clear for not solving it swiftly. Win. Win.

She smiled. "Okay. So first thing Monday we contact Elliott's place of work and see if he filed a will. Which I assume he has. He *was* a lawyer."

"Why a will?" Adam asked as if he was testing her, but really, he was curious. He hadn't thought about checking out the will.

"Elliott must be loaded if he lives here. His beneficiary could have motive. It'll give us someone to question."

Check the will for suspects? Now why hadn't he thought of that? Because he never had to think of it, that's why.

Celia checked her watch. "Looks like I'll be able to salvage Sunday after all."

"Not true." He might be a lousy detective, but he knew how to make it look like he was gathering evidence. Which they'd have to actually do this time. "Since the cameras don't work, we need to question everyone in the building."

Her shoulders sagged. "I should have known that."

Adam smiled. Maybe he could teach her after all. "But we don't have to start right away. It can wait until later. Like after church, if you do that sort of thing." Which meant he could still get a few hours of sleep and take Sabrina to brunch like he'd promised. However, that didn't mean he had to go back to his apartment, and his awful couch, to sleep.

There was a better option out there and he planned on using it.

Chapter 3

Adam let himself into the Tudor-style home, hung his wet overcoat on the hook by the door, and collapsed onto the couch in front of the large—and currently cold—fireplace. After kicking off his shoes, he propped his head on one armrest and his feet on the other. While this couch was shorter than his own, it was way more comfortable. He could go upstairs and use the guest room, but then he might never leave. He had that brunch date with Sabrina, after all.

He'd texted her earlier letting her know he would be home later. That's if she got the text. When he tried calling, he'd gone directly to her voicemail, as if she had turned off the phone. Or maybe it had just died. In that case, it would be her own fault if she worried about him. He'd done his part.

"I see you still refuse to use the guest bedroom." Zane Grey, owner of the home, strolled into the room carrying a mug, the contents steaming. He wore a plush, royal blue robe over a set of matching pajamas. Adam didn't own pajamas. Heck, he usually wore nothing unless it was cold, and then it was an old pair of sweats and a T-shirt. Which would probably be his pajamas until Brina found her own place. But even Spencer Elliott didn't have a matching set on when he died and he'd been rich.

"The guest bedrooms are for guests. You told me I wasn't a guest." Actually, Zane had said that Adam was like family ever since the guy had practically adopted him once he discovered

Adam could see ghosts, too, but hey, if Adam couldn't tease the old guy, who could he tease?

Zane shook his head as he placed the mug on the table and settled into the chair catty-corner to the couch. At the age of 67, he would be considered by some a silver fox with his salt-and-pepper hair and trim build. But the man refused to date. Losing Allie two years ago still affected him. Case in point: it was close to four in the morning and the man was up, if he'd slept at all. "No, I said you were family. I also told you not to sleep on the couch, and yet, here you are. Still wearing your suit coat, I might add. Shouldn't you hang that up?"

Ah shit. Adam jumped to his feet and removed his coat. He probably should have hung it up, not that it could look any worse sleeping in it. He draped it on the coffee table. "You'd rather I get my sleeping bag? Because—"

"Stop. I'm not going to have this argument again. So why aren't you at home? Has George become…difficult?"

Adam fell back onto the couch, not sure he wanted this conversation, but wouldn't lie to his friend, either. "George is fine. Still patiently waiting for Emily to pass." And he probably had a long wait. His wife wasn't even sick. But did George care? Of course not. Sometimes ghosts just couldn't be helped. "The reason I don't want to go home…" *Spit it out, just spit it out.* "Sabrina and her kid are there." Who said confession was good for the soul? Didn't make him feel any better. "Think I could live here awhile? I promise to use the guest bedroom."

Zane leaned forward and smiled. "Sabrina's visiting? For how long? Will I finally get to meet this sister of yours?"

Adam tensed. His nightmare could become reality if that happened. "No offense, but no. She doesn't know."

"Know? About me?"

"About you. About what I can see." And he wanted to keep it that way.

Zane crossed his arms. "You never told your sister? Why?"

"Why would I? She would have blabbed it all over school." And to anyone who would listen to her. It was bad enough his parents thought he was crazy.

"You were children then. She's an adult now. Don't you trust her?"

"Secrets don't stay secrets if you tell people."

"But you told me."

"Only because you convinced me to." Zane had been the one to approach Adam. Suspected what Adam could do. Could see, actually. Introduced him to HeSMO—Helping Spirits Move On—a semi-secret organization Zane had founded that gathered ghost seers like him. And he'd wanted Adam to join. Knowing he wasn't alone, that he wasn't a freak, was the only reason Adam had confided in Zane.

"So how long is Sabrina visiting?"

"Indefinitely? She told me she left her husband. That's all I know right now." He rubbed his face. He was so far out of his element. If only they had parents who could be counted on. Who cared. But neither parental unit gave a damn about him and Sabrina. Why they bothered having kids at all was a mystery he'd never solve.

"Did you know her marriage was failing?"

Adam lowered his hands. "No. I haven't heard from her since she had the baby. Everything seemed fine then. But now I don't know what to do. What to say. I'm thinking she needs some space, and me living with her in my tiny one-bedroom apartment isn't giving her that."

"Or maybe she doesn't want space. Maybe she wants her brother. Ever think of that?"

To be truthful, he hadn't thought of that. Damn it. He wouldn't be like his no-good parents. He wouldn't abandon her, too. "Fine, I won't live here, then. But I'm not telling her. So don't bother visiting. You hear?"

"I hear just fine. I don't wish to make your life harder. Only easier."

And of course easier was telling everyone his secret. Easiest way to get fired. To be ridiculed. Adam propped his right ankle on top of his left knee. "So what are you doing up? I didn't wake you, did I?"

Zane picked up his mug. "Couldn't sleep, so I made some tea. Want some?"

"I'm good. Thanks." He needed to change the subject; stop this awkwardness with Zane. "I got another case. Unfortunately, this one says he doesn't know who killed him."

"He wouldn't be the first ghost we've come across who didn't know how they died."

"Yeah, but not on a case I'm assigned to."

"Ahhh, so you feel your reputation is at stake, is that it?"

"I wouldn't go that far. But why ruin a good record? So I gave the case to Celia."

"Is she ready?"

Adam shrugged. "I don't know. But she asked for it. Why not give it to her?"

"You don't think that's cheating?"

"Cheating? What I do for a living is cheating." He certainly couldn't claim experience. He'd never solved a murder case without a ghost's help.

"How is it cheating when you solve the crime? You don't plant the evidence, do you?"

"You know I don't." Plant the evidence? How insulting! "But I have an advantage over everyone else. An advantage they don't know about."

"Only because you don't tell them."

Adam grimaced. Apparently he hadn't changed the subject after all. He stood and paced about the room. "What do you think they'd do to me if they knew? Huh? Not only would I be laughed out of the department, all my cases would be suspect. I can't have that happening."

"But you did nothing wrong. You gathered the proof, did you not?"

"Only after I was told who to investigate. I've never had to investigate a case to determine who the killer is."

"Never? You passed the detective's test, right?"

Adam stopped and placed his hand on his hips. "What's your point?"

"My point is that you're more than capable to do the job." Zane took a sip of his tea. "But if you need my help—"

"Are you kidding? How the hell would I explain you? Celia already suspects something's up with me."

Frowning, Zane placed the mug on the table. "Do you really think so little of me? I didn't mean openly. I meant discreetly."

All the muscles in Adam's body just...deflated. If he hadn't been standing in front of the couch, he might have plopped onto the floor. Instead, he landed on a soft cushion. "I'm sorry. I didn't mean to imply..." *Shit.* "You're my best friend. I think the world of you. But you're part of my secret. You understand that, don't you?"

"I do understand, Adam. I may not agree, but I do understand. So use me as a friend. Bounce ideas off me. You say the ghost doesn't know who killed him..." Zane motioned his hand for Adam to continue.

Maybe it wouldn't be so bad to bounce ideas. "No. He *says* he doesn't know. And maybe he doesn't. He seemed truly surprised to learn his death was not an accident. But he wasn't entirely truthful, either. Otherwise, why hang around?"

Zane smiled. "See? Already your detective skills are at work. Could he be protecting someone?"

Adam nearly slapped his head. He should have noticed before. Spencer Elliott was in love with Evie. And if he thought Evie was in danger because he knew who his killer was... "That's it. He's protecting Evie."

"Evie?" Zane raised an eyebrow. "It's unusual for you to use first names. Unless... Would this Evie be the same Evie you knew once before?"

Ah shit. That's what he got for spilling his guts to a friend. A friend who had a computer disk for a memory. "She would. She's his roommate."

"Roommate or more?"

"She called herself his roommate. Said that Elliott, that would be Spencer Elliott, was like a brother to her. Nothing romantic."

"But Spencer doesn't feel the same?"

"I don't think so. I think he's in love with her."

"Does he know your past relationship with Evie?"

"Probably. It was mentioned when she realized who I was. But it's not like we hugged or anything."

"Mmm, mmm."

"What's that supposed to mean?"

"If Spencer has an attachment to her and suspects you have an interest, it could turn ugly."

"I don't have an interest. Okay? She left *me*, remember?" But had that stopped him from thinking about her ever since his niece pulled out those photos? Nope. None, whatsoever. He was such a dope. And apparently this dope still had feelings for her.

Zane tilted his head back in thought. "How sure are you that she didn't kill him?"

"Pretty sure." Well, more like hopeful. He didn't want her to be guilty. "The door of her condo has one of those motion detector cameras and she never left the condo. Plus, she seemed genuinely shocked to hear he died."

"Just because she didn't do the deed doesn't mean she's not involved."

Which was exactly what Celia had implied after they left the condo. And she wasn't wrong.

Adam leaned forward. "Elliott is adamant she didn't do it. Even got a little angry when I asked if she had killed him."

"Angry? How angry?"

"Nothing substantial. A few glasses rattled, that's all." Which was more than most new ghosts exhibited, but then he'd always done his best to keep them from being angry.

Zane stood, his face scrunched in worry. "He made the room shake? That's not good."

Usually, Adam would agree. "I calmed him down before he went too far. No one noticed. Not even him."

"You better hope you can *keep* him calm. I don't relish the thought of another Aldridge incident, and you better nip this before it gets that far."

Aldridge had been one nasty ghost. Maybe if he hadn't been executed at his place of work, the building would still be standing and all those people would still be alive. Adam didn't care about the guilty ones so much, but the innocent hadn't deserved that kind of wrath. Would Elliott be just as bad? Without his cooperation, Adam wasn't all that sure he could nip anything.

If only he *did* have a crystal ball.

Chapter 4

Evie emerged from her bedroom and approached Spencer's office. It was ten a.m. and she was still in her jammies. Heck, it was a rare day she'd slept in late as it was. Why was grief so…exhausting?

She entered the office and shivered. Sunlight shone through the uncovered window, but did nothing to warm the room. It was practically freezing. Ever since she'd been told about Spencer's death, she'd been nothing but cold. Did grief do that, too? Take away the heat? Or maybe it was just time to turn on the furnace, but that would be admitting summer was over and she wasn't quite ready to admit that…yet. At least the day wouldn't be dreary looking, even if it wasn't warm. If only it would raise her spirits. But would anything do that? Spencer was gone. For good. And she'd be homeless in a matter of days.

She shuffled over to the bird cage and uncovered it. "Good morning, Bailey. Why don't we get you some food?"

The African grey parrot scooted toward the door. "Spencerrrr!"

Evie jumped. He'd done the same thing yesterday and had startled her then, too. "Damn it, Bailey. Can't you see Spencer's not here?"

Spencer had been so proud to get Bailey to say his name upon entering a room, whereas she'd been merely annoyed. Because Bailey couldn't just say Spencer's name. Oh no. He had to shriek it.

But Bailey had never mistaken her for Spencer before, so why start now?

"Uh oh. Curse jar. Uh oh. Curse jar."

Another merely annoying trait Spencer had taught Bailey. Anytime she'd say shit or damn or fuck, he'd keep it up until she put a dollar in the Cookie Monster jar. Because Heaven forbid they'd put cookies in there. It got so bad that she made sure not to curse any other words in front of Spencer in case he got it up his ass to have the bird recognize those, too.

"Spencer is gone, Bailey. I can curse if I want."

Bailey spread his grey wings and flapped. "Spencerrrr here."

"Spencer is not here!" And now she was arguing with a bird. Was this what her life would be like without Spence? He'd been there for every bad moment in her life. The loss of her parents. The loss of her brother. He'd been such a good friend. Unfortunately, it was impossible for him to console her for his own damn death.

Pulling up the neckband of her sleep shirt, she dabbed at her constantly weepy eyes and stared at the bird. Maybe she was using the wrong tactic. "Bailey, cursing is good."

"Cursing bad."

"Noooo. Cursing gooood."

"Spencer say, cursing bad." Bailey lifted the latch and pushed the door open with his beak.

She clenched her jaw. He expected her to extend her arm so he could exit. Yeah, he knew how to open the door, but get out? During his one and only attempt, he'd damaged his wing. Hadn't tried again. Sometimes his memory was a good thing and she refused to extend her arm and give him what he wanted "And I say, if you want to eat, cursing is good."

The silence was unnerving. Not even a squawk. She went to close the cage door when he said, "Cursing good. Bailey eat."

"That's more like it." She extended her arm and Bailey hopped onto it. Now maybe she wouldn't have to stick a dollar in a jar for a trip she would never take.

She headed down the hall, proud she'd built up muscles in her arms so she could hold Bailey. It was deceiving just how much strength it took to hold the one-pound bird for any length of time. Spencer had laughed at her when he'd noticed she'd only used her dominate arm to carry the bird. Said she'd end up lopsided if she didn't switch it up. Afraid that might actually happen, she'd made an effort to use each arm equally. No one was going to accuse her of having lopsided arms. Not that anyone would notice now, would they? What a lonely life she led.

She walked around the dinette table and placed Bailey on the top branch of a fake, leafless tree situated in the corner. After grabbing an apple off the kitchen counter, she pulled a knife from the butcher block. The calendar on the wall stared at her, today's date even more so since it had a written note from Spencer to pick up his cleaning.

She wiped her face again as new tears fell. "Damn it, Spence. Why'd you have to die? And who the hell would want to kill you?"

She still couldn't believe he'd been murdered. Spencer didn't even handle criminal cases. Just wills and contract stuff. If someone had an issue with their will, it wasn't like they could come back from the dead and demand retribution.

"Bailey hungry." Leave it to the bird to snap her out of her musings.

"Sorry." She cut the apple, placed the wedges in his dish, and set the dish on the floor mat. There was also a shelf on one of the top branches, but experience had taught her that Bailey ate less messy on the floor. Usually. At any rate, she wouldn't get beaned in the head when he threw his food. Because he always threw his food.

The bird jumped down branch by branch until he landed on the mat and proceeded to peck away at the apple pieces. After putting the cutting board in the sink, she blindly grabbed a K-cup from a drawer and popped it in the Keurig. She inhaled. Ahhh, hazelnut. Today was a good day for hazelnut. Oh hell, it was a good day for coffee. She didn't relish looking for an apartment, but she couldn't very well keep living here. Someone from Spencer's family would eventually arrive and kick her out—especially after the will was read. She just wanted to beat them to the punch.

The doorbell chimed.

She groaned. Now what? She couldn't even look at her phone to see who was calling since she'd left it on her nightstand. Yesterday, everyone and their brother seemed to phone to pay their respects, especially when Spencer made the news. All she wanted was to be left alone. But if she didn't answer the door, they'd only come back. Or worse: keep pounding until she answered it. If only she could push a button and make them go into her voicemail. She probably had dozens of messages to return, but she could do that on her own time. A physical visitor was another matter. Better to get it over and done with.

"Be right there!" She rushed to the bedroom, blew her nose, and slipped her coat on as she headed back to the foyer. Her penguin T-shirt and leggings weren't exactly appropriate hosting apparel. Hell, she hadn't even left the condo since Spencer's death. Good old Spence had taken care of all his final arrangements. All she had to do was make a phone call to get the ball rolling.

Her phone! It was still on her nightstand. So much for checking who was at the door. It was what they made peepholes for anyway, right? She peeked through the hole and was instantly transported back to the best day of her life before it had turned into one of the worst.

Adam Fox stood in the hallway. She'd only known him by Adam; they never had exchanged last names. Or phone numbers. But then she'd thought they'd have time for that later. His eyes still reminded her of the morning sky after a storm blew through. He hadn't smiled the other night, but back when he was a teenager, his smile made those eyes even brighter. She didn't think it was possible he could be hotter than he was that summer night so long ago, but he proved her wrong there.

He knocked. "Miss Harper? Evie? Hello?"

Shit. How long had she been staring at him? She zipped her coat half-way and opened the door. "Hi."

Now he smiled and she was right. Brighter eyes. Of all the times to get a lady boner.

"Good morning. Is this a bad time?" He gestured to her coat. "Are you getting ready to leave?"

Spencer would have had a fit if she'd tried to leave the condo dressed like this and here was Adam assuming this was her everyday wear. She didn't know whether to be complimented or insulted. "No. I'm in for the day."

Every day until the funeral or she found an apartment to inspect. A place that would take parrots in case she was allowed to keep Bailey. The reading of Spencer's will couldn't happen soon enough, but she'd been told it would occur after Spencer's funeral. And apparently his body wouldn't be released for that to happen until the police were good and finished with it.

"May I come in? I'd like to ask you some more questions."

A cold draft blew past and Evie shivered. Damn. First the office, now the doorway. Could it be the air conditioning was on? "Yeah, sure." She motioned him inside. "Where's your partner?"

He walked past her and she got a whiff of his cologne. Or aftershave. Or maybe it was just him. Musky and yummy. Oh, it had been too long since she'd been with a man. And now Adam was here. After eleven years. Was he hoping to reconnect? She could go for that.

"Sick kid. Husband out of town. Do you normally wear your coat in the house?"

"I don't own a robe." She shut the door and glanced at her reflection in the side mirror. Holy shit. Her eyes were bloodshot, her nose rivaled Rudolph's, and hair that had escaped her braid was shooting every which way. And he assumed she was leaving the condo like this? What he must think.

As if that should matter. Because she had to be realistic. He was here to investigate Spencer's death, not hook up.

Why'd it have to take Spencer's death to finally find Adam? That just didn't seem fair.

"You okay there?" he asked. "You look a little lost."

She was a lot lost, but that was her issue, not his. "I'm fine. Still processing his death. Would you like some coffee?"

"That would be great. Thanks." He followed her to the kitchen and skidded to a stop when Bailey flapped his wings and squawked. "Whoa. That's a bird."

Evie laughed at Adam's surprised expression. "Actually, he's an African grey parrot. His name is Bailey."

"I don't remember seeing him the other night. Where'd he come from?"

"He sleeps in Spencer's office. Don't worry about him. He's mostly harmless."

He took a step back. "Mostly?"

"Just keep your hands to yourself and he'll leave you alone." No use warning him about his toes. Unlikely he'd be walking around barefoot. At least today. But would there be any tomorrows?

She hated they had lost all those yesterdays. He'd turned into such a handsome man from the cute boy she'd fallen for. His blond hair was trimmer, he'd grown a few more inches, and he seemed more solid, like he exercised regularly. While it seemed he wore the same wrinkly suit as before—something Spencer would never have done—he certainly filled it out nicely. Wide chest. Nice butt. He was probably married, though. And why wouldn't he be? He'd been a great guy eleven years ago.

On that sad thought, she opened the K-cup drawer. "What kind of coffee would you prefer? I have French vanilla, caramel vanilla, wild mountain blueberry—"

"How many flavors do you have?" He kept the dinette table between him and Bailey and maneuvered to a seat farthest away from the bird.

"Lots. But I do have some non-flavored ones." Those had belonged to Spencer. If it wasn't plain old coffee, it wasn't coffee to him.

"Huh. Surprise me."

"Wow." He was still doing it, even after all this time. Being perfect. For her. But could a seventeen-year-old really find their soul mate at an amusement park? If only she hadn't left him, and so rudely, too. She'd been sure he would have forgotten all about her, except he had remembered her the other night. Could that be a sign? Maybe he wasn't married.

"What, wow?"

"Oh, nothing. Spencer hated being surprised." He hadn't even been able to handle an impromptu lunch visit. She blindly grabbed a cup—ooh, southern pecan—and inserted it into the machine. "After you left the other night and I went through a box of tissues, I pulled this from my wallet."

She grabbed the old photos from the counter and placed them on the dinette table.

He sat as he fingered one frayed edge. "You kept them?"

"Yeah. What girl wouldn't keep a memento of a beautiful night?" Because it had been beautiful, until it turned ugly.

He turned toward her. "I'd hardly call it beautiful. You left me."

It was worse than she'd thought. He hadn't forgotten her. He hated her.

* * * *

Adam had gone over that night a million times, always wondering what it was he'd done wrong. She never came back. No goodbyes. No exchange of numbers. She'd just…left. And she'd known he'd been waiting.

"Not on purpose," she said. "Things might have been different if you didn't hear my phone ringing."

"I remember the phone call." He'd jokingly told her her purse was ringing since she didn't seem to realize her phone was going off.

Evie lowered he head momentarily. "I felt kind of foolish not recognizing my own ringtone, but to be fair, I'd never heard it ring before that night. It was a graduation present, so I'd only had it for a day. But I never meant to leave you that night. You gotta believe me."

He might, if her story rang true. "You never told me who called."

"Because I didn't think it mattered…at the time. It was my brother. He was at the gate to pick me up. Before I could tell him I'd find another way home, he'd hung up. So I decided to just tell him in person. Figured I had time since we were in line for ice cream. I really thought I'd be back."

"You saying he dragged you off without your permission?" What kind of brother did she have?

Evie shook her head. "No. Not at all. He told me our parents were in an auto accident and came to take me to the hospital. He didn't tell me on the phone because he didn't want me to be alone when he gave me the news. I guess I was in shock or something, because it wasn't until we were on the road that I remembered I'd left you. I begged Lee to return to the park, but he refused. Said there wasn't much time. And he'd been right. Any later and I wouldn't have been able to see them before they passed. I wanted to get back to the park after, but wouldn't have made it back before they closed. So I called the park to see if they could page you, but they wouldn't do it without your last name."

Wow. Talk about feeling like a schmuck. He should have known there was a valid reason behind her disappearance. But what eighteen-year-old didn't jump to conclusions? "I'm so sorry for your loss. If I had known, I would have been there for you."

Her smile bordered more on sad than joy. "You were, in a way. Hold on." She got up and dashed from the room. A moment later she returned with a frame, the front held against her chest. "You kept the best picture, I thought, so I drew it for myself. You've always been there for me."

She handed over the frame that contained a drawing of them kissing, like the picture he had buried in his wallet. And just like the other morning, his heart ached at seeing it. "You did this from memory? That's remarkable." More than remarkable, really, it was exquisite. The details were unnerving, and all done in pencil. "But wouldn't seeing this make you sad that we never hooked back up?"

She placed a mug in front of him. His coffee. "Yeah, I was sad that happened, but it's not like I could do anything about it. Remembering that night, before it turned bad, always makes me happy. It was the best night of my life...until..." She shrugged and returned to the kitchen. "I try to remember the good things. Otherwise, I'd just cry all the time. Wouldn't you?"

That she could say that when it most likely had been the worst day of her life, too, meant something to Adam. His heart thawed a little. Knowing he hadn't done anything wrong was a huge relief. "You know, I did look for Evies and Eves after that night, but never had any luck. But with your name being Evelyn, no wonder I struck out. I would have thought Evvy would be a nickname for Evelyn. Why Evie?"

"Evie isn't a nickname for my name. It's a nickname for my initials, E.V. Evelyn Violet. My dad thought Evelyn was too grown-up a name for a baby, especially since I was named after his mother, so he started calling me Evie and it stuck. But you tried looking for me? For real?"

"Yeah. Without success, of course." But now he was here investigating Elliott's murder and she was most likely involved. Unless he proved she wasn't involved. Elliott seemed sure, but how sure? Adam had more questions for the ghost, but first he needed answers—or rather, reactions—from Evie. And he prayed she'd react correctly.

* * * *

Evie placed the creamer and sugar on the table. Now that he understood her reasons, maybe they could finally hook up again. Contingent on his marital status. But she still couldn't bring herself to ask.

"At least I was able to clear the mystery of your name. And your disappearance. Again, I am sorry for your loss." Adam placed the drawing on the table, face down. "But I guess I better get to why I'm here."

Also contingent on Spencer's murder case. Why else cover up her best work? Or maybe he just needed to focus and she was a distraction? She sat catty-corner to him with her own mug. "Are they finally releasing Spence's body?"

"I don't know, but I can find out the status for you." He pulled out a pen and notebook from inside his coat and jotted down "Body" on a clean sheet of paper. Then he flipped to a page with lots of writing on it. "I have a few more questions, if you don't mind?"

"Go ahead. I want to help however I can."

"Do you know your building doesn't have functional security cameras?"

"Yes, isn't that the stupidest thing? Spencer was furious when he found out they were there as a deterrent only. I only found out when he installed our door camera, though, because I had asked him if there was security in the building why we needed it at our door. He said he did it for himself, but I know he wouldn't have bothered if not for me since I work from home."

Adam picked up his mug and took a sip, foregoing the creamer and sugar just like she did. "What do you do?"

"I'm a graphic artist. I create websites and stuff. Like logos, ads, that sort of thing. I don't have to leave this place unless I want to." And even then, she didn't leave for long. When a person lived with their only friend, why bother going out?

"Sweet. I guess it makes sense, since you seem to be an extraordinary artist."

"That's kind of you to say, but I'd only go so far as saying I'm good. Not extraordinary."

"You're extraordinary to those who can't even draw a stick figure." He chuckled. "Did you work for Spencer?"

"No. But I did do work for his firm. I designed their logo and website."

"Noooo…" His eyes widened. "You're responsible for the ACE Team?"

She laughed, something she was sure she'd never do again. "I am not. I tried to talk them out of that, but was overruled. And you don't argue with paying clients."

"I suppose you're right about that. Did Spencer get the job for you?"

"He suggested they use me. It helped that I wasn't as expensive as the others."

"Spencer was into contract law, right?"

"Contracts and wills, yes." She sipped her coffee. He could have found this information on the web. Maybe he *was* here to find out what had happened eleven years ago and now that he knew… Inwardly, she smiled.

"So how come he's in all those ads for the firm? They're not exactly aimed at people needing a will."

"Because he's a nice guy?" She cupped her hands around the warm mug. "The partners wanted someone to become the face of the firm. They didn't want the added expense of hiring an actor, thought it would look phony, and they were right. But Mr. Ashe and Aaron Callahan didn't want to have their face 'splattered all over the place.' Their words, not mine. Spence volunteered, even though he's not the typical lawyer who advertises. But he is a partner. Or was." Her eyes watered. "Damn."

He grabbed a napkin from the holder and held it out. "There's nothing wrong with being sad. He was your friend, right?"

"Yes, he was. My best friend." Okay, only friend. She took the napkin and dabbed at her eyes. At this rate, they would never stop leaking. She picked up her mug and took another sip.

Adam folded his arms on the table. "Did you know you're inheriting Spencer's estate?"

Inheriting? She nearly choked on the liquid and swallowed hard before it went down the wrong pipe.

"I take it you didn't know."

"No, I didn't know!" Aaron never mentioned that during their phone call. "It can't be a lot, though. Right? I mean, all his money must be tied up in the condo." But she wouldn't have to move. That would be great. She did like living here.

He leaned back and wrapped his hands around his mug. "He was a millionaire."

"On paper. Right?" When Adam shook his head, she dropped her mug. Luckily, it didn't have far to land and remained upright, but some of the contents splattered on the table. She grabbed a napkin and sopped up the mess. "Why would Spencer do that?" She hadn't meant to say that out loud, but apparently her mouth decided otherwise.

"You tell me."

Oh. Right. Because she was probably looking like their number one suspect now. Great. Adam wasn't here for personal reasons or to get her help on the case. All her hopes deflated. "Not much to tell. I was told they would read his will after the funeral. How did you find out?"

He lifted his notebook. "Murder investigation?"

"Right." She stared at her mug. The hazelnut wasn't working as she'd hoped. But then, she didn't think she was going to be arrested for murder when she'd made it, either.

* * * *

Adam couldn't stop staring at Evie. Her untamed hair, her flawless complexion, and that penguin T-shirt. Everything about her turned him on. Especially now that he knew she hadn't deserted him, hadn't left him on purpose. And he believed her story.

But man, he had to get a grip. He was here professionally and must act professionally. Anything else was unconscionable.

She couldn't be guilty. She just couldn't.

He must focus on the case. Without Elliott's help, Adam's inadequate abilities would be put to the test. Right now, Evie was the prime suspect, especially now that it seemed she had a big motive—money—and Celia was doing everything to prove Evie was guilty.

Whereas, he was going to do everything to prove she wasn't.

Since this was Celia's case, she'd told him to come here and continue questioning while she worked from home. Even gave him a list of questions to ask.

Most of the questions he'd already gotten answers to online, but Celia wanted to know Evie's reactions. And to be fair, Adam wanted to see her reactions, too. So far she didn't seem to be lying about anything, and she wasn't acting guilty. Two plusses in his world. But one big minus practically erased those: she knew the cameras in the foyer were fake.

But would Evie admit to such a thing if she were guilty? Man, he hated this case.

"I didn't kill Spence," she said. "I loved him. He was my best friend. And you know I didn't leave the condo that night."

Didn't mean she hadn't hired someone to do the dirty work. He wanted to believe her. Wanted to tell her he believed her. But what kind of detective did that? "Can you think of anyone who wanted him dead?"

She ran her thumb along the edge of her mug. "I wish I did. I'd only been to his office a couple of times. Everyone seemed to like Spence. He was a great guy."

"I'm sure he was." As she lifted her mug for a sip, he pictured those lips of hers on parts of his body. Which was a stupid thing to think because now his pants were growing uncomfortably tight and there could be a ghost getting a good view. He shifted in his seat and took a sip of his own coffee. The nutty flavor was quite tasty, too. "What kind of coffee is this?"

"Southern pecan. Why? Don't you like it?"

"No, I like it. Might get some for home." His crotch became a little roomier. Thank goodness. "What did Spencer do away from work? What did he do for fun?"

"Fun?" She chuckled. "Sorry. I just never associated that word with Spence. Besides watch football, he did play video games, if you consider that fun. Or rather, one game. Some online thing." Her eyes widened. "Do you think I need to let them know he died?"

"I wouldn't worry about it. How is he with the neighbors?"

"Fine, I suppose. He never complained about anyone."

"Do you know of anyone who might've wanted money from him?"

She frowned. "You just said he was a millionaire. Why would he be dealing with a loan shark?"

"No, no. You misunderstood. I'm not saying he owed someone, but that maybe someone was asking for a hand out and it got out of hand. You know, like a friend. Or a relative?"

He waited. Would she take the bait? Or stick with the story she gave earlier?

"I told you. Spencer doesn't have any close relatives. He has some cousins in Ohio, but he never visited them. And they didn't come out for his mother's funeral, which was a sticking point for him. As for friends, no one close that I know about. That's why we marked each other as the in-case-of-emergency contact."

They marked each other? "You don't have family in the area?"

"No. Mom was from South Korea. I've never been and her family never visited us. I'm not even sure if she ever communicated with them after she left the country with Dad. I know they didn't approve of her marrying a soldier, especially one who was Black. She never talked about stuff that would upset her, so I assumed it was upsetting to her. Dad has a brother who lives near Charleston. Close to the beach. We vacationed there almost every summer when Lee and I were kids—free place to stay, Dad would always say. But since my parents died, I haven't visited. Oh, my cousins asked me to move down there when they came up for Lee's funeral, but Chicago is home. I can't see living anywhere else."

He couldn't argue that point. One of the reasons he lived in the city, if not the only reason: it was home. Thankfully, his rotten parents had seen fit to move to Florida, so he didn't even have to worry about running into them. Like that was even possible. Look how long it took for him to run into Evie.

She cupped her mug and stared at the contents. "Anyway, Spence never mentioned anyone needing money. He never did anything with friends, so I assumed he didn't have any close ones. I suppose I shouldn't be surprised he left me something. He did seem to think I was his responsibility, although I wasn't. I *can* survive on my own. Basically have been. But to leave me that kind of an estate? And not tell me what he was worth? What the hell was he thinking?"

Adam didn't know how to take her response. She seemed clueless, but wouldn't someone guilty act that way? "He never mentioned his half-brother? Connor?"

"Spencerrr!"

Adam jumped. The bird had climbed up that fake tree and was practically eye-level. "He talks?"

"All the time. But he's usually quiet around people he doesn't know. I think he misses Spence. He's been acting like he's in the room and keeps shrieking his name."

If this parrot was like most animals, he probably saw the ghost. "Does he just repeat stuff he hears or can he hold a conversation?"

"A conversation? No, he doesn't work that way, unfortunately. He can repeat words you say to him and understand certain phrases through action and repetition. And he can put names to people and things if you tell him enough times. Think of him like a toddler learning to talk. That's about where Bailey will always be. He belongs to Spence, well, I guess he's mine, now. But Spence taught Bailey everything he says."

Damn it. Meant he couldn't ask the bird what happened. As if a bird's testimony would stand up in court. Of course, neither did a ghost's, but Adam always managed to get around that. "Did you hear the bird when Spencer left the other night?"

"No, but then Bailey was in the office in his cage, and the cage is covered and the door closed. Unless Spence was loud, Bailey wouldn't have heard him." She stared at the bird. "But Spence sure was in a hurry to get out of here. Don't you think?"

"He did seem…anxious." Certainly wasn't in a hurry to get the mail, since the videos proved he'd gotten it earlier. Elliott was lying and Adam needed to question him some more. Without getting him angry. Would that be possible?

She sat up, alert. "Could he have gotten a phone call and went downstairs to meet someone?"

"That's a possibility." And something he would ask the ghost. "He didn't have his phone on him."

"It might still be on his nightstand." Evie stood. "Come on."

He followed her down the hall. Elliott's room was the last one on the right. Curtains covered the windows—making the room dark—and she flicked on the light. The king size bed looked tiny in the huge room. A bathroom was situated to the left, beside a large walk-in closet. She entered like she'd owned the place and zeroed in on the nightstand. Bingo. Smartphone.

She picked it up and punched in a code.

"You know how to open his phone?"

"He gave me his code in case of an emergency. This is an emergency, isn't it?"

"Well, it's not like he's going to argue." Not with her in any case. Adam moved beside her as she brought up the phone log.

"Nothing. His last call was Friday. Damn it." Her shoulders sagged as if she'd been hoping the phone had held the answers to all her questions and had failed. She placed the cell back on the nightstand. "So what about this half-brother you said he has?" She shivered and hugged her coat closer. "I swear, there must be something wrong with the A/C. It shouldn't even be on." She headed for the door.

There wasn't anything wrong with the A/C. Just a ghost who apparently didn't want anyone talking about Connor. Adam pulled out his phone as if he'd just gotten buzzed with a text. "May I use your office? I need to make a call."

She looked over her shoulder. "Yeah, sure. It's next door. Help yourself. I'm going to check the thermostat."

He followed her as far as to the door to the study and waited until she turned into the kitchen and was out of sight. A moment later, materializing out of thin air and hovering near the kitchen, was Spencer. Adam needed to get his attention.

Chapter 5

Spencer hovered near the living room. Evie headed toward the dining room, which was where the thermostat was located, and Fox needed to make a phone call. A phone call. About who? Evie? Connor? And why was he interrogating her? He already knew she wasn't guilty.

Spencer paced, as well as he could without touching the floor. Should he listen in on Fox's conversation? It's not like he hadn't been listening to their conversation all morning. Who would know?

The detective might. He said he could see ghosts when no one else was around. Like he had the other night when they first spoke. So unless Spencer wanted his presence to be known, he'd just stay right where he was. In the living room. Doing nothing.

Damn it! What was that detective up to? And why did he keep asking about Connor?

Fox was still standing in the hallway, but staring at Spencer. Gave the follow-me gesture. Follow? Oh. There was no call to make, was there? Maybe the guy wasn't a genius at solving cases, but he certainly knew how to go about getting privacy.

Instead of floating through the wall, Spencer popped into the office. He kind of enjoyed moving around like that. Certainly made it easier to not run into Evie by accident, especially when she didn't see fit to wrap a towel around her after coming out of the bathroom.

Awwwwkward.

"So glad you could make it," Fox said as he closed the door.

"Is that how you always talk to ghosts? Fake a phone call?"

"Not always. Comes in handy, though."

"But how did you know I was here? You said you couldn't see me with her in the room."

"I can't, but I can tell when she feels you. And then there's Bailey."

"Bailey can see me? But Evie was there." Although…now that he thought about it, Bailey had called out his name whenever he'd entered the room regardless of Evie's presence.

"Doesn't seem to matter to pets." Fox strolled over to the window. "Nice view."

It was a nice view. Lake Michigan sparkled in the morning light. Spencer had offered this room to Evie as her own when she moved in, but she insisted he keep this as his office. Maybe she didn't like the morning sun shining in her eyes. Or maybe she'd felt like she'd disrupted his life as it was. As if having her live with him was an imposition. Far from it.

If anyone was an imposition, it was this detective.

"Why are you interrogating Evie?"

Fox turned around. "You know why. She became the main suspect after we found out you left her everything."

"But she didn't kill me. You know this. You saw, she never left the condo!"

"Yeah, but she could have masterminded the whole thing." Fox held up his palm in a stop motion, and as much as Spencer wanted to argue with the guy, he obliged the man. "Not that I believe it, okay? But we need to think realistically. What if she was involved?"

"But she wasn't."

"Spencer. Stop thinking with your heart. Think with that lawyer head of yours. Is it possible she knew you were leaving her everything?"

Hard to think with his head when everything to do with Evie involved his heart. But Fox was right. They had to prove she wasn't involved so that they could go after who was. "No. I told Aaron, Aaron Callahan, my partner, he witnessed my signature, not to breathe a word of it to anyone. He has the original, locked in his desk."

"Does his secretary have a key?"

"I doubt it. I'm sure his spare key is kept at home. Like mine is."

Fox pulled out a little notebook from his inside coat pocket and wrote something down. "Do you have a copy of your will?"

"Yes. It's at work. Locked in my desk."

Fox wandered over to the desk, his arms behind his back. "Are your work desk keys in this desk?"

"They are now, but they're on my keychain, which I always have with me when I leave the condo. The spare is in my dresser."

Fox spun around. "So she has access to it."

"No. I mean technically, yes. But she doesn't know about the key. And if she did and she took it, I'd know. It's taped to my sock drawer so I wouldn't lose it."

"Are you sure there isn't anyone else in your firm who could have told her about the will?"

O'Hara? No, that couldn't be right. O'Hara couldn't have known. And he and Evie were no longer a couple. Thank God! Spencer shook his head. "I didn't tell anyone, and Aaron wouldn't have betrayed my trust."

"Did she ever hint that she'd be desolate without you? Hint that she couldn't survive if anything should happen to you?"

Spencer snorted. "You may have spent one day with her eleven years ago, but you don't know her. She thinks having too much money is evil. And no, she never hinted at anything like that. She doesn't even know half of what I own."

"And yet, you left it all to her. Why? And why specifically mention your brother gets nothing?"

Seemed the detective actually had read the will. "Just because we share the same father doesn't mean shit. It certainly didn't mean shit to Connor, okay? And if I hadn't put that in, he could come back and claim I hadn't known about him. I didn't want that. As for leaving everything to her…besides feeling it was my duty to fulfill my promise to her brother, who happened to have been my best friend, I had no one else I could leave it to. No one who wouldn't waste what I took so long to build. Is that so hard to understand?"

"Did she know about this promise?"

"No. Lee asked me in confidence, just before he left for Afghanistan. And he didn't ask me to help her financially. He just wanted me to watch out for her."

"Did he know you were in love with her?"

"What makes you think—" Spencer shook his head. What was the point in denying it any longer? Wasn't like anything could happen about it now. "Well, if you can see it, I'm sure he could, too. But I never told him. Or her. She thinks of me like another brother."

Which he'd been okay with. It meant he would be in her life.

Fox looked at the desk as he walked around it. Not that there was much to see. A laptop. A small stack of mail. The pen Evie gave Spencer when he became partner. That was it. Fox stood behind the chair and faced Spencer. "Who did you go downstairs to see? Who shoved you?"

Spencer's moment of truth? Whatever. Better to throw his useless brother under the bus instead of the woman he loved. Because she hadn't killed him. He knew it. "Connor. He called from an unknown number and left a message. She didn't find it on my phone because I deleted it."

"Why?"

"Why else? I didn't want Evie to know about him."

"She goes through your phone calls often?"

"It's not like that. I usually have my phone on me, anyway. Or had. It was just a case-of-an-emergency kind of thing."

"So what happened with you and Connor?"

If only he had ignored Connor's call... But if he had done that, Connor would have just come upstairs since there wasn't anything to stop him. "I went downstairs to meet him. Told him he could save his breath, he wasn't getting any more money from me. That's when he shoved me into the mailboxes. But he didn't have a tire iron or anything heavy like that on him. I would have noticed."

"Not if he'd hidden it."

"But that would mean he came specifically to kill me, right? Connor may be a bastard, but he's not a killer."

"Unless he knew about the will and made a deal with Evie."

Spencer fisted his hands. How dare this detective even hint that Evie would stoop to something so low? And that Connor would even go for it.

Fox raised one palm out while slamming the other over the pen rattling on the desk. "Calm. Down."

"What was that?" Not only had the pen been rattling, but so had the picture of Evie and Lee on the bookcase. Spencer couldn't blame it on a bump to the counter this time. Were they having an actual earthquake?

"You need to watch your anger."

Anger? *He* was doing that? "What are you talking about?"

"Your anger outburst causes some kind of disturbance. Do you want to scare Evie? She'll leave if she sees this kind of shit. And you won't be able to follow her. You're stuck in a quarter-mile radius of your death."

No. No. Spencer shook his head. He couldn't have that. "Why are you provoking me, then?"

Fox removed his hand from the pen, which no longer rattled. "I don't want to provoke you. But you must know this scenario will be investigated. Help me refute that claim, because I can guarantee you my partner is thinking along those lines. Could Connor have known about Evie?"

"I don't know. It's not like I kept her a secret. I certainly didn't tell Connor about my will. If anything, he would assume I was leaving everything to him."

Fox straightened and blinked as if he was processing data. "Because you never told him differently."

"Right."

"So he could have hidden a weapon. It could have been his backup plan all along."

Could Fox be right? If so, what did that mean for Evie once Connor discovered he was left out of the will? "Is Evie in danger?"

"She's fine until the will is read." Fox's phone buzzed and he looked at the screen. "Shit. What the hell is she doing?"

"Who's doing what?"

"Celia. She says she got a warrant." His thumbs got to work at texting something back.

Spencer wasn't close enough to see the texts. Wasn't sure he wanted to be. "A warrant for what? Evie's cooperating with you."

"I know." Fox's phone buzzed again. "Damn it. I told her this wasn't necessary. She's got a warrant for all the electronics. Guess she's concerned that Evie will do something with them. Who knows? I'm to stay with her until someone arrives with the warrant. This is just great."

Spencer hated to think how Evie would react to a warrant, but he was more optimistic. "That's good, though. Right? You all will see that Evie had no contact with Connor. That she wasn't involved in my murder."

"I'll do my best to steer this case toward Connor. He seems the likely suspect in any case. But don't get your hopes up. Just because you feel it in your heart doesn't mean Evie isn't involved."

Spencer didn't believe that. Was pretty sure Fox didn't either. Unfortunately, they needed more than feelings to protect Evie.

* * * *

Adam rushed to the living room. He still had questions for the ghost, but with the warrant on the way he had no time. At least he got Elliott to cooperate. And to see reason. Maybe now the building wouldn't crumble from his anger.

Even with their brief conversation, Adam had gotten some good info. And he wasn't lying when he said he'd try to steer this case toward Connor. He only had to get Celia on board without realizing he was manipulating her. But was it manipulation if it caught the bad guy? Adam had been manipulating his cases ever since the first one. This one was no different. Well, except for the part of knowing exactly who had committed the murder. That left figuring out the motive and opportunity to narrow down the suspects. Something he had no experience with. It was easier to determine those two things once he knew who to investigate.

Evie emerged from a room across the hall in what he could only assume was her bedroom. She'd changed into something a little less…lounge-like. Her jeans hugged curvy hips and the yellow T-shirt was partially tucked in. She had pulled her hair up into a messy bun. Damn, she looked sexy. Then again, she looked sexy in her lounge-wear, too.

To think he'd come here as a semi-disinterested male. But once he discovered the truth about her disappearance, it was like a switch had been flicked and he became a horny male. She still seemed to like him, too. Even after all these years.

She shoved her cell into her back pocket. "That must have been some phone call. You were in there a long time. Is everything okay?"

"Not really. Would you please sit in the living room? There's a search warrant on its way and I was asked to detain you."

"Wow. That was fast, huh? Whatever. I don't have anything to hide."

And he hoped to Heaven that was true, because he didn't want to lose her again. Not before he had a chance to know her. If she was still like that girl at the amusement park, he definitely wanted to know more of her. "Maybe so, but you might want to think about getting a lawyer."

God, if Celia heard him now, she'd have a coronary. Or at least blame him for sabotaging her case. And she'd probably be right if Evie were guilty. Except she wasn't acting guilty. Although, would he notice the difference? Shit.

Evie stopped on her way to the far chair. "A lawyer? Like Aaron Callahan?"

"No. Not Spencer's lawyer. Your own lawyer."

"Won't that make me look guilty?" She sat in the chair facing him.

Before he could debate on the pros and cons of obtaining a lawyer, someone knocked. She stood, but he indicated for her to stay. He opened the door. Celia and two officers stood in the hallway.

"Hey, I'm surprised to see you. Thought you had a sick kid."

She barged her way in and indicated the officers follow her. "Got a babysitter when the warrant came through."

"What are we looking for?" He hated being out of the loop and apparently Celia had been busy working at home. Even with a sick kid.

"Any device that shows she might have communicated to someone to set up the murder. You know, procedure."

Adam scratched his head. Procedure? Celia must have gotten that from the detective handbook, if there was such a thing. Hell, he never followed procedure. Never had to.

Celia sent the two officers to start searching. She walked into the living room and handed Evie the paperwork. "Here's your copy of the warrant."

"Thanks?" Evie's tone and expression contradicted her words, but she took the papers.

Celia settled on the couch close to Evie and pulled out her smartphone. "How long did you know Spencer?"

Evie looked up from reading the warrant. "Since I was twelve. He was friends with my brother longer, but that's when I first met him."

"How long have you lived here with him?"

"About five years. Not long after my brother died."

"Were you two ever an item?"

Evie smiled and shook her head. "No. There was never anything physical between us. He was like another brother to me."

Adam lowered his head, hoping to hide the smile that threatened to form. He was thrilled she never felt anything but brotherly love toward Spencer.

"How about his half-brother? Were you and Connor Elliott involved?"

The knick-knacks on the bookcase rattled. The floor vibrated. Oh shit. Spencer didn't seem to have a problem knowing Evie only had brotherly love toward him, but his brother? Yeah, that could be a problem.

Celia looked around. "What's happening? Are we having an earthquake?"

Oh, if only it were that simple. So much for thinking he had the ghost under control. Adam moved behind the empty chair and discreetly put his palm out, hoping Spencer not only saw but got the message. The rattling stopped.

Evie surveyed the walls and ceiling as if she were looking for damage. "I never heard of such a thing in Chicago. Do you think the building is safe?"

Adam walked around the chair and sat beside Celia on the couch. "I highly doubt it was an earthquake. I bet your neighbor is moving furniture and hit the wall." He mentally crossed his fingers that they both bought it and steered back to the subject Celia started. "Have you ever met Connor Elliott?"

Evie stopped her surveying and focused on him. "No." She turned to Celia. "Like I was telling Adam, I didn't even know Spence had a brother, or half-brother, until Adam asked me about him. And I certainly didn't know Spence had left me everything."

Celia gripped her smartphone and cast a wary glance his way. "Who did you think he would leave his estate to?"

Evie shrugged. "I don't know. His mother until she died. I didn't even know he had that much money."

"You'd have me believe you've known and lived with Spencer for all these years and didn't know his financial status?"

No, no, no. Evie shouldn't answer any more questions. But how could he get through to her without making Celia suspicious? He couldn't. Damn it.

Apparently, his thoughts got through to Evie. "If you don't mind, I'm not going to answer any more questions without my lawyer present."

He almost let out a sigh of relief. "That's your right."

Celia didn't even bother to hide her white-eye look his way. "Can I talk to you in the hallway?"

Had he gone overboard? No, he was okay. He didn't say or do anything to jeopardize this case. But at least Evie was going to call her lawyer. He couldn't protect her otherwise. He followed Celia to the hallway, but she made sure his back was to Evie. Almost like Celia didn't trust him to watch her.

"Why are you helping her? You told me she was nothing to you."

Whoa. Helping? Really? "What makes you think I am?" Before he could let her answer, he continued. "Listen, you sent me here to ask her questions. I did that. I even have the notes for you." He pulled out his notebook and waved it in her face "My gut says she didn't do it."

"Your gut or your dick?"

"Excuse me?" What had he done in front of Celia to make her think he'd acted unprofessionally? Nothing, that's what. But if he pulled her off this case now, she'd complain and then *he'd* be pulled off the case. And that wasn't happening.

Celia lowered her head. "I'm sorry. That was uncalled for. It's just that when she called you by your first name…"

So that was what she was upset about? His name? Or was it more? "What? Don't stop now. You think we have something going on, is that it?"

"Well, don't you?"

"No." He kept his voice low, but let the anger seep out. "She knows me as Adam from eleven years ago. And we reminisced a little. So sue me for getting her comfortable to talk to me. Maybe if you hadn't come down on her like she was guilty of murder, she wouldn't have thought of calling her lawyer. Ever think of that?"

"You have to admit, she's our prime suspect."

"Yeah, but she doesn't need to know that. Does she?" If Spencer was eavesdropping again—and Adam highly doubted it as the room didn't shake and Celia wasn't complaining about the cold—he would explain later. Right now he just wanted Celia to back off.

"Okay, I get it." She nodded. "So who does your *gut* say killed Elliott?"

Now was his chance to steer her in another direction. "The brother. Connor. It's possible he would assume he's Spencer's beneficiary. Don't you agree?"

"That makes sense. Or she and Connor could be in on it together."

Okay, so he only partly steered Celia. It was a start.

* * * *

While Adam and Detective Delavau were having some kind of heated discussion in the hallway, probably because Evie had dared to utter the "L" word, Evie pulled out her cellphone. She'd briefly read the warrant, but what Adam suggested made more sense now: call her lawyer. It had sounded good on her lips, but who the hell should she call? She didn't keep one on retainer.

Spence had always taken care of anything legal. What little legal business she had. But now he was gone and the only other lawyer she knew who wasn't associated with Spence was the last person she wanted to talk to. But the thought of going to prison scared her more than her pride, so she texted a contact she should have deleted months ago.

He'd left a voice message yesterday, but she'd deleted that without listening to it. Now maybe she should have. Then she might have been prepared.

She texted, *"Hi Keith. Can you come over to the condo? The police are here and I think it's best I have a lawyer present. Please don't call me. I just need to know if you can come over."*

Keith responded sooner than she'd expected. *"Why are the police there?"*

Of course he would ask questions instead of just saying "Be right there." She texted back, *"They think I killed Spencer and they're looking for evidence."*

"What? Do they have a warrant?"

"Yes, they have a warrant. I'm not stupid." Okay, maybe a little stupid. Hadn't she let Adam have free reign of Spencer's office? Damn it. Could he have planted evidence? No, he wouldn't have done that. Not the Adam she remembered, in any case. And he certainly wouldn't have suggested she call a lawyer if he was trying to set her up.

"Are they going to take you in? Should I meet you at the police station?"

Again with another question. *"Not that I know of. I have evidence that shows I never left the condo that night. But apparently that doesn't exonerate me. I just don't know what I should do. Can you come over?"*

"Don't say anything to them. Wait until I get there. Okay?"

Finally, an answer. *"Thanks."*

Had she made a huge mistake texting him? Surely he wouldn't take it as a sign that she wanted to get back together. More like he'd take it as a sign to move in on her again. Be dominant. Be the macho-man. It had seemed fun at first, then it had just gotten annoying. She wasn't some stupid damsel in distress. She could take care of herself.

Well, except for nearly getting arrested. Then she was out of her element.

Detective Delavau held out her hand. "I'll take that."

"What? This is my phone."

"Part of the search warrant. We're taking your computer, too."

What? She should have read that warrant more closely. She handed over her cell. "How am I supposed to work without my phone and computer?"

"You'll get them back in a couple of days." Delavau put the cellphone in a small bag. "What's the pass code?"

"If I don't tell you, are you going to break my phone?"

"If you haven't done anything wrong, what's the problem?"

"Fine." She gave the detective her code. "Are you going to take Spencer's phone, too?"

"Is that the one they found on the nightstand?"

"Yeah. His pass code is 0630."

Detective Delavau typed something on her cell. "Why do you have his pass code?"

"He thought I should have it in case I needed to get something from his phone." Not that she had. Ever. He'd used her birthday so she wouldn't forget it, either. But damn it, she shouldn't have answered. Should she? Hopefully, Keith would arrive soon.

The detective rubbed her arms as cold air blasted the room. "Got the air on a little high, don't you?"

"It's broken." When Evie had changed into a T-shirt and jeans, combed her hair, and applied a little makeup—hoping to look more appealing to Adam—she'd left her jacket in the bedroom. She highly doubted they'd let her get it now. Instead, she moved to the couch and curled into a ball. "Damn air conditioner," she muttered. Guess she would have to call Tony to get it fixed. Or rather, go downstairs and tell him since she didn't have a phone.

Adam picked up the afghan from the stand in the corner and opened it up. He moved as if he were going to drape it around her shoulders, but seemed to have second thoughts and handed it to her instead.

"Thanks." She took the afghan and snuggled under it. The chill dissipated. "You don't think I killed him, do you?"

He sat on the chair and whispered, "Please, don't talk to anyone without your lawyer present."

She leaned her head back as the chill returned. Great. Even Adam thought she was guilty.

Bailey shrieked, "Spencerrr! Spencerrr!"

"Holy shit!" Detective Delavau jumped away from the bird, who had wandered in from the kitchen, probably feeling neglected. "What the hell is that?"

"Uh oh. Curse jar. Uh oh. Curse jar," Bailey said.

Evie laughed. Guess old habits were hard to break. Even for a parrot.

Chapter 6

The officers left the condo with two laptops, one tablet, and two smartphones. They hadn't found anything resembling a murder weapon, not that Adam expected they would. No burner phones, either, much to his relief. If there was any incriminating evidence, it would most likely be on the items they confiscated.

Adam asked Evie to sign all the appropriate forms. He wanted to tell her it would be okay, but Celia—not to mention Evie's lawyer—might have had an issue with that.

Spencer hadn't mentioned Keith O'Hara. Did he know the guy? He must, since it appeared Evie knew him before today. So would Elliott call the guy a jerk? O'Hara had barged in like he owned the place and not once tried to get on Adam's, or even Celia's, good side. But at least the lawyer did his job. He'd pretty much told them that Evie was done talking until he got the whole story from her and that they better not take anything that wasn't specifically mentioned in the search warrant. Adam had never been so relieved to see Evie being protected. Even by a jerk.

Adam took the signed papers and stepped out into the hall. The door nearly closed on his backside. *Yeah, jerk.*

Funny how quickly his attitude had changed. He'd come here looking for an answer, thinking she'd tell him she wasn't interested, that she'd left that night on purpose, and that would be the end of it. Then he wouldn't have cared so much if she was guilty. But now that he knew what had happened...

This could be his second chance. She just couldn't be guilty. Couldn't. Hopefully the evidence Celia gathered today would prove Evie's innocence. It just had to. He'd never wanted anything more.

He headed toward the elevator, where Celia was standing. "You waited for me?"

"You're my ride." She pushed the down button. "I don't like that guy. I feel greasy just being in the same room as him."

Adam couldn't argue that point. "Yeah, he's a tool, isn't he?" And if the evidence came back clean, he wouldn't have to deal with the lawyer again.

"And what was with that bird?"

"Bailey?" He chuckled. Celia's expression had been priceless. "What about him?"

"He kept screaming Spencer's name. I thought he was going to puncture my eardrums."

"A little dramatic, don't you think?"

"Well, maybe. But then you don't have little ones screaming all the time. My ears have gotten sensitive."

Kids did seem to scream. A lot. Even his niece had a small screaming fit during brunch. Made it impossible to talk to Sabrina. Not that she was saying much of anything.

The elevator doors opened as loud as usual—Wookiee-style. Celia took a half step and stopped. "Do you think it's safe?"

"Why wouldn't it be safe? The doors are just noisy. Not broken." He entered the car to prove his point.

"I'm not talking about the doors. I'm talking about the earthquake."

He resisted rolling his eyes. "I told you there wasn't an earthquake. Did you hear the other officers talking about it? No. Because they didn't feel anything." Spencer's little anger blast had been contained to the living room and made Adam's explanation more believable. "I told you, it was the neighbor. But hey, if you want to take the stairs, be my guest."

She palmed the doors as they squeaked closed, causing them to reopen. "You don't have a death wish, do you?"

He scoffed. "No. Which is why I'm not taking the stairs."

She nodded and entered the elevator. "You have to admit that was strange. The walls shaking like that."

"Walls shake all the time. You just live in a house. Try living in an apartment."

"If you say so."

Adam rubbed his palms together. "So, boss, what do we do next?"

Her eyes widened momentarily. "You don't have to call me *that*, but thanks for asking. We should go check out Connor Elliot, right?"

"You asking or telling?"

"Telling. Definitely telling." Her smile seemed to take the starch out of her stance. "Thanks for being so patient with me."

More like prudent, but he wasn't going to argue the case. She'd want to know why. "Hey, I'm new at this mentoring thing, so don't sweat it. We're learning together. So, who's watching the kids?"

"The kids have names."

And the conversation had officially turned course. He hadn't lost his touch after all. "That they do. So, who's watching Emmaline and Bastian?"

"My sister. The extortionist. She apparently thinks I'm made of money."

"And yet, you still paid her more than you should have."

"Do you think I did the right thing?"

"Are you asking me for parenting advice or how to deal with an extortionist?"

That got a chuckle out of her and she rarely laughed at anything. "Neither, I guess. But it does make me wonder about Elliott's brother, though."

Finally, he was getting through to her. "Your gut telling you something?"

"Don't know if it's my gut. I mean, my sister needs money, but I can't see her killing me to get to it."

"Yeah, but you're not a millionaire and she's not desperate. Is she?"

"You think Connor is desperate for money?"

"Won't know until we check him out." But if Elliott was right, it would be an easy discovery.

The doors squealed opened and they headed for the garage where Adam had parked his car. All he'd had to do was push a button and the gate had let him in. No keycard. No keypad. Amazing other non-residents weren't parking inside. Maybe those fake cameras worked after all. One was situated at the garage opening with a sign underneath it stating RESIDENTS ONLY. ALL OTHERS WILL BE TOWED.

"You really think Connor thought he was a beneficiary?" Celia asked. "Wouldn't Spencer tell him he wasn't since it's in the will?"

"Not if they weren't talking. What better way for Spencer to stick it to Connor and have him find out when he can't do anything about it? Kind of brilliant, if you ask me. Connor can't contest the will and claim that Spencer never knew about him. So I could see Connor expecting to get something. He was the closest blood relative. If you were him and didn't know about Evelyn Harper, wouldn't you think you'd get it all? Even if you knew about the roommate, wouldn't you still think you'd get most of it?"

"Harper was surprised? Really surprised?"

At least he didn't have to lie about that. "She nearly spit out her coffee when I told her."

"She could just be a good actor."

There was a time he'd thought the same thing, but now his gut *was* telling him something. That she was innocent. Didn't hurt that the ghost believed her. Believed in her. He reached the driver's door and folded his arms across the top of the car. "Would you prefer I investigate Connor on my own so you can relieve your extortionist sister?"

Celia smiled and shook her head. "I promised her a flat amount and I'm taking advantage. Not my fault if she didn't set a time limit."

"And you call *her* an extortionist?"

She shrugged. "Who do you think I learned it from? Let's go."

* * * *

Evie leaned back against the armrest and stretched her legs across the couch, only to keep Keith from sitting next to her. He'd tried it a couple of times when the police were here. Now they were alone. Why couldn't he have gone with them?

Keith sat in the chair by her feet. "Did you do it, Evie?"

She bolted upright. "I'm sorry, what? You think I had Spence killed?"

"I have to ask."

"You have to ask? We dated for over a year and you have to ask? Apparently you don't know me at all." And she apparently had picked the wrong lawyer. Damn it.

"You have to admit, money makes people do strange things."

"Aside from the fact I didn't even know he had an estate and that I was inheriting it, I don't need his money. I would rather have him in this room than have his money."

Bailey squawked from his perch by the window. "Spencerrr!"

Keith stood. "Why are you keeping that stupid bird?"

"Bailey's not stupid. You're stupid."

"Evie… Would you calm down? You asked for my help."

Oooh, she hated when he said that. As if she weren't allowed to be upset. "And how is calling me a murderer and my pet stupid helping?"

"I apologize, okay?" He paced to and from the window, keeping clear of Bailey. "That bird never did like me, though."

Because Bailey had sense. Or Spencer had trained him. She wouldn't have put it past Spence to do such a thing. He never cared for Keith. Especially since she'd started dating him. Before that, those two had worked together. "Did you know Spence had a brother?"

Keith stopped his pacing. "He has a brother?"

So, that would be a no. Did the guy even know how to answer questions? "Weren't you two friends at all? Even before?"

"You mean before he fired my ass."

"He didn't fire you. Aaron did."

"Only because Spencer told him to."

She did not want to rehash this and was sorry she'd brought it up. Spence had told her it was Aaron's idea, and she'd believed him. "So you weren't friends? At all?"

"We weren't enemies. We were co-workers. Acquaintances. Hell, he only introduced me to you because I wouldn't stop bugging him to."

At the time, she'd been happy Spence had. Served her right for following her eyes instead of her ears. But it was the company Christmas party and she wanted to have fun. Spence had tried to warn her about Keith, but she listened to him about as much as she'd listened to her brother when it came to dating: she didn't.

Even now her eyes were happy with the view. The dark hair. Cobalt blue eyes. Sharp features. The man could be a model for Armani and knew it. That's all Keith would ever be to her, though: eye candy. Eye candy that gave her indigestion.

Keith turned toward the window and looked out. "I think if he'd have known you would agree to date me, he never would have introduced us." He rubbed his arms. "How cold do you have the air on?"

"The thermostat is broken."

"Or the A/C unit is on the fritz. Man, this place is falling apart. I see you still don't have any kind of security at the entrance. And those fake cameras? Did they really think they'd deter people? I'm surprised Spencer never moved. He certainly had the millions to do it."

The police had never mentioned to Keith how much Spence was worth. "How do you know he had millions?" He hadn't lived like any millionaire. Hell, he hadn't even bought his cars new. And the fact that he'd actually bought his car instead of leasing it said a lot to Evie.

"I know what was in the will."

"How?" Why had everyone else seen this will but her?

"After you texted me, I called Aaron. Told him the situation and asked for a copy. He wouldn't send it to me, but told me basically what's in it. You're a millionaire, sweetheart. Or will be once we clear your name."

Evie didn't care for the grin on Keith's face. As if he'd just hit the jackpot. As if she were the jackpot. She stood and held her arm out for Bailey, who jumped on it. "Can you take me to Aaron's office? I want to see this will."

"Sure, but you might want to call first. He might not be free."

She hadn't thought of that. She placed Bailey back on his perch. "Can I use your phone?"

He opened it and handed it over. "Were you planning on taking the bird with you?"

What the hell kind of question is that? "Sure. I take Bailey with me everywhere I go. Didn't you know?" She shook her head. Served her right for dating him in the first place. Maybe Aaron could recommend another lawyer to represent her. She wasn't sure Keith was the smart way to go.

∗ ∗ ∗ ∗

Adam drove toward the Midway Airport. The storm that blew through on Sunday brought clear skies and crisp temps. Some trees were already showing their bright fall colors and stood out against the blue sky. He enjoyed the changing of the guard, but not the arrival of winter, as that was sure to come early. It always seemed to.

"What the?" Celia bent over and picked up the empty glove box. "Don't you throw things away?"

"Hey, put that back."

"Why?" Although she did drop it back into the footwell.

"It's my reminder to get another box. If I throw it away, I'll forget."

"Couldn't you just write yourself a note? Like a normal person?"

That would require reading the note, and where would he keep that exactly? "That *is* my note, okay?"

"You are one strange dude."

Maybe so, but his process worked. Most of the time.

Connor's last-known address was in an old trailer park. And by old, Adam didn't believe one trailer on the lot had been made after the '90s. Or possibly the '80s.

"His brother lives here?" Celia frowned as she peered out the window. "Maybe he *was* desperate for money."

He pulled up to Connor's trailer, the tires crunching on gravel. Weeds overpowered the dinky green space given to the lot and the wooden steps leading up to the door were nearly rotted out.

As Adam approached the door, a breeze kicked up a scent of mildew. Black streaks marred the side of Connor's trailer. Adam could only imagine the stench inside.

Staying on the ground, he reached up and knocked on the door. No answer. No movement from inside. Tried the knob. Locked.

"If you're looking for Connor Elliott, he hasn't been here the last two days."

Adam spun around. An old woman wearing a threadbare coat was sitting on a frayed rattan chair in the lot across the drive. Her trailer wasn't in much better shape than Connor's.

"You know Connor?" Celia asked.

The woman folded her arms across a substantial bosom. "Wouldn't go so far as saying that, but I know what he looks like. We talk occasionally. Mostly about how much of a dump this place is, but when the funds are low, what's a person to do? Better than being homeless, I say."

Celia pulled out her smartphone and started typing. "Was he struggling for funds?"

"Who isn't around here? Does this look like the Taj Mahal?"

Celia didn't seem to have an answer to that, or a backup question, so Adam stepped in. "Has he ever had any visitors?"

"Nah. Just a loner. Like me."

"When was the last time you saw him?"

"Saturday afternoon as he was leaving. Said he had a job interview." She cackled, displaying a mouth that was missing several teeth. "I don't know what kind of job he was interviewing for, but he certainly wasn't dressed for nothing fancy. I mean, who wears old jeans and a hoodie to an interview? I never heard him return, and he's none too quiet, that boy. Is he in trouble?"

Celia appeared to come back to her senses and answered, "We just need to talk to him. About his brother."

"He has a brother? Hmmm… Never mentioned him."

Celia held out her business card. "If you happen to see him return, would you please call us?"

"Now, missy, do I look like I can afford a phone?" The woman took the card anyway.

Adam reached into his pocket and pulled out two quarters. "I see there's a payphone by the manager's office. Why don't you use these to call?"

She snatched the coins from his fingers as if they were going to disappear. "*If* I see him and *if* the phone works, I'll call. But don't hold your breath."

Adam followed Celia back to the car.

"Guess your gut was right," she said.

"My gut?" What had he said? He climbed inside and buckled up.

She did the same on the passenger side. "About Connor. If he was innocent, wouldn't he have come home?"

As much as Adam wanted to agree with her, keep her headed in that direction, deep down he knew a good detective couldn't focus on one thing. "Yes, my gut is saying Connor is involved, but his not being home could be due to other reasons. We don't have a witness who saw him at the crime scene. We're just going on possible motive."

"True. We'll know more once we're able to go through Harper's electronics."

That couldn't happen quickly enough. Adam needed proof that Evie wasn't involved. Otherwise, he'd have to deal with one angry ghost.

As if that was the only reason to speed things along.

Chapter 7

Adam parked at his apartment complex, grabbed his clean suits and the pizza box, and headed toward his building. Once inside, he climbed the stairs. No fancy elevator existed—not even a squeaky one. Then again, his building was only three floors tall, not twenty. He refused to live on the first floor, though. Luckily, an apartment on the second floor had been vacant. And the whole area was ghost free.

Well, it was when he had moved in.

George appeared on the landing. "Hi, Detective. I see you have some visitors."

At least the ghost was harmless. He was usually more interested in staying with his wife, Emily. Waiting for her eventual passing. Unfortunately, Emily was unaware of George's presence and was living a pretty decent life. Adam had tried to convince George to move on and wait for her there. That it might be a decade or more before she passed. But George was one stubborn ghost and he refused to leave.

"Hi, George. My sister, Sabrina, and her daughter are staying with me for a while."

"Becca, right?" He leaned in close as if someone could overhear. "She could see me. I wasn't expecting that. I think I might have scared her."

Some children tended to see what adults couldn't. Same with pets. "So you went in my apartment?"

George lowered his head in guilt. "Emily went out shopping. I got…bored. I didn't mean to intrude. But Adam. She could see me. So I just had to see if I could…"

"Touch her?"

He nodded.

"And?"

He shook his head. "She's not like you, is she?"

"No, she's not. So I know you can't hurt her."

"I didn't mean to hurt you."

"I know you didn't." When George had died, nearly two years ago, Adam had been at the wrong place at the wrong time. And alone. Freaked out from dying, George had slammed into Adam in the hallway and sent him flying down the stairs. Luckily, he came away with only a hip bruise. The worst was having George know they could touch. The last ghost who touched Adam had nearly killed him. But then he was angry. Fortunately, George wasn't an angry ghost and he only cared about Emily, so his refusal to leave until it was her time wasn't as bad as it could be. Still, Adam would feel safer if George moved on and waited for Emily elsewhere.

"Do you mind if I visit her again?"

"I don't have a problem with it. But what about Emily?"

"I love Emily. But she doesn't see me. I didn't realize how much I missed being seen."

"Even by a two-year-old?"

George smiled. "Yeah. Even by a two-year-old."

"You know, if you moved on—"

"Ain't gonna happen without Emily. How many times do I have to tell you?"

"At least one more time. Enjoy your visits with Becca."

"Thanks, Adam. That means a lot."

George floated through the wall to his own apartment, leaving Adam alone in the hallway. He unlocked his door. As he stepped inside his apartment, he froze. Music was playing from the kitchen and his living room had been taken over by…toys. And in the middle of the melee sat one tiny human: his niece. Or rather, George's new friend.

"Mommy!" she screeched.

Sabrina came rushing from the kitchen. "What is it now?" Stopped when she saw Adam. "Oh hey! It's okay, baby. You remember Uncle Adam." She kissed the top of her daughter's head and straightened. "I would have fixed dinner, but you don't have much to cook. And that store on the corner is pretty pathetic."

Not so pathetic when he just wanted a quick run for chips and a six-pack of beer. But groceries? Only if he was desperate. He lifted the box. "I got dinner. Hope pizza is okay. I tried calling, but kept going into your voicemail."

He placed the box on the dining table, which no longer was covered with his mail. Huh. As he walked around the toys to hang his suits in his bedroom closet, the music died. Since when did he have a radio in the kitchen? He closed the closet door and headed back to the living room, pausing as he passed his dresser. It was still cluttered with ties and mismatched socks, but the spot in the back corner was clear. Oh yeah. He did have a radio there. Not that he used it much. Actually, not at all after he'd moved in.

"I'm sorry," Brina said. "I turned off my phone to save the battery. And I'm sorry about the mess. Becca isn't happy playing with her toys unless they're all out of the box." She opened a colorful cloth bag and tossed toys into it.

"Don't bother. It's fine."

"It's not a bother. I'm really sorry. I should have been watching her better."

Her attitude worried him. She'd never been so…nervous before. He grabbed her by the arms. "Brina, stop. You have nothing to apologize for. They're just toys. And it's not like I'm a clean freak."

She froze and winced.

Shit. How hard had he grabbed her? He let go and stepped back. "Did I hurt you?"

"No." She rubbed her arm. "I pulled a muscle carrying all my crap. Guess I should have left some of it behind, huh?"

She really hadn't brought that much with her. Pretty much what she could carry on a bus, which begged the question… "Why didn't you drive here?"

She indicated they move into the kitchen, as if it was surrounded by soundproofing. Or that Becca could actually understand what they were talking about.

As he stepped inside the kitchen, he couldn't believe what he was seeing. The dishes had been washed and put away. The front of the oven no longer had the grease stain he'd made that one time he attempted to cook hamburger, and the yellowed refrigerator he'd left her with was actually white. Even the small appliances on the tiny counter looked spiffy. So did the floor.

"You've been busy."

"It's the least I could do. I just wish I'd realized you didn't have any food or I would have suggested we go shopping after you bought your new couch."

Yeah, a couch he wouldn't get until Wednesday. He pulled out a chair from the small table, which was also clean of sugar, or salt, or whatever it was he'd spilled the other day. "Sit. Tell me why you didn't drive."

She sat and spoke softly. "My car is registered in Glenn's name. I didn't want to be accused of stealing it."

Adam always thought there was something off about Glenn, but he seemed to care for Sabrina and she'd been so in love with him. Then again, why wouldn't she fall for him? He'd been the only person—besides Adam—to throw any kind of attention her way.

"You should have called me. I would have helped you move."

"Wasn't necessary. I had a bus ticket. We made it here, didn't we? I feel bad taking over your apartment, though. Once I get a job, I'll get out of your hair."

"Brina, you're not in my hair. Okay? It's fine. We'll manage. If you have more stuff to bring here, we can drive there some weekend and get it."

Her eyes widened. "No. That's not necessary. I have all that I need. I don't want to be a bother. If I had anywhere else to go, I'd go there. You know that, don't you?"

What kind of brother had he been for her to say that? Maybe one who had wanted to escape to a friend's house instead of being at home and helping? Thank goodness for Zane's wisdom or he'd screw this up for sure. "Stop it. You're staying here. We're family. Mom and Dad never understood that, but I do. I'm always here for you."

She lowered her head. The breath that escaped her pretty much loosened every muscle in her body. "Thanks. I appreciate it."

He needed to lighten the mood. She seemed on the verge of tears. "Hey, I don't know about you, but I'm starving. Open up that box." He got up, pulled three plates from the cabinet, and stopped. "Shit. Does she eat pizza?"

Sabrina laughed. "Uh…no. But I already fed her. If you tell me where the closest grocery store is, we can go there tomorrow and I can stock up."

"It's too far to walk." And it was probably too late to take Becca out shopping. Didn't kids have an early bedtime? "I can go tonight. Just make a list. What kind of phone do you have?"

"Why do you need to know that?" She opened the pizza box and inhaled. "Oh man, I haven't had pizza in ages. Sure smells good."

He handed her a plate. "So I can get you a charger."

"I don't need—" She stopped and lowered her head again.

"Brina…" Damn it. Only one reason why she'd turn off her phone. "Are you afraid to talk to him?"

She straightened. "Of course not. I just don't want to. Not yet, anyway."

"Why don't you just block his calls?"

"I can do that?"

"Yeah. Gimme your phone." She handed it over and he showed her where to do it. "When you're ready to talk to him, you can un-block him."

"Oh wow. That's great. Thanks. Maybe I'll feel like talking with him after I see the lawyer tomorrow. By the way, do you know which train I should take downtown? It's been so long since I've been in the city."

"You have an appointment? Already? Wow. You've really thought this through."

"I've been thinking it through for over a year now." She slid a slice of pizza onto her plate. "He changed after Becca was born. Or maybe I did. He never wanted her, and I can't have her grow up in a family like we did."

Adam kissed his sister's forehead. "I'll do whatever I can to help. You just have to tell me."

And one of the first things he could do was find a larger apartment.

Chapter 8

Evie stared at the lone child's shoe lying on the sidewalk. She'd been pretty much walking in a daze since meeting with Spencer's lawyer, Aaron Callahan.

Provided she wasn't convicted for Spencer's murder, she would become independently wealthy. She never would have associated those two words with her. Never. Graphic artists didn't usually generate that kind of income. Especially no-name artists like her. Lawyers, though, apparently did. Or rather, smart lawyers did. Spencer had inherited the bulk of his estate and invested wisely. His brother Connor had spent his share. Or so she'd been told.

Why could Spencer share that bit of information with Aaron and not her? She'd thought they'd been friends. More than friends. Family.

But some child was missing a shoe. Possibly the one in the stroller up ahead?

"Ma'am?" She picked up the shoe and rushed up to the blonde woman pushing the stroller. "Is this your child's?"

The woman turned around. Her eyes were red and her cheeks were wet with tears. "Oh, thank you. I didn't notice she'd kicked it off."

"You okay?" Maybe today was the day all women cried. It had taken Evie forever and lots of cold water to finally get her eyes white and puff-free again.

Crying Woman swiped her cheeks and took the shoe. "Not really. I think I'm lost."

"That can happen. What are you looking for? The L?"

"No. I'm supposed to meet my brother at Coffee Perks, but I can't seem to find it." She hit her cellphone. "Stupid map isn't working."

Evie glanced at the cell and turned the woman around. "Might help if you're situated properly. See? It's down that street over there. Come on, I'll show you."

"Oh geez. I passed it?" She placed her hand over her heart. "Thank you. I can't believe how stupid I am."

"You're not stupid. Just looks like you've had a rough day."

The woman slipped the shoe back on her daughter's foot. "I've had better. Lawyers. I don't know whether to hug them or hit them."

"I know the feeling." Evie walked with the mother as she pushed the stroller. When they turned the corner, Evie pointed up ahead. "There it is."

"Are you busy? I mean, I'd like to buy you a coffee if that's okay. And maybe talk to an adult? My name is Sabrina, by the way. This little one here is my daughter, Becca."

Busy? Maybe if she had her phone and computer. But without those there wasn't much she could do. She'd already drawn out her ideas on the few projects she had. "Sure, why not? I don't have anywhere to be right now. I'm Evie."

Sabrina pushed the stroller to a free table and placed the diaper bag on a chair. "I'll buy. And don't argue. It would have cost me more to buy her new shoes. Do you have a favorite?"

Evie smiled. It wasn't worth pointing out that Sabrina would have probably found the shoe on her own once she realized she'd passed the street she wanted. "I'll take the flavor of the day if they have one. Regular if not. Black is fine."

"I'll be right back." Sabrina kissed the top of her daughter's head and moved to the end of the line.

Evie slung her purse over the back of the chair next to the stroller and sat. Becca squirmed to see where her mother went, so Evie turned the stroller giving Becca the view she desired.

Evie leaned back in her chair. A coffee was nice, but what she really wanted was something stronger. Something to forget Keith ever existed. Now there was a lawyer she'd love to smack, but it seemed she was stuck with him. Aaron had nothing but good things to say about Keith, lawyer-wise. When she asked why he'd been let go, Aaron had grimaced and said, "Some of the employees had issues with him, true. It created a hostile environment. But he was always very professional and meticulous with his cases. You're in good hands with Keith and I do hope you can get this settled."

Had Spence gotten Keith fired because she'd been dating him? It was beginning to look that way.

Sabrina returned with two cups and a bag and placed them on the table. "Hope you like chocolate-chip cookies. I couldn't resist." She moved the stroller so it was to her right instead of between her and Evie. She pulled out a sippy cup from her bag and gave it to her daughter as she took her own seat. "You know, the more I look at you, I get the feeling I know you from somewhere. Are you an actress or a model?"

"No. I'm just a plain old graphic designer. I don't get in front of the camera. Are you from Oak Park or did you go to Northwestern?"

"No. I didn't go to college." Sabrina shrugged. "You must just look like someone I know. It'll come to me eventually. Do you still live in Oak Park?"

"No. I live just south of here, actually. I was here seeing a lawyer, too."

"Divorce or none of my business?"

Evie chuckled. This was nice, just sitting and chatting with a total stranger. Was this how the real world did it? Maybe she *should* get out more. "Not a divorce. My, uh, roommate passed away. He left me his estate."

"Wow. Nice roommate. I mean, I'm sorry for your loss, but still…nice roommate. I was seeing a divorce attorney. He didn't seem to give me much hope, though."

"About getting a divorce?"

"No. I was able to get that filed. He told me not to expect to get full custody of Becca." Sabrina grabbed a napkin and dabbed her eyes.

"Then maybe you need to find another attorney."

"Yeah, that's what I was thinking. But he's in my price range. I wish I could afford to be picky, as if I'd know who was good and who wasn't."

"Join the club. My roommate was a lawyer and yet I couldn't tell you who is good or not. It's a crapshoot."

"That's what I'm afraid of."

"So is this your first trip to the city?"

"No, but it's been awhile. I used to live here. Moved when I got married. I'm staying with my brother until I get my life all straightened out. I was living in Springfield when I finally decided to leave my jerk of a husband."

"It was nice of your brother to take you in."

"He is nice. And single." Sabrina's eyes widened. "You wouldn't by any chance be single, too, would you?"

"I am." Except there was this guy she wanted to get to know better. A guy who could end up arresting her for murder. "But I'm not really looking for a relationship."

"No one ever is when they find one, right? Just stick around. Meet him. See what happens. Who knows? Maybe it was fate we met today."

Fate. Right. She'd thought fate had brought Adam into her life all those years ago. Did it also have a hand in taking him away? And now he was back in her life and she could be arrested for murder. Fate could take a shit bath.

"Seems you don't have to wait long. There he is now." Sabrina stood and waved. "Adam, we're over here."

Adam? Evie twisted around in her seat. *Holy shit.*

* * * *

Adam spotted his waving sister, and when her table mate turned around, he ran into a chair and nearly face-planted the floor.

Smooth, Fox. Smooth.

Evie Harper. They lived in the same city for how many years and now he runs into her? What were the odds? Really, what were the odds? And what was she doing with his sister?

Sabrina sprinted toward him. "You okay?"

"I'm fine. Didn't expect you to have company." Because yeah, every idiot plowed into a chair when they ran into unexpected company.

"This is Evie. I got lost and she helped me, so I bought her a coffee. Evie, this is my big brother, Adam. He's a police detective."

"Yes, I'm well aware." Evie stood. Yesterday her hair had been up. Today the silky strands were down, its length nearly reaching her butt. And what a luscious butt. "I'll leave you two alone. It was nice meeting you, Sabrina."

"No!" Sabrina grabbed Evie's arm. "He doesn't mind if you're here, do you, Adam? And you haven't finished your coffee. Please stay."

He'd never seen Sabrina so clingy for friends. He really should let Evie go, even though the circumstances had changed, but he hated seeing his sister so distressed. "Yes, please stay. Don't let me shoo you off. I have good news about the case."

Sabrina turned her baby blue eyes his way. "What are you talking about? Are you investigating her roommate's death?"

"Murder. I'm investigating his murder."

Evie grabbed her purse. "And he thinks I did it, so I'll just go now. Good luck with your lawyer."

He should let her go. His sister would survive. But, damn it, he'd rather have her stay. And not just for Sabrina. "Wait. I told you I had good news. You've been exonerated."

Sort of. They'd found no evidence of her involvement, in any case. That was enough, wasn't it?

Evie stopped and turned around. "That fast? You two seemed pretty sure I had something to do with it."

"Which is why my partner put a rush on the contents of your computer and phone. And guess what? There's no evidence to suggest you were involved. You'll be able to pick up your stuff tomorrow morning."

Her eyes widened at that. "That *is* good news."

Adam hoped he hadn't jumped the gun. Celia wasn't totally sure of Evie's innocence, saying something about how evidence could be hidden or manipulated. That Evie knew about computers because she worked on one. Well, he worked on one, too, and didn't know jack shit about how to manipulate data. Celia was reaching, hoping for an easy case. But this case was anything but easy.

Regardless of Celia's feelings, he wanted to be closer to Evie. Maybe pick up where they left off. Once the case was solved. He held out her chair. "You gonna make my sister happy and stay?"

She stared at the chair for a bit, glanced at Sabrina—who was grinning and nodding—and finally met his gaze with a hint of a smile. "Sure. Why not?"

Adam resisted the urge to run his hand alongside her shoulders as she sat. It was one thing being seen in public with her, quite another to appear intimate. So he sat opposite her, faced the door—his preference—and kept Sabrina between them. It was safer this way. Safer for his career.

Sabrina returned to her seat and eyed Adam. "Did you think she did it before you had proof?"

He frowned at his sister. "What does that—"

She cut him off. "Just answer the question, detective."

Well, hell. Was he under investigation now? "No, I didn't think she was guilty."

That news seemed to surprise Evie, but then he'd never given her any indication otherwise. Not with Celia hanging around.

Sabrina slapped her hand on the table. "I knew it! He'll tell you it's because of his gut, but I think he has some kind of sixth sense."

Evie turned her attention toward him. "Sixth sense? Like how?"

"Like my sister is full of it." He laughed, trying to ease the chill going down his spine. This conversation was getting way off course. "A little dramatic there, aren't you, Brina?"

"How else do you explain how you solve all your cases?"

"Good skills? My gut? I didn't realize my record was known in Springfield." Because he certainly hadn't told her.

"Glenn mentioned it. He thinks you're cheating somehow, but I think you just have ESP or…" Her eyes widened and she snapped her fingers. "I know! You see ghosts. Yeah, that's it. The ghost tells you who killed them and you arrest the culprit."

The room became brighter and he nearly choked on air when Evie started snickering.

"You can't be serious," she said. "Ghosts don't exist. They're just a myth."

Evie couldn't be more wrong, but no way was he going to correct her. Instead, he went along with it after he took a calming breath. "What she said. Nice to know what you think of my abilities."

Bad enough he thought he sucked. He nearly rubbed the pain in his chest but didn't want to show how much her words had hurt.

Brina frowned. "Oh, Adam. No. I didn't mean it like that. You're the smartest person I know. I was just trying to understand how you knew about that boy, that's all."

"What boy?" Evie asked.

"Adam knew where this boy was buried. Back when we were kids. I heard Mom and Dad talking about it one night when I couldn't sleep."

Shit. Seemed she eavesdropped on their parents as much as he had. "Well, you missed some essential information. Like I'd told them about an argument I'd heard mentioning the kid." So what if that argument was with the ghost kid. Did that make it a lie? "And Glenn thinks I cheat at everything. You're divorcing the man. Do you believe everything he's told you?"

Sabrina shook her head, clearly unhappy that he had debunked her theories. "Fine. You're good because of your gut. Okay? You have to admit, it would be kind of cool if you did communicate with ghosts. Right?"

If it weren't for the fact Sabrina would spread that news to whoever would listen, it was nice to know she wouldn't think him crazy for seeing ghosts. Still, it kind of hurt that she believed he wasn't doing the job on his own. That her mind instantly went in that direction. A correct one, but still…

"I think anyone who says they communicate with ghosts is missing an essential part of their brain, or their wires are crossed," Evie said.

Well, hell. Maybe his sister wouldn't think he was nuts, but Evie would. Great. Just great.

"You don't believe at all?" Sabrina asked. "What about all the different stories?"

"Exactly. They're stories. Fiction. They're great for entertainment, but real life? No. Once you're dead, you're dead. And your memories or whatever is inside of us dies also."

"Sounds like you don't even believe in Heaven," Brina said.

"I don't believe in religion. It was created to control people."

"You're not wrong there," Adam injected. "But I think there is something beyond death. Just haven't figured out what."

Evie smiled. "Is that what your gut says?"

"I guess you could say that. It hasn't been wrong yet." He patted it for effect.

"Touché!" Evie's laughter brought back wonderful memories of their time at the amusement park. "Someday, you'll have to share your theories with me."

A customer passed, stirring up the air. Adam got a whiff of a dirty diaper. Before he could say anything, Sabrina wrinkled her nose.

"Oh, Becca! You're supposed to tell Mommy before." She got up, lifted the child from the stroller, and stood her on the floor.

"Excuse me while I go clean her up. You won't leave while I'm gone, will you? Adam, please make her stay."

"Don't worry," Evie said. "I'll still be here."

Grinning, Sabrina grabbed the diaper bag in one hand, her daughter's hand in the other, and headed to the restroom.

"Is she always…persistent like that?" Evie asked.

Adam was sure she'd meant "clingy" but her word worked, too. "I don't think she has many friends. I blame her husband for that."

"He abused her?"

He was beginning to wonder about that himself. "I don't know. She never said." Because she knew he'd kill the bastard? "Funny how she ran into you today."

"I know. What are the odds, right?"

"That's exactly what I was thinking."

She took a sip of her coffee. "Keith will be furious I'm here talking to you."

The mention of that lawyer's name almost made Adam groan out loud. There was someone he hoped to never see again. "Why? You probably don't need him anymore."

"Yeah, it does seem that way, huh?" Evie propped her elbow on the table and rested her head on her hand. "So your gut said I wasn't guilty? Or was it the lack of evidence?"

He couldn't help but chuckle. "Let's just say I was thankful the lack of evidence confirmed my gut feeling."

"If you didn't think I was guilty, why did you want me to get a lawyer? You seemed…desperate, almost."

"I was. Celia was so sure you were involved. That was the only way I could think to protect you. O'Hara seemed…familiar with you, though. Are you and he friends?"

"We know each other, yes, but we're not friends."

Yet, she'd called him. Had his number in her phone. "Was he friends with Spencer?"

She scoffed. "No. Definitely not. Keith and I used to date. Okay?"

What? Was that why Spencer never mentioned O'Hara? Certainly explained O'Hara's attitude toward Evie. But why hadn't Spencer said anything? Damn it! Adam fought to remain nonchalant. "Is that so? Who broke it off?"

"I did. He had a hard time believing that my relationship with Spencer was strictly platonic. Keith got especially paranoid after

Spencer's mother died. Two weeks later I called it quits. I got tired of defending myself all the time."

Hmmm… Could O'Hara have known, or even suspected, that Evie would inherit everything? No, that couldn't be. He'd have to work at the same firm and Elliott would have mentioned that. Adam hated this not knowing bit. "He seemed kind of…possessive. Like he might want to get back together."

"Oh, like he can trust me now that Spencer is dead?" She shook her head. "It doesn't work that way. Not for me, anyway. Trust is important in a relationship. Don't you think?"

"I suppose." Not that he'd had many relationships. None that lasted more than a couple of months. "So you trusted Spencer, but didn't love him?"

"I loved him, just wasn't *in* love with him. And apparently I didn't know him at all. Why would he leave me everything but never tell me he had money? Or a brother? Half-brother, but still…a brother."

He hated seeing her so down. Assuming her question was rhetorical, he changed the discussion by pointing to the bag on the table. "What's in there?"

"Cookies. Sabrina bought them."

"Oh?" He opened the bag and found three large chocolate-chip cookies. Man, they smelled great. Certainly one was for him. If it wasn't, too bad.

"Have you been able to find Connor yet?"

He spread out a napkin and pulled out a cookie. "No, but we're still looking. If he comes by the condo, call Celia. Not because I don't want you to call me, but because it's her case."

Boy, did that sound lame or what? He broke off a piece of the cookie. Maybe if he stuffed his mouth, he'd stop spouting nonsense.

"Doesn't matter. I only have her number. Not yours."

He'd brought the treat half-way to his mouth and stopped. Hell. Was she asking for his number? He put the cookie down and grabbed his wallet. "I can resolve that."

"Nice to know you can take a hint." Her lips curled slightly as she took his card and placed it inside her purse. A moment later, a frown replaced the smile. "Do you think he'd hurt me?"

And she was back to Connor. "I don't know. You're certainly fine until the will is read. And then? If he's smart, he'd look for a way to discredit you first."

"How would discrediting me help him?"

"Connor could say you coerced Spencer into changing his will. Especially after his mother died. Then presto-bingo, he inherits it all. I've seen stranger things happen."

She laughed. "Presto-bingo?"

"Yeah. It's a legal term. Never heard of it?"

Her smile crinkled her eyes and he was transported back to that summer night again. When they'd had their pictures taken. When he'd kissed her. If only he'd found her under different circumstances.

He picked up the cookie just as a commotion over at the counter became loud.

A man pulled a gun from his backpack. "What is it with you people?"

Oh shit. Adam had been so intent on Evie—and the stupid cookie—he hadn't realized what was going on in the café. Sabrina emerged from the ladies' room. He waved her back. Her eyes widened as she clutched Becca and retreated into the restroom.

He put the cookie down. Guess it was time to be a real cop.

* * * *

Evie turned around after a white guy yelled at the counter. Not just a guy, a gunman. Wearing jeans and a hoodie, he held a backpack strap in one hand and a gun out in the other. If not for the weapon, she would have thought he was a college student. And maybe he was, but who took a gun to school? She gripped the table while he waved his weapon at the barista.

Adam leaned over and whispered, "Crawl over to the exit while I distract him."

Distract him? Before she could question what he meant, he stood and walked to the middle of the café, away from the door. He pulled out his gun and pointed it toward the gunman. "Chicago Police. Put down the gun and backpack and we can talk."

The few customers sitting inside the café dropped to the floor and hid behind their chairs. The ones by the door rushed outside. She slipped off her chair, keeping the table between her and the gun.

The gunman swung his weapon toward Adam and her heart nearly stopped. "Talk about what? How they're always disrespecting me? Waiting on their own kind before they wait on me?"

Okay, the man didn't seem intent on killing Adam. Thank God! But it seemed to take forever for her heart to start up again, and when it did, it beat overtime. Evie crawled alongside the windows, getting closer and closer to the door. Two tables were in her way, but unoccupied. *Please don't let him see me. Please.*

Adam kept his gun pointed at the customer. "I'm sure that's not true. Now, put down the weapon."

"It is true! They're taking over our country. They need to go back where they came from!"

One more crawling step and she'd be free.

The door opened and a bell jingled. The loudest freakin' jingle ever. Evie cringed.

A man stumbled over her. "What the hell?"

The gunman spun around. "You! Stop!"

"Fuck." The man beat feet. The door jingled shut.

Evie froze. The gun was now pointed at her. Holy shit. She was going to die.

Adam yelled, "Drop the weapon. Now!"

"I'm allowed to own this."

"But you're not allowed to point it at innocent people or bring it into this establishment. There's a notice on the door. No weapons allowed."

"She's not innocent. She's one of them. They don't belong here!"

"You want to talk about that? Drop the weapon."

"This isn't right," the gunman grumbled, but he placed the gun and backpack on the ground and raised his hands.

Oh thank God. Evie breathed easier as her blood pressure lowered a few digits. Uniformed police officers rushed inside and handcuffed the gunman. The few patrons in the store clapped, as did the barista. She leaned back against the wall. That was too damn close. She tried standing, but her legs refused to work properly and she slid back to the floor.

Adam trotted over to her. "Hey, it's over. You're okay."

"I thought he was going to shoot me." She covered her face. Would anyone even miss her if that had happened? Who would claim her body? Who would bury her? She had no one.

"Come on, let's get you to a chair." He wrapped his arm around her and guided her upright, away from the wall.

God, he smelled good. Better than she remembered. She rested her head on his shoulder. Slid an arm around his waist. Probably the wrong thing to do, but it just felt so right. He felt so right. So familiar. So calming.

How messed up was that? He was investigating Spencer's murder. Sure, she wasn't a suspect anymore, but should she get involved with him? Hell, being seen with him couldn't be good for his career. Could it?

As Adam helped her sit, Sabrina returned from the ladies' room and gave him a sisterly smack in the arm. "Thanks for letting me know it was clear."

His face turned bright red. "Gee, Sabrina. I'm sorry. Are you okay?"

Sabrina looked between Adam and Evie and smiled. "I'm fine. Good thing I called 9-1-1. Would you believe no one else had, but yet, they all had phones? What was all that about?"

"Just another dissatisfied customer." Evie tried to laugh it off, but couldn't stop the tears from escaping.

Adam crouched beside her. "Hey. It's okay. It's over now."

Was it? Sure, the actual crime was over, but she kept seeing that gun.

"We need to give her a ride home."

It took a moment for her to realize Sabrina was talking to Adam. "I don't want to inconvenience you. I can call an Uber."

"Don't be ridiculous," Sabrina said as she put Becca back into her stroller. "I'm a wreck and I didn't have a gun pointed at me. We're taking you home. No questions."

Well, as long as Sabrina came along, it wouldn't look too bad. Would it? "Thank you. That would be kind."

Chapter 9

Sabrina waved at Evie as Adam drove away. He had offered to walk Evie up to the condo, and while part of her wanted that more than anything, another part needed to go up on her own. To stop leaning on the guy. Like at the café. She had to be realistic. Any association with Adam couldn't help her case any. Or his job. And she wanted him to do his job.

On the drive over, she'd even sat in the backseat with Becca—felt it was safer that way—but had been behind Adam, with his handsome face visible in the rearview mirror. It seemed he'd glanced at her more than he had the road. His expression not only of concern, but care. Of course, she wouldn't know such a thing unless she'd been staring back. But she couldn't help it. She had it bad for Adam Fox, and this past incident hadn't helped any. If not for Sabrina's much-needed rambling, the drive might have been awkward.

Evie turned toward the entrance on rubbery legs. She was still feeling the effects of the near-death experience and a nice soaking bath sounded good. Spencer's bathroom contained a huge soaker tub and he'd always told her she could use it anytime she wanted. She'd never wanted to before. Now? She couldn't wait to try it out.

She entered the foyer and stopped. It finally hit her. Spencer had died here. Someone had killed him. Here. They just walked inside and did it. Was she safe? Were any of them?

"You're Spencer Elliott's roommate, Evelyn Harper, aren't you?" a man asked from behind her.

Clutching her chest, she spun around. An older gentleman with hair several shades whiter than his skin stared at her. She didn't recognize him. "Where did you come from?"

"Sorry. Didn't mean to startle you like that. I just left the manager's office. Thought I closed the door rather loudly."

"Guess my mind was elsewhere." Spencer's death. Her near-death. But to not hear a door slam? Damn, she really needed to get her shit together.

He looked at the mailboxes. "Understandable. I'm Marvin Holt. I live on the tenth floor. Spencer told me about you. I visit Marie a bit, but I believe this is the first time I've actually seen you in person."

He most likely meant her neighbor, Marie Diamante, who became a widow about two years ago. "I don't get out much. So you're the reason Marie's cooking again, huh?"

Evie hadn't realized how much she'd missed the scents emanating from Marie's condo. That woman knew how to cook delicious-smelling food.

His face turned pink. "Well, I doubt that. But she loves to cook and I love to eat."

Evie laughed and her muscles relaxed. Maybe it wasn't a bath she needed. Just normal conversation. "Sounds like you're made for one another."

"Yeah? We'll see. It's a shame what happened to Spencer. I warned the board that something like this would eventually happen."

"You thought someone would be killed? Here? The neighborhood isn't that bad." Or was it? Look what happened at the café. Granted, that was a different neighborhood, but still... Maybe it was a good thing she didn't go out all that much.

"Killed. Mugged. It happens everywhere. These are violent times. We need better security." He eyed the black globe on the ceiling. "You know those aren't real, right?"

"Spencer told me." One of the few things he'd managed to tell her.

"Yeah, well, maybe this will be their wake-up call. I doubt anyone will be able to sell their unit now unless this place becomes more secure."

"Sounds like you should join the board."

"Right. Like they'd want me. Although, now that there's a spot open, maybe I will run. If I decide not to sell."

"Oh? Someone left the board recently?"

He looked at her as if she'd grown a horn. "Ummm…Spencer?"

What? Spencer was on the board? How come he never bothered to tell her that? She recovered enough so she didn't look like a total dunce, although she certainly felt like one. "Oh, right. Silly me. I wasn't thinking."

"I get it. Still in shock, right? Man, I still can't believe he was killed."

Killed. By Connor. Or could it be someone in the condo? "Do you know if anyone hated Spencer, since he was on the board?"

Marvin shook his head. "Can't really say. I mean, who doesn't hate someone for some stupid reason or another? But if someone held a grudge against the board, they picked the wrong guy. Should have gone after Hugh Latimer. He's the stupid chairman and doesn't give a rat's ass about the owners. And he is one!"

Evie held back a smile. Was Marvin's hatred for Hugh stupid or warranted? "He's worth killing over?"

"Not for me, but who knows about someone else? I mean, they should have better security here. Might have prevented Spencer's death."

Which meant that whoever killed Spencer must have known the cameras didn't work. "I think you need to run for the position. Make things better."

"Yeah?" He puffed his chest out and nodded. "Maybe I should."

A blast of cold air hit Evie and goosebumps formed on her arm. "Wow, they have the A/C on rather high, don't they? It's not even that warm out anymore."

"What are you talking about?"

"You didn't feel that? The cold air?"

"I didn't feel anything." Marvin took a few steps back. "Maybe you're coming down with something."

How could he not have felt it? Was she going crazy? "Maybe someone walked over my grave." That's what her mother had always said about sudden chills. But those chills seemed to be happening more often. She pushed the up button for the elevator.

"I know it's none of my business, but will Spencer's unit have to be sold?"

She wasn't in the mood to talk about the inheritance and he was right, it wasn't his business. But she didn't need to sound rude about it. "I don't know yet."

"I'm sure whoever owns it now won't get much for it. Even as nice as it is. Not when we've had an actual murder in the foyer. When is Spencer's funeral? I'd like to pay my respects, if that's okay."

The request caught her off guard. She'd never considered anyone here would want to attend. Then again, she hadn't known Spencer was on the board. That would definitely make a difference. "The funeral won't be scheduled until the police are done with his body. I'll be sure to post the details on the board." She pointed to the bulletin board that held notices of one sort or another.

The squeaky elevator doors opened and she stepped inside.

"Thanks. I'm sure others would like to know, too." He waved as he exited through the garage door.

Yeah, others. Because Spencer apparently had friends here she knew nothing about. She had lived with the man. Considered him a brother. Shouldn't she have known more about him? His life? His family?

Instead, she knew nothing.

As the doors squeaked to close, she wedged her arm and reopened them. She'd almost forgotten about the faulty A/C in the condo. Tony should also have a list of the board members. It would be nice if she contacted them separately about the funeral.

Evie walked to the manager's office and entered. The small room was unoccupied, but there was a buzzer on the counter. She pushed the button.

Tony appeared moments later. "Hey, Ms. Harper. What can I do for you?"

"Something is wrong with the A/C. I thought it might be my own unit, but I can feel it in the hallway and foyer, too. Do you have it turned on really cold or is it just malfunctioning?"

He shook his head. "I haven't touched it. It's all automatic. The system determines whether the air or heat should be on."

"Well, you might want to check out the system. It's been freezing. Even in my own unit. And I don't even have it turned on."

"I'll report it. Sure. Anything else?"

She was tempted to ask if there were any owners who disliked Spencer, but figured Tony probably didn't know. "Do you happen to have a list of the HOA board members?"

"You looking to run after…" He lowered his head. "Sorry. Forgot you're not an owner." He pulled out a sheet of paper behind the counter. "This is the only list I have. You'll have to take a picture of it."

"I don't have my phone. Do you have any paper?" She grabbed a pen out of her purse. Heaven forbid she carried paper of any sort. What kind of artist was she? The kind who didn't go anywhere, that's what.

"Sure." He ripped a sheet from somewhere behind the counter and placed it on top.

Seven members. And there was Spencer's name, so Marvin hadn't been lying. Not that she thought he had. As she wrote down the names and contact info, she asked, "Were you the one who found Spencer?"

Tony crossed his arms and lowered his head. "Yeah. I shoulda come out when I heard the arguing, but figured it was none of my business. But then I heard some weird noises, like banging. I was sure someone was messing with the mailboxes again. I sure wish I had come out earlier. Maybe then I coulda saved him. You know? I feel real bad about it."

This was the first she'd heard about a fight. Not that Adam would have told her the details, not with her being a suspect. "Was Spencer arguing?"

He shrugged. "I don't know. Most likely he was, but at the time it was just two guys arguing. I couldn't make out what they were saying or who they were. Just guys' voices."

She dropped the pen in her purse and folded the paper. "Thanks for the list."

"Yeah, no problem. And I'll be sure to let the maintenance company know about the A/C."

She left and headed back toward the elevator. Spencer had been fighting. With Connor? Seemed the most likely candidate, especially since Spencer had specifically not included him in the will. Or had Spencer made an enemy with an owner?

Just the thought that Spencer had enemies seemed preposterous, but then how well had she really known the man? And how many more secrets would she uncover?

* * * *

Adam pulled into a parking spot at his apartment complex and gripped the steering wheel. His nerves were still a bit jumpy, his hands a little shaky. Man, how close had that guy come to shooting people? To shooting Evie?

Sabrina unbuckled her seatbelt. "You're her hero, now, you know that, right?"

He stared at his sister. "What are you talking about?"

"Evie. I saw the way she looked at you…after. And you like her, right? I haven't seen you look at someone like that since…" Her eyes widened and she smacked her forehead. "Oh my God! That's it! That's why she looked familiar. She's the girl in the picture, isn't she?"

Adam shook his head as his vision went spinning out of control. He'd forgotten how his sister could jump from one topic to another at zippy speed. "Slow down there, Brina. Again, what the hell are you talking about?"

"Watch your language. I don't need Becca picking up those words."

"She's asleep." Not that he'd actually checked before cussing. "And stop changing the subject."

"I haven't changed the subject. I'm talking about Evie. She's the girl in your picture. The one from your grad party at Six Flags."

"How do you know about—"

"Relax. I wasn't snooping. You'd just come home from the party and I came into your room to see how it went, but you'd gone into the bathroom. That's when I saw the picture. It was on your dresser. I was so happy you'd found someone, but then you came back to your room, in a bad temper, and told me to scram."

"I remember that." He'd been so frustrated that he couldn't find Evie's friends. "You never said anything."

"I wasn't going to bring it up in front of Mom and Dad. And then you seemed sad all the time. I just figured it didn't work out. So what happened?"

"An emergency came up and she left before we could exchange our full names or phone numbers."

"Oh, Adam. And this is the first time you've seen her since?"

He scoffed. "Yeah."

"And now you're her hero."

"I'm no one's hero. She was freaked out. That's all." He jumped out of the car and retrieved the stroller from the trunk. As Sabrina pulled Becca from the back seat, his phone rang. *Celia. Now what?* "I gotta take this call. You take her upstairs. I'll bring the stroller and car seat."

"Okay…hero."

"Would you stop calling me that?" He didn't want to be a hero in Evie's eyes. He wanted to be an equal. But he couldn't do anything about it until the case was solved.

He answered the phone and leaned against his car. "What's up, Celia."

"What the hell were you doing with her?"

"My sister?" Seemed the logical answer, but for the life of him he couldn't figure out how Celia knew about her.

"Not your sister. *Her.* Evelyn Harper. It's all over social media."

Adam palmed his face. The incident. Of course it was on social media. Because that's what people did nowadays. Forget about calling 9-1-1. Let's get it on video! "It's not what you think."

"Oh? So what am I supposed to think when I see you hugging her? I thought you said you knew her a long time ago. That there was nothing between you two."

"I wasn't hugging her. I was helping her to her seat." Okay, maybe he had been hugging Evie. Once he'd wrapped his arm around her, all he'd wanted to do was protect her. He'd been ready to become her shield when that gunman pointed his weapon at her. "It was a traumatic experience. For all of us."

"That doesn't explain why you were with her in the first place."

He had to settle this calmly. See it from Celia's point of view. "I wasn't with her. My sister was. I was meeting my sister at the café. I didn't know Harper would be there. Okay? And why does it matter? She's been cleared."

"Temporarily, you mean."

Of course she would say that. She still had it in for Evie. "Celia, there's no evidence to indicate otherwise. You have to stop focusing on her. Start focusing on Connor. Or better yet, Keith O'Hara."

"O'Hara? Why?"

"I talked to Ev—Ms. Harper about him." Ooops. Quick slip there, and a rotten thing to say for sure. Evie certainly hadn't thought he was interrogating her, but maybe it would get Celia to cool down. "I wouldn't be surprised if he was involved in this somehow."

"Just because he's sleazy doesn't mean he's a killer."

"Wouldn't hurt to do a background check on him."

"Oh, this is just great. You still like her, don't you?"

"I don't even know her." Like that made a difference.

"Okay, bad choice of words. You're attracted to her."

Why lie? Apparently he couldn't hide it. "So what if I am? She's a beautiful woman. I don't plan on dating her." At least not until the case was solved. "Relax, would you? Nothing happened."

"That might be true, but pictures tell a different story. Do you have Twitter or a Facebook account?"

"What does that have to do with anything?"

"It has to do with everything. Hero."

Hero? No. "Why'd you call me that?"

"You might want to check out Twitter or Facebook, then you'll know why I called you that. You better not have done something to get me taken off this case."

"I didn't do anything wrong. You didn't either."

"And you know just as well as I do that perception tells a different story. And right now, it's saying Evelyn Harper is your girlfriend. And the fact we haven't been able to solve this so quickly makes it look even worse. That maybe you're trying to protect her."

"You don't believe that, do you?"

"No, of course not. But you have to admit, it looks suspicious. I know I told you I didn't want you using your voodoo or witchcraft, but I'm rethinking that. A good detective uses all resources, right? So if your gut knows something, spill."

Oh, if only his gut were involved.

Chapter 10

Evie emerged from the tub. That bath had been just what the doctor ordered—if she had a doctor and the bath was ordered. She would have soaked longer except the water was getting cold and she was turning all wrinkly.

Someone pounded on the front door. "Evie, open up!"

Not someone. Keith. Damn it. What was he doing here? It would have been nice to have that security door now. But no, just any old body could come inside the building. She found Spencer's robe—a royal blue plush terry-cloth kind—on the back of the bathroom door. He wasn't here to use it any longer; she might as well. The thing was much too long, but it was soft and wasn't see-through at all, so it would do.

She rolled up the sleeves as she shuffled her way to the front door, but refused to open it. "What do you want, Keith?"

"Open up. We have to talk."

"About what?"

"About you and your boyfriend."

Boyfriend? Had Keith gone bonkers? She no sooner unlocked the door when he barged in.

"You should have told me."

She shut the door and wrapped the robe around her tightly. "Told you what?" Unless… No, he couldn't know she'd been at the coffee shop. No one had taken her name.

"This." He shoved his phone into her face. It displayed a picture of her and Adam with a headline that read, "Detective saves girlfriend from a potential mass shooting."

She stormed past him and plopped down into one of the chairs. This was just great. What her soothing bath had managed to relax, that article, and Keith, undid.

"Well?" he said. "Don't you have anything to say?"

"People see what they want to see. I am not his girlfriend." Although, maybe later it might happen. She wouldn't be opposed to that. "He was helping me to my seat. And he saved everyone in that coffee shop, not just me. I just happened to be one of the few the gunman pointed his gun at."

And she still had trouble erasing that image from her head. If she ever would.

"What?" He rushed to her side. "Are you okay? Did you get hurt?"

If she thought for one second his concern was real, she might have been nicer. But she learned a long time ago that Keith was only out for himself. And now that she was possibly worth millions, he probably saw dollar signs instead of her. "I'm fine. No one got hurt. Because Detective Fox managed to stop what could have become a mass shooting."

Keith sat on the couch, close to her. "What were you doing there with him?"

"I wasn't with him. I was with his sister. Who I happened to meet accidentally. I didn't even know he was her brother until he showed up at the coffee shop."

"That seems awfully convenient. For him."

"What? You think he staged it so Sabrina's daughter kicked off her shoe and I would be the first one to pick it up? Don't be a jerk, Keith. It was a coincidence. That's all. Besides, he told me I was cleared as a suspect. See? Good news. You won't have to worry about me anymore."

Keith stood. "You believed him?"

"Why wouldn't I believe him?"

"Shit." He rubbed his head. "I bet you talked to him, too."

"Of course I talked to him. I'm not rude."

"What did you talk about?"

"I told you. That I'm cleared. Really, Keith. He wasn't there five minutes when that gunman came in. And it's a good thing

Detective Fox was there. I'd hate to think how many people would have gotten hurt, or worse, died. That man was angry. About a stupid cup of coffee. I don't get it."

Keith paced and rubbed his face, mumbling. "Maybe this is a good thing. We can get him taken off the case."

The man was seriously deranged. Hadn't he heard a word she'd said? "Why would I want him off the case? I'd like to know who killed Spencer, and he seems pretty good at his job."

"You can't be serious. They think you did it."

Nope. Not a word. She might as well have saved her voice. "I just told you they cleared me."

"Please don't get all naïve on me. He wants to gain your trust so you'll talk to him without me around."

"That's ridiculous." Or was it? Adam did seem to have a lot of questions. Was he trying to pick up where they left off or had he been interrogating her?

* * * *

Spencer hovered in the living room, keeping his distance from Evie, but not so much from O'Hara. Anything to get the lawyer to leave. He'd done nothing but upset Evie.

All because of a photo. The detective sure did seem rather intimate with Evie. And she wasn't exactly pushing him away by putting her head on his shoulder. But if Fox had actually saved her life—and she had seemed rather shaken when she returned home—Spencer would give the man a hug if he had the capability.

"Spencerrr!" Bailey screeched from his perch by the window.

Spencer floated over to the bird. "How you doing, fella?"

"Bailey fine."

Wow. Fox had said that Bailey could see Spencer, but didn't say anything about hearing him. But then why wouldn't the bird be able to hear him? Fox could.

"Who is that thing talking to?" O'Hara said as he sat back on the couch, much too close to Evie for Spencer's liking.

Evie frowned at the man. "That *thing* is the best parrot in the world and his name is Bailey. And maybe he's talking to Spencer's ghost."

Spencer moved to Evie. "Since when do you believe in ghosts?"

"Ghost? Really?" O'Hara said.

"Not like that," she said. "I think Bailey's mind believes Spencer should be here, so he is. Probably pretending Spencer is talking to him. Which means Bailey would reply in kind."

Spencer deflated a bit. Figured she still didn't believe. But maybe he could do something to make it interesting. He went back to Bailey and repeated several times, "Keith is a jerk."

"That's the…weirdest thing I've ever heard," O'Hara said.

Spencer continued spewing the phrase. It had worked in the past, why not now?

"Weird or stupid?" Evie asked.

"I didn't say stupid," O'Hara said. "You're not stupid. But come on, it's just a bird. You can't believe it actually—"

"Keith is a jerk," Bailey said.

Keith bolted from the couch. "What the hell, Evie."

"Uh oh. Curse jar. Uh oh. Curse jar," Bailey said.

Evie snorted. "Better watch your language. He's on a roll."

"Why'd you teach him that?"

"I didn't teach him anything. I swear! That's all Spencer."

Spencer laughed and put his palm out. "All right, Bailey! Give me five."

"High five." Bailey lifted his claw, just the way Spencer had taught him.

Couldn't leave the bird hanging, but when he patted the claw, his hand went right through. "Awww, Buddy. I'm so sorry."

"What is he doing?" O'Hara asked.

Evie smiled. "High-fiving Spencer?"

"She thinks I'm here? Bailey, she thinks I'm here! Do it again, Bailey," Spencer said. "Keith is a jerk."

Bailey repeated, "Keith is a jerk. Keith is a jerk."

"This is ridiculous," O'Hara said. "Why'd he teach the bird to say that?"

She snickered behind her hand. "Maybe because Spencer didn't like you?"

"Did you tell him why we broke up? Is that it?"

"I didn't tell him you thought we were sleeping together, no."

Spencer hovered to O'Hara. "You thought she was cheating on you? You didn't trust her? You jerk!"

"Keith is a jerk," Bailey said.

O'Hara scowled. "Then why would he teach him that?"

"Maybe because he didn't think you were husband material."

He pounded his chest. "Hey, I'm great husband material."

"No, you're not, Keith. Not for me." She stood and tightened the robe around her. "I think you need to go now. I have work to do."

O'Hara grasped Evie's arms. "That was one time. One time. You're never going to forgive me for that?"

Ooooh, if Spencer could land a punch, he'd land it on O'Hara's face. Although, he could make the room shake. Should he? Probably best not. It would only scare Evie and he didn't want to do that. Besides, she seemed to be handling things pretty well on her own.

"It's more than one time, now, isn't it? What was your first thought when you saw that photo? Huh?"

"Okay, so I jump to conclusions. Doesn't mean I'm not willing to hear you out. And I believe that nothing is going on between you and Fox. I believe you. Doesn't that count for something?"

Evie yanked free from his grasp. "It counts that we can be friends. But don't ask for more than that. Now, would you please go so I can get dressed and make a living?"

O'Hara laughed. "Living? Honey, you don't have to work anymore."

Of course he would say that. O'Hara had been nothing but a money-grubbing…lawyer. And he apparently didn't know Evie at all.

"Did you ever think that maybe I like working? And if you didn't notice, the will isn't finalized until Spencer's case is solved. So yeah, I have to work."

"But how? You don't have your computer?"

"I still have my pencils and paper. I can draw out my ideas. Now go." She practically shoved O'Hara out the door.

Spencer kicked the guy's butt, just for the hell of things.

"Wait just a minute," Keith said. He fumbled in his pocket and pulled out a cellphone. "Here. This is my old phone. I reactivated it so you can use it until you get yours back. This way I don't have to come over here when I need to get in touch with you. My number is already added as a favorite."

Evie sighed, but took the phone. "Thanks Keith. I appreciate it. Now will you go?"

"I'm going. I'm going."

While Evie went to her room to get dressed, Spencer followed O'Hara down the elevator, making sure to give the creep a chill or three. If only he could give someone frostbite. Now that would be something.

This day was turning out pretty good. She wasn't interested in getting back with that creep and he'd taught Bailey a new phrase.

Spencer "escorted" O'Hara to the garage just as Hugh Latimer, the chairman of the HOA board, and Fox both pulled inside and parked. Fox emerged from his car in the visitor section, saw O'Hara, and quickly climbed back in. It wasn't until O'Hara drove away that Fox exited his vehicle. Why the subterfuge? Was he planning on visiting Evie because they *were* dating and he didn't want O'Hara to know?

Fox followed Hugh into the foyer. Hugh went to his mailbox and Fox pushed the up button.

"You're one of the detectives on the case, aren't you?" Hugh asked.

Fox turned around. "I am."

"I spoke with Detective Delavau earlier. Any leads yet?"

"I'm not at liberty to say."

"Like I told her, it's a shame the cameras don't work. I'm chairman of the HOA board here and I've been trying to get the owners to see reason, but no one wants to spend the money. I say you can't put a price on security, though. Maybe this will loosen up their purse strings."

"What the fuck?" Spencer blurted out loud, as if anyone could hear him. He had been the one trying to get the cameras installed. He was the one who wanted security to enter the building. He'd even gotten enough votes to approve it. Hugh had been the hold up, not the members. The man was full of it.

"Maybe it will," Fox said. The elevator doors opened. He stepped inside and held the door. "You coming?"

Hugh looked up from his mail. "I gotta go talk to the building manager. Thanks."

Spencer floated inside the car as the doors closed shut.

Fox jumped back a bit. "Well, you just made my job easier. Is there a place we can talk and not be disturbed?"

The detective was here to see him? "The roof. You can get to it from my floor. I figured you came to see Evie."

"I would have, if I didn't find you first."

"I heard about the incident at the coffee shop. Did you really save her from getting shot?"

"I stopped a gunman from doing something stupid. That's all. How's she doing?"

"She was a bit rattled when she came home, but the bath seemed to relax her."

Fox frowned and placed his hands on hips. "You watched her bathe?"

Hmmm… The man was rather…protective, wasn't he? "Don't be ridiculous. I'm not a perv." Although, what would it matter? Who would notice? She would, that's who. Because she felt cold whenever he was around her. He hated that he affected her that way, but no way would he invade her privacy. Cold or no cold. "How come your partner talked to Hugh? He has nothing to do with Connor."

"It's procedure to question everyone in the building, especially once we learned the cameras were fake and that you were on the board. She just happened to get his floor."

The elevator doors opened. Spencer pointed to the stairwell that led to the roof and then popped his way up there.

Fox emerged from the stairwell. "Nice set up."

One of the better perks of living in the building. Especially on warm summer nights. Several seating arrangements of rattan furniture were scattered so that more than one group could come up here and not disturb the others. There used to be a grill up here, but no one cleaned up after using it, so the board had it moved to the pool area, where it could be monitored more easily. Or rather, the users could be more easily identifiable since more people used the pool than the roof.

"Some owners have parties up here when the weather is nice. I don't expect anyone will come up here tonight." Not that Spencer could feel the weather. Hell, he couldn't feel anything. But the sky had been an ugly grey all day and the air must be chilly since Fox was wearing an overcoat. "Why the clandestine moves with O'Hara?"

"Oh, you saw that, huh? I didn't want him to know I was here. He'd think I was visiting Evie."

"So you're not here to see her? At all?"

"I'm thinking she's had enough of me for one day. I really just came here to see you. I have more questions."

Questions, questions, questions. Well, he had questions of his own. Questions he needed answered if he were to ever…move on. "I'll be happy to help any way I can. But first, what was that picture all about? You two looked all cozy."

* * * *

Adam grimaced. That damn picture was going to get his ass handed to him. "Please don't be mad about that."

"I'm not mad. O'Hara was, though."

O'Hara was mad, huh? Damn it. Did the guy think he still had a shot with Evie? Or could the two of them be involved with Spencer's death? That's what Celia would think in any case. "Yeah, about that. How come you didn't tell me Evie used to date him?"

"Because it didn't seem relevant. And they broke up because he didn't trust her. With me." Spencer leaned back and barked laughter. "Can you believe that? The man must be blind to see she didn't look at me like a person in love. That she treated me more like a brother than a lover. And you know, at first that bothered me, but then I realized if I couldn't accept being her surrogate brother, she wouldn't be in my life at all. So I tried to be her brother. I really did. And that meant biting my tongue when she dated that creep."

"How did she meet him?" Adam meandered to a chair and ran his hand along the cushion. Good, it was dry. He sat and faced the ghost.

Spencer lowered his head. "I introduced them."

"You? How?"

"At the company Christmas party."

Adam bolted to his feet. "Wait, what? O'Hara works at your firm?" How had he not known this? He'd specifically told Evie to hire someone outside of Spencer's firm.

Spencer shook his head. "Not anymore. But he used to work there."

Adam paced in front of the chair. Maybe it wasn't as bad as he thought. "When did he leave?"

"Back in March."

"Was he still dating Evie at the time?"

Spencer lowered his head again and spoke softly. "Yes."

"Spencer… What aren't you telling me?"

"I might have…had a hand…into getting him…fired."

"What? You don't think that information would be *relevant?*" If O'Hara and Evie were involved, wouldn't that be motivation? Oh hell, this case was just getting worse and worse. For Evie.

Spencer folded his arms across his chest. "No, I don't. He has a better job now. Probably making more money, too. He might have been mad then, but he has no reason to be mad now. Certainly no reason worth murdering me."

"Would he suspect you'd leave everything to Evie? Especially after your mother died?"

"They broke up shortly after her death. If he was aiming to get some action, he sure went about it wrong."

"Could their breakup have been an act? If he knew, and told Evie…" Adam closed his eyes. God, those words practically curdled on his tongue. "And now that you're out of the picture…" She couldn't be involved with O'Hara. She just couldn't.

"Will you relax? She and O'Hara are not an item. Okay? So don't go there. Oh, yeah, he hoped to get back with her, but she nipped that in the bud. That's when I found out *why* she broke it off. You don't know how happy that made me."

"Oh?" Adam plopped back onto the chair.

"Yeah, I can see it makes you happy, too."

More than happy. Relieved. Meant Evie and O'Hara weren't in this together. If only he had proof, though. Something he could take to his captain. Something to keep Celia pointed away from Evie.

"Besides, I don't think O'Hara has the guts to kill anyone. He's more the flight than fight kind of person. My brother, though…" Spencer shrugged. "Who knows. Any luck in finding him?"

"No. He hasn't been at his trailer since Saturday. We checked with his mother. Claims she hasn't seen him in months. Do you remember any of his friends?"

"We were hardly close. And the only time we spent any time together was when Dad had us both for his two-week-long vacation. Almost like he put us together to get his obligation over with quicker. Or maybe he'd hoped we'd keep ourselves busy so he wouldn't have to do anything."

"How come you never told Evie about Connor?"

"Not just Evie. I didn't tell Lee, either. I was so envious of the relationship Lee and Evie had. The family they had. I wanted that with Connor, but Connor had—has—anger issues and didn't want anything to do with me. Said I was Dad's mistake. Said he was the one Dad wanted. I couldn't fault him for that reasoning, because at the time I had thought the same. So when it came time to talk about family, I just pretended Connor didn't exist. It was what he wanted anyway."

"You don't think the same now? About your father?"

"My inheritance? It was from Dad. He'd left half of his estate to me and half to Connor. I figure he must have loved me after all if he included me in the will. Connor, however, was livid. Thought it should have all gone to him. Which is why I worry about Evie. He would definitely think she wasn't entitled to my money."

"Until the will is read, she's safe." And thank goodness. By then Connor should be behind bars. Adam looked at the time and stood. "I gotta go. You don't have any other secrets to spill do you? Any more ex-boyfriends?"

Spencer chuckled. "No more ex-boyfriends. She really didn't date before O'Hara and no one since."

"Good. Then I'll see you later." Adam headed for the door.

"Wait. You've dealt with a lot of ghosts, right?"

Adam stopped. "I have. Why?"

"What kind of abilities do I have?"

Spencer probably possessed several abilities, but Adam wasn't going to mention them. A ghost left in the dark made for a safer ghost. Usually. "Hard to say. Every ghost is different. Why do you ask?"

"Well, I made stuff shake earlier. How did I do that?"

"I told you my theory. Anger. You don't have the body to maintain pressure, so it just…goes outward. I have no proof that's why it happens. Not every ghost I've met got angry."

"Can I control it?"

"I'm sure with practice you could control anything. Wouldn't you rather move on, though? And be at peace?"

"I can't be at peace until I know Evie will be okay."

"I understand. But if you want to practice controlling your anger so you can move things, you might want to do it outside. Away from the buildings. You don't want to give Evie a reason to move, now do you?" Adam headed back for the door and debated whether he should ask or not, but right now he needed all the help he could get and if that meant giving a ghost some knowledge, he'd have to risk it. "Have you run into any other ghosts?"

"Here? In the building?"

"In the building. In your bubble. Yeah."

"I have a bubble?"

"I told you that, too. You're stuck within a quarter-mile radius of your death. You go beyond that, you'll pop back to your place of death."

"That doesn't seem fair, now does it?"

"Maybe it's to force you to move on. Ever think of that?" At least, that was his and Zane's theory. "So have you? Seen another ghost?"

"I don't think so. It's not like I go out much. Today was the first day I actually ventured from my condo. I mean, look at me. What if someone saw me dressed like this?"

Adam shook his head. "The only someone who can see you besides me is another ghost. And if there's one in your bubble, they might have seen your murder."

"Oh. How would I recognize them, though? I see everyone."

"Because they're not solid."

Elliott looked down at his chest. "You can see through me?"

"Yep. And you'll be able to see through another ghost the same way. So do me a favor, okay? Check your bubble for other ghosts." Adam opened the door to the stairs.

"Are you a good guy, Adam Fox?"

He held the door and turned around. "I'd like to think so."

"Evie mentioned you have a sister. Sabrina? Are you close?"

"She mentioned her? To you?" When Elliott raised his eyebrows, Adam realized his blunder. "She mentioned her to O'Hara, right?" The ghost nodded. Yeah, that made more sense. "I'm not as close to Sabrina as I'd like. She married someone I didn't really trust, but she's getting a divorce now and I'm helping as best as I can."

"Then you're a good guy."

"A good guy wouldn't have let her marry him."

Spencer chuffed. "I'm sure you couldn't have stopped it any more than I could have stopped Evie from dating O'Hara. You like Evie?"

Keep the ghost calm. Zane's warning came blaring into Adam's head. He wasn't sure what answer would work best. A lie or the truth? "Where are you going with this questioning?"

"After you find my murderer, do you have any intention of pursuing her?"

"Why do I get the feeling there's no right answer to that question?"

Elliott sighed. "I'm not mad that you like her. Okay? I'm glad. You're a police officer. A detective. You care about your family. You're a good guy. Evie needs a good guy."

Whoa. Not at all what he expected. "Matchmaking, are we?"

"I just want what's best for her."

"Then maybe you should let her decide that for herself. But to answer your question, I would very much like to know her better. Provided she wants to do the same with me."

"Did you see that picture of you two on Facebook?"

Adam covered his face. "Oh please, don't remind me."

"Look at it more closely next time. You'll see why people think you two are involved."

Chapter 11

Evie rode the elevator back up to the condo and thumbed through the mail. Remembering to get the mail was going to take some time. Spencer always got the mail on his way in from work. Always. And on Saturdays, he'd make a special trip downstairs. Like it was his favorite part of the day or something. She never cared. No one ever wrote to her. And she had no bills. Not even a credit card. She wasn't going to get into that trap. Ever.

Her parents had. She and Lee had to sell their house just to pay off their credit card debt. What little remained from the sale, Lee insisted she use for college since he was joining the Army. So she had. But had Lee learned anything from that? Nope. She'd had to sell his house to pay off his own damn debt, which had left her homeless. Oh, she would have eventually found an apartment to live in, but with needing first and last months' rents up front, it would have been a long eventually. Spencer had been a life saver offering a room, but she'd been reluctant to take him up on his generous offer. Then he'd told her how much he missed Lee, making it hard for her to say no. After he'd agreed she'd pay her fair share—rent and food—and would only stay until she could afford her own place, it had made sense to move in. But by the time she'd saved enough money, Spencer's condo had become home. Spencer and Bailey had become family. He'd never asked her to leave and she never did look for her own place.

Spencer had so much mail. And it'd only been two mail days since…well, *that* day. She stopped at the electric bill. Should she pay it or Spencer's estate? Would Spencer's estate take care of the bills? And what about any bills that he got online? She would have to ask Aaron Callahan about that.

But since she no longer had to pay rent, and no one was going to kick her out—yet—she should probably pay the utilities. They couldn't possibly be more than what she'd been paying Spencer. Provided she could still make a living. And why wouldn't she? She'd been cleared as a suspect—and, unlike Keith, she believed Adam—so her business should be safe.

Or rather, safe again. Provided the two days offline wasn't disastrous. She never realized how much she depended on her phone and laptop. Not only for her business, but to keep her mind off of things. Things like Spencer's death. Or his upcoming funeral. Or Adam.

Especially Adam.

She flipped through the rest of the mail—mostly junk—and came to one piece that wasn't Spencer's. Oh, the condo unit was correct, but it was addressed to the building manager. "Damn it. Note to Evie: look at the mail before stepping into the elevator."

The squeaky doors opened on her floor. Adam stood waiting to embark.

That they'd found each other after all these years was a miracle. That it happened under these circumstances was unfair.

"Our elevators must have passed in the shaft. Huh?" she said. At least they hadn't passed a second time. Although with the way she looked—wearing leggings and her penguin T-shirt, and her hair in a messy bun—maybe it would have been better if they had passed.

"Actually, I've been here awhile. Questioning. People. I didn't want to bother you." He pointed to her hands. "You got the mail."

Despite her dishevelment, disappointment still burned in her chest. So he hadn't come to see her. "Yeah. Forgot all about it when I came home."

The doors started closing and he put his hand out to stop them. "Aren't you coming out?"

"Actually, I got someone else's mail by mistake, so I was headed back down." Now, why did she go and say that? He was going to think she was some kind of idiot not checking the mail beforehand.

"Bummer. I've done that. Mind if I tag along?"

"Not at all." Wow. No ridicule. Spencer would have seen fit to correct her. That always irritated her, but in a sibling kind of way. Like her brother Lee had always irritated her one way or another. Didn't mean she didn't love him. Just that she wanted to smack him every now and then.

As Adam stepped into the car, he transformed it into some kind of safe space. His presence filled her with peace, just like he had all those years ago. Just like he had at the café.

She pushed the button for the first floor. The squeaky doors closed slowly.

He chuckled. "Okay, is it just me or do those doors sound like a Wookiee to you?"

"A Wookiee? Like Chewbacca?" She'd never really thought about it, but now that he mentioned it… She laughed. "I guess they do. Thanks for that visual."

"You're welcome. Nice to know you understood what I said. Would you believe some people haven't seen *Star Wars*?"

"Kind of hard to imagine."

"Right?"

The car started the slow descent. Spencer had hated how slow the elevators were, and she might have, too, if she was in a hurry, but today she had nothing to complain about. She could use some more alone time with Adam. "Did you get taller?"

"What? Since this afternoon?"

She laughed. "No. Since…then. You were eighteen, right?"

"Yeah. And you were seventeen, or rather, how did you put it? 'One month from your eighteenth birthday.' See? I didn't forget. I grew a couple more inches since then. I'm officially six-two and one quarter. You haven't changed at all."

"I doubt that." Sure, she was still five-six in her bare feet, but she did have a little extra padding in the butt region. Probably from sitting all day on the job. Too bad she didn't inherit her mother's butt genes. She really should get out more often. Or use that fancy bike machine in Spencer's bedroom.

Something exploded in the distance. The lights flickered and the elevator jolted to a stop. She grabbed the rail to keep from falling. For a moment they were in pitch darkness. Her throat closed up. Air. She needed air.

The emergency light came on.

Oh, thank goodness. Even though she knew she was still in the elevator, the lack of light made a huge difference. And now that there was light, she could relax. She took a deep breath. "What happened?"

Adam turned to the control panel. She could have sworn he muttered, "Spencer."

"Excuse me?"

"Power outage?"

"That's not what you said."

"It's not?" He opened a tiny door. Picked up the emergency phone. "This is Detective Fox with the Chicago Police. You got two people stuck on elevator two." Pause. "Evelyn Harper." Another pause. "Okay. Thanks." He hung up. "Seems the whole building is out. Electrician has been called." He pulled out his cellphone.

"You probably won't get a signal in here. I never do."

"You're right. It's useless." He shoved it back into his pocket. "Might as well get comfortable, huh? Probably be here awhile."

Comfortable? Awhile? If the power was out… "Air can get in here. Right?"

"There's plenty of air. We won't suffocate."

Good to know. And as long as she could see, she should be fine. "How far up are we? Should we try to escape?"

"Oh no. We're safer inside. Besides, I think we stopped around the tenth floor."

"Tenth floor?" That was a long way down. "And the cables?"

"They're secure. We aren't going to fall. It's just a power outage."

"You sound pretty confident."

"Not my first outage. Or stuck elevator. Just relax. Someone will get us out. They know we're in here."

"How long do you think?" Maybe if it only took ten minutes she could survive without looking like a psycho.

"Depends on the traffic and how far away they are. Probably an hour. At least."

"An hour?" Way longer than she anticipated. But she could see. And Adam was here. That should make a difference. She hoped.

The emergency light dimmed for a few seconds before going out for good. Blackness. All around her was blackness.

"Are you fucking kidding me?" This wasn't happening. Not again. "I need to get out of here." She pounded on the doors. "Help!"

Something touched her arm and she screamed.

* * * *

Adam had been stuck in an elevator three times before. Once due to a mechanical issue and twice due to a power outage. None of those incidents were caused by a curious ghost, and Adam would bet his last nickel that Spencer was the cause. But for the emergency lights to also go out?

Some condo building.

Evie was losing it, though. Adam touched her arm and she screamed.

"Evie, it's me. Adam. You're panicking. Close your eyes."

"I can't be in here. I have to get out. Get me out of here!"

"Take some deep breaths. I'm going to touch your face." He ran his hand up her arm. Along her neck—oh sweet Jesus, her skin was as silky smooth as he remembered—and covered her eyes. "Close your eyes and sit. Pretend you're looking out your living room window."

Her breathing slowed and he guided her to the floor. She was a quivering mess and he wanted to hold her tight. To ease her mind. As if he had the right. Although he wouldn't mind having the right.

"You got your eyes closed?"

"Yes."

He removed his hand. "What do you see out your window?"

"The boats on the lake. Crystal blue sky." She was in the process of leaning into him—and he was ready to take advantage of that—when she jerked upright. "What the hell is wrong with me?" she muttered.

"Nothing is wrong with you. Lots of people are afraid of the dark." And it was definitely dark. Not a speck of light shown through the cracks.

"Kids, you mean. And they grow out of it."

"Not true. Believe it or not, I don't know that many kids. But I do know a lot of adults. I had a roommate who needed a light on in the room in order to sleep."

"You're just saying that to make me feel better."

"Sort of true. I'm telling you his story to make you feel better. He'd kill me if he knew I had. Oh shit. I'm so stupid." He pulled out his smartphone.

"Why are you stupid?"

"Because I have a light." He turned on the flashlight app. His battery was at 30%. Damn it. Hopefully it would be enough. He set the phone down. The light wasn't much, but at least it didn't feel like they were stuck in a tomb. "How's that?"

She opened her eyes and looked around. She wasn't shivering anymore. Either the light did the trick or Spencer had left. If Spencer had even been here to begin with.

"Better?" He resisted the urge to rest his arm across her shoulders. To pull her in close and offer comfort. Because if he didn't resist, he might do something stupid. Like kiss her.

"Yes. Thank you. Although, closing my eyes helped, too. Something you learned from your friend?"

"Something I taught him. I learned it from my grandma."

"You were afraid of the dark?"

"I had a bad experience as a kid. Grandma helped me get through it. She'd say, 'When you close your eyes you can transport yourself anywhere. Or fall asleep doing it.' She wasn't wrong."

Evie laughed. "She sounds wonderful."

"She was." Saddest day of his life was the day she'd left him for good. He'd always wondered how she ended up with a daughter who lacked any kind of empathy.

"I'm sorry for your loss."

"Thanks. It happened a long time ago, though. Doesn't mean I don't still miss her."

"I know what you mean. I miss Lee every single day. Oh, don't get me wrong. I miss my parents, too, but Lee was my buddy. My friend. We could tell each other anything."

"Spencer wasn't that person for you?"

"I thought he was. Now? I'm not so sure. I'm learning so much about him that he never shared. I don't get it."

"Probably because he was in love with you and knew you didn't feel the same."

Evie scrunched her forehead. "What? How would you know?"

Yeah, how would I know that? Idiot! "Just a feeling I got."

"That gut of yours, huh? Is your gut saying your battery will last until help comes?"

No, no, no. No talking about their situation. "Let's think positive, okay? You're not worried about Bailey, are you?"

"No. He'll be fine. Probably prefers the dark. He can see out the window better that way. No reflections. Unless the whole block is out. Do you think the whole block is out?"

"I doubt it. You don't call an electrician for a large outage. How long ago did Spencer get the bird?"

"Oh gosh, years ago. Years before Lee died, even. Spencer had seen the bird in a pet store and became enamored. He'd always wanted a pet. Figured a bird wouldn't be as messy as a dog or cat." She snickered. "He was wrong."

Keeping her light hearted was his one goal. "Are you going to keep him?"

"Of course I'm keeping him. He's a great bird. Funny thing is that Spencer bought him because of their long lifespan. Said he and Bailey would grow old together." She frowned. "Shit. Guess that's not happening. I can't believe he's gone. Although sometimes it feels like he's never left."

"Wait a minute. I thought you didn't believe in ghosts." If she did believe, telling her about his gift would be easier. But not now. After this case. Definitely after this case and after Spencer moved on. And only if she'd have him.

"Ghosts? Who said anything about ghosts?"

Okay, that stung. He had hoped she'd changed her mind. "I just assumed, especially after what Brina said." Now he was rambling. He needed to just shut up.

"Sabrina has an active imagination, for sure. What I meant is… It's just that Spencer's stuff is still there. And then there's Bailey. Can a bird hallucinate?"

"I have no idea. Why do you ask?"

"Something Bailey did. It was like he was playing with Spencer. Which is crazy, right?"

"Playing? How?"

"When Keith was over, Bailey started yelling, 'Keith is a jerk.' That is something Spencer would teach Bailey. I almost laughed out loud."

Adam didn't bother restraining his laughter. *Good one, Spencer.* "When did he teach him that? When you were dating Keith?"

"I don't know. Bailey had never said that before. And then he raised his claw. He only ever did that when Spencer said 'High five.' It was really strange."

Damn it. What was that ghost up to? Was he trying to get Adam to confess? Like that would do any good. If anything, she'd move away. From him. From the strange occurrences. From Spencer. And then Spencer would get angry and blame Adam, when it would have been his own damn fault. He needed a plausible excuse. Like maybe…

"Could it be possible Bailey doesn't like Keith and just said it? And maybe he wanted to high five you?"

That made her think. "Spencer would say it was. He always thought Bailey spoke as if he knew what he was saying. I think Bailey just mimics what he hears. Although…"

"Although, what?" Adam crossed his fingers that she'd come to another conclusion. One that she could accept.

"I did sort of have a conversation with Bailey the other morning. One-sided, that is. Maybe Spencer was right. That Bailey is smart and can communicate. He just has to learn the words. And I did call Keith a jerk. Maybe that's all it takes. And now I feel bad that I didn't high five him back."

Adam hid his relief. One day he'd tell her the truth, but that day wasn't today. And after they got out of this elevator car, he'd have a serious conversation with Spencer.

* * * *

Once Fox had turned on his flashlight app and calmed Evie, Spencer popped back to the foyer. Even the emergency lights were out. The only light in the foyer came from outside, through the front door.

He should have practiced first, like Fox had suggested. But when Fox and Evie rode down the same elevator, Spencer got an idea.

Some idea.

He had popped down to the basement. Floated through the locked utility door and had found the electrical panel. There had been just enough light from the emergency EXIT sign to see.

All he had to do was focus on the breaker for the elevator. Simple, right? Wrong. He'd blasted the whole box instead. Now he was sorry he'd even tried. He hadn't meant to scare Evie like that.

Didn't even know about her fear of the dark. And he made the emergency lights go out, too? What an idiot.

He thought for sure the elevator malfunction would have been fun. Cause the two of them to get close again. Like they had when they were kids. Instead, he freaked out the one person he never wanted to freak out.

He so much wanted to give her a hug. But then she'd get cold and Fox would notice and so, he kept his distance. They didn't need to know he was spying. And he never planned to stay long, just long enough to make sure she was okay. Which she wasn't.

But Fox was taking care of her. Calmed her down. That was enough for Spencer to leave them alone.

Two repairmen loaded with electrical equipment and working flashlights came through the front door and headed for the basement. Spencer followed. When they reached the door to the utilities, they punched in a code and entered.

There was a freaking code box for the utility room, but not the garage or building? If Spencer had known about that box when he'd been alive he'd have let loose on the board. He couldn't imagine it would have cost that much to have a damn keycard system. But he never got the chance to investigate costs. Hell, he never got a chance to do any good on the board.

The electricians shined their flashlights on the electrical box.

If only he could repair the damage he'd done. But that box sure looked like a done deal. If one were looking to cook a box.

"Damn," Worker One said. "Looks like lightning struck it."

It sure did look that way. Had the bolts come from his eyes? That would have been cool to see. But actually, Spencer couldn't recall any light source before the bang. So whatever he threw at it was invisible. At least to him.

"We're gonna need a whole new box," Worker Two said.

"Not only that, look at this. The wires are practically melted. What the hell caused this, do you think?"

"I'd say a power surge, but I ain't never seen a surge only hit one building like this."

A power surge? Hmmm… Spencer placed his hands on his hips. "Just call me Spencer, the Power Surger."

"Yeah, me neither," Worker One said. "We're not going to be able to help those people in the elevator."

"Not anytime soon, that's for sure. Come on, let's go tell him the bad news."

Spencer followed the repairmen to the building manager's residence.

Worker One knocked. Tony opened the door. Candles were lit inside his apartment. "What's the word?"

"It's gonna be hours before we can get it fixed. If not tomorrow."

Tony's eyes widened. "What? It's that bad?"

"What?" Spencer mimicked. Adam was so going to kill him. Wait. He was already dead. Still, he didn't want to be scolded like some child, dead or not.

"We gotta replace the whole shebang," Worker One said. "Wires, too. Let the elevator people know they have a rescue to perform. Then notify the residents, in case they want to stay somewhere else."

Tony pointed toward the dark EXIT sign. "What about the emergency lights? Why are they out?"

"I'd say the battery died. When was it checked last?"

"Hell if I should know."

"You're the building manager, aren't you?"

"That's my job?"

Spencer palmed his face. He knew he should have bought the management company out right when he couldn't get the HOA to find another one. Then he could have hired someone who knew his ass from a hole in the ground.

At least he knew he wasn't responsible for the emergency lights going out. Unless his surge caused the battery to die. Shit.

Spencer popped back into his condo. The two UPSes—uninterrupted power supplies his electronics were plugged into—were beeping. They'd beep until the power came back on or they died, whichever came first.

All night. The power could be out all night. Would Evie leave? Of course she'd leave. Why stay here when the electric was out? She wasn't about to walk up and down twenty flights of steps—without emergency lights, no less—now was she? But where would she go?

Not O'Hara's. Please, not O'Hara's. Shit. That man was useless.

But wait. She didn't like him. She didn't look at him the way she looked at Fox. So maybe staying with O'Hara wouldn't be all bad. She wouldn't let him make a move. Right?

Spencer laughed. He needn't worry. Wherever Evie went, Bailey went. O'Hara would not want the bird in his apartment. Hmmm… Spencer hovered over to Bailey.

"Spencerrrr!"

"That's right. It's your good ole buddy, Spencer." It was nice that Bailey could see and hear him. Apparently, so could another ghost. He'd never bothered to search the other floors. Why would he? His home was here. But once the power came back on, he'd check them out. Until then, maybe he should teach the bird a few more phrases. Seemed he had a few hours to kill.

Chapter 12

Evie stared at the light source. How long would that phone stay lit?

It wasn't that she hated all darkness. She was okay with nighttime. She could sleep without a light on. Oh sure, she kept the drapes open—who was going to see inside the twentieth floor anyway?—because it was never dark in the city. Even in her old room, when she lived with her parents, the street lamp had been enough for her.

But pitch dark? Where she couldn't see anything? It was too much like being trapped in that box. Why closing her eyes made it better, she didn't know. Didn't want to know. Still, if that light went out...

"How long has it been?" she asked.

Adam glanced at his watch. One of those old analog types. The type her dad used to wear. "About thirty minutes."

"Only thirty minutes?" Why did it feel like hours already?

"Have I grown boring in my old age?"

"Hardly. If it weren't for you, I don't know what I would have done. You're keeping me sane." As was the light from his cellphone. It hadn't dimmed any, had it?

"I'm glad I could be of service. What happened to cause you to be afraid?"

"What makes you think something happened?"

"Because fear comes from experiences. We're all basically fearless until something happens to cause us to be afraid."

"Did your grandmother tell you that, too?"

"No. Believe it or not, I figured that out myself. See, I used to love to dive. Not just in pools, but in lakes. From any height. The more dangerous it looked, the more thrilling it was. When I was 13, I got hurt and realized I wasn't invincible. Now? If it doesn't look safe, I ain't jumping. Why risk it?"

"But you became a cop. That's a risk, isn't it?"

"Except I'm not doing it for the thrills. I'm helping other people. Big difference. So what happened to you? If you'd rather not say—"

"No, that's not it." She'd always wanted someone to confide in, but never did for fear it would come back to her parents. Now that her whole family was gone, did it really matter? She might have told Adam-from-the-amusement-park, if the subject had come up, so why not tell him now?

"My mother always said, 'We don't talk of such things.' She was a big believer in family secrets. Why she felt this should be one, too, I don't know. So of course I never told anyone, not even Spencer. If Lee told him, I'm not aware of it. Lee blamed himself, so I couldn't see him spilling his guts, and since my parents never wanted to talk about it, we didn't, but when I was twelve, I nearly died."

"What? How?"

"Stupidity?" It sure seemed stupid now that she looked back on that day. "Lee thought I was old enough to leave alone for a few hours even though my parents didn't. And clearly, they were correct. He wasn't gone ten minutes when I got bored. So I went to the backyard to set up the sprinkler. I think it was close to ninety degrees that day and we didn't have air conditioning. Probably why Lee wanted to get out of the house.

"Anyway, I was pulling the hose from the storage box—one of those long plastic ones with the cushions on top so it could be used as a bench, too—when some kind of swarm came through the yard. I panicked at the buzzing noise and jumped inside the box. When the buzzing stopped, I went to open the lid and it wouldn't budge. The latch had hooked around the loop and locked me inside."

"Shit."

"You're telling me. It was dark in there. Felt like I was in a coffin and I panicked. I pounded and screamed what felt like forever, but if anyone heard me, they didn't come to my rescue. And then it got hotter and hotter and I found it harder to breathe. By the time Lee came home, I had passed out. Thankfully, he was concerned I wasn't there and called my friends. After he struck out, he finally caved and called Dad. Dad's the one who noticed the hose was not where it should be. Another hour or two and I might not have survived. I was diagnosed with heatstroke. Spent the night in the hospital. Where there was air conditioning."

"And you never climbed in that box again, huh?"

"Dad wanted to toss the box in the trash. Mom said that wasn't necessary. That I'd learned my lesson. She wasn't wrong. Instead, Dad yanked that latch free with his bare hands. Lee said he'd never seen Dad so scared. And Lee couldn't apologize enough. Especially when I'd wake up screaming from a nightmare."

"How long did those last?"

Had they ever really stopped? It had been almost a year since the last one. At least she handled them better now. "I suppose the nightly one lasted a few months."

"Did you see a shrink?"

"A shrink? You mean a therapist? Are you kidding? My mother believed that if you didn't talk about it, it didn't happen."

"But not your dad?"

"He would never go against her wishes, and frankly, I don't think he knew how to talk to me about it. Instead, he just gave me hugs and told me everything was fine." A hug from him now would come in pretty handy, too. He'd always made her feel safe. "You think I should see a therapist about my fear?"

"That's up to you. But if it's controlling your life, might not be a bad thing."

She couldn't say it was controlling her life, but then what kind of life did she really have? Maybe it was time to find a professional to consult with. Talking to Adam about it had helped a little, but should she be using him that way?

"Keith still thinks I shouldn't talk with you. That you're only being nice to get information out of me. I told him what you told me, that I'm cleared as a suspect. But he thinks you lied to me to get me to open up to you without him being there to protect me."

"I didn't lie. You aren't a suspect anymore. He can call Detective Delavau to confirm it."

"You mean, until you find evidence to say otherwise."

"Will you stop? You have an alibi. And there isn't any proof to show you're involved. You wait and see. It'll all turn out fine."

"And you know this, how?"

He patted his stomach. "Gut feeling."

He used that answer a lot. What exactly did he mean by it, though? Intuition? Or was he just very good at his job? Guess he'd have to be since he'd solved all his cases.

A phone rang. Not his cell, the emergency one. He popped to his feet and answered, "We're still here."

He smiled at her while he listened, but after a bit his eyes weren't looking as happy as his lips. Something was wrong. Would he bother telling her?

"Got it. Thanks." He hung up and sat back beside her. "It's going to be at least another hour."

"What? Why?" No way would that light last that long.

"The electricians are going to need several hours to fix the outage."

"We're stuck in here all night?" *Oh God, oh God, oh God!*

"No. We're stuck here until someone comes to get us out. They were hoping the electricity could be fixed easily and the car would run. Apparently, it's not an easy fix. In fact, he suggested you find another place to stay until it is."

"Another place?" Where the hell would she go?

"You know, like a hotel."

"I know what you meant. But no hotel is going to allow Bailey."

"I know you don't have family here, but don't you have a friend you could stay with?"

She lowered her head. "I don't have anyone."

"Not even…Keith?"

Was he fishing, was that it? "Oh please. He'd be the last person I'd ask."

"If you don't like him, why pick him for your lawyer?"

"Because he's the only lawyer I know who isn't associated with Spence. And I was scared."

"Well, now you can just tell him to scram. You don't need him anymore."

She'd like to believe that, but a tiny voice—one that sounded way too much like Keith—said it was better to keep him…just in case. Because maybe Adam thought she was in the clear, but his partner might have other ideas.

Adam brought a knee up. "If you can't find someplace that will allow Bailey, I can always take him to my place. I'm sure Sabrina wouldn't mind watching him."

She almost thought he was going to ask her to stay at his place. And she would have jumped at the chance. But that was crazy, wasn't it? They hardly knew each other. "Thanks for the offer, but I don't need to go anywhere. Not if we're only talking about one night. Now if it were out for a week, I might take you up on it."

The light dimmed. She hadn't imagined it this time. "Oh no. No, no, no."

"It's okay." He stood and nudged her shoulder with his leg. "Scootch forward."

She moved away from the elevator wall. "Why? What are you doing?"

"Distracting you, what else?" He settled behind her, his legs alongside hers, his presence comforting. Protecting. And a little stimulating. "Now, close your eyes." He placed his hands on her shoulders and leaned forward. "They're still open."

That they were. And if they weren't stuck in an elevator with their light source fading she might have taken advantage of their situation. "It's getting dark."

"Yep. But we're not going anywhere. You're still in the elevator car. And we have plenty of air. Now close your eyes."

"I don't know if I can keep them closed that long." But she lowered her head and did as he commanded. Concentrated on the way his legs rubbed up against hers. On the way his hands covered her shoulders. It took everything within her not to lean back against his chest.

He massaged her shoulders, sending her into nirvana. The man had serious finger ability. She could so get used to this. But would he have bothered if not for their current situation?

"Then try to sleep. I got you, okay? Relax. Enjoy. Pretend you're at some posh spa. Or better yet, we're on that water ride at Six Flags. Remember that?"

"How could I forget? You purposely had us sit up front so I would get all wet." And boy, had she. Thank goodness the night had been warm.

He chuckled. "Yeah. Good times."

"So you admit you just wanted to see my bra." Because when her shirt had gotten wet, it became nearly transparent.

"I'm not admitting anything." He leaned forward and whispered, "But it sure was a pretty shade of pink. Now relax."

She probably could go to sleep if he kept massaging her shoulders. And would that be so bad? Using him as a pillow? He certainly smelled great. Hell, she'd nearly kissed him earlier, and when she'd questioned what she was doing, hadn't realized she'd said the words aloud. Thankfully, he thought she was talking about being afraid of the dark. If he only knew how much she wanted to kiss him now. But that was a bad idea.

Wasn't it?

* * * *

Adam was pretty sure Heaven existed. He'd heard enough stories from ghosts. Ghosts who had seen other ghosts move on to believe in its existence. And while Adam was alive and well on planet Earth, he felt like he was in Heaven all the same. Who knew being stuck in a darkening elevator with the most beautiful woman in the world would be that for him? It certainly wasn't a dream.

He leaned over Evie's shoulder. Finally, she'd closed her eyes. To save his dying battery, he turned off the flashlight app with one hand while continuing to massage her slender shoulders with the other. When he'd started the massage, she was stiff, her shoulders like rocks, but after a minute or three, she'd relaxed. Might have even fallen asleep. Yet, he kept massaging. Because touching her was bliss and he wouldn't stop until she said to.

"You think we'll ever get out of here?" she asked.

Okay, so maybe she hadn't fallen asleep. "I can say confidently that we will."

"I meant alive."

He chuckled. When had she become so…pessimistic? "So did I. Will you stop worrying? You're making me feel inadequate."

"Inadequate? How?"

"That my calming techniques aren't working."

"Oh, this massage thing is working. I just wish your flashlight was still working."

Yeah, that would have been nice. It had been keeping her calm. Talkative. He wanted her to keep talking. Even though they were in the worst of circumstances, he couldn't remember the last time he enjoyed having a conversation with a woman that didn't include the subject of sex.

No, he took that back. He could remember. It was with her. Eleven years ago.

"What prompted you to start a graphic artist business?"

"Well…money." She laughed. "I wasn't into that starving-artist thing. I like to eat too much."

"But you had Spencer."

She stiffened. "I didn't *have* Spencer. I leaned on him for a little bit, sure, but not for long. And I paid him rent and my share of living expenses from the day I moved in. He was my friend. Another brother, actually. At least I thought he was."

Adam massaged the new knots in her shoulders. "Sorry. I didn't mean to upset you."

"It's not you. He just makes me so damn mad."

That made two of them, for completely different reasons. "Because he had money and didn't tell you?"

"What? No. I mean, well, maybe. He knew how I felt about money. It was the secrets. He had so many damn secrets."

Spencer had certainly kept a lot from her. "I'm sure he didn't tell you he left you his estate because he knew what you'd say."

"I suppose," she grumbled. "But what about Connor? He had a freakin' brother I knew nothing about!"

"I got the impression they weren't close. Else, he would have left Connor part of his estate, if not all of it. So maybe Spencer was embarrassed because he didn't have the same kind of relationship with his brother like you had with yours."

"Okay, that might make sense, too. So, smartypants, do you have a reason why he never bothered to tell me he was on the HOA board?"

"You didn't know?"

"Not until after he died. But you knew, right? From your investigation."

"The building manager mentioned it. If Spencer didn't tell you, who did?"

"It doesn't matter. I swear, it's like I never even knew him. He only shared the happy stuff with me, if he even shared all of that. Why do you suppose he did that?"

Adam didn't have a clue. It wasn't like any of Spencer's secrets were all that important. "He didn't want to burden you with it?"

"But isn't that what friends are for?" She leaned her head back against his chest. "I probably know more about your childhood than I did of his and I grew up with him. You didn't seem to have a problem sharing that information with me."

"Well, when you're trying to get to know someone, you share the good and bad. Right?" Not that he'd shared all the bad. It wasn't like he was hiding anything insignificant, like Spencer had. And he would tell her…eventually. Once they declared their love for one another. If that day would ever come.

"Exactly—wait."

His fingers froze on her shoulders. What the hell had he just said?

She twisted in his lap, placed her palms on his chest. "If I hadn't left that night, would you have asked me out? Asked for my number?"

Oh boy. Her touch was wreaking havoc with his body and he was growing hard. Why'd she have to go open that door? But did it really matter? He would have opened it eventually. "Yeah, I would have."

"Why?"

He covered her hands with his. "Besides finding you irresistible? Because you listened to me. Didn't laugh when I told you I wanted to become a police detective. You made me feel like I…mattered." Something he'd never gotten from his parents. They had never taken him seriously. On anything.

"You did matter. To me. You don't know how often I wished I could have changed things. Given you my last name. My number."

"And I wished I would have gone with you. So many times I wished that. But we can't change the past. We can only move forward." And when this case was over, he was moving full steam ahead.

"If only I weren't a suspect."

"You're not." But it didn't really matter what he thought, now did it? She would be considered a person of interest until they discovered proof that showed otherwise.

"But what if—"

He gripped her hands, keeping her close to his chest. "Will you stop? You didn't kill Spencer. You didn't have anything to do with his death. I know this."

"How? How do you know? Keith doesn't know. He actually asked me if I killed Spence. How do you know I'm not a good con woman? How do you know I didn't talk Spence into leaving me all his money? What proof do you have? And please don't go saying it's a gut thing."

Well, he wasn't going to tell her the truth. She didn't know him well enough. "It's complicated, okay?"

She ran her hands up his chest, to his face. Palmed his cheeks. "How is it complicated?"

Her touch was glorious and messed with his brain. Thinking coherently became difficult, if not impossible. But telling her the truth was out of the question. "You're not guilty. I will find out who killed him. Please have some faith in me."

"Faith." Her forehead touched his. "Adam?"

Damn, he wanted to kiss her. To see if she tasted the same. "Yes?"

"Kiss me?"

Holy shit. If only he could see her face, her eyes. But did he really need that confirmation? She'd asked him. So he palmed her cheeks and covered her lips with his. Had hoped to make it gentle, but as soon as they touched, a fire ignited inside him. And apparently inside her, too.

She wrapped her arms around his neck and opened her mouth to him. He dove in and tasted her. Just like eleven years ago, she was like a drug in his system. He ran his hands through her silky locks and continued to devour her.

He'd thought he was in Heaven before, but he'd been wrong. So, so wrong. This was Heaven. This. And he never wanted to leave.

Someone above cleared their throat. Adam quickly broke away and opened his eyes. The car was no longer in darkness. The access panel had been removed and he raised his hand to block the light.

"Sorry," said the man holding the flashlight. "Didn't mean to intrude. Should I come back later?"

Evie opened her eyes and squinted at the workman. "Are you here to get us out?"

"If you want me to?"

Oh hell no. But he had to think of Evie. "We do," he said. "What's the plan?"

Chapter 13

The insistent beeping of the batteries was driving poor Bailey nuts. He'd already shit a few times by the front door—something he did whenever he was mad. If Spencer could mute the alarms, he would. But between the beeping and the bird squawking, even Spencer was going nuts, so he did what Bailey couldn't: popped up onto the rooftop and hovered there. Ahhh, peace and quiet. Well, almost. Somehow the white noise of the city was calming. Certainly less jarring.

He moved to the front of the building. If he hovered out over the street, would he be able to stay there? Or was the ground or flooring keeping him at a certain distance? He'd never really moved through the building. He'd always just popped from floor to floor. He leaned over the edge.

A truck had parked in front of the building. Could he fly down there and check it out? If he fell, he could always pop back into his condo. Right? He took the chance and dove down.

The angle disoriented him and he stopped. Whoa. He flapped his arms—because it seemed the thing to do not because he had to—and righted himself so the world wasn't upside down. He lowered himself at a reasonable rate. This was so cool. It was like flying. Wait, not like flying. It *was* flying. Damn. He could fly!

He stopped beside the truck. Ahhh, the elevator company. Probably here to rescue Evie and Fox. Had a sufficient amount of time passed for them to get close again? Rekindle their youthful infatuation? Spencer sighed. Guess he would find out soon enough.

He popped up to the ninth floor and found a crowd. Between people leaving their units with small overnight bags and the rescue team at the elevator, the trapped occupants became a curiosity. Battery-powered lights were up on either side of the elevators. The doors to the shaft were open. The younger residents were filming on their phones.

"Big news tonight, huh?" Spencer said to no one in particular.

If there was another ghost in the area, would they check out the commotion? Maybe he wouldn't have to go searching after all. Wouldn't another ghost be curious?

He cupped the side of his mouth. "Hey! Is there another ghost here?"

No one replied. Which meant there probably wasn't another ghost in the building.

The elevator cab was lowered. Spencer popped up a flight and poked his head through the shaft on the tenth floor, where a worker was bleeding the line. Fox and Evie were sitting on the floor inside the cab.

Spencer returned to the ninth floor. When the cab was lined up, the rescuer held his arm out to the occupants. Evie and Fox debarked to a round of applause and Evie gave Fox a big kiss. Right on the mouth.

"Hey, it's the couple from the coffee shop," said one teen.

"Oh my God. Did you make out in the elevator?" asked another.

That question caused Fox to step away from Evie, but he didn't answer. Spencer wasn't sure what that was all about. Sure, Evie kissed Fox, but… Upon closer examination, Evie's and Adam's mouths were a bit on the reddish side. One kiss wouldn't have done that.

Holy crap! They'd been kissing. That was good news. Wasn't it?

Tony came up to Evie. "I'm so glad you're okay."

"Me, too." She placed an envelope in his hand "Your mail."

Adam pointed to the flashlight hanging on Tony's belt. "Can we borrow that? She'd like to go up to her condo. And I'm guessing the emergency lights aren't working in the stairwell, either."

"Yeah, apparently the battery's dead and I can't figure out how to recharge it. I left a message with my employer." Tony slipped the flashlight free. "But yeah, here. Be my guest. It's the least I can do."

Fox and Evie thanked the workers and approached the stairs. Instead of popping to his condo, Spencer followed them up the stairwell. He kept his distance so as not to give Evie a chill, but turned out he needn't have bothered following them at all. Neither one talked. They didn't stop to kiss. Did nothing but climb up stairs. What the hell was wrong with them?

When they reached the twentieth floor, Evie turned toward Fox. "You really didn't have to accompany me up here. I'll be fine."

"Actually, I was hoping to talk you into leaving. I could help. Carry Bailey's cage."

Leave? Oh, the power outage. Well crap. How could he protect her if she left the building? Not that he *could* protect her, but he could zap electricity and cause walls to shake. That would be enough, wouldn't it?

"That won't be necessary. I'll be okay for one night." She reached the condo, unlocked the door, and opened it to beeps.

Fox covered his ears. "Damn, that's loud."

"Aren't they? I really should get rid of them. Poor Bailey. Excuse me while I go turn them off." As she rushed inside, she slipped on the bird crap. "Shit!"

Fox caught her before her butt hit the floor. "You okay?"

"Yeah. Should've known he'd be angry." She straightened and removed her shoes. "Watch your step."

Shining the flashlight on the floor, he closed the door and stepped around the mess. A piece of paper floated off the table. He picked it up. "I need to talk to you."

Spencer turned around expecting to see Evie, but no one was behind him.

"Yeah, I'm talking to you, ghost."

"Oh. What about?" He tried to play it innocent, although he guessed Fox wanted to chew him out for the power outage. Not that he didn't deserve it.

"Not now. Later. When I'm alone."

Right. Because of Evie. That made sense.

The beeping from the office stopped. She returned and silenced the living room battery used for the television. "I'd offer you something to drink, except all I have is tap water. No, that's wrong. There's a bottle of bourbon in Spencer's desk. Why do people put booze in the desk?"

Fox shrugged. "So they aren't tempted to drink it all the time? But I'm good. What's this?"

She took the paper from his hand and placed it back on the table. "Just what it looks like. A list of the HOA board members."

"Why do you have it?"

"It was brought to my attention that they may want to attend Spencer's funeral. You know, since I just found out today that he was on the board. Is there some reason I shouldn't tell them?"

Spencer hovered by the window. What did she mean she just found out? Hadn't he told her? Shit. Maybe he hadn't. But why did it matter?

"No reason I know of," Fox said. "You sure you're going to be okay here without power?"

"Yeah, I'm sure. See? The city is enough light for me. But…" She wrung her hands as she headed Spencer's way.

What the hell? Could she see him now? *No. Of course not, idiot.* She was walking to the window. Spencer poofed to the dining area before she could feel the cold.

"But what?" Fox asked.

Evie turned. "Do you have to go? Can you stay?"

Spencer placed his hand over his heart. She wanted Fox to stay. Yes! This was more like it. Not only did Fox like her, she liked him back.

Fox smiled. "Ah, Evie, you tempt me. I need to make a phone call first. I probably have enough juice to do that, too. Can I answer after that?"

A phone call? Who would he need to call? Oh wait. Not a call. A ghostly discussion.

She nodded. "If you need privacy, you can use the office."

"Thanks. I'll be right back."

That was Spencer's cue. But before he popped away, he watched Evie. She was actually straightening up the place as she headed toward Bailey. And grinning. This had to be one of her worst days and she was grinning? He'd do anything to make sure she stayed happy.

She found Bailey on the tree in the dining room. "Ah, Bailey. I'm sorry you were scared. How about a treat?"

Spencer left her to the bird and popped into his office—or rather, former office—and knew Fox wouldn't yell at him. The walls weren't that thick.

* * * *

Adam stepped into the room, shut the door, and placed the flashlight on the desk pointing upward to light the room. Evie had asked him to stay and he was seriously considering it. But what about Spencer? How would the ghost feel about that?

A ghost who most likely caused this whole power outage to begin with.

Spencer appeared by the window, his back to the room. All that was missing was a popping sound announcing his arrival. Ghosts were too damned quiet for Adam. Other seers had admitted to getting headaches or feeling pressure in their ears whenever a ghost appeared. Adam had never felt any difference. Their sudden appearance always startled him.

The ghost turned around. "Do you really need to make a phone call or was that your excuse to talk to me?"

"Well, considering I told you out in the foyer that I needed to talk to you, what do you think?" Adam whispered.

"I think if you had the chance, you'd yell at me. I swear, I didn't know that was gonna happen."

Adam shook his head. "So you *did* do this. I told you to practice outside. Do you see why now?"

"I didn't have time to practice. And I was in the basement. I thought it would be safe there. Hell, if I was outside, I might have taken out the whole block. I didn't know I had that kind of power. You could have warned me."

Adam had learned that every ghost was different when it came to their abilities. Some could move objects. Some could possess. And some could create force fields. It was a rare ghost who could do more than one. Was Spencer one of those rare ones? Adam really didn't want to find out. "What do you mean you didn't have time to practice? What the hell were you doing then?"

"Getting you two together. I thought that was obvious. And it worked, didn't it? She kissed you and asked you to stay. So if you're looking for my permission, you got it."

Adam scrubbed his face. Instead of encountering an angry ghost, he got one who was into matchmaking. "You're something else."

"Hey, I just want her to be happy. You make her happy. And as long as she's with you, she's not in danger."

"She's not in danger unless Connor finds out about the will before we catch him."

"Which will be when? At my funeral?"

"That's a possibility."

"Hey, can you tell her I don't want her to invite any of the board members?"

Adam closed his eyes and took deep breaths. He couldn't afford to raise his voice. "How the hell am I supposed to do that? And why? What's wrong with the board members?"

"Besides being power hungry? Nothing."

This was the first Adam had heard anything negative about the board. Celia had interviewed them and said they all checked out. But maybe she hadn't asked the right questions. "Explain."

"I joined the board to make changes. But every time I suggested something, I was always outvoted. By everyone. I was going to suggest we have term limits, but never got around to that. They probably would have thought I was asking them to commit suicide. Really, it's just a board."

The current board didn't have term limits? That couldn't be good. "Did the board members know you were thinking along those lines?"

Spencer shrugged. "I don't know. I suppose. Does it matter?"

"You tell me. If some of the members were getting kickbacks, would they want to lose that cash cow? Would they kill to keep it?"

"You don't think Connor is responsible anymore?"

"He's still a suspect. I'm just looking at all angles. Finding anyone who might hold a grudge. Which you should be doing, too."

"Well, I can't imagine anyone on the board capable of murder."

"You're telling me no one on the board is in financial trouble?"

Spencer spread his arms wide. "How the hell would I know? I'm not their accountant."

"You're a ghost. Have you checked them out since your death?"

"Checked them out? What do you mean?"

Surely the ghost wasn't that dense. "Go into their condo. Spy on them."

Spencer's eyes widened. "No, of course not. That's rude."

Adam stifled a laugh. A ghost afraid of being rude. Now that was something he'd never heard. "You're here. With Evie. How is that not rude?"

"That's different. I lived here. And I never spy on her. She still has her privacy. I am not a pervert. So if you want to stay, I'll leave you alone. I promise."

Did the ghost know how to stay on topic? He had a case to solve and all Spencer cared about was Evie's love life. "You surprise me, Spencer. I thought for sure you'd be mad since you love her and all."

"Well, if you hadn't noticed, I'm not really here anymore, am I? So why should I be mad? She likes you. She's always liked you. I just never realized that was you in the picture she drew. I'm happy she found you again. Don't let me be the reason you don't stay."

"I promise to not let that be the deciding factor if you promise to start spying on the board members."

"What if they see me?"

Gah! Why was he acting like a five-year-old? "I told you, no one is going to see you except another ghost."

"You do."

He'd never had the urge to hit a ghost. Never. And not because hitting them would have been pointless. Because he could hit a ghost. He just couldn't win if the ghost decided to retaliate. So it was better if the ghost didn't know what could happen if they touched a seer. Still, Adam was tempted to smack some sense into the guy. "Fine. Say someone sees you. They can't hurt you. Hell, maybe you can get information from them that I can't. Take advantage of your situation, Spencer. You can do so much more than I can. You can narrow the field for me."

"You really think someone on the board could have killed me?"

"I don't know. Maybe it was an owner taking it out on one of the board members. The maintenance in this building is shoddy. Don't the owners complain?"

"Oh, they complain. Until they're told their HOA fees will increase. Then they shut up. It's why I'm always outvoted. I was told it costs too much." Spencer used air quotes on that last sentence. "Thing is, I don't think the money is getting spent correctly. I offered to find another management firm, but got outvoted on that, too."

Another interesting tidbit that Celia hadn't uncovered. "Then start there. Start with Tony. Spy on him a bit. He might be able to give you insight as to who to spy on next."

"This just seems wrong. Shouldn't you have a warrant?"

"Will you stop acting as if you're alive? The rules changed for you the moment you died. Try to remember that."

Adam's smartphone vibrated and he pulled it from his pocket. "Oh great." Figured he'd have enough power left for her call. He tapped the answer button. "Hey, Celia. What's up?"

"Oh, don't give me that innocent voice. How the hell did you end up in the elevator with Evelyn Harper?"

Boy, that didn't take long. Social media struck again. Celia must live on it or something. "Purely coincidental."

"And the kiss? Was that coincidental, too?"

Oh crap. Figured someone caught that. "It wasn't planned." But it sure was welcomed. And to think he could be kissing her again tonight. Doing more than kissing. "She was just thankful."

"Sure, thankful. Most people hug, not kiss."

"Is there a reason for this call or did you just want to harass me?"

"Captain wants to see us first thing in the morning. If you've gotten me kicked off this case—"

"You didn't do anything wrong. I'll handle the captain. Stop worrying."

"I can't help but worry. Connor Elliott is a ghost. I swear, he disappeared without a trace."

A ghost? Sure, Celia meant it a different way, but was it possible Connor met with a similar fate as his brother?

"I did put out a BOLO on him," Celia said. "As a person of interest only."

Be On the Look Out. Adam had never resorted to doing that. Guess there was a first for everything. "Then there's nothing you can do right now. Get some rest. I'll see you in the morning."

"Eight a.m. Don't be late."

Adam chuckled. "Yes, boss."

He disconnected the call and stared at his phone. If he stayed, he'd have to call Sabrina. Did he have enough juice in his phone for that?

"There's a portable charger in the top left-hand drawer of my desk," Elliott said. "Should be fully charged. I believe we have the same make of phone, so the charge cable should fit. You know, if you plan on staying and want to charge your phone."

Adam raised his head and nearly laughed at the silly grin on Elliott's face. "You really want me to stay the night, don't you?"

"Don't you?"

He did. He really did.

* * * *

Evie fiddled with a loose thread on the couch. She should go and get scissors before she did any damage, but that would require getting up and looking for said scissors and she was determined not to leave the room. Not until Adam returned.

In the time he'd been gone, she'd cleaned up the mess by the door and fed Bailey, who seemed content staying in the kitchen. And she'd lit several candles, which were now situated on the coffee table giving the room a nice mellow glow. She figured Adam would have finished with his call by now. Was he making arrangements? Making excuses? Would he stay the night?

She couldn't believe she'd actually asked him. But when would she get this opportunity again? Right now she was in the clear. But after they caught Connor, he might say something to make her look guilty again. And then what?

Adam appeared in the hallway. Finally. She stood. Waited.

"I was all set to bring out the bottle of bourbon. Then I talked to Sabrina. I'm afraid I won't be able to stay long. I'm sorry."

"Sabrina doesn't want us together?" That didn't seem like her. She'd been all happy at the cafe.

He shook his head. "No. I didn't tell her where I was. Didn't want her to feel guilty. She just needs me at home and I can't…"

"Abandon her?"

"Something like that." He stepped into her personal space. Placed his hands on her shoulders. "She still hasn't told me what's going on between her and Glenn, and that kind of scares me. I really shouldn't leave her alone if I can help it."

Disappointment burned, but his reasoning lessened the pain a little. "Family comes first. I get it."

"Thank you." He touched his forehead against hers. "Rain check?"

"You got it." Tears threatened to fall and she willed them away. He'd wanted to stay. That had to mean something. Unless he'd been using her all along. Damn Keith and his stupid suspicions. They were rubbing off on her.

He kissed her. Too quick. Too gentle. Before she could react, he stepped back and pulled the flashlight from his back pocket. "Do you need this?"

"No. I have candles. See?"

He looked around as if he hadn't noticed them. "I'll return this, then. You sure you're okay? Because I can help you move if you want."

"Thanks, but Bailey and I will be just fine here. Tell Sabrina I said hi. And if she needs a friend to talk to, maybe I can help. Provided you're okay with it." Evie held her breath. If he rejected her help, maybe he hadn't really wanted to stay. Maybe he'd been using her all along.

"That would be nice. I'll be sure to pass along the offer."

She breathed in deeply and smiled. Keith could go suck rotten eggs.

Chapter 14

The next morning, a little more than an hour before his meeting with the captain and Celia, Adam slipped into the stairwell of Evie's condo and went down to the basement. Apparently the workers had come and gone. Power had been restored to the building.

He hated that he'd had to leave Evie last night. But his couch had been delivered early and Sabrina was sounding so needy he thought it best not to leave her alone for the night. If only she would tell him what was up between her and Glenn. But she'd clammed up. Again. That Evie had offered to talk to Sabrina had meant a lot, but Sabrina hadn't seemed all that interested. Which wasn't like her at all. What had Glenn done to her? Adam was tempted to drive out to Springfield and confront the guy just to get some answers.

"You're not wrinkled," Spencer said.

Adam ran a hand down his suit coat. "Yeah. Sabrina insisted on ironing my suit. And no, I didn't ask her."

"I didn't think you would. You don't seem the sort to care what you look like when you leave your home."

"Yeah. Whatever. Did you have any luck?"

"Not really. Kind of hard to see things when the power is out and I can't touch anything. Tony did call Hugh, though. Just to tell him he was staying elsewhere. Hugh asked if there was any news, but didn't elaborate and Tony just said no."

News, huh? Might be nothing, then again, it might be something. He wrote it down in his notebook. "Keep on that, okay? Did you check Hugh's condo?"

"Yeah, but he wasn't there. None of the members stayed the night. But I guess that'll change now that the power is on."

"I know I asked you this before, but is there any other place Connor could have gone? Someplace of your father's maybe?"

Spencer's eyes widened. "Oh crap. The lake house."

"The rental property mentioned in the will? He knows about that?" Adam wrote down the information.

"Yeah, he knows. Man, I forgot all about that. He could be there. It's not currently rented out." Spencer hovered back and forth. "When he finds out he's not even getting the house he's going to blow his top."

"Why? What's so special about a rental property?"

"It was our father's."

"Your father didn't leave part of it to him?"

"Oh, Connor got half. But he wanted money more. I tried to tell him we could make money renting it out, but he didn't want to hear it. Said he needed the money now. So I paid him for his share. A year later he accused me of tricking him to sell his half. I don't know what kind of world he lives in, but it's messed up for sure. And I really didn't think about what Connor might do to Evie when I left everything to her. This is all my fault."

"It's not your fault. The fault lies with the killer." He checked his watch. Celia would have his hide if he arrived late. And if he got caught in traffic… "I gotta go. I'll be back later. Keep spying. The sooner we get some answers the sooner this case is solved."

But now he had a captain and partner to appease. Man, he better not be late.

* * * *

Evie lay in bed while her phone rang—or rather, the phone Keith gave her—for the third time, at that. Since he was the only one who had this number, she'd been reluctant to answer. But if she didn't answer the phone he'd just keep calling. Or worse.

He'd come over.

Oh hell no.

She whipped off the blankets and picked up the cell. "What's so important that you have to call me at seven in the morning?"

Although, that was a pretty stupid question. Only one thing—person—would get Keith riled up. But Adam hadn't spent the night, so what was Keith's problem?

"It's seven-fifteen."

"Like that makes a difference. Call me back in an hour. Make that two. I might be awake then."

"Stop. Don't hang up."

She really shouldn't poke the bear, but it was kind of fun. "What do you want, Keith?"

"Tell me how you were stuck in the elevator with him. How? *How?*"

The elevator. Of course. It probably made the news. Or at least social media. "It was just a coincidence, okay? Now call me—"

"Don't give me that bullshit. Two coincidences in one day?"

"Hey, you don't need to talk to me that way. And it *was* a coincidence. He was here questioning the owners. I wouldn't have even known he was here if I didn't go down to get the mail."

"And you had to ride down the elevator with him?"

"What? I should have waited for the other car to arrive? What sane person does that?"

"Fine. Fine. So it was a coincidence. But what about that kiss? Huh?"

So the kiss made the news? Or just social media. Keith must be on it 24/7. "I panicked in the elevator. Okay? He kept me calm. When we were rescued, I gave him an appreciation kiss. That's all. Can I go now?"

"Did you talk?"

"Of course we talked. How do you think he kept me calm?"

"Damn it, Evie. I wouldn't be surprised if he caused that elevator to jam so he could get information out of you."

"How many times do I have to tell you? I'm not a suspect anymore. Call Detective Delavau. She'll tell you."

"I did. It could still be a ruse. To get your guard down."

Holy shit. He couldn't have meant that. Could he? "My guard down? For what? I. Didn't. Kill. Spencer. So even if it is a ruse, and I don't believe it is, why does it matter? Besides, Detective Fox didn't cause the building to lose power, so stop making things up in your head."

"What? You lost power? How?"

"I don't know. Apparently the electric box blew up or something."

"The electric box blew up? How?"

"I have no idea. How do they normally blow up? Can I go now?"

"So you're staying at the lake house?"

Evie rubbed her forehead. "I think you've mixed me up with another client. I don't own a lake house." Really, what had she ever seen in him? "Yes, you do. Well, Spencer did. His father left it to him. Didn't he ever tell you?"

What? Another secret? What was it with Spencer and his secrets? "No, he didn't tell me. But apparently he told you?"

"No. I only know because of the will."

"A will I don't have a copy of. A will that won't be read until Spencer's funeral. Aaron didn't mention anything about a lake house."

"Well, he read the basics of the will to me when I told him I was representing you. You have one. And if you decide to go over there, call me. I can drive you."

"You make it sound so easy. Like I know where it is and I have a key."

"I'm sure Spencer has a key in that desk of his and Aaron has the address. Just call me and I'll take you there."

Good thing she wasn't on Face Time. He would have seen her scowling. "That won't be necessary. The power's back on. But if I do decide to go there, I'll take Spencer's car."

"You can drive?"

"I have a license." Sure, it'd been years since she'd been behind the wheel. The clerks at the motor vehicle office never asked how often she drove whenever she'd renewed her license because she always renewed on time. "Now, if you'll excuse me, I gotta go pee."

She disconnected the call to his objections and silenced the ring. Because he would call back. She was sure about that.

* * * *

Spencer popped back to his office. The sun was rising and the sky was a fiery orange. He'd never noticed the sunrises when he was alive. Always too busy getting ready for work or too busy at

131

work. Would it have killed him to enjoy the view every now and again?

Evie entered the office and went to the window. "Oh wow." She went to Bailey's cage and lifted the cover. "Good morning, handsome! Would you look at that sunrise."

"Spencerrrr!"

"I thought we went over this. I'm not Spencer. I'm—" She rubbed her arms and turned around.

Ooops. He'd gotten too close. He popped over to his desk.

"Spencerrrr! Here!" Bailey squawked.

"Is he?" She stuck her hand out and moved away from the window. "Where is he, Bailey? Over here?"

What the hell? Did she believe he was here now? He should leave. Get out of the room. But something inside of him wondered if she'd notice the cold. If she put two and two together. Wouldn't that be great? Then he could tell Fox and then Fox could tell her the truth.

Evie stepped up to the desk and waved her arm. Another foot and she'd wave it through him. Instead, she looked down at the desk and sat in his chair. Yanked open the center drawer.

She pulled out his car keys and placed them on top of the desk. Then rummaged through the rest of the contents and uncovered the envelope labeled LAKE HOUSE.

"Whaddya know. Keith was right." She opened the envelope, dumped the keys on the desk, and pulled out the slip of paper containing the address and code to the alarm—her birthday.

What did she mean, 'Keith was right'? He'd told her about the lake house. Hadn't he?

"Oh Spencer. Why didn't you ever talk to me? Wasn't I a good enough friend?"

"We talked. Lots of times. Didn't we?"

"Didn't you think I'd ever want to visit your lake house? If you loved me, why didn't you share your life with me? Why didn't you try to make me fall in love with you? Instead, you pulled this kind of stupid shit. And then gave it all to me. I'm so freakin' mad at you!"

Apparently death wasn't the cause of his faulty brain. Life was. His life. He never thought about sharing his life with her because he didn't think she'd be interested. She hated money, so why talk about it? And the bad stuff? Who talked about that? It just got to be a habit not to share anything. To think he might have had a chance with her if he had. He could only laugh.

But was she going to go to the lake house? Now? Connor might be there. He glanced at Bailey. Could he help?

He got the parrot's attention. "Repeat after me. Do not go to lake house."

Bailey flapped his wings. "Go to lake house."

Evie snapped her head up. "What?"

"No, Bailey." He waved his hands. "Do *not* go to lake house."

"Go to lake house."

She stood. "You know about the lake house?"

Spencer grabbed his hair. "Why can't you get it right? I thought you were my friend."

"Spencerrrr friend."

"Of course he was, sweetie." She looked at the paper again. "A lake house. I own a lake house. Wonder what it looks like?" She shoved the paper and keys in her pants pocket. "I'm going out for awhile. Will you miss me, Bailey?"

"Bailey eat."

"Yes, I'll feed you first." She opened the cage and Bailey landed on her extended arm.

Oh great. Now she not only thought he hadn't cared about her, she was thinking about going someplace that wasn't safe. If only Fox would tell her he could see ghosts. Maybe he should be working on the detective instead of the parrot.

* * * *

Adam tossed his overcoat onto the back of his chair and froze. Dozens of sticky notes were stuck on his desk. Each one with lipstick stains. Or rather, someone went to the trouble of kissing each paper with red lips. Celia?

"Wow, you made it here on time," she said from behind. "And not a wrinkle—what the hell is all that?"

He turned around. Okay, so not Celia. "A practical joke, I'm sure. You think the captain was in on it?"

"You better hope he was. I'm impressed. You actually pressed your suit."

"They don't come wrinkled from the dry cleaners."

"True, but you wore that yesterday. Trying to impress the captain?"

The woman had some mad observation skills. If he was looking to impress, that was certainly a way to go about it. But when had he ever had to impress anyone?

"Fox. Delavau. Get in here." The captain was a man of few words and a booming voice to go with them.

Adam indicated Celia lead the way. "Ladies first."

"More like chickens last," she said.

"Whatever." He followed her into the office and closed the door without being asked. "Morning, sir."

Captain Nevin sat behind his desk, and while the desk was the largest in their department, he made it appear tiny. With that big body and booming voice, he had probably scared a lot of perps during interrogation when he was a detective. One of the reasons he had moved up so quickly was because he got the job done. Adam got the job done, too, but the last thing he wanted was to be Captain. He wouldn't be able to help half the ghosts he helped now. Oh sure, he couldn't solve their murder without their help, but he became a cop to help them move on. The accolades were just a bonus.

"Want to tell me why my detective was caught consorting with a suspect?" Captain Nevin asked.

Adam chuckled. "Well, she's not a suspect anymore. And I wouldn't exactly say consorting."

"No? What would you call it, then?"

"We were stuck in the elevator. Quite by chance, by the way."

"And the kissing?"

"One kiss. From her to me. A kiss of gratitude. That's all." And that's all he would say. Only one other person saw them actually kissing, and Adam was fairly certain he wouldn't tell the captain or Celia. "She'd been very nervous in the elevator and I kept her calm."

"Uh huh."

Yeah, Adam could see the guy believed every word—not. "We did manage to talk, though. About Elliott being on the board of the HOA. Seemed he wanted to make major changes, but none of the other board members did."

Okay, so that was a minor lie. Evie hadn't told him, Spencer had. Hopefully no one would confirm his story.

"Why would that matter?" Celia asked.

"Because the HOA fees are high and none of the work appears to be done. The cameras don't work. Even the emergency lights didn't come on during the outage. And the building manager doesn't seem to have a clue. Elliott was even looking into buying the management company. It's possible someone on the board is getting kickbacks from the current company and might have killed Spencer to stop him."

"That's quite a supposition," the captain said.

"But it's worth checking into. Right?"

"Everything is worth checking into. What have you found out about the brother?"

Celia spoke up. "Nothing, sir. He hasn't been back to his trailer, and no one knows where he could have gone. He has no credit cards, so he'd be dealing strictly with cash, if he even has any. I put a BOLO out on him, but no word so far."

"Actually," Adam intervened, "it's possible Connor's at Spencer's rental property. The one listed in the will. Seems it used to be owned by their father. I was going to suggest we go up there and check it out."

"I'm surprised, Fox. I figured by now your gut would have said who killed the vic. Unless you know and there's some reason you're not sharing that information."

Oh great. The captain thought he was covering up for Evie, too. "My gut does seem to be uncooperative this time. But Connor and the management firm are top of our list."

"You don't think Miss Harper is involved with Connor Elliott?"

Which was all the more reason to find Connor. Just so Adam could debunk that theory. "There isn't any record of them ever meeting or corresponding. No record of Connor coming to the condo prior to the night of Elliott's murder. And Miss Harper isn't known for leaving the condo."

"And you know this how?"

"Building manager. Said that when Miss Harper leaves the building, she's usually standing outside waiting for her Uber or Lyft ride. And she only does that maybe twice a month."

"Probably meeting up with the brother," Celia said.

"No. That's when she goes to the library. She gives classes on using Photo Shop. I checked it out yesterday. No one there has ever seen Connor loitering about."

"You've been busy," Celia muttered.

Busy finding the proof he so desperately wanted. "Just doing my job. She works full time in the condo. Orders her groceries online. I tell you, she rarely leaves the condo."

"And yet, you managed to run into her twice in one day. Outside of her condo," Captain Nevin said.

"Well, technically, one was inside the condo building. I went there to question a tenant and she was going down to get her mail."

"Enough. Get out of here. And don't let me see another video of you two together. Got it?"

Adam opened the door for Celia. "Ready to take a trip?"

Celia exited the office and he followed her out. Once they reached their desks, she grabbed his arm and pulled him into the break room. She inspected the empty room, spun around, and nailed him with that white-eye look. "What the hell, Adam?"

He'd never seen her so mad at him before. "What's the matter?"

She put her hands on her hips. "Are you trying to make me look foolish?"

"How the hell did I do that?"

"By not telling me about what you uncovered."

"I just did."

"No. You told the captain. I just happened to be in the room." She paced back and forth. "I thought I had lead on this case."

"You do."

"Then why don't you treat me like I do? You should have told me first. Like when I called you last night. But no, you have to be the big man on campus. The hero. The savior."

Adam put his palms out. He needed to fix things. And fast. "That is not true. Can we sit and talk? Please?"

She pulled out a chair, the legs scraping against the linoleum, and plopped down. "Are you falling for her? Is that it?"

Not falling. Fell. Eleven years ago. He sat across from Celia. "I hardly know her."

"Yet, you kissed."

"She kissed me. In gratitude."

"Oh cut the bullshit. I bet you were kissing in the elevator. What I want to know is would it have gone further than a kiss if you hadn't been rescued?"

"Eeew. In the elevator? No. Who does that?"

"Lots of people."

"You mean in your books." Celia had been caught reading a romance novel once and some of the guys at the station still wouldn't let her forget that.

"Not just books. Try shining a black light inside one of those things. Then tell me no one has sex in the elevator."

"You carry a black light with you?"

"No, but my last partner did. Seen semen in more places than I care to know."

Adam would like to think the elevator was cleaned every now and then. But with how lax the maintenance was, maybe it hadn't. And to think he'd been sitting on that floor. Eeew. "Well, nothing happened, okay? She freaked out when the power went out. I kept her calm. That's the end of it."

"And the information you learned last night? Why didn't you tell me first?"

He sighed. "You're right. I should have told you. And it won't happen again. I guess this internet thing messed with my head. And the fact I have no idea who the murderer is. I've never been this stymied before."

"If you hadn't met Harper previously, would you still think she wasn't guilty?"

"Yes. Because none of the evidence is pointing to her. Connor is the likely candidate, but we can't rule out someone on the HOA board, either. So which road do you want to take first?"

He was fine with either, because neither led toward Evie.

Chapter 15

Spencer hovered in the garage as Evie drove away. Couldn't be happier knowing she wasn't heading for the lake house. Instead, she was driving to the police station as her computer and phone were more important. That didn't mean she wouldn't venture over there someday, but hopefully after Fox found Connor. Then it wouldn't matter.

A few residents had returned to the condo building, including the board members. Tony must have called them with the good news. Now it was time to find out if any of them were responsible for cracking his head open.

Honestly, he didn't know anyone who hated him that much.

Might as well start on the first floor and work his way up. Which meant Tony won the prize. It wasn't really his condo, per se, as the residence came with the job. The HOA owned his condo and the guest suite. Tony might not be responsible for murder, but it was possible he knew more than he had told the police.

As Spencer approached the residence, Connor came strolling through the front door.

"What the hell are you doing here?" Spencer barked. Not that Connor could hear to answer. "Back to gloat at the crime scene, is that it?"

But Connor didn't stop at the mailboxes. He headed straight for the elevators and pushed the up button. When the doors squeaked open, he boarded the car. Spencer followed. He didn't bother keeping his distance and gave Connor a real cold shoulder. After pushing the button for the top floor, Connor crammed his hands inside the hoodie pocket.

Thank goodness Evie was gone. Would his brother try to break in?

The elevator doors opened. Connor stepped out and read the condo numbers until he came to Spencer's. He knocked on the front door. "Open up, Spencer. I need to talk to you."

Okay, if Connor was his killer, why would he call out for him? Or was he covering his tracks and making it seem like he didn't know about Spencer's death?

Marie, his neighbor, opened her door. "Are you here to see Evie? I believe she just left."

Connor turned toward the woman. "No. I'm here to see Spencer."

"Oh. I'm sorry to have to tell you this, but Spencer died."

"What? When?"

"He was killed late Saturday night. Technically Sunday morning. Right downstairs in the foyer. I believe the police are still investigating his murder."

"Saturday? In the foyer?" Connor scrunched his forehead momentarily until something clicked inside that head of his. His eyes widened. "Holy shit! Excuse my language, ma'am. But why are they still investigating? Didn't the cameras record who did it?"

Why would he ask that if he had committed the murder?

"Would you believe those cameras don't work? I couldn't believe it when I heard it. Boy, did we let the board know it, too. Was told they would be operational within the week. A little too late, if you ask me. Were you close?"

"He's my brother. Or rather, was."

Marie placed her hand over her heart. "I'm so sorry for your loss."

Spencer ran a hand down his face. When did the board meet? How come he didn't know? Probably because he was too busy mooning over someone who wasn't his to begin with instead of finding out who killed him. Ah, hell. What else had he missed? His brother seemed clueless, so did that mean he was in the clear? Or just a good actor?

One good thing. Once Evie retrieved her phone, she'd see the notification and know someone was here. She'd probably let Fox or Detective Delavau know right away, too. Spencer floated over to the elevator. If only he could hold his brother until the police arrived. And not damage the building in the process.

* * * *

Celia had chosen the lake house after she'd given another officer instructions to investigate the HOA board members. While she drove, Adam researched the house on his tablet. "Says here that Jonathan Elliott owned most of the land surrounding the lake. Brian Elliott was his only son and inherited the land upon Jonathan's death. Brian turned around and sold most of the land to a real estate development company, but kept a huge chunk for himself, where he had a house built. Upon his death, the house was inherited by his two sons: Spencer and Connor."

"Both inherited the house? But the deed is in Spencer's name only."

"Yeah. He bought his brother's half. For more than it was worth at the time, too."

"And yet, Connor is broke and Spencer is a millionaire. How?"

"Gambling? Drugs? A combination of both? Remember, they were raised by different mothers. Probably different values. I don't think the father was in the picture all that much."

Celia turned down the street of the lake house. "Damn. These are some huge estates."

"Oh, didn't I say? Cheapest here is valued at over one point five million. When Brian Elliott sold the land, he made sure it was to be used for high-end homes."

"So people actually live here?"

"Some. Most are rented out by the week. Spencer's house is listed that way."

"Is someone renting it now?"

"No. Next customer on the schedule is next week. Don't know if Connor knows that or not, but if it's empty, it's likely he's staying there."

She pulled to the side of the road, one house down from Spencer's. "Stealth or not?"

"Stealth works for me. Why give him a reason to run? If he's here."

Her smartphone went off. She scrunched her forehead and answered, "This is Detective Delavau. What can I do for you Miss Harper?"

Evie was calling Celia? Whatever for?

"What?" Celia put the call on speaker.

"Someone was at the condo." Evie's voice came through clear. "I just got my phone back and saw the notification."

Adam didn't know whether to be happy she called Celia or disappointed. Granted, she was doing her best to keep their personal life distant from this case. He so much wanted to take over the conversation, but then his feelings might get in the way, which was probably why she called Celia. Besides, it was Celia's case and he needed to remember that.

"How long ago?"

"Fifteen minutes? He spoke with our neighbor, Marie."

"He's probably gone, but I'll go over and check it out. Can you hold tight until you get the all clear? Just in case he has a beef with you? It'll probably take me an hour to get there."

"I have to go over to the funeral home to set up Spencer's service. I was told they sent his body over already. I won't be going home any time soon."

"Good. I'll call you once we check out the condo. Thanks for calling."

Adam's smartphone went off. Oh hell, Evie wasn't calling him now, was she? But the number on his display wasn't hers. "This is Detective Fox."

"Detective, this is Linda. Mr. Callahan's secretary."

Adam put the call on speaker. "Hi, Linda. What's up?"

"I just got off the phone with Connor Elliott."

He and Celia stared at each other. "What did he want?"

"He was calling to confirm Mr. Elliott's death."

"Confirm? He said that?"

"He said he'd heard that Mr. Elliott died and wanted to know if it was true. Then he wanted to know if the will was read. When I asked who was calling, he said he was Mr. Elliott's brother, Connor. I told him the will would be read after the funeral and for him to contact the funeral home for the date since it hasn't been scheduled yet. I didn't tell him you were looking for him, just like you asked."

"You did good. Do you know if anyone called for Spencer there, say, within the last hour or two?"

"As a matter of fact, we did. Since we've already contacted all his clients, we just tell whoever calls that he no longer works here. Should we say differently?"

"No, that's fine. Thanks, Linda. You've been a big help." Adam disconnected the call. "So, Connor Elliott calls the firm, finds out Spencer doesn't work there and comes to the condo to confront him. Finds out he's dead and calls back to confirm?"

"We don't know he called the first time," Celia said. "But it makes sense if that was him at the condo, which means he's not at the lake house. We need to see that door-cam video."

"Agreed. And we need to talk to that neighbor. But first, let's just check out the house since we're here. Make sure he hasn't been squatting."

Finally, a break. Sort of. But if Connor was in the clear, then who did kill Spencer?

Chapter 16

Standing in the hallway of the twentieth floor of the condo building, Adam pushed the down button for the elevator. After he and Celia checked the lake house and came up empty—no sign that anyone had stayed there—they'd come back to the condo and questioned Marie Diamante, who confirmed what Evie had told them. After which, Celia called Evie to meet in the rec room downstairs.

Celia pulled her coat closed. "Man, is it cold in this building or what? I thought Mrs. Diamante was crazy to have her air on, but it's cold out here, too. I don't think it's even this cold outside."

Yeah, that would be Spencer. Not being too tactful, either. Adam had to figure out how to get alone to speak to the ghost without looking like he was waiting for Evie. "The maintenance in this building is kind of wonky."

"We need to see that video. That girlfriend of yours better not change her mind."

Adam bristled. "She's not my girlfriend." At least, not publicly. "And if you keep calling her that, it's a sure-fire way to get us taken off this case."

She lowered her arms and let out a sigh. "You're right. Sorry. But it might help if you didn't go looking all dreamy whenever you see her. Or hear her. Or when her name is mentioned."

Dreamy? More like happy, but whatever. He'd just have to work at not reacting at all. If that was even possible. "So I like her. It's not a crime. But I won't let it interfere in solving this case. If it turns out she had something to do with Elliott's death, then she's not the girl I remember. Okay?"

"That's fair. But you really need to watch your reaction to her. Especially in public."

If public meant around Celia, then, yeah, he needed to watch it. Right now, though, he really needed to talk to Spencer. The elevator doors squeaked open. Celia entered. Adam waited. It was now or never.

She blocked the doors from closing. "Aren't you coming?"

"I'm thinking of…" He patted his stomach. "Putting my gut to the test."

She narrowed her eyes. "You have a key to her place now?"

"Will you stop? I don't have a key. I just have a feeling, okay? Can I be alone with it?"

"Fine. Whatever." She unblocked the doors. "If it'll solve this case, I'm all for it. Just tell me what your gut says before you tell the captain, okay?"

The doors closed on her retort. Yeah, he had that coming.

"It's about time," Spencer said.

"Not here." Adam pointed up and took the stairs to the roof.

He'd barely opened the door to the roof when Spencer blurted out, "Connor didn't do it."

"You don't know that." Although, even Adam had to admit that scenario was looking likely. But if not Connor, who killed Spencer?

"No, don't you get it? He was surprised I died."

"You don't think he was acting?"

"I thought that at first, but why would he act with Marie? And why was he yelling for me to answer the door? Hell, he thought the cameras were real."

"He could be covering his tracks, though. But if Connor is innocent, that means someone else is guilty. How's your search going?"

"Slow. Not many people are home during the day."

Adam was afraid of that. "And other ghosts?"

"No one showed up during the rescue."

He didn't like what he was hearing. "Did you check all the units? And every residence within your bubble?"

"Why would I need to do that?"

Adam rubbed a hand over his face. "Spencer, how badly do you want your killer caught?"

"I…I don't know. If Connor is innocent, Evie's safe. Right?"

No, this was not happening. Spencer had to see reason. "Yeah, but what if Connor isn't innocent? When he finds out he's out of the will, he'll go ballistic. Most likely on Evie."

"But you'll have caught him by then."

"And he could get out on bond. We don't have any tangible proof that he's guilty. We have nothing. Zip. Nada. Our only hope is if another ghost saw something for us to investigate. Which means you have to track them down. You can see all the ghosts all the time. I can't."

"But one didn't appear during all that commotion. If they were nosey, wouldn't they come?"

"Not if seeing you die caused them to be scared. You need to check every room within your bubble. And you need to do it quickly. Your funeral will be any day now. Evie was making the arrangements."

"Okay, okay. You're right. I'm sorry. It's just…this is all new to me."

Adam nearly banged his head against the door. Not only was he failing to mentor his partner, he couldn't even help a ghost move on. God, he sucked! "No, you're right. I'm sorry. I don't mean to push you. It's just—"

"You're frustrated. I get it. I know you're only trying to help." Spencer chuckled. "I swear I wasn't this dense when I was alive. I'll do better. I promise. Is it okay if I'm at the meeting downstairs? After you leave, I'll start searching. Promise." He crossed his heart with his index finger.

Adam couldn't help but smile. Like stopping the ghost was even possible. "Just don't take your curiosity to mean another ghost would be the same, okay? And try not to hover too close. You're making them both uncomfortable."

He descended the stairs and pushed the down button for the elevator. He figured Spencer would have just popped down to the rec room, but instead he tagged along.

"Why don't you tell Evie you can see ghosts? Don't you trust her with that kind of secret?"

If only that was the issue. He really didn't want to see her expression. Have her laugh at him. He needed to establish a relationship first. The doors Wookiee-squealed open and Adam stepped inside the elevator car. He waited for the doors to close before answering. "Okay, let's say I tell her. Let's also say she doesn't laugh me out of the building and tell everyone at my work that I'm crazy. How do you think she'll react when she realizes you're still hanging around? Think she'll stay in the condo, where she has some kind of security with the door camera? Or do you think she'll leave and go someplace where it isn't so safe?"

"Why would she leave?"

"Why would she stay if she believes you're in the condo? Watching her."

Spencer's forehead scrunched, then his shoulders sagged. "But you could tell her I'm not watching. You could tell her the cold is from me. She'd know then."

"She feels the cold when you're close. But say she's in the tub. She wouldn't be able to feel you if you just stuck your head inside to watch."

"But I wouldn't do that. She knows I wouldn't do that."

"Does she?"

Before Spencer could answer, the elevator doors opened and he vanished. Adam stepped out just as Evie emerged from the garage, her laptop bag hanging across her body. His heart warmed at seeing her. Another part of his body got excited. At least Spencer didn't care. His partner was another issue. Good thing Celia wasn't present. He really needed to keep it together.

Evie wiped her eyes.

"Hey, everything okay?"

She looked up and smiled. "Yeah. Just missing Spence. Where's Detective Delavau?"

Missing Spencer, huh? Adam bet the ghost just loved hearing that. "She's in the rec room. I was just…looking around."

"Right. Because if you were actually waiting on me, you'd get in trouble?"

"No. I really was just looking around. But I also really want to see you tonight, too. It's just, between this case and Sabrina…"

"She still hasn't told you anything?"

"No. But can I take you up on your offer? Why don't you come over tonight and talk with her?" That would certainly help, wouldn't it?

"As much as I would love to come over, she still might not say anything with you around. I could take her and Becca out to lunch tomorrow. Just us girls. How about that?"

Disappointment stung. He'd really wanted her to come over, but he had to think about his sister, first. "I think she'd like that very much. Thank you."

"You're welcome. Guess we better get to the rec room before your partner comes searching for us, huh?"

"Yeah. After you." He followed her to the meeting room where Celia was busy with her smartphone. She frowned when she saw them enter together.

Evie walked around the table and sat beside Celia, placed her laptop bag on the table, and pulled out her smartphone. "Here's the video you wanted to see."

Adam stayed on the other side of Celia, although every inch of him wanted to sit beside Evie. He settled for looking over Celia's shoulder instead.

"That's Connor Elliott, all right," Celia said. "And he's talking to Mrs. Diamante, just like she said."

"Too bad you don't have sound," Adam said. "He does look surprised, though."

"Do you think it's safe to stay here?" Evie asked.

"I can't imagine he'd come back. Not until he's learned what's in the will. When is the funeral?"

"Monday. At three p.m. After the service, they'll read the will and play the video."

"Video? What video?" Spencer hadn't mentioned any video. Neither had the lawyers. Damn it.

Evie shrugged. "I don't know. I just learned about it today, when I called Aaron about the funeral arrangements. I don't know if I can handle seeing him on the screen. Do you think Connor will be there?"

"Pretty sure. He called the lawyer's office."

"Don't worry, Miss Harper," Celia said. "We'll have plenty of police on site. You won't be in any danger."

And if Adam could swing it, he'd be sticking close to Evie's side. Her personal bodyguard, if it came to that.

* * * *

Spencer stayed across the room. He really didn't need to see the video of Connor since he'd been there, but he still itched to stand with everyone else. To feel like he belonged. Which was stupid. He was a ghost and they couldn't see him. How "belonged" could he possibly be?

Evie missed him, though. Wouldn't she be relieved to know he was still hanging around? Or would she be freaked out like Fox said and move? It wasn't like he had any say in the matter, though. Fox wasn't going to tell her he could see ghosts.

"Guess I'll see you at the funeral, then," Evie said as she stood and picked up her laptop bag.

"If you don't hear from us before," Celia said. "Please call me if Connor Elliott shows up at your door."

"Oh trust me. I will." Evie smiled at Fox and mouthed "Call me later" when Celia wasn't looking.

Just that little action made Spencer happy. She had found someone. Her someone. And he'd be damned if he let his murder get in her way of happiness. But how could he help her?

After Evie left, Celia pulled out her cellphone. "Those lawyers are really pissing me off."

Fox turned around after watching Evie leave. "Who are you calling?"

"The lawyers. They knew about the video Elliott made and didn't tell us."

Spencer covered his face. He'd forgotten about his video. A stupid, stupid video. He figured he'd be gone and it wouldn't matter. And while he wouldn't be able to be there and see anyone's expression, he sorely wished he could turn back time and not have made the damn recording.

And while he was at it, maybe not have gotten himself killed.

"Oh. Yes. Good idea. I need to use the restroom. I'll meet you out by the car." Adam moved his head in a follow-me manner. Not that Celia was looking at him. And why would he want her to follow? No, this had to do with the video. Damn it.

Spencer popped into the restroom and waited for Fox to enter.

"What's on the video?"

No beating around the bush for this detective. Of course not. Spencer grimaced. "Me?"

Adam palmed his face. Couldn't blame the guy for being frustrated. But he should try being a ghost. "What are you saying *on* the video?"

"Right. *On* the video." Spencer laughed, but Fox wasn't buying it. "I was just talking about the will."

"Details, Spencer. I need details."

There were details and there were details. Maybe he could confess about one of them? It wasn't like Fox wouldn't see the video, but why get him angry now? "Stupid stuff, okay? Everything I wanted to tell her but was too scared to say. Figured I wouldn't see her reaction, so why not? You know?"

"You still won't see her reaction. The funeral home is outside your bubble."

"Oh, I know. I'm not talking about the initial reaction. But I'm sure she'll talk to you about it. Or Bailey. She talks to him a lot. Makes me sad to think she doesn't have a friend she can talk to. Why is that, do you suppose?"

"Don't change the subject. How mad is your brother going to be with this video?"

Spencer hovered back and forth. Damn it. Well, they do say that confession is good for the soul. And it wasn't like Fox could actually do anything to him. Just yell. "How mad would you be if your brother told you that you were a no-good piece of shit?"

Fox grabbed the counter and leaned over. "Shit, Spencer."

"I know." Although, at the time he'd made the video, it had felt…empowering. "If I could, I would take it back. But I can't, now can I?"

"Does your lawyer know what's on the video?"

"No. I gave the DVD to him in a sealed envelope. To be opened and played after the reading of the will." Spencer hovered closer. "You could warn her."

Adam looked up. "Warn her? About what?"

"About what's on the video. You just have to tell her you can see me."

"Or we can watch the video prior to the reading of the will. And then I warn her."

That probably would be a better way. What if Fox was right and Evie left because she didn't trust Spencer wasn't peeping on her? "Don't leave her side. Please. Stay by her during the reading."

Adam straightened and headed for the door. "Trust me. I plan on doing just that."

Chapter 17

Adam grabbed his coat from the office chair. His stomach was demanding lunch, especially since breakfast only consisted of coffee and a bagel. Celia had an errand to run before their appointment with Aaron Callahan and he was on his own. He so badly wanted to join Evie and Brina, but he'd promised Evie he'd stay away. If his absence got Brina to talk, then it would be all good. But damn, he really wanted to see Evie in the worst way.

Their phone conversation last night was…nice. If only he could solve this case now, then he could stop playing games in front of Celia and the rest of the department.

As he stepped outside, his phone went off. The number was unknown, but the city listed Springfield, IL. If the person on the call was who he thought it was, maybe he could get his answers another way. He answered the call. "Detective Fox."

"Okay, you piece of shit. You've gone too far."

Being called a piece of shit wasn't new. Glenn never did like him. Especially since the day he kept Glenn from becoming a CPD detective. But he was confused about the second statement. "Hello, Glenn. I don't know how you got my number, but you're going to have to clarify. Exactly what have I done?"

"I am a private investigator. I know how to get someone's number. And don't play dumb with me. You talked her into leaving me. Into divorcing me."

"If I had that kind of control over her, she never would have married you. So why don't you tell me what you did to cause her to leave?"

"I didn't do anything. I left on a case and came home to an empty house and divorce papers! This is all your fault. You have no right to interfere in our marriage."

"I haven't interfered. In fact, I haven't even heard from Sabrina since she had the baby. If you're such a great investigator, you'd have known that." Adam winced at the dig. He was probably making things worse for Sabrina, but he just couldn't help himself.

"You asshole! It's all because of you that she won't take my calls. I need to talk to her, and apparently you're the one who can get her to cooperate."

"Cooperate? She's not a slave."

"Oh, it's just like you to twist my words. Guess I should have known better than to ask *you* for a favor."

At least Sabrina was smart enough to block Glenn's calls. Or was that smart? Shouldn't she talk this out with him? "Listen, Glenn. I agree she should talk to you, but I can't force her and neither can you. She'll talk to you when she's good and ready. And I guess she's just not ready now."

"Liar! Stop interfering!"

"I'm not interfering. I'm far from interfering. I want to stay out of it."

"Like hell, you do. Where is she? Is she staying with you?"

Adam wasn't going to lie, but he wasn't going to tell Glenn the truth, either. "You need to leave her alone for now. I don't know what's going on between you two, but if you love her, you'll give her some space."

"She's my wife. Mine. She shouldn't have left."

"Are you abusing her, Glenn? Is that why she left?"

"How dare you insinuate… I've never laid a hand on her!"

"There are other forms of abuse. Like, verbal. Controlling."

"Don't go making shit up. I want to talk to her. Where is she?"

"I'm not going to tell you. But I'll let her know you called."

"You piece of shit." The call ended.

Adam wondered if Glenn was always angry like that. If so, he could see why Brina left. The man was on the verge of exploding.

* * * *

Evie knocked on the door to Adam's apartment. She couldn't believe how close his place was from where Lee and she used to live. They would have frequented the same supermarket, provided Adam was living here then. Just how close had they come to finding each other sooner?

Sabrina opened the door and grinned. "Come in. Come in. I have a favor to ask before we go to lunch. You're not that hungry, are you?"

Evie stepped inside the small apartment. "I'm not starving. What do you need?"

She'd promised she'd help Adam figure out what was going on with Sabrina. Although, the woman didn't seem sad or depressed at all.

"Adam said we'd look for a larger apartment when his lease was up, but I found out that a larger apartment is available here. His landlord said that Adam might be able to transfer the lease. But I need to check it out first. Can you watch Becca while I do that? It won't take long."

"Sure. Why not. But won't Adam need to see it, too?"

"I'm not even sure if the apartment is large enough. Why bother him until I know all the details, right? He's so busy, what with your roommate's case and all. I still can't believe he hasn't solved it yet. That's so unlike him."

"How would you know? I thought you hadn't seen each other in years."

"We haven't. But I read the internet. Not too hard to follow his cases. I used to brag to Glenn, my soon-to-be-ex, but after Becca was born, I stopped. It always put him in a grumpy mood and I didn't want him to take it out on the baby."

"He was abusive?" Could that be why Sabrina left her husband?

"He never hit me."

Hmmm… There were other forms of abuse. Could Sabrina just not realize it? Or maybe she did subconsciously, which is why she left. "Well, that's good. I guess. Go on ahead. We'll be fine."

Sabrina kissed the top of her daughter's head. "Mommy is going out for a little bit. Be nice to Auntie Evie. When I get back, we'll go to lunch."

"Lunch!" Becca said.

"That's right, sweetie." Sabrina stood and opened the door. "I won't be long. Thanks for watching her."

She blew out of the apartment like a mini tornado. If ever Evie had seen someone sorely wanting to change the subject, it was Sabrina. Looked like she might be able to get some information to Adam after all. Evie had barely gotten comfortable when Sabrina returned, scowling.

"No luck?"

"Bad luck. The landlord can't show it now. Damn it."

"Won't the landlord hold it for you to see later?"

"Yes." She let out a huge sigh. "I was just hoping to get this done before Adam came home. Now I'll have to take Becca, and I really didn't want to take her."

"Or…you can try again when we get back. I can still watch her."

Sabrina's face lit up. "You'd do that?"

"Sure."

The hug came out of nowhere, and Evie didn't know if she should hug back. Before she could decide, Sabrina released her. "I forgot what it was like to have a friend. Thank you so much."

"You don't have any friends?"

"Oh, I do. But I'm always with Glenn."

Yep, definitely controlling. "Let's go eat. Need me to carry anything?"

"You can take the car seat. That would help."

Evie picked up the seat while Sabrina slung a diaper bag over her shoulder and picked up Becca. When they made it to the parking lot, Evie used the fob to unlock the doors of Spencer's Lexus sedan.

"Wow. Nice car," Sabrina said.

Evie opened the door to the passenger back seat. "It *is* pretty fancy, isn't it? It can even parallel park on its own."

"No kidding! Your business must be doing pretty good, huh?" Sabrina put Becca down and took the car seat. Within seconds she had it secured.

Kind of felt neat that someone thought she was successful enough to purchase a car like this. If only… "Not that good. This was Spencer's car."

Sabrina lifted Becca and put her in the seat. "Ah, yes. The lawyer, right? Bet he got a new car every year, huh?"

"Actually, he didn't. He bought this one last year after his other car died. His colleagues wanted him to get a Mercedes, but he talked them down to this. He was fairly frugal with his money." One of the things Evie had liked about Spence. He never flaunted his wealth. Probably because she wouldn't have stuck around if he had. He'd done so much because of her, because he apparently *loved* her, but couldn't trust her to tell her his true feelings? Why did men have to be so…stupid?

Sabrina closed the car door and opened the front passenger side. "He's a rare one, then. By the way, where are we going for lunch?"

"A diner not far from here. I used to live in this area and there's this great place I haven't been to in ages. Hope you don't mind. It's not fancy or anything."

"Do I look like I'm dressed for fancy? A diner sounds perfect. They won't care if Becca becomes fussy."

Evie drove the short distance and pulled into the parking lot.

Sabrina stared at the diner. "How long ago did you move out of this neighborhood?"

"About five years ago. Why?"

"Adam took me to this diner."

"Oh. If you'd rather go someplace else—"

"No. Don't you see? He said this was his favorite diner. Comes here all the time. If you hadn't moved, you might have run into him. He's only lived here for four years."

His favorite diner? Four years? Damn. "He told you about us?"

"Well, not exactly. I just remembered your picture when he came back from the amusement park. I asked if you were the same person. That's why you looked familiar to me. I'm so sorry you two have been apart for so long. Maybe now you can get back together? I mean, you still like each other. Don't you?"

"Did you forget about the case?"

"But you're not guilty."

Before Evie could get into how it wouldn't look good for Adam's career, Becca screamed.

"Lunch! Lunch! Lunch!"

Sabrina shook her head. "Alright already. Sheesh. You'd think I never feed her."

* * * *

Not understanding his boundaries, Spencer floated outward from his place of death, slowly—paying attention to details—until he popped back in the foyer of his condo building. Not only popped back, but was on the floor, leaning against a wall he couldn't feel. He straightened. Fox had said that would happen and he hadn't believed him. Which meant Fox was probably right about being able to spot a ghost easily.

Spencer popped back to his boundary and looked around. If he was in a bubble—and he didn't doubt that any longer—it meant he couldn't just walk in a straight line. Or go straight up.

Yeah, up. The buildings blocked his view of the sky. The ground was easier to cover compared to up, what with all the condos and office buildings around, but it would take him forever to check them all. Then there was the lake, or rather, dock.

So many boats. Would he have to check those, too?

It was all so overwhelming. Too many places. Too many people. If he had died up at the lake house, it would have been so much easier. Might be the same amount of square yardage, but fewer people and fewer buildings. And nothing higher than two stories.

Yeah, definitely easier.

There was so much happening in what was appearing to be a huge bubble, it was a wonder he hadn't found another ghost. Could it be the detective was right? That most ghosts stick to their place of death? Hell, he hadn't even bothered checking his surroundings until he was told to. If he had wandered around and saw something he didn't like, would he have bothered returning? Probably not.

This was going to take forever. If only he could use a map and cross off the buildings.

Fox was also right about no living person noticing him. The few people who walked through him apparently felt the chill—if rubbing their arms was any indication—but that was about it. No, "Who are you?" or "What are you doing here?" from anyone. Not even another ghost—if there was even one inside Spencer's bubble. His luck? The ghost he wanted—if they truly existed—had a bubble that barely overlapped Spencer's place of death. Which is why he screamed out for all ghosts as he traversed the border. Did a ghost's hearing improve upon death? Probably not. Spencer hadn't noticed any difference.

The sun was high in the sky as he completed the trip around his border. Well, the border on land. What was the use in going out over the water? It wasn't like he could get a reference there. He was surprised he could make it to the shore as it was.

This was ridiculous. He should just start with his condo and work his way out. Wouldn't that make more sense? Besides, wasn't he also supposed to be checking to see who in his condo wanted him dead? Maybe some of the residents worked from home now.

He popped inside his condo. Might as well start here and work his way around and down. But before leaving, he took a moment to himself. This was home and the stress of the last few hours melted away. The only thing that would make it better was if Evie were here. The place was really empty without her. And according to Fox, this is what it would be like if she discovered he was a ghost. She'd leave. Did Spencer want to risk that Fox was wrong? Nope. Not one bit.

He floated into Marie's condo. She was a widow, but her college-aged children were over for lunch. If only he could smell what Marie was cooking. Instead, he could only go by memory. And he remembered how delicious everything she cooked smelled. Oh, Evie was a good cook, too, when she cooked something he liked. Unfortunately, she liked to experiment a lot and he'd end up being a guinea pig for most of those meals. It got so bad he insisted she didn't need to cook all the time and that he'd bring in takeout at least once a week. Or, he'd find a reason to stay late at work and miss dinner at home altogether. Which was a rotten thing to do, but he had to think of his mouth, didn't he?

"Hello, hello, hello. Don't mind me. I'm just looking for a ghost." No one paid him any mind.

He searched the premises for ghosts and came up empty. Then he went back to the study, or office, or whatever Marie called it, and looked at the desk.

If only he could open the drawers or move the papers around—and there were a lot of papers. A stack of bills to pay. A stack of medical receipts. But nothing to indicate she had a reason to kill him. If he'd even recognize it.

An eight by ten picture of two young teenage girls hung on the wall behind the desk. A new, elaborate frame but an old photo, by the looks of their clothing. '80s, maybe? The oldest looked like Marie, in a way, and going by her age now, it was possibly her as a teenager.

Marie's daughter dragged her brother inside the room and closed the door. "Why didn't you tell me she has a boyfriend?" she asked.

"What are you talking about? She doesn't have a boyfriend," Marie's son said.

Daughter placed her hands on her hips. "Then who's Marvin?"

"Marvin? Oh, him. He lives on the tenth floor. He came over when I was helping Mama rearrange her furniture. Said he came to help, but I think he just wanted to help himself to Mama's cooking."

Spencer laughed. He couldn't blame Marvin. He'd wanted to sample her cooking for a long time, too.

"Did she look all dreamy at him like she does when she talks about him?"

"Dreamy? How the hell should I know? What does that even look like?"

Spencer had always wondered about that look, too. Until he'd seen the way Evie looked at Fox. She'd never looked at him that way.

He left the siblings squabbling over their mother's love life and continued on his floor, going back and forth across the hallway. When he reached the end of the other wing, he went down a flight and continued in the same manner.

He was amazed at how many people worked from their home. He was also amazed at how many of them were in debt up to their eyeballs. Granted, it wasn't cheap to own one of these units, but apparently it was a status symbol of sorts. Spencer didn't need to work to live here, he just wanted to. What else would he have done all day?

He floated down to the tenth floor and entered Marvin's condo. He knew Marvin pretty well—except for the part where he'd been hitting on Marie—since the guy always liked to complain about everything. Not that Spencer didn't agree with the man. He did. He'd tried his best to at least get more security.

Marvin was on the phone and Spencer hovered close so he could listen in on the other end of the conversation. "When are you going to at least fix the cameras? We were told it would be done by the end of the week. Doesn't his death mean anything?"

"Mr. Holt, I can't fix what isn't broken," Tony said on the other end. "Those cameras aren't wired in. They're just there for looks. If the board approved an actual installation, they didn't tell me."

Spencer laughed. The board members were spewing their lies again, it seemed. They hated to spend money. Wouldn't even consider taking a poll of the owners, either.

"The boss is a piece of shit. A man was killed. In our building! Doesn't anyone care?"

"We all care, but that doesn't mean I have the authority to install a security system. You'll just have to take it up with the board."

"You're useless." Marvin disconnected the call and scrolled through his contacts. Found Hugh's name and pushed to call.

"What can I do you for, Marvin?"

"You lied to us. You said we'd get security by the end of the week."

"No, we said we would look into getting security. Not that it was going to be installed."

"When is the next board meeting? I want to be there."

"Not until January."

"What? That's too late. Then I want to call an emergency board meeting."

"We just met this week. I'm not calling another—"

"This week? Why wasn't I informed? Why wasn't a notice posted in the lobby?"

"There was a notice. I can't help it if you didn't see it."

"Did you discuss the security in this building? Are we finally getting cameras?"

"As I said, we're looking into it. That's all I can say—"

"Looking into it? A guy was killed in our foyer and you're just looking into it? Don't you think that's a message? That we should do something now? Or are you waiting for the next owner to be murdered?"

Hugh's sigh was loud enough for Spencer to hear through the speaker. "Marvin, if you hate it here so bad, why don't you move?"

"Like I can sell this place after there was a murder downstairs? Yeah, right."

"Goodbye, Marvin."

Marvin tossed his phone on the side table. "Why couldn't it have been you down there that night?"

"Well, he wasn't," Spencer said. "And why would that matter? Someone wanted me dead, not Hugh. You do understand that, don't you?"

But of course, Marvin didn't answer. Maybe he just thought someone wanted a board member dead and Spencer had been the unlucky candidate. That could almost make sense, except he'd been trying to change the rules. None of the other board members were. If someone were targeting a board member, wouldn't they have gone after one of them?

Spencer was heading for the bedrooms to continue his search when a girl appeared in the living room. A translucent girl of about fourteen. He pointed at her. "You're a ghost!"

Her eyes widened just before she vanished from sight.

* * * *

Sabrina placed her napkin on the table. "That was one good sandwich. And these chips are awesome!"

Evie smiled. "I think they make them here. At least, they used to."

Sabrina's phone rang. She leaned over to read the screen. "My lawyer. Wonder what he wants?" She answered the phone. "Hello?"

Evie couldn't hear the conversation, but Sabrina grew extremely pale, pushed a button, and nearly dropped the phone on the table.

"What's the matter?" Evie asked.

Sabrina's eyes watered. "That wasn't my lawyer. That was…" Her phone went off again. She picked it up. "Adam, oh thank God—" Her eyes widened more. "Stop calling me!" She turned off her phone and covered her face.

"Sabrina? What's the matter? Talk to me."

"How did he do that? How did he make me believe it was someone else?"

"Your phone?"

She stood and grabbed Becca's bag. "We have to go. He knows we're here. We're not safe."

"Hold on." Evie grabbed Sabrina's arm. "Let's not get ahead of ourselves. Exactly who called?"

"My husband, but it wasn't his number on the screen." Sabrina whispered as if saying it out loud would make him appear.

"Sounds like he spoofed another number."

"Not just another number. My lawyer's. Adam's. I can't trust my phone! And he knew I was here. That means he's here somewhere!"

"Sit down. You're freaking out Becca." Which was saying it kindly. Becca was on the verge of tears.

Sabrina slowly sat and lifted Becca from her seat. "It's okay, baby. Mommy's okay." Patting her daughter seemed to calm them both down.

"Now, look around you. Do you see him?"

There weren't that many people in the diner. Sabrina shook her head.

"Okay, then. He probably tracked you with the Find Me app."

"No. I turned that off."

"Well, he apparently has other ways of tracking this." Evie picked up the discarded phone and held it out. "Call Adam. Let him know what's going on."

Sabrina shook her head. "I can't turn that on."

"You can. He already knows it's here. Just ignore any incoming calls. You can call your brother."

"But won't I get…*him*?"

"No. Adam's number is Adam's number. You can still call him." Evie stood and walked around the table. "Why don't you give Becca to me? Then go into the bathroom and make your call. No one will bother you there."

"You're sure?"

"Positive. I've got you. Adam's got you. It's gonna be okay." Evie took Becca and hugged her close, hoping she hadn't just lied to the woman.

Chapter 18

Adam pulled into the driveway of Zane's house. After lunch, he'd planned on going to the condo unit to talk to Spencer, but Sabrina's panicked phone call had changed all that. Bringing her here would be best. Glenn wouldn't be able to track her—if she followed Adam's advice—since there wasn't any link anywhere to show that Adam and Zane knew each other. Seemed his secret became beneficial in other ways.

He'd called Zane ahead of time to make sure Sabrina and Becca were welcome, although hadn't the guy already asked when he was going to be able to meet them? Still, it was the polite thing to do and Zane had no issues being a host, as he put it. He seemed to relish the idea, in fact. Adam had asked his friend to wait inside for introductions, since he had a lot of explaining to do with Sabrina.

Evie and Sabrina were parked on the street, waiting for Adam. As soon as he pulled in, Sabrina exited the car and ran to him. Adam barely got his feet on the ground when his sister gave him a huge hug.

"I'm so scared."

"I know you are. But it'll be okay. He can't find you here. Did you dispose of your phone like I asked?"

"I... It's not here."

"Brina?"

"It's still at the diner."

"Destroyed. Yes?"

"Um…no. My pictures are on the phone. Evie said she'd go back and get it and copy the pictures over for me. Then she'll destroy it."

It was just like Brina not to upload them to a cloud. Then again, she probably didn't trust Glenn not to delete them if the mood struck. "Why didn't you just leave it at the apartment? Glenn already knows you've been staying there."

"Because Evie wouldn't be able to go back and get it. Duh!"

"You shouldn't even be involving her."

"It's okay," Evie said. "I don't mind."

Adam turned. He hadn't heard her leave the car, and she was holding Becca's hand to boot. "Thank you for bringing her here. I appreciate it."

Brina stepped back and picked up her daughter. "This house is huge. How do you know this guy and why did you never mention him to me?"

"Zane is an old friend." The how really wasn't that important. Not to Sabrina and especially to Evie. And Zane knew to keep that part quiet. "And it wasn't like we communicated all that much since your marriage."

"That's because *he* hated you. And he monitored my calls."

Adam noticed Brina couldn't even bring herself to say Glenn's name. Was it because of Becca? Probably. "No, he monitored your phone." He looked at Evie. "After you've copied her photos, turn it off and call me. I'll come pick it up. I'm curious to see what…*he* did to her phone."

Evie smiled. "Not a problem."

"I thought blocking him and turning off the finding app would have been enough," Brina said.

"Yeah, enough for any regular person. Not necessarily for a private investigator. Come on, let's go meet Zane."

Adam opened the door.

Brina grabbed his arm. "Aren't you even going to knock?"

"He knows we're coming."

Zane approached as they entered his home.

Adam closed the door and braced for any gushing from Zane once he introduced the trio. "Zane, this is Evelyn Harper, my sister, Sabrina, and her daughter, Becca. Ladies, this is my old friend, Zane Grey."

But Zane was the gentleman he always was. Just stood there and smiled.

Brina, however, scrunched her face. "The author?"

Zane laughed. "Not hardly. He died back in 1939. But my mother was a huge fan of his writings and couldn't resist naming me after him, since we already had the last name. It's very nice to meet you, Sabrina." Zane rubbed Becca's chin. "You too, Becca. I wish it were under better circumstances."

"Are you sure it's okay that we stay here? I don't want to be a bother."

"Nonsense. You won't be a bother at all. This house craves company. Come on in. Make yourself comfortable."

"Did you pack up everything?" Adam asked.

Brina nodded. "It's in the car."

"Evie and I will go get your stuff, then."

"Actually, you'll get the stuff," Evie said. "I have an errand to run."

Brina went to Evie and hugged her. "Thanks for lunch. And for being there. And for the pictures. And for…everything."

"Hey. You have my number. Call me anytime, okay?"

Adam felt ridiculous being jealous of his sister. She got to hug Evie without any repercussions. Someday, hopefully, he'd be able to do the same.

He ushered Evie out the door and to her car. "Spencer's car?"

"Yeah. When I took it the other day, I surprised myself that I could still drive. It's been awhile."

"But you still have a license?" He couldn't resist the question. The cop just came out of him.

She laughed. "Of course I have a license. They don't require you to take the driver's test when you renew it. Or didn't you know that?"

She pulled out the fob and unlocked the car and trunk. Adam grabbed the car seat and stroller from the back seat while Evie grabbed Sabrina's meager belongings from the trunk.

"I didn't want to say anything in front of Sabrina, but I can't believe this is all she has."

"I know. Apparently, it was all she could carry to the bus station. I'm really surprised she got this much." And if he had known she was leaving on the sly, he would have picked her up. He would have helped more.

Some brother he was.

He took the bag from Evie. "Did she tell you why she left him?"

"To be honest, I was hoping we'd have that discussion after lunch, but that's when Glenn called. From what little she did say, I'm thinking maybe he's been abusing her. But not physically. Mentally."

"Yeah, that's what I was thinking too. God, I wish I'd seen that side of him before they got married."

"I'm sure he's very smooth around other people. Sabrina's lucky she got away when she did."

"Thank you for being there with her. I just hope you don't show up on Glenn's radar. You have enough stuff to worry about."

"I'll be fine. You go take care of her. I'll go get her phone. And don't worry. I'll pick up my laptop first and I'll keep her phone off until I get to the library to transfer her photos. Okay?"

"Call me when you're done. I want to see what the bastard put on her phone. Oh wait. I have an appointment with Aaron Callahan at two. Can you sit tight for that long?"

"I can, but why are you seeing Aaron?"

"Spencer's video. Celia and I need to see it before the funeral."

"Oh." She lowered her head. "You gonna tell me what's on it later?"

Spencer had wanted Adam to warn her, but now he wasn't sure. "I don't know. Depends on what's on it, I guess. If it's personal, maybe it's best you hear the words from him first. If it pertains to the case, I'll tell you what I can. Okay?"

"Sounds fair. I'm sorry I couldn't help you more. Regarding Sabrina, that is."

"You're doing more than I ever expected." He stepped closer, fighting the urge to kiss her. But out on the street? If they showed up on another social media site, it would be his ass.

"I so badly want to kiss you," she said.

He chuckled. "I was thinking just the same thing. But not out—"

"In the open. I get it. However…"

He narrowed his eyes. "What however?"

"Are you free this weekend, or do you need to stay with Sabrina?"

"Frankly, I want to keep my distance from her. If I know Glenn, he'll probably try and sic a PI on my ass to track her down that way. I can usually spot them easily enough, but why take the chance? She's safe here. That's what matters. So, I guess that means I'm free. What do you have in mind?"

"Well, I have this lake house. Actually, it's Spencer's, but I have the key and it's available this weekend. Maybe we can spend some private time together there? Well, as private as it can be with Bailey. I can't leave him alone that long."

Adam grinned. A whole weekend with Evie? Privately? "I'd like that very much."

And just like that, his rotten day had just turned awesome.

* * * *

By the time Evie made it back to the diner, it was after two. The lunch crowd had really thinned and there were only two other cars in the lot. Why'd she think picking up her laptop at the condo would be a quick trip? But if she hadn't stuck around for a little bit, she'd come home to another mess on the floor. Sure, she could have put Bailey in his cage, but she would have also had to lock it if she wanted him to stay inside. And if she did that, who knew what kind of racket he'd make. She didn't need to put her neighbors through that.

So she'd fed the bird, and reassured him—as best she could—that she wouldn't be gone long. She'd left a towel by the front door, too, just in case.

Evie entered the diner and headed to the cashier. "Hi. Remember me? I came to pick up my friend's phone."

"Oh, yes." The cashier reached under the counter and pulled out the phone, all pink with sparkles on the back. "I can't believe her husband was tracking her like that. Is she okay?"

"She's better now, thanks. I appreciate you keeping it safe. She didn't want to lose her pictures, so I'm off to copy them for her." Evie put the phone in her purse as the man at the counter jumped down and headed outside. That left only one table occupied in the building. A couple. She remembered this place always being packed. Of course that was what, five years ago? Maybe it was the time of day? "Business always this slow?"

"On a weekday between lunch and dinner? Usually. Well, maybe not this slow. If it weren't for the to-go orders, we'd probably be closed."

"Well, I'm glad you're still open. I'll try and make it here more often. I forgot how good your food is." And now that she knew someone who lived nearby… Well, she could dream.

Evie drove to her library and settled in. Within minutes of turning on the phone, it rang. She was tempted to take the call—tell that man to fuck off—but it really wasn't her business, and why make life any more difficult for Sabrina? Because Glenn would certainly take it out on Sabrina if he could. Instead, Evie silenced the phone and went to work.

It took longer than she expected to upload the photos to her laptop. And even longer to transfer them to the flashdrive. Make that flashdrives. Good thing she came prepared with five of the suckers. And some work to keep her busy.

It was after three when she texted Adam that she was on the last batch, just in case he couldn't take her call. And then she thought about Spence and his video. What could that man possibly say on a video that he couldn't tell her in person? Probably some stupid secret that certainly didn't mean anything now.

Secrets. Man, she hated secrets.

* * * *

Adam walked into Zane's house and was bombarded with the scent of food cooking. He rubbed his stomach. He never really got to eat lunch today. But staying here with Brina wasn't a good idea. He just needed to drop off the photos, her new phone—which he had picked up earlier—and scram. Glenn might not be in the area yet, but he didn't trust the guy.

But damn, whatever was being cooked, it smelled wonderful. Garlic, onions, and oregano—if his nose could be trusted, and it usually could.

Zane met Adam in the living room. "I wasn't expecting you back so soon."

"I figured it was safe for now. I got her pictures and a new phone." He placed a bag on the side table. "How's she doing?"

"She's doing fine. And a wiz in the kitchen. We're having lasagna tonight. Care to join us?"

"I'd love to, but maybe that won't be such a good idea. I really shouldn't stay long."

"Nonsense. You've been here lots of times before. Not showing up now might look more suspicious."

"Maybe so, but still…"

"You want to see Evie." Zane smiled as if he were a mind reader. "Do you have dinner plans with her?"

"No. Seeing her while I'm investigating Spencer Elliott's case isn't exactly beneficial to either of us." At least, not publicly. Privately was a whole 'nother matter. And they would definitely meet privately this weekend. He couldn't wait.

"So you *can* stay for dinner." When Adam's stomach replied with a loud rumble, Zane raised an eyebrow.

"Okay, okay. I'll stay for dinner. Gotta eat anyway, might as well eat well. Right? I suppose Elliott can wait a little longer."

Zane snapped his fingers. "Yes. That. Come into my study. We need to talk privately."

Privately? About Elliott? Adam followed Zane. Zane closed the door and locked it.

"Locking the door? This is serious."

"I didn't think you wanted Sabrina to overhear our conversation, since it's about our favorite subject."

Oh, not Elliott specifically. Ghosts. Maybe it was Zane's favorite subject, but it had never been Adam's. "So…what? You find another ghost you need me to investigate?"

"Actually, I've been researching Spencer Elliott's neighborhood."

"Yeah? That's what I have him doing. Looking for another ghost in his bubble. So far he hasn't found anyone, but I haven't seen him in a couple of days. Which is why I need to go over there, see if he's had any success." Not that he expected anything, but it was best to check in regularly. Wasn't like he could phone the guy.

"Well, you might want to be on the lookout for the ghost of a fourteen-year-old girl."

"What?"

Zane went to his laptop and started typing. "In April of 1985, a fourteen-year-old girl's body was found when they broke ground in Elliott's condo complex. Her name is Erin McCallister."

"Just because they found her body there doesn't mean she died there. And I haven't seen any sign of another ghost in Spencer's building."

"Which we both know means nothing, especially in downtown Chicago."

Adam couldn't refute that. Skyscrapers gave ghosts plenty of places to haunt. And hide. "So why do you think Erin is still around?"

"On August 18, 1984, her family reported her missing. Erin's sister accused their step-father of wrong-doing, but without a body, there wasn't anything the police could do. Plus, Erin had been known to run away before. Once the body was discovered, the police found the evidence needed to put the step-father away."

"They caught the killer?"

"Seems so."

"Sounds like closure to me. What proof do you have that she's still hanging around? If she hung around to begin with."

"The accidental deaths out on the lake, near the condo."

"People die on the lake all the time. You're saying she's responsible for them all?"

"No, but don't you find it interesting that there's an accidental death every August 18 since 1985?"

"Every August eighteenth? The day she went missing?"

"Probably the day she died. I can't believe I haven't noticed this trend before. But they've all been reported as boating accidents. Those don't necessarily get media coverage. Last August some journalist noticed the trend when his friend died on that date. He's calling it the curse of Erin McCallister."

"Was this in one of your rags?" Zane subscribed to every tabloid, because that's where the unexplainable was usually reported. Sure, most of the articles were for entertainment purposes only, but every once in a while a real account of a ghost sighting showed up. One where Zane could help, or assign someone to help.

"No. Actually, I stumbled across his blog in my research. The journalist was certain foul play was involved—someone associated with the girl—but couldn't prove it. The paper wouldn't print his story and he thought he was above the tabloids. I wish it had been in one of my magazines. I might have been able to do something earlier. I'm thinking Erin McCallister is involved with those deaths."

"Zane, that doesn't make sense. Her killer was found."

"What if she doesn't know that? What if she doesn't care? If she is responsible and Spencer finds her, you might want to be careful."

"Well, if she does exist, you think she's going to teach him some bad habits? Spencer is a goody-two-shoes. I had to beg him to spy on his neighbors."

"When a new ghost meets an older one, the new one can learn things. Pretty quickly. And I'm not comfortable with all the so-called accidental deaths that have occurred on the lake near the condo."

"They might be accidents. The dates can be coincidental."

"And we both know nothing is coincidental when a ghost is involved. I know you have enough on your plate right now, so I'll investigate it further. But be careful. If Spencer Elliott finds her—"

Adam interrupted. "Spencer doesn't have a mean bone in his body. If anything, he'll bug her with his questions."

"And what have we learned when we bug an older ghost?"

Ahh shit. "I could have a dangerous ghost on my hands."

"Exactly."

* * * *

Spencer hovered back and forth on the rooftop as the sun set. No spectacular colors tonight. Just the same grey it had been all day. Dreary, dreary, dreary. Eventually, Fox would return, wouldn't he? For once Spencer had news and was ready to burst.

He popped back down to the empty foyer just as Fox emerged from the garage. "Finally! I got news!"

But Fox didn't react. He just pushed the up button for the elevator. Spencer waved his hand in front of the detective's face. Nothing. He looked around. Who was watching? The only person who could: Tony.

Spencer popped into the manager's office and sure enough, there was Tony, peeking through the window. "Why couldn't you have been that curious on the night of my murder?"

The man was useless. That much was clear.

The elevator arrived and Fox stepped inside. Spencer followed. The doors closed and Fox jerked. "Damn, you startled me."

"Sorry. Tony was watching the foyer. But I got news. I got news! Meet me on the roof, okay? See you in a sec."

He popped up to Marvin's condo. The ghost was right where he left her earlier—watching TV. But instead of the news—which Marvin had been watching—an episode of *The Brady Bunch* was airing. Marvin was napping on the chair, a dirty plate in his lap and the remote in his hand. Weird.

"What are you doing back here?" she asked.

"You said to come get you when Detective Fox came back. Well, he's here. Heading toward the roof as we speak. Let's go."

She looked up at him. "I changed my mind. I don't wanna."

She must not have been a ghost for very long, she still acted like a kid. Although, he couldn't remember anyone dying here since he moved in. And she would have had to die here to be a ghost here. Right? "I thought you wanted to prove me wrong. Come on. It won't take long."

"What's in it for me?"

"Something to do besides watch TV? Doesn't that get boring?"

She stood and sighed. "Fine."

Spencer popped back up on the roof. Fox was sitting on the bench, waiting. Spencer expected her to appear simultaneously, but no luck. Damn it. How was he going to get her up here?

"What's going on?" Fox stood. "Did you find some—" Before he could finish, she finally appeared. Fox plopped back down on the bench. "Erin McCallister."

"Wow. I guess he *can* see me," she said.

"Wait. What? You know her? You knew there was another ghost this whole time and didn't tell me?"

"I didn't know. I just found out about her today and came here to tell you. I wasn't even sure she was here. How did you two meet?"

"In Marvin Holt's condo while I was searching. She popped in, saw me, and left. I figured she came to his condo for a reason, so I stuck around and waited. And ta-da! She returned. She wouldn't tell me her name, though." Spencer placed his hand on his hips and faced the other ghost. "Erin McCallister, huh? Why does that name sound familiar? Come to think of it, you even look familiar."

Erin shrugged.

"If you're a reader of blogs, you might recall an article about the Erin McCallister curse," Fox said.

"That's it! Not that I read blogs, but Keith does. He showed me one about my condo building. Oh my God!" He turned to Erin. "That's why you look familiar. You've been a ghost a long time. Has someone been taking revenge on your death?"

"Before we get into that," Fox said, "did you happen to see who killed Spencer?"

"She says she didn't. I already asked."

"Will you let her speak for herself?"

"Sorry." Spencer got the feeling that Fox wanted to smack him. And probably would have if he could.

Fox smiled at Erin. "Do you ever leave Marvin's condo?"

"Only when he's gone. He turns off the TV then. But sometimes he leaves and forgets to turn it off. Then I stay."

"You like TV."

She nodded. "And I like Mr. Marvin. He doesn't seem to mind the cold."

"Yeah, I noticed that, too," Spencer said. "I got into his face when he was talking to Hugh and he didn't shiver or anything."

Fox sat up. "He was talking to Hugh?"

"Complaining. He was complaining to Hugh. But only after he complained to Tony. He's mad that no one is taking security in this building seriously. Can't really blame him."

"Where do you go when Mr. Marvin turns off the TV?"

"Sometimes I go lay by the shore and look at the sky. Especially if the moon is out. I like the moon."

"Wait? You can lie down?"

Erin rolled her eyes. "Duh!"

"You're gonna have to show me that."

"Erin," Fox interrupted. "Why are you still here? Are you waiting for your killer to be caught?"

"He was caught. Went to prison. He's still there, isn't he?"

"He is. So why are you still here?"

"Yeah," Spencer said. "Detective Fox told me I'll move on once I know who killed me. But if you know and you're still here…"

"I told you that you'll move on once you determine Evie is safe. And you won't feel that way until your killer is caught." Fox turned to Erin. "What's keeping you here?"

Erin frowned. "You think I have a choice? You don't know shit!"

She looked at them both and vanished.

"Erin, come back!" Spencer turned toward Fox. "Damn. How can we help her?"

"My friend is already looking into her case. I'll let him know what I found out." Fox stood. "You need to be careful around her."

"She's just a girl."

"No. She's an old ghost. I'm guessing an angry ghost. It's possible she's killed. Many times."

"What? You mean the curse? You think she's responsible? How?"

"I don't know how. But if she tells you, promise me you won't attempt to do the same."

"You make it sound like a drug. A bad drug."

"How often have you wanted to try and blow the circuit again?"

Okay, maybe the detective had a point. That had felt good, but blowing the circuit would only hurt Evie and he didn't want to do that. "I'm not going to risk Evie moving out if that's your concern."

"Just concentrate on finding out who killed you. That way you'll know Evie will be safe and you can move on. Trust me, you don't want to be stuck here."

He certainly didn't want to be like Erin, watching TV all day. That would be torture.

"By the way, I saw your video today." Fox shook his head. "I don't know your brother, but...ouch. Did it make you feel better knowing you wouldn't see his reaction?"

"Actually, I didn't really care at the time. I certainly hadn't thought he'd come after Evie, but now... Are you going to warn her?"

"No. Not much to warn her about. We'll catch Connor before he has a chance to see the video, anyway. That's if he decides to show at your funeral. And I'm betting he will. So you don't need to worry about Evie anymore. This will all be over soon."

Only if Connor was guilty of murder. Spencer still wasn't convinced his brother was responsible.

Chapter 19

Evie pulled into the driveway at the lake house. She had pictured some small cabin, not a huge estate. Of course, after discovering what Spencer charged to rent this place, maybe she should have known it wasn't some dinky cabin.

Damn. Spencer *was* rich. No wonder Keith said she wouldn't have to work another day if she didn't want to. Not with that kind of income.

Of course, that meant she'd need to actually inherit Spencer's estate to receive the income. That was still up for debate, now, wasn't it?

Since the lake house address was listed in the car's GPS system—which she never noticed from all the times she'd been in the car—she assumed the button underside the rearview mirror would open the garage door. Sure enough, the button worked.

Which meant Spencer had been here. Probably more than once. And all that time he hadn't thought to tell her about this place. Had he been afraid she'd judge him, him having money when she didn't? Hadn't he known her better than that?

Of course, knowing Spencer the way she did, he most likely never even thought about this place being his to use. It was just a form of income. Gosh, when was the last time he'd taken a vacation? Or even went away for a long weekend?

Never. He'd never taken any kind of vacation since she moved in. True, she hadn't either, but she could take a break from her work any old time she felt like it. Whereas Spencer had gone into his office every work day. Sometimes even the weekends and holidays.

That was no way to live. She realized that now, and she'd pretty much fallen into the same rut.

She could change all that, though. Hopefully with Adam, but if not him, she wouldn't continue to isolate herself. It just wasn't healthy.

She was kind of disappointed that Adam couldn't make the drive with her. She'd stopped by to pick him up, but he declined. Said he was basically on call and needed his own car, but that he'd follow her. As she pulled into the garage, he pulled in beside her. She'd barely pushed the button to close the garage door when Adam yanked her door open and pulled her out for a kiss.

His lips were demanding and she opened up to him. He thrust his tongue inside her mouth and she sucked on it. They had never kissed like this at the amusement park. Because if they had, she'd have given up her virginity that day. Somehow, some way. It was like the man had a key to her soul and all he was doing was kissing her.

She grabbed his head and broke the kiss. "Can we unload the car first? Bailey would appreciate it."

"If we must." He gave her a quick peck on the lips and opened the back door. "Why is he covered up?"

"Would you believe he hates driving? The speed freaks him out." She opened the trunk and pulled out her bag and Bailey's perch.

Adam laughed. "Well, I guess he can't fly at sixty miles an hour."

"Or even twenty. The first time Spence and I took Bailey to the vet, you'd think we were killing him once we got on the road. So Spence covered him up. Bailey calmed down. Good thing, too. I don't know anyone who'd want to babysit a bird."

"Not even one of your neighbors? Like Marie?"

"You know, I never really thought about that. We rarely talk. Just doesn't seem right to ask that of her." But maybe it was time she got to know her neighbors better. "Of course, once you catch Spencer's killer, maybe I could ask Sabrina to move in with me. Think she'd like that? You wouldn't have to find a bigger place, then."

Adam was reaching for the cage, but stopped after her comment. "What?"

Maybe she shouldn't have said anything. At least, not until she'd had a chance to think about it first. But when an idea struck, she hadn't been known to think. She just acted. Or in this case, blurted it out. "It was just a thought."

"You want my sister and her kid to live with you?"

"Apparently you don't. Am I not good enough for them?"

"It's not that." He grabbed the cage and headed for the door leading to the house.

"Then what is it?"

He opened the door that led to a huge, open kitchen. A larger family room with sliding glass doors to some kind of sun room was also visible. While the alarm beeped for the code, he placed the cage on the island and lowered his head. "You're gonna think I'm crazy."

She placed her bag and the perch on the floor and punched in the alarm code to silence the beeping. "I doubt that. Spill."

"Oh, I was just hoping…that after we catch Spencer's killer, that, maybe, I could visit you more often. But if Brina was there…"

She laughed. She hadn't thought that far. And he was right. It would be weird.

He pointed at her. "See? You think I'm crazy."

"No. Not at all. I think you're sweet. And I totally get it. I want you to visit me more often, too."

"You do?"

She wrapped her arms around his waist. "What can I say? It's a dream of mine."

"Oh Evie." He palmed her cheek and leaned down to kiss when the doorbell rang. "What the hell?"

"Probably groceries. I ordered them to be delivered. That way we didn't need to go out again."

He smiled. "Always planning ahead. I like that. Be right back."

Adam headed for the front door while Evie moved the perch to the window to give Bailey a nice view of the backyard. And it was a nice backyard. The lake glistened. She pulled the cover off of Bailey's cage and prepared herself for the wailing. "Hey, Buddy. How you doing?"

But the bird didn't wail. She held out her arm for Bailey to exit the cage and placed him on the perch. He just looked around. "Spencer gone."

"That's right. Spencer is gone." She blinked back tears. Had this trip done what she'd failed to do back home? Was he finally getting it?

Funny how she missed his wailing, though.

* * * *

Adam took the plastic grocery bags and folded them while Evie put the groceries away. He wanted to take her upstairs and devour her body, but it seemed that every time he started in on that, something interrupted them. He was afraid to start up again. What else could interrupt them? He really didn't want to know.

"I meant to ask earlier," Evie said as she put the milk in the fridge. "Are you able to tell me what's on Spencer's video?"

Oh yeah. The video. It was probably best not to worry her about Connor, but she had to be prepared. The funeral was Monday. "Most of it is personal for you, so I'm not going to go into that. There is some…stuff aimed toward Connor, but if he shows at the funeral, and that's a big if, we'll get him before he has a chance to view it."

"Stuff?"

"I think Spencer had some issues with his brother, and well, it was probably cathartic for him to air it out on the video. Unfortunately, there wasn't anything on the video to actually prove Connor killed him."

"Do I need to worry about him?"

"No. We'll have the funeral covered. He won't get near you. Actually, I'm hoping it'll all be over then. We'll get his confession and you'll be home free."

"You sound awfully confident about that."

He had to be. Anything else was unconceivable. "I am. As long as you follow our orders."

"Well, I certainly don't want to do anything foolish. And I trust you have my best interests at heart."

"I do. I do."

"What did you find on Sabrina's phone?"

He still couldn't believe that Evie had wanted Brina to move in with her. While he was flattered that she cared, he was still uncomfortable about the whole situation. He didn't need Glenn involved in Evie's life, and Glenn would certainly get involved if he thought it would get Brina back. "Bastard downloaded an app that made it possible for him to track her without her knowledge. The app wasn't even shown on her screen. It was all working in the background. I got her a new phone on my plan and she was able to upload the pictures you copied for her—thanks for that by the way. We both really appreciate it. At least Glenn won't be able to reach her or track her now."

"That's good. I know she was worried." She pulled out a carrot and a knife and started cutting.

"Is it snack time?"

She nodded. "For Bailey. Gotta keep him busy."

"Oh? Why?"

"Because I don't want him interrupting us."

At least he wasn't the only one who thought they'd be interrupted. And while he was pretty sure what she had in mind, he couldn't resist teasing. He leaned his elbows on the counter. "Oh? What are we going to do?"

"Well, if you have to ask..." She smiled. "I thought maybe we might go for a swim. I noticed this place has an indoor pool. Can you believe it? Indoor!"

Not exactly what he had in mind. Could he convince her otherwise?

She put the knife down and carried the plate of carrot strips to Bailey's perch, where she placed it at the foot. The bird jumped down and attacked the vegetable.

Adam came up behind her and wrapped her in a hug. "Swimming sounds like fun. But I thought..."

She turned in his arms. "What did you think?"

Seemed it wasn't something outside to interrupt them. It was inside. Inside his mind. Suddenly he couldn't form a coherent sentence. She was glorious and in his arms. He should kiss her. Carry her upstairs. But he couldn't seem to move.

She palmed his cheek. "What's the matter?"

"Are you as nervous as I am?"

"A little." She smiled. "Why are you nervous?"

"Because I don't want to screw this up."

"Me, neither."

"There's no way you can."

"I could say the same to you."

He laughed. "We're a pair, aren't we?"

"Yeah. Why don't we go upstairs and see how good a pair we are." She kissed him, her lips doing wonderful, erotic things throughout his body.

Oh yeah. They were going upstairs for sure now. He lifted her in his arms.

"What are you doing? Put me down before you get hurt."

"Hey, I'll have you know I lift more than you weigh." He approached the back stairs. They were awfully narrow. "Okay, this looked so much better in my head."

She laughed as he lowered her to the ground. "It's the thought that counts, I suppose. I take it we're going upstairs?"

"It's like you read my mind!" He took her hand and led the way. Light filtered in from the open rooms. When he reached the top, he scooped her up again. "Let's try this again."

Since his and Celia's visit—looking for Connor Elliott—he knew where the owner's suite was located. Just past the front steps. Which were way wider. Shoot. He could have carried her up those. Then again, it wasn't like his brain was actually thinking right. He carried her into the sitting room.

"This place is huge," she said. "Who needs this much space?"

"Apparently people with money to spend." Keeping her in his arms, because it was awesome just holding her, he headed over to the French doors, where a huge deck overlooked the backyard and lake. "Can you imagine living here?"

"No. Not really."

"Just a city girl at heart, are you?"

She leaned her head against his shoulder. "I guess I am. But I don't mind getting away every now and then, either. You gonna hold me all day or did you have something else in mind?"

Oh, he had a lot of something elses in mind, and they all required being naked.

* * * *

Evie was excited and nervous. Excited because she was with Adam. Nervous because she was with Adam. It was nice to know he was nervous, too.

He lowered her feet to the floor and kissed her. Her erogenous zones woke up and she palmed his pecks. His nipples were just as hard as hers. "We need to get naked."

"Your wish. My command." He slipped his T-shirt over his head.

She'd wondered if he had a hairy chest. Not that it really mattered, but she preferred non-hairy, and what do you know? No hair. Everything about him was perfect for her. She ran her palms over his smooth skin and kissed a nipple. He smelled wonderful. Tasted even better.

"Oh God. What are you doing to me?"

"Hopefully getting you in the mood?" she joked.

"There's no getting. I'm there." He tugged on her shirt. "Next?"

She lifted her arms. "Be my guest."

Cool air caressed her hot skin. She went to remove her bra, but he took her hands.

"Let me admire you in this sexy bra first, okay? You're beautiful. So beautiful."

"My bra is far from sexy." Heck, she hadn't even thought to wear sexy underwear.

"Everything you wear is sexy, okay?" He kissed her, plunged his tongue into her open mouth.

She was getting wet just from his kiss and didn't realize he'd removed her bra until her nipples were rubbing up against his bare chest. "Oh God. What are you doing to me?"

"Having my way with you. What else?" He moved her toward the bed and slowly pushed her back, keeping his mouth busy on hers. Once she was down, he nibbled his way to her breast and teased her nipple with his tongue.

Her leg rubbed against his erection and she reached down to undo the button to his jeans. But he moved lower and her fingers only met his shoulders. Nice shoulders, but not her goal. He pulled off her jeans and kissed the juncture of her legs. "You smell wonderful."

His breath caused ripples of pleasure. And a lot of teasing. *Touch me. Just touch me already.*

Jeans discarded, he widened her legs and did exactly what she mentally demanded: he licked her core. Man, had a tongue ever felt so sensual? Could she come just from that alone? He didn't give her a chance to find out. With his wicked tongue, he flicked her clit and stuck one of his long, glorious fingers inside her. She rode waves of ecstasy.

"I love how you're so wet. And tasty. I could eat you all day long."

And she wouldn't mind. The sensations he erupted inside her overtook all thought. She was just…being. Being adored, being worshipped, being special. She loved it.

He had masterfully removed his jeans without her knowledge. "Do I need a condom? I have one just in case. I'm clean. I promise. I got tested after…well, after my last time."

"I'm clean, too, and I never stopped taking the pill after…well, you know." Telling him she just liked to regulate her periods seemed a little bit TMI. "I would love nothing more than to feel all of you inside me right now."

He grinned. "Keep talking like that. I don't think I've ever been harder."

She sat up and palmed his length. All smooth and hard and ready for her. Touching him, knowing he wanted her, was almost overwhelming.

He closed his eyes and moaned. "If you keep that up, I'll be a goner soon."

"Oh, I think you have better control than that."

"Sweetheart, I'm living my fantasy right now. I don't know how much control I got left."

She was living her fantasy, too. She scooted back on the bed and he followed, his kisses melting away any anxieties she had.

He took his penis and rubbed it against her clit. It became so sensitive she nearly exploded. His mouth worshipped her body: her breasts, her mouth, her neck. Since when had that become an erogenous zone? She almost begged him to enter her when he did. Ripples of euphoria spread throughout her body. If he thought he was almost a goner, he had no idea that she was already there. She'd gone and went to Heaven.

* * * *

Adam stared down at Evie. After their last bout of love making, she had pretty much collapsed on top of him. Hell, he'd worn himself out, too. Lying in bed with her was a dream come true.

If he had known eleven years ago what he discovered today, he wouldn't have given up so soon. He would have knocked on every door to find her. He should have knocked on every door. Why the hell hadn't he?

He had just lived his wildest fantasy. Lived it. So why couldn't he just be happy? Why did he have to dwell on the past?

Evie opened her eyes and lifted her head. The smile on her face created weird, wonderful feelings in his chest. "You're still here."

"Where would I be? You're lying on top of me."

"Hey, you said you lifted more than I weigh."

Oh crap. He didn't mean to insult her. "That's not what I meant and you—"

Her laughter stopped him. She was teasing.

"You're incorrigible."

"Nah. I just like having fun with you."

"I like it, too. Honest." Oh, life with her could be splendid. An adventure every day. Fun every day. He just had to find Spencer's killer first. Easy-peasy.

"Good." She ran her hand across his chest, sending warm tingles throughout his body. "Want to go for that swim now?"

"I hate to break it to you, but I didn't bring a suit." Hell, he wasn't even sure he owned a swim suit. He couldn't remember the last time he needed one.

"Who said anything about a suit? The pool is indoors." Her grin was nearly evil.

"You want to skinny dip?" Oh hell, he was getting hard again.

"You have something against that?"

"Nope. Not a thing. Let's go!" He jumped off the bed and took her hand. As he pulled her to the door, he stopped and she collided into him. "Wait. I guess we'll need towels?"

She chuckled and wrapped her arms around his torso. "There are some in the pool room. I already checked."

"I have a feeling you planned for everything."

"Not everything. But close."

He nearly floated down to the kitchen and spotted the bird on the floor. "Hey, Bailey."

The bird approached him. Said, "Uh oh!" and bit Adam's big toe.

"Ouch! What the hell?"

Evie covered her mouth to stifle a chuckle or two. "Sorry. Meant to tell you. He likes to bite toes. At least he warns you before he bites."

"Would have been nice if you had warned me about his warning."

She kissed his cheek. "Did he spoil the mood?"

He spun around and pulled her into his arms. "He could never spoil the mood. Got it? As long as I'm with you, I'm in the mood. I'm like that song by Weezer, 'If You're Wondering if I Want You To, I Want You To.' That will never change."

She blinked several times. "Never? That's a long time."

He kissed her. "Not long enough. Not nearly long enough. I love you, Evie." Oh shit. Did he just admit that out loud? It was too soon, wasn't it? He was going to scare her away. "Wait. You don't have to say it back. In fact, forget I said anything."

She palmed his face. "Like hell I'm gonna forget. Shut up and kiss me again. I love you, too, you silly guy."

Okay, this had officially become the best day of his life. How'd he get so lucky?

Chapter 20

Evie emerged from her bathroom, naked as the day she was born. It was kind of freeing, walking around this way, knowing her privacy was safe. It had been super nice doing that at the lake house, too. With Adam. Who had said he loved her. Loved. Her. And then proceeded to show her all weekend.

She practically danced her way to the bedroom. Talk about the best weekend ever. Everything she'd imagined being with Adam had come true. But now she was back at home, getting ready for a funeral she really didn't want to hold.

Kind of made Spence's death real. She would say her final goodbyes to him. *Oh, God!* If she didn't stop thinking this way, she would start crying, and if she started, she might not be able to stop. This day was going to be difficult.

She opened her closet, pulled out the black pantsuit, and laid it out on the bed. She'd almost gone with a dress, but didn't really feel all that dressy. Plus, the weather had turned colder. According to her weather app, fall was pushing its way through.

At least she got to celebrate the end of summer with Adam, when he told her he loved her. He. Loved. Her.

Yeah, she would never tire of running those words through her head. Was he feeling the same way?

Hopefully this funeral would be the end of all her legal problems, Connor would be arrested, and she could get on with her life. With Adam.

Her phone rang and she smiled at the number as she answered it. "Hey."

"Hey! I miss you," Adam said. "I never realized how empty a bed felt until I slept with you. I kind of want you there all the time now."

She laughed as she sat on the edge of her bed. She could say the same. Waking up beside Adam had been the best part of the weekend. All that love making before and after sleep was a sweet bonus. "Then you're just going to have to hurry up and solve this case so we can sleep together more often."

"Trust me, I'm doing the best I can. I wish I could drive in with you."

"Don't you think I can drive to a funeral by myself?" It was meant to sound teasing, but somehow it didn't come out that way. She could really use his shoulder today but wasn't about to sound needy. Plus, he had his job.

"You shouldn't *have* to drive by yourself. I know how rough this day will be for you. If it weren't for Connor, I'd be with you during the whole event."

She knew that. He had his job, a job she wanted finished more than anything. But without Adam there, she'd most likely be alone during the funeral. Or worse, Keith would hover around her. Oh hell. She'd rather be alone. "Will I at least see you there?"

"If you come outside you will. I'll be at the front entrance until Connor shows. Celia will be at the back. We got you covered."

"Spencerrrr!" Bailey squealed from the living room and she jumped.

She'd been so wrong. She hadn't missed him squealing like that.

"He's in fine form today, isn't he?"

"He's been doing that ever since we got back. I thought for sure he'd stop. He was so quiet at the lake house." Suddenly, sitting naked on the bed didn't feel freeing. What if ghosts did exist and Spencer was one? What if he was watching her right now? Could that be why Bailey squealed his name? He actually saw Spencer? She grabbed some panties from her dresser.

"He probably wasn't comfortable there. Or he hates me. I still can't believe he bit my toe."

Evie laughed as she slipped on the panties. "And I told you he just bites toes. He doesn't care whose toes they are." She pulled a fresh bra from her dresser and couldn't put it on fast enough. She'd love to ask Adam about Spencer's spirit, but she knew how he felt about the subject. Hell, hadn't she told him she thought ghosts were just myths? But still, Bailey didn't say one word to anyone at the lake house. Get home and that's all he'd been doing. And the only person he talked to like that was Spencer.

And the cold spots. She only felt them here. Not at the lake house.

Could ghosts be real? Could Spencer be one?

She shook the shiver from her body. Maybe she shouldn't walk around naked anymore. Just in case.

* * * *

Spencer stayed in the living room where it was safe. He hadn't meant to see her walking naked in the hallway. He hadn't meant to stare.

Damn, she was beautiful. And he was a pervert. Just because she didn't know he was there didn't give him a right to spy on her. To ogle her. Oh, if he could only cut out his eyes, he would.

Because he apparently had no willpower not to see her.

Evie appeared at the hallway entrance wearing black. Well, almost all black. A bright turquoise blouse peaked behind her blazer, a color he loved on her. Had she known? Was she wearing it in his honor? He'd like to think she was.

She hesitated, looked around. Why was she acting so weird? She'd been walking naked earlier as if she didn't have a care in the world. Now? Had Fox's call upset her? She had sounded happy talking with him. That's when Spencer high-tailed it to the living room. And then Bailey had seen him.

"Spencer? Are you here?" she asked.

Why would she ask that? Had Fox finally told her the truth?

She walked over to the bird. "Hey, Bailey. Do you see Spencer?"

Or maybe Fox hadn't told her the truth; she was just figuring it out by herself.

Should he get the bird to say his name or not? Maybe now wasn't a good time. If ever. Because if she even thought she lived with a ghost, she would leave. He just knew it. As he moved away, she rubbed her arm and stepped back.

"Spencer? Is that you I feel?"

No, no, no. He popped down into the foyer, the scene of his death. What was he going to do? He couldn't stay away from her.

She was all he had. But he couldn't stay with her if she knew he was there. He grabbed his head and screamed.

"You okay?"

Spencer jerked upright. Oh, it was Erin. Of course. Who else? "A little frustrated."

"I understand. It'll go away. Eventually."

"What will go away?"

"The frustration. Once you figure out all the neat stuff you can do."

"The only neat stuff I've done so far is make the power go out in this building." And even that didn't seem all that neat now. "What kind of neat stuff can you do?"

The grin on her face reminded him of a character in a horror movie. He'd gotten chills then and he was getting them now. "I can make things move."

"Yeah? What kind of things?"

"Small things. Like keys." She giggled. "It's fun hiding them from people."

He could see the humor in that. For her. Not for the owner. How many times had he misplaced his keys? Had she been responsible? "You can control it?"

She nodded.

"How?"

"You just have to concentrate. Find the energy inside you and use it."

That sounded easier said than done. "The last time I found the energy inside me, I melted the circuit breaker."

"That's because it has energy, too."

"So I overloaded it? Makes sense, I guess. How long did it take you to control your energy?"

She shrugged.

Yeah, time probably didn't mean much to her now. Would it be the same for him once Evie moved on? Or would he move on once Evie was taken care of, like Fox said? "How come you're still here?"

Erin blinked as if she didn't get the question. "Mr. Marvin turned the TV off. I think he's going to your funeral."

"No, no. I mean how come you didn't move on? What are you waiting for?"

"Who says I'm waiting for anything? Being a ghost is fun. Don't you think it's fun?"

Spencer shook his head. "No, I don't."

"That's because you can't do neat stuff yet."

"If you can move things, how come you don't turn Marvin's TV back on?"

"I need Mr. Marvin to do that. And he notices when I move his hand to turn on the TV when he's awake."

"What? You can't just use the remote?"

"No. It has energy."

"Doesn't Marvin have energy?"

"Different kind of energy. I can't melt him."

"Ohhh." He was starting to understand. "You'll melt electronics just like I melted the electric panel?"

She nodded. "Thanks for that, by the way. Ruined a good day of TV."

Hmmm… Wonder if he could do something simple like open Bailey's cage? Or lock a door? He'd have to give it a try.

The elevator dinged. Marvin Holt stepped out.

Erin's unsettling grin reappeared. "Want to see what else I can do?"

She stood in Marvin's path as he headed toward the garage. As he passed through her, she disappeared. He swerved and ran his shoulder into the wall. A moment later, she emerged from his body.

Marvin rubbed his arm. "Damn wall. Where'd you come from?"

Erin giggled.

"You did that?" Spencer asked as Marvin left the foyer and managed the door to the garage without another incident.

She nodded. "Doesn't work on everyone. Only those who don't feel me."

Holy shit. Could that be how she killed those people? If she killed them. "But how?"

"Easy. When he walked through me, I grabbed onto him. With my energy. Can't hold on for long, but long enough to get him to turn on the TV. Or run into the wall. Neat, huh?"

Neat or creepy? Spencer was leaning toward the latter.

* * * *

Adam watched the front entrance of the funeral home while Celia watched the back. So far the only people who'd arrived were Evie, Keith, and Mr. Holt.

Oh, and the male ghost he'd spotted earlier when he'd checked the grounds surrounding the funeral home. It had only been a brief moment; just long enough to realize what he was seeing before the ghost disappeared. He could return later when the area wasn't so busy and investigate. Or he could call Zane and have him do it.

As if his hands weren't already full investigating Erin McCallister. That ghost gave Adam the creeps. The quiet from Erin was…unnerving. He'd told Zane about his encounter, which had only excited his friend. It had been years since he'd been able to help a local ghost, and he was determined to help Erin.

Evie stepped outside, saw Adam, and walked over. "I guess if you're still here, he hasn't appeared."

He turned off his mic so Celia wouldn't overhear. "And you'd be correct." Evie's bloodshot eyes worried him. "You okay?"

"I expected more people to come."

"It's early, yet. It's just the viewing now, right?"

She nodded. "That's why I thought there'd be more people. I don't expect a lot to actually stay for the funeral. Even his cousins aren't planning on coming. Shows you how close they were, huh?"

"Not surprising." The only blood family Adam could count on was Brina. Everyone else he considered family were not related by blood. "But he has friends at work, right?"

"Yeah. Keith said the office was closing at four."

Adam had been irked that Keith had shown at all, but there wasn't much he could do about it. And at least Evie wasn't alone. Keith was better than no one. "There you go. I bet you have a full house."

"I wish you could be inside. With me."

He eyed Celia, who had come to the side of the building probably because she couldn't hear him anymore. The frown on her face said she was wondering what they were talking about. Well, she could keep wondering. "You know I wish that, too. Right? I'm surprised Keith isn't glued to your side."

"He is. I lied and told him I was going to the ladies' room." Evie pulled a tissue from her pocket and wiped her eyes. "I have a feeling I'm going to go through a box of these today."

He so much wanted to give her a hug. To say the hell with Celia. With the CPD. To just be a boyfriend. Instead, he took a step back. This case was almost over and he just needed to be patient. Although patience was becoming harder and harder to achieve in her presence. "Want me to come over tonight? After we're through with Connor?"

"I'd like that. I can even have dinner for you."

Dinner? Spencer had told him about some of her dinners. At this point, he really didn't care if she was a good cook or a bad cook. He wasn't one to judge. All he wanted was to spend some time with her—however it was spent. "I don't want you going to any trouble, but I'd love to have dinner with you."

She smiled. "I wasn't planning on cooking. I doubt I'll have time for it, anyway. You like Giordano's deep-dish pizza? I haven't had one in ages, but it was Spencer's favorite. We can have it in his honor."

Spencer would sure get a kick out of that. If he hadn't moved on before then. "That sounds good. It's a date."

O'Hara emerged from the building, scowling. As if he had a right to Evie.

"Don't look now. Keith found you."

Her shoulders fell. "Shit. If your partner wasn't in viewing distance, I'd kiss you just to irk him."

"What? You don't want to kiss me? I brushed my teeth. Honest."

She shook her head, but her lips curled into a smile. "You know what I mean."

He did, but he got her to smile and that was his goal. "Go on. Let me do my job."

She nodded and headed inside.

Since Spencer was going to be cremated after the funeral, there wouldn't be a need for a funeral procession, so people just parked wherever there was a free spot. By four o'clock, only a few parking spots remained. Still no sign of Connor.

Celia spoke through his earpiece. "He's here. Coming in through the back."

Finally.

Adam sprinted to the back as Celia approached Connor and displayed her shield. "Connor Elliot? Chicago PD. We need to ask you a few questions regarding your brother's murder."

Had Adam spooked the guy by running around the building? Or was Connor just guilty? Whatever his reason, he turned and dashed inside the building. Adam rushed after him, following the sounds of screams and shouts. A path of toppled chairs led him to Connor, who stood beside Spencer's casket. Evie had moved to the back of the room, as had most of the other attendees. Except Keith.

"What is the meaning of this?" Keith bellowed.

Adam held his hand out toward the lawyer, but concentrated on Spencer's brother. "Connor. Don't make a scene. Just come with us nicely."

Someone from the back said, "Oh my God! Is he the murderer?"

Celia approached the attendees and held her arms wide. "Please exit out front."

A few people grumbled, Keith being the loudest, but they all filed out through the front door.

Connor looked inside the casket. "He's dead. He's really dead?" Placed his hand on Spencer's arm. "I'm sorry, Spence. I'm so sorry."

Adam pulled out his cuffs and read Connor his rights. He didn't fight. He was crying.

* * * *

Evie thanked the remaining guests for attending. After Connor's brief disruption, the viewing and funeral continued without a hitch. Still, this day couldn't end soon enough.

"You ready to watch the video?" Keith asked.

She sighed heavily. "Do I have to do it here? Can't I just take it home with me?" That way she could watch it with Adam present. And cry all over his shoulder instead.

Aaron Callahan held out the disc. "Since we've already seen it and you're the only beneficiary, I don't see why not. We already made a copy for Spencer's brother. If he's ever able to collect it."

She took the disc. Adam had mentioned Spencer had said some stuff toward Connor, but that was all. She couldn't imagine it was anything good. And if the guy had killed Spencer, he didn't deserve any final words anyway. He deserved to be put away forever. "Thank you. Now, if you don't mind, I'm going home." She had a pizza to pick up.

She went into the backroom, grabbed her purse, put the disc inside, and followed the men outside. Sunset was officially in less than an hour, but with the surrounding buildings, the parking lot was completely shaded.

The funeral home attendee locked the door behind them.

"Where's your coat?" Keith asked as he slipped on his overcoat.

"I didn't bring one."

"But it's getting chilly out here."

"I'll be fine in the car."

Of course, Keith had to be right. It was chilly outside. But she was right, too. She'd be in the car. It had a heater and heated seats.

She had parked on the opposite end of the men. Or rather, they had parked opposite of her, since she'd gotten here first. After a final goodbye and wave, Aaron strolled toward his car, but Keith tagged along as she headed toward hers.

"You sure you don't need some company tonight? We can grab dinner first."

He was worse than a puppy. She stopped and faced him. "In case you forgot, we're not dating anymore."

"Does that mean we can't be friends?"

Friends? Really? "Yeah, that's exactly what it means."

"Ah, Evie. Don't be that way."

"Keith, don't think I haven't appreciated you being there for me when I needed a lawyer. But you're not my lawyer anymore, either. Frankly, I hope this is the last time I ever see you."

He huffed. "I help you out and this is the thanks I get?"

"You want me to thank you properly? Send me a bill." She opened her car door.

"It's that detective, isn't it? You got the hots for him."

"It doesn't matter what I have. It's none of your business. You don't like the way we turned out? Then maybe you trust the next woman you date more than you trusted me. Although, I think the only reason you ever saw any interest in me was because you knew Spencer had a lot of money and that I was his beneficiary."

"I knew no such thing!"

She laughed. "See? I think that's a lie. You'll just have to find another way to get your millions."

"What a bitch." Keith stormed off toward his car. "I don't know what I ever saw in you!"

"Dollar signs. You saw dollar signs," she yelled back.

She tossed her purse into the car. Man, that had felt good. She should have told him off months ago. It probably would have made Spencer ecstatic. Instead, she'd make Adam ecstatic. She resisted giving Keith the finger as he drove off.

A man ran up the driveway. "Miss? Were you here for the funeral?"

Another mourner? She hadn't recognized half the people who attended and she thought no one would show. Boy, was she wrong. "Yes, but it's over. I'm sorry."

"Ah, damn it. I tried to get here on time, but the traffic was horrendous. Are you family?"

"I was a close friend."

"Spencer was my lawyer. Well, sort of. I used his services once. But I always saw him at the gym. I couldn't believe what happened. That he was killed in his own building."

The only gym Evie knew that Spencer used was the one at his work. "Which gym is this?"

"The one in our office building. I work for the mortgage company on the third floor. The Smith Brothers."

She recognized the name and relaxed. "Spencer said that gym was one of his best perks."

"I'll say." He came closer. "My name is Bill, by the way. And I'm sorry for your loss. Working out just won't be the same anymore."

"I'm sorry for your loss, too. But I have to go."

"Oh, yeah, sure. Before you do, do you know Evelyn Harper?"

She'd be a fool to admit she was the one and only. "I do. Why?"

"Spencer lent me his charger the other day and I wasn't able to give it back to him. Can you see that she gets it?"

"You could just keep it. I'm sure she wouldn't notice."

"But I'd notice. Please? If it's not an imposition."

She got the feeling the guy wouldn't leave until he gave it to her. And since she wanted to be on her way… "Sure. Why not?"

He smiled. "Great," he said, stepping forward as he pulled something out if his pocket. Sprayed something into her face. The world became fuzzy and she fell asleep.

Chapter 21

Adam stood in the observation room while Celia started with the interrogation. Should he be in there with her or would she see that as encroaching into her case? And it was her case. She had every right to lead the interrogation. He was confused as to what to do. It had never gotten this bad for him before. The fact the case had gone on this long wasn't looking all that good, either.

Did Connor kill his brother? Based on Spencer's account, Connor was there and Spencer had died. Spencer was sure if Connor had killed him it was an accident. Except his head wound didn't come from being shoved into the mailboxes. So where was the murder weapon? And if Connor was innocent, who else could have done it in such a small window of time?

Until Connor actually admitted he'd been there that night, their case was at a dead end. They had nothing. Nothing on Connor. Nothing on anyone. Nothing.

God, he was the worst detective ever!

Celia left Connor and came into the observation room. "I don't know if he's playing dumb or he is dumb."

"He's not dumb."

She crossed her arms. "Well, he hasn't asked for a lawyer yet, either."

"Because he doesn't believe he needs one. He knows the cameras are fake. Marie told him that. So he knows we can't prove he was there that night."

She narrowed his eyes at him. "And how do you know he was there that night?"

Oh shit. What did normal detectives say? They certainly didn't say a God-damned ghost told them. "It was a hunch."

"Oh my God!" She paced inside the tiny room. "Are you purposely making me look bad?"

"How am I doing that?"

"I believed you when you said Connor was our guy."

"He could still be guilty."

"No. I mean, I *believed* you. Thought you had evidence you were holding back and pointing me in the right direction. Now I think you want me to look bad. Don't you think I deserve this promotion? Or don't you want me to because I'm a woman? Or is it because I'm black?"

He held his palms out. "Whoa, hold up there. I have no issues with you getting promoted."

"Then how come you're sabotaging my case?"

"How am I doing that? You said you wanted to solve this on your own. No voodoo, you said."

"So you admit you use voodoo?"

"No!" Damn it. How was he screwing this up royally?

"Then tell me how it is you can solve all your cases within hours, yet you let me go on for days? I could see you letting me flounder along for a day or two, but it's been over a week and I'm no closer to finding the murderer."

She had a point, but by this time, even if he confessed all—and he wasn't about to do that—she still wouldn't believe him because what proof *did* he have? None, that's what. "It's not just you, okay? I'm no closer than you are."

"What? You saying I get the one case you can't solve either? Great. Just great." She eyed him. "Or is it that you're covering for *her*?"

Again? He was so sick and tired of her accusations. "I'm not covering for anyone, and you know Evie didn't do it."

"So it's Evie now?" She paced. "Damn it, Adam. This is why you gave me the case, isn't it? You didn't want me to solve it so your girlfriend goes free."

Adam scrubbed his face in frustration. He needed to calm down. Getting upset wasn't helping anyone. Although, a good yell would feel good right about now. "No. I gave you the case because you asked for it. You asked for it before we knew she was even involved."

"Yeah, but you gave it to me after you knew she was involved. And you've been misdirecting me ever since."

"I'm not misdirecting you. I honestly don't know who killed Spencer."

"So she could be involved."

"You know she isn't involved. There isn't a shred of evidence to suggest that, either. But let's say Connor wasn't there that night. What else have you uncovered in your investigations with the HOA? Anything look hinky there?"

"Everything looks hinky, but nothing I can prove. None of the board members are hurting for money, but that's not a surprise. All their income seems legit. On paper, anyway." She snapped her fingers. "But the property maintenance company..."

"What about it?" Spencer was sure that was where the issues were concerning the HOA.

"It's owned by a company, which is owned by another company, which is owned by another. I got so dizzy after the third layer of companies that I gave it to legal to look into. They're supposed to get back to me today. Maybe."

He snapped his fingers. "That has to be it."

"What has to be it?"

"If Spencer suspected the HOA funds were being misappropriated he would have the ability to check into it. The person responsible would want Spencer out of the equation." He pointed toward Connor. "I still think he was there that night. The fight Tony heard. Why else would Spencer go downstairs? Anyone else in the building, such as a board member or building manager, would have just gone up to his condo."

"Okay, I guess that makes sense. But we have no proof!"

"No, but *he* doesn't know that. We've been approaching him all wrong. Stay here." Adam entered the interrogation room but didn't bother taking a seat. "Listen. We know you were there. You were seen leaving the building. Just tell us what happened."

"No, no, no," Connor said, shaking his head. "There's no way they saw me..." He lowered his head. "Shit."

So someone could have seen him? Finally. Adam sat in the chair. "Connor, talk to me. Tell me what happened between you and your brother."

"I didn't kill him."

"But you pushed him. Didn't you?"

"I didn't mean to! He just got me so mad. Damn it."

"Tell me what happened."

"Nothing happened! He came storming into the foyer. Wouldn't even listen to what I had to say. Told me to leave him alone. He pushed me first. I swear. I only reacted. Over reacted, but reacted."

"How long did this pushing match take?"

"Not even a minute. When he hit the mailboxes he must have… I mean… He was still breathing when I left!"

"Where did he land? After you pushed him?"

"On the floor?"

Adam fisted his hands. Was this a brotherly trait, evading questions? He felt like he was talking to the ghost. "Did he fall over on his side? Slide down onto his back?"

Connor shook his head. "He just sat there. His eyes were closed, but he was breathing. I saw his chest move."

"What caused you to leave your brother sitting unconscious on the floor instead of finding someone, like the manager, for help?"

"I…uh…I wasn't thinking. I heard someone shut a car door in the garage, so I hightailed it out of there. It looks bad, I know, but I didn't kill him. He was still alive."

"You heard a car door shut. Not a condo door?"

"It sounded like a car door. It echoed from the garage. Not in the foyer."

"And you ran knowing there was a camera in the foyer?"

"I told you I wasn't thinking, okay?"

"What did you do with the murder weapon?"

Connor frowned. "Weapon? What weapon? I didn't have one. Ask your witness. They'll tell you I wasn't carrying anything. Damn, I really didn't think anyone in that SUV saw me, either."

Finally, a clue. "What SUV?"

"The one your witness was driving!"

"I never said my witness was driving a car. But the killer could have. What SUV? Color? Make? Model? License?"

Connor's eyes widened. "Killer? Shit. I didn't see the license. Wasn't really looking, either. But it was white. Lit up when it drove under the street light. Kind of small, hell all those small ones look the same to me, but it had the spare hanging on the back door, so I guess it's an older model. The newer ones don't do that anymore. It turned down the lane to the garage."

Not only one clue, but maybe two. Whether he could do anything with them was still debatable. He left Connor and returned to the observation room.

"Nice to see you were wrong," Celia said. "He *is* dumb. I can't believe he fell for that."

"I know, right?" Adam ran a shaky hand through his hair as the adrenaline coursed through his body. "And he may end up being our witness. We know Spencer went downstairs at 12:17. Tony called 9-1-1 at 12:35. If what Connor says is true, that he was only there a couple of minutes, why wouldn't Tony have come out sooner and called 9-1-1?"

"That's if you believe Connor. He could be lying. Or he can't tell time."

"Someone's lying, but I'm not sure it's Connor. Marie Diamante had to park her car around the same time Tony discovered Spencer since she entered the foyer while Tony called 9-1-1. If Connor heard her slamming the car door, why did it take so long for her to come into the foyer? And who was driving the white SUV? We're missing time."

"Not much. Is it?"

"Enough time for someone to knock Spencer over the head with something heavy and leave. Maybe that's what Tony heard."

"Or Tony's involved," she said.

Holy shit. He stared at Celia as his brain cranked information. "Tony works for the maintenance company."

Her eyes widened. "Motive?"

"Exactly. Good call! Still doesn't explain two possible people stumbling over the crime scene and not saying anything."

"Time to go find out if someone in the building owns a white SUV?"

"And we need to talk to Marie again." He pulled out his cellphone.

"Calling the girlfriend to tell her you'll be late?"

Adam sighed. No use in denying it any longer. "Okay, fine. We're dating. But I'm not calling her. I'm texting. You might want to do the same with your husband. I'm not quitting until I figure this out. We're close. I know it."

He texted, "*I have to cancel tonight. Sorry. Gotta break in the case. I'll call you when I'm done.*"

After taking Connor back to holding, they headed to their desks. Adam found the paperwork on the owners. Scrolled through the list and stopped at a familiar name. "Marvin Holt owns a white 2010 Toyota RAV4. What year did they stop putting the tire on the back?"

Celia checked her smartphone. "Looks like 2013, so that might be our car. But who's Marvin Holt? You make it sound like you know him."

"He was at the funeral. Lives on the tenth floor." With a ghost by the name of Erin McCallister, but Celia didn't need to know that. He searched through the rest of the list. "No one else owns a white SUV and the only other white vehicles aren't owned by board members."

"Let's start with the SUV, then." She grabbed her coat. "I hate this weather. It was so nice this past weekend, and now we're supposed to get highs in the forties? Doesn't seem right."

"That's Illinois for you. Ever think of moving?"

"Once. Both our families let us have it. Said we weren't taking their grandbabies away." She chuckled as she pushed the elevator button. "Have to admit, it's nice having family around. Some actually babysit for free."

He was starting to feel the same about his family, something he never thought he'd actually have. Brina was home. Now Evie. Life was turning out pretty sweet. It would be perfect once he and Celia got this case solved.

She drove them to the condo building. Parked in the visitor space. Spencer's space was empty. It was nearly seven. Maybe Evie decided to get that pizza anyway and was eating at the restaurant. That was possible.

They rode up to the tenth floor.

Celia knocked on Holt's door. When he opened the door, she whipped out her badge. "Mr. Holt, I'm Detective Delavau with the Chicago PD. I'm with Detective Fox. We have a few more questions to ask regarding the night of Spencer Elliott's death."

"Like I told that other cop, I'll help any way I can. Come on in."

They came inside the cluttered living room. This unit was a lot smaller than Spencer's. In fact, the lower the floor number, the more units, so it would make sense they'd be smaller.

This was where Erin McCallister liked to stay? The TV was on, so she was most likely in the room, too. Not that he would notice. But if Celia started rubbing her arms, that would be his answer.

* * * *

Spencer hovered inside the parking garage waiting for Evie to return. What was taking her so long? Had the funeral run long? Had she had an accident? It had been ages since he'd last seen her drive, maybe she forgot how. Or had she and Fox gone off somewhere after? He hated not knowing what was going on. It wasn't like he could call anyone, either.

Fox and his partner drove inside the garage and parked in the visitor space. So much for thinking Evie was with the detective. What were they doing here? He couldn't imagine Fox was here to see Evie, not with his partner tagging along. Had they gotten a break in the case?

Spencer followed them to the elevator. Fox punched the tenth floor. No way were they coming to see Erin. If Fox was alone…maybe. So who were they seeing on the tenth floor?

He followed them to Marvin's door. What did Marvin know of his murder? If only he could talk to the detective. Instead, all he could do is hover and listen in.

Erin was settled in front of the TV. When Detective Delavau walked through her, Erin scowled and the detective rubbed her arms. At least Spencer didn't need to worry about Erin possessing the detective, since she felt the chill. He wouldn't put it past Erin to do it just to even a score in a game no one knew they were playing.

"Mr. Holt, would you please repeat for us where you were on the night of Spencer Elliot's death?" Detective Delavau asked. "Between midnight and twelve-thirty?"

Erin turned her head and stared at the detectives. "Why is she asking him that?"

Spencer shrugged. The less he said to her, the better. Speculation didn't seem to sit well with her, in any case.

"Wow, that's pretty specific. But like I told that other cop, I was here. Watching TV. Actually, I might have fallen asleep watching TV. That happens sometimes."

"You didn't drive your SUV anywhere that night?"

"My SUV? No. Oh, wait. I lent my car to Marie. She had some kind of function to attend and her car was in the shop. I offered to drive her, but she didn't want to put me out. Not that it would have been an inconvenience. It's not like I go out all the time, you know? I just wish she would have remembered to lock the car. I don't know how many times I have to tell her to lock it. It's not like there aren't crooks in our neighborhood."

"Would that be Marie Diamante? Spencer's neighbor?"

"Yeah, that's her. She stumbled across the whole scene that night. Found Tony calling 9-1-1. Of course, I didn't find out any of that until the next day, when she returned my keys. I sure wish I'd known. I could have comforted her or something."

"I bet you would," Erin mumbled.

"You have a problem with Marie?" Spencer asked. When Erin ignored him, he prodded her some more. "More like a problem with Marvin and Marie? You afraid they'll become a couple and you'll lose your TV?"

She glared at him. "Don't you have something better to do?"

Actually, he did. The detectives were leaving and he still needed to talk to Fox. Back to the elevator. Next floor: his. Probably to see Marie. And he was right.

Although, Fox discreetly glanced at Evie's door. Did he know Evie wasn't home yet? He had to have seen the car wasn't in the garage.

Marie answered, smiling. "Hello, detectives. What can I do for you?"

"We're missing some details on the Spencer Elliott case and hope you can clear it up," Detective Delavau said.

"Come on in. I'll help however I can. Would you like some coffee? Tea?" Marie closed the door and indicated they take a seat.

Fox remained standing, but Delavau sat on the couch and opened the notebook on her phone. She'd been doing all the questioning at Holt's and apparently was going to do the same here, too. "That won't be necessary, but thanks. We've been told that you were driving Marvin Holt's SUV that night. Is that correct?"

Marie sat on a chair across from the couch. "Yes, that's right. My car was in the shop and Marvin lent me his."

"Did you see anyone leave the building when you returned that night?"

She shook her head. "Leave the building? No. I wasn't really looking, though. My friend called as I was turning onto our street."

"Do you know what time that was?"

She picked up her phone on the side table. "That would be 12:21. I didn't answer it because I was driving, but that's the time listed on my recent call list."

"12:21? But you didn't enter the foyer until 12:35, when Tony Fiori was calling 9-1-1. It took you 14 minutes to park and exit the car?"

"No, of course not." She rubbed her temple. "I clearly remember parking and turning off the engine. But then…"

"Then what?"

"The next thing I remember, I'm lying on my side inside the car. Like I fell over? I thought maybe I passed out. I did have a slight headache, but I went and saw a doctor later and she couldn't find anything wrong with me. But it was the strangest thing."

Spencer couldn't believe that Marie had anything to do with his death, but with the way Erin acted whenever Marie's name was mentioned, could she have done something to Marie? Like make her kill someone? But Erin would have had to possess Marie.

He ran his hand through Marie. Nothing. Not a single reaction. Holy shit. He needed Fox's attention. Now.

Spencer concentrated on the picture of Marie's late husband displayed on the side table. Nothing. He tried to find the energy, but had no idea what that even felt like. Instead, he yelled, "Move, damn it. Move!"

The picture fell onto its front.

Hallelujah! He finally did something right.

"I'm sorry," Delavau said. "Did I knock that over?"

Marie stood and adjusted the frame. "Don't worry about it. It doesn't take much to knock over. I think I need a sturdier frame."

Damn it. He'd been so sure it was him. Now how was he going to get Fox's attention?

Fox pulled out his cell. "Excuse me. I need to take this call."

Spencer grinned. Guess he got the detective's attention after all.

* * * *

Adam was certain the frame fell over because a certain ghost had something to say. He headed for the door.

"You can't take that call later?" Celia asked.

"It might be important. I won't be long."

He stepped out into the hall. Spencer was hovering there. Adam nodded toward the elevators, away from any inquisitive ears. Namely, Celia's.

"What do you want?"

"I'm so glad you noticed that picture. That was me! Neat, huh?"

"I don't have time for this. What do you want?"

"Yeah, okay. A couple of things. One, Erin might have controlled Marie that night."

Of all the things Spencer could say, that one was out in left field. "What? She can possess people? How?"

"She says she can make a person do things for a brief moment. But only to people who can't sense her. Like Marvin. And apparently Marie. She didn't feel me when I ran my hand through her."

Possession. It figured. "You say brief. How brief?"

Spencer shrugged. "She didn't specify, but she possessed Marvin for less than a minute. Long enough to get him to walk into a wall. Could she have used Marie to…kill me?"

Adam palmed his face. He'd never heard of a ghost possessing someone who was awake. The victims had always been asleep or unconscious. And he'd never heard of a ghost making someone do something they wouldn't normally do. "Why would Erin want you dead?"

"I don't think it's me so much as wanting to do something bad to Marie. She doesn't like her for some reason. Well, there is a reason. Marvin."

"Do you know where Erin is now?"

"Probably still in Marvin's condo, watching TV. She didn't care for the interruption earlier."

This was just great. More ghosts involved. Couldn't anything go easy for once? "What's the other thing you wanted?"

"Oh. Evie. She's not back yet."

Adam took a deep breath. "I suspect she stopped at Giordano's on her way back from the funeral home. She wanted to get a pizza there to honor you. I'm sure that's what's taking her so long."

"To honor me? How sweet. I really did love their pizzas."

His phone actually rang. "See? That's her now." He answered. "Hey, what's up?"

The voice that came over the phone was not Evie's, but a man. "Not your girlfriend. In fact, she's down. Down for the count."

"What? Who is this?"

"I'm hurt that you don't recognize your brother-in-law's voice."

"Glenn?" Why would he have Evie's phone. And what did he mean down for the count?

"Bingo! Give the man a prize."

"What do you want? Where's Evelyn Harper?"

"Your girlfriend is hidden safely away. As for what I want, I took you to be smarter than that. Who do you think I want?"

Sabrina and Becca, of course. "You think I'm going to trade my sister for Evelyn Harper? Why would I do that?"

"Oh, don't play dumb with me. I know what she is to you. I know what you did at that house by the lake. And if you want to see her alive again, I suggest you do as I say."

"Just because you have her phone doesn't mean—"

"I knew you'd say that. Check your messages."

Adam opened the message. Evie was in some kind of container. Her hands were tied behind her back and her mouth was taped shut.

"Oh my God," Spencer said. "What's he done to her?"

Evie. His Evie was hurt and it was his damn fault. Adam slid to the floor. "You're not going to get away with this."

"I think I will. Because you're going to let me."

"Sabrina doesn't want anything to do with you. She filed for divorce—"

"I know what you made her do. That can easily be rectified. And she'll do what I say for fear of losing her babies. That's right. I said babies. I plan on keeping her barefoot and pregnant, and if she even thinks about leaving me, I'll take one of her babies. I happen to know she'd do anything for them."

"You're insane."

"No. I'm just a man who will do anything to get his family back. Wouldn't you do the same? If you want to see your precious Evie again, I suggest you send Sabrina and the kid to Wrigley Field."

"I'm not sending them anywhere."

"See? I knew you'd be unreasonable. If they're not in front of Wrigley Field by—"

"You think I'm stupid? What possible reason would I do that? It's not like I can trust you to give me Evelyn's whereabouts. For all I know, you've already killed her."

And that thought soured his stomach.

"That's true. You just have to take my word for it. She's not dead. Yet. And I don't want to kill her. I just want back what's mine. This is all your fault. If you hadn't meddled in my affairs, none of this would be happening. You should be glad I'm such a forgiving guy. Wrigley Field. Nine p.m. If I see one cop near them—"

"It's not going to happen. It's over, Glenn. Just tell me where she is and go home. I'll forget the whole thing."

"You want to play that game? Fine. When she dies, it's on you." Glenn disconnected the call.

Adam stared at the phone. When she died? What had he done? How could he find her?

"Nooo!" Spencer said. "You need to call him back—"

Spencer vanished as Celia came around the corner. Several lights flickered in the hallway.

She looked up at the light show. "What is going on?" When she turned back toward him, she frowned. "Adam? What's the matter?"

Everything was the matter. "Glenn took her."

"Who's Glenn? And who did he take?"

"My brother-in-law. He took Evie." And he had absolutely no idea how to go about finding her.

Chapter 22

Evie moaned. The throbbing in her head wouldn't go away. Was she getting a migraine? She opened her eyes. Couldn't see a thing.

Oh God. Not again. Not again.

She struggled to sit up and failed. Her arms were bound behind her. Her ankles were bound together. She screamed, but her mouth was taped shut.

What was happening? Why was she taken? Connor had been caught. Who was that guy at the funeral home?

She needed to calm down, but how? Wait, what had Adam said before? Her eyes. She closed her eyes. The headache was still there, but now she could be anywhere. Anywhere that had a hard floor and smelled like fish. No, not floor. It moved.

Think. Think. Why would it move and smell like fish?

Water. She was on a boat on water. Lake Michigan? Or something smaller? Was she floating freely or tied to a pier? She opened her eyes to darkness.

Oh crap. She closed them again. Calm thoughts. She must think calm thoughts.

Spencer had a boat docked at the lake house. It was small with a blue tarp. Could she be there? She slowly got to her knees and pushed upright. Hit a hard surface; not a tarp. Damn it. It was like she was in a box.

A box. Oh God. Not another box.

Calm thoughts. Calm thoughts. She took several deep breaths through her nose.

Not a box made of wood. The surface was smooth. Like plastic. A cooler? Some of those big fishing boats had a cooler in the back. Maybe that's why it smelled like fish. Oh God. There weren't dead fish in here with her, were there?

Calm thoughts. Calm thoughts. Dead fish couldn't hurt her.

Could she force the top open? What did she have to lose?

Getting leverage. That was the key. But if the top was locked…

Oh great. Was it air tight? Would she suffocate?

That was the wrong thought. She cried. "Let me out!"

Yelling was pointless since her mouth was covered. Plus, she'd use up precious air. She jerked upright. Her hands and back hurt, but the top didn't budge.

A light breeze touched her face. She opened her eyes. Light. When she turned her head a certain way, a light came through a crack, where the breeze initiated. Had she cracked it? She inched closer.

No, she hadn't cracked anything. Appeared to be the seam where the lid met the cooler and something was wedged between them. Whoever had kidnapped her didn't want her to die. At least, not right away.

She lay back onto her side. She wasn't going to suffocate. But could she die from exposure? It was cold and she didn't have her coat. Her fingers were already going numb. Was it from the cold or had the restrains cut off the blood to her extremities?

The night was supposed to get into the thirties. She could survive that, couldn't she?

Yes, she would survive. Because whoever put her in here was using her for leverage. That had to be it.

But who? And for what?

* * * *

Adam continued staring at his phone as if it would bring Evie back.

"Adam, get up." Celia grabbed his arm. "Tell me what happened."

"I told you what happened. Glenn took Evie."

The funeral home. That had to be where he abducted her. And that ghost probably saw what happened. Could say where they went.

"We need to go back to the funeral home."

"We aren't going anywhere until you explain—"

"I'll explain on the way, okay?" He pushed the down button. "I should have known he'd do something like this. I shouldn't have left her alone."

"Why would your brother-in-law take Evelyn Harper?"

"Because he thinks I had something to do with my sister leaving him. The man is an abusive jerk. And he's apparently insane, too. Why else would he do something so stupid?"

The elevator doors screamed open. He stormed inside and pushed the button for the lobby.

"You need to calm down," Celia said. "Being upset isn't going to help. Why do we need to go to the funeral home?"

Calm down? Yeah, that was a joke. "That's the last place Evie was. A place he would have known about. Maybe someone saw something."

"If I recall correctly, Spencer's funeral was the final one for the day. I'm sure everyone is gone by now."

There wasn't anyone at the home he needed, although they might come in handy, too. Did he have to share his secret? Would she understand? But he couldn't do this alone. He needed help.

"There's something about me no one knows about."

The doors opened to the lobby. "Yeah? What's that?" Celia rubbed her arms. "Damn, that's quite a breeze."

Adam didn't feel any breeze. The temperature hadn't changed a bit. Spencer? Probably. Hopefully. He'd hate to think Erin was following them down. Maybe it was better to say this where he could use the ghost's help. But the foyer was not the place today. Several people milled about the mailboxes, talking. "I'll tell you in the car."

As she stepped out of the elevator, he waved for Spencer to follow. *Come on, buddy. Don't fail me now.*

Celia climbed in and started the car.

Adam stood outside and whispered, "I need your help, Spencer. Please, get inside and do what I say." He climbed in and spoke to Celia. "Don't go anywhere yet. I need you to stay here."

"To tell me your secret?"

"You always wondered how I can solve cases so quickly, right?"

"Yeah…"

"Well…you see… I get help." Damn, this was harder than he'd thought.

"Help from who?"

Spit it out, stupid. "The deceased."

Celia blinked at him. "Meaning what exactly?"

"Meaning I can see their ghost, okay? The ghost tells me who killed them."

She looked ahead through the windshield. "Do you take me for a fool, is that it?"

"No. I'm telling you the truth and hopefully can prove it. You know that frigid air you keep feeling in the building?"

"Yeah…"

"That's Spencer. Now, before you go rolling your eyes, I want you to look at your right shoulder."

She hesitated a moment, then did as he requested. "Why?"

"Spencer, touch her shoulder, please."

It seemed to take forever. Was he wrong and Spencer hadn't been following? Then her eyes widened and she jerked back against the door. "What was that?"

"Touch her other shoulder now."

She jerked back his way. "How are you doing that?"

"I'm not. Spencer is."

"He's sitting in this car? Now?" She gripped the steering wheel. "You can see him?"

"I can't see him right now. I can only see and hear ghosts when I'm alone with them. The cold air you feel tells me he's here." Or rather, a ghost was here. Whether or not the spirit was Spencer, they were being very cooperative. "Spencer, why don't you touch her some more."

She squirmed in her seat. "Stop it! Stop it! I believe you, okay? That's why you go off on your own, huh? Not due to any phone calls or your gut, huh?"

Adam shrugged. "What was I gonna say? I don't want anyone to know I can see ghosts. I'd be laughed out of the department. Or worse, the department would become a joke. All those cases I was on could come under scrutiny. You can't tell anyone. If you do, I'll just deny it. My word against yours."

"You didn't plant evidence, did you?"

Why did everyone always ask him that? "No. Of course not. I was just told where to look."

"Okay, say I believe you. How come you haven't solved this case if you're communicating with his ghost?"

"Because he doesn't know who killed him. He remembers Connor pushing him, but didn't see him with any kind of weapon. When Spencer departed his body, he saw Tony and Marie in the foyer. That's it. He thought it was an accident. That he'd hit his head against the mailboxes."

"So what are you hoping to find at the funeral home? If Spencer saw something, why doesn't he just tell you here?"

"Spencer wasn't at the funeral. Ghosts are stuck in a quarter-mile radius of their death. I need to talk to the ghost I saw there earlier. I'm hoping he saw something."

"Damn. Just how many ghosts are out there?"

"Unfortunately, too many. I help who I can. I help those whose cases I have. It's why I became a cop. I have access I wouldn't normally have. Now please, can we go to the funeral home?"

"Who else knows you can see them?"

"No one." No one she needed to know about.

"Not your sister? Or Evelyn Harper?"

"I haven't told them, no."

Celia laughed. "So the voodoo thing wasn't too far off, was it?"

"Not voodoo, but yeah, it's unusual."

"Unusual? I'll say. Although, now maybe I need to apologize to my aunt. She's always claimed to see spirits. I just thought she was telling stories or maybe drinking too much. So all this time, all those cases—"

"I know. I'm a fraud."

"No, you're not. You still had to find the proof, right? Just because you know who, you still have to prove it in court. You did that."

He nodded. "Yeah, I guess so."

"So we know Glenn took Evie. Let's go find out what he did with her."

"Thanks, Celia. I owe you."

"Damn straight you owe me. You owe me a case that I can get credit for solving quickly."

"You don't think that's cheating?"

"If it gets the killer off the streets sooner? No. What's cheating in a murder investigation, anyway? Besides planting evidence. Hell. Is there even *any* evidence in this case?"

"Hell if I know."

"So will this case go cold?"

"I don't know. Spencer just found out that it's possible another ghost caused his death. How the hell am I going to prove that?"

"Another ghost? There's another ghost in this building?" Celia couldn't drive out of the garage any faster.

* * * *

Spencer hovered in the garage as the detectives drove off to find Evie.

Damn, if only he could help. He thought he could protect her, but what a joke that was. She had to be all right. She just had to.

But while he couldn't help Fox find Evie, he could help Fox find his killer.

He popped into Marvin's condo. Marvin was dozing in his chair, but the TV was on and Erin was perched on the floor in front of it. She glanced at Spencer briefly as if he were an annoyance.

Well, if he was going to be treated as an annoyance, he might as well be one. He stood between Erin and the television set.

"You make a better door than a window," she said. "A screen door, but still. Would you move?"

He decided to just skip the getting-to-it questions. "You killed me, didn't you?"

"What made you come to that conclusion?"

"That Marie lost time down in the parking garage. That she thought she'd fallen asleep or something. That you can possess people who can't feel you. And Marie can't feel ghosts. You possessed her and killed me."

"Came up with that all by yourself, did you?"

"Why did you do it?"

Erin shook her head. "You got it all wrong. I was trying to keep her from killing you."

"Who? Marie? Why would she want me dead?"

"Because she doesn't want Mr. Marvin to move. No one in their right mind would buy a condo here now. Would they?"

"That seems rather extreme, doesn't it?"

"Hey, people do extreme things when they're not thinking. If you don't believe me, you can find your murder weapon in Mr. Marvin's car."

"Why didn't you tell me this before?"

"What, like it matters?"

"Of course it matters. I thought someone was going after Evie next." Except someone had gone after Evie. Just not the someone he'd expected.

"Now that you know, does that mean you're leaving?"

"I'm not going anywhere until I know Evie's safe."

"If she lets you go, that is."

"What's that supposed to mean?"

"Nothing." She vanished.

Damn ghost. Spencer popped back into the garage. Found Marvin's SUV. At least he didn't need a key to see what was inside. A flashlight might have helped, though. He stuck his head through the back end. A blanket was crumpled up in the corner. He stuck his head through the blanket, but it was just black. Could he move the blanket?

He concentrated on the edge. If he could only flip it up a bit, he'd be able to see. He scrunched his face, certain that if anyone could see him, they'd laugh at his expression. Nothing happened. Damn it! Erin would have been able to flip it without a problem.

What was he doing wrong? Maybe it was his eyes. He pictured the energy flowing from them and concentrated on the corner of the blanket. It flipped up. Wow! It worked.

The bloody tip of a tire iron was exposed.

Spencer backed away. "Holy shit!"

* * * *

Adam pulled behind the black Lexus. Celia and he decided that it was best if they split up, since she couldn't help spot the ghost anyway, and she would stay at the station and help with tracking Evie's phone. When she dropped him off, Celia admitted that she'd never removed the tracker from Spencer's car. Something they should have done once Evie was no longer a suspect. But he could have kissed Celia for such an oversight if the tracker had led to Evie. Instead, it showed the car was parked a couple of blocks from the funeral home.

He climbed out of his car. Walked over to hers. It was locked, but her purse was in the footwell of the passenger seat and her phone was on the seat.

Her phone! He gripped the handle. Shit. Could she be in the trunk?

He rushed to the trunk and pounded on it. "Evie! Are you in there?"

Someone slammed Adam into the car. He spun around. "What the hell?"

A slender, white male in his mid-twenties hovered in the street. It was the ghost Adam had spotted earlier. And his eyes were popping wide as he stared at his hands. "I should have gone through him. Why didn't I go through him?"

"Because I can see you," Adam said. *Please be on the friendly side. Please, please, please.* Otherwise…

"What? You can see and hear me? How?"

Adam shrugged. "It's a gift, what can I say. You were at the funeral, right? Did you see what happened to the woman who drove this car?"

The ghost hovered closer. "You didn't seem to notice me at the funeral home."

"I saw you briefly. Before people started arriving. I can only see you when there isn't anyone nearby. I'd love to stop and chat, but right now I need to know what happened to the woman who owns this vehicle. Is she in the trunk?"

"She was, but isn't now. Over at the funeral home, some guy sprayed her face with something and then shot her up with some drug. Tied her up and put her in the trunk. Then he drove off. I tried following, but he went too far."

Adam pulled up a picture of Glenn and Sabrina. "This man?"

"Yeah, that's him. Luckily, I just happened to catch him driving over here. He parked the car and removed something from the bumper. Then he opened the trunk, like he was making sure it was clean, tossed the phone on the seat, and took off in a truck. You just missed him."

Damn. Glenn had been tracking Evie? No wonder he knew where they'd been. "What kind of truck? Make? Model?"

"Sweet ride. Ford F150 with all the bells and whistles. Ugly silver, though."

That sounded like Glenn's truck. "Did it have Illinois plates?"

"No. Ohio, I think."

"You think?"

"The frame kind of covered the state, but it said 'Birthplace of Aviation.' That's Ohio, right? It was also dirty. Like it had been in the front of the car at one time."

So maybe it was his truck and he'd just stolen the plate. "You don't happen to remember the number, do you?"

"Started with an F or maybe an E. Last two numbers were 42. What are you? A cop?"

"Yeah, a homicide detective." A lousy one, but it was his title. "What's your name?"

"Michael. Michael Watterson."

"Thank you, Michael. You've been a big help." At least he had more information than he arrived with. But damn it, it still felt like he was back at square one. Adam headed back to his car, but couldn't leave the ghost just yet and stopped. "Were you killed? Recently?"

"I don't know. Maybe? I died on March 12, 2017. Is that recent?"

"Recent enough. Listen, I can't help you right now, but I will try and help you later. I promise. It's just that I need to find that woman before that man kills her."

Michael's eyes widened. "You can help me? How?"

"I'll tell you later, okay? Where can I find you? Behind the funeral home?"

"Yeah, that works. I hope you find her in time."

"Me, too." Adam climbed in his car and called Celia. "We need an APB on Glenn's truck and a forensics unit on Elliott's car, just in case he was stupid and left some evidence behind."

"I don't know. Sounds pretty stupid to use your own car."

"Well, it does have an Ohio plate. Likely stolen." He gave her the information. "Evie's phone is inside her car. I can get it if you need it for anything." And frankly, he wouldn't mind smashing something right about now. Glenn's head would be preferable, but a window would do.

"Do you really want to tamper with the crime scene? Let forensics take care of that, okay?"

"I can't sit here and do nothing!"

"Then come back here. Benny will be here shortly. Listen, I was looking at the picture. The one Glenn sent you."

"Yeah? And?"

"The container she's in looks an awful lot like a cooler."

"That's one big cooler."

"It's the kind they use on some fishing boats."

"Do you know how many fishing boats are in the Chicago area?"

"I know. I know. But it's something. Right? And if her phone has location turned on, Benny might be able to find out where the photo was taken."

"That would be better than something. That could be everything. While you're waiting on Benny, do me a favor. Look up Michael Watterson. Probably went missing in March 2017."

"The you-know-what?"

He nearly laughed. She was being so careful not to say ghost. Someone must be nearby. "Yeah, the ghost."

"Sure. Oh. Benny's here. I gotta go."

Adam pocketed his phone. If Evie was stuck in a cooler, how much air did she have left? Glenn said he wasn't going to kill her, but that didn't mean shit. She could be suffocating right now and there wasn't a damn thing he could do about it.

Chapter 23

Evie leaned the back of her head on one end of the cooler and stretched her feet to the other end, causing her knees to bend. Not a whole lot of room to move around, but enough for her to investigate. She'd found four spots where something was wedged between the lid and cooler. That had to be a good sign her kidnapper had no intention of killing her. But it was cold and she couldn't stop shivering. Did he plan on having her freeze to death instead? Or maybe die of starvation? How long could she go without food or water? If she was on a boat, the season was practically over and the owner might not come out for weeks. Or months. No way could she survive that long.

No, no, no. She had to stop thinking that way. If she was being used for leverage, leverage for what? Did this have to do with Spencer's death? Could it be someone looking to get Connor free from jail? Right, like the police would trade him for her. So if she wasn't being used for leverage, what else could it be? Nothing was making sense.

A car drove up. Oh thank God! She kicked the cooler wall. They had to hear her, they just had to.

The boat rocked.

She kicked harder. Yelled behind her gag. *Please open it up. Please.*

"You're awake, huh?" It was the man from the funeral home. She recognized his voice. Was he ready to free her now? Or finish the job?

The boat shifted. Colder air brushed her face and she took a deep breath through her nose. Air. Fresh air.

She opened her eyes. The man from the funeral home towered over her.

"No use yelling. No one's gonna hear you anyway." He leaned down and ripped the tape off her mouth.

Her lips stung something fierce and made her eyes water. She sat up, wiped her mouth along her shoulder, which brought some relief, and checked her surroundings. Boats and water. Lots of water. That was about all she saw. But it wasn't her lake. More like a marina on an inlet of Lake Michigan. Wherever they were, it was deserted.

"Where's my wife?"

Evie had thought this guy had something to do with Spencer's death, but wife? "I don't understand. Who's your wife?"

"Don't go playing games with me. I gave your boyfriend a choice and he chose wrong. Don't make the same mistake. So I'll ask you again. Where's my wife?"

Boyfriend. He must mean Adam. So what would his wife have to do with… Oh shit. Glenn had kidnapped her. How was she supposed to help him tied up inside the cooler? And did she want to help him?

"Answer me! Where. Is. Sabrina?"

Definitely had to be Glenn. "Adam's sister? What makes you think I know her?"

He pulled out his phone and shoved it toward her face. "Because you had lunch with her. Where is she?"

The picture had been taken at the diner. Glenn hadn't been there, but someone was. Apparently another private investigator.

"I don't know."

He smacked her across the face and she fell sideways, her face burning. Now she really had tears in her eyes. Damn, that hurt. No one had ever hit her before. Had he done this to Sabrina, too? No wonder she was leaving his ass.

"See, I think you're lying." Leaning over the edge, he gripped her shoulder, sat her upright, and got into her face. "So let me tell you this. If you don't know, you're no use to me. How about I just leave you in this cooler without the air holes. Is that what you want?"

"No." She just wanted to go home. But she wasn't about to give up Sabrina and Becca to do that.

"Fine. So let's try this again. Where is my wife?"

What could she say? Where could she say that would be believable? That would help her? Wait. The police still had Spencer's phone. Would they see the notification from the doorbell app? What other choice did she have? "She's at my condo."

"Your condo? Like shit she is. Tell me the truth!"

"I am telling you the truth. She's staying with me. Her and Becca. But you'll never get to her without me. My place is being watched."

As he sat on the bench molded to the side of the boat, his holster and gun were exposed. God, she'd love to jump out of the cooler and tackle the guy, but without the use of her hands and feet he'd probably just shoot her. Hell, he might do that anyway.

"Why should I believe you?"

"Because I don't want you to hit me again." *Please believe me. Please…* The only way to stay alive was to go with him to her condo. Someone there would be able to help her. They just had to.

"Who's watching? Where are they?"

"The police. Outside my building."

"I know you were exonerated for Spencer Elliott's death. They have no reason to watch your building now."

"Oh, they're not looking for me. They're looking for you. After your little stunt with Sabrina's phone, Adam asked some friends to keep watch off duty. Guess he had a reason to protect her after all." She flinched, waiting for another slap to the head, but he stayed seated.

He pulled out a set of keys from his coat pocket. "Is this the key to your place?"

"If that's my car fob, yeah."

"What's the code to your alarm?"

"I don't have an alarm."

He slapped her again. "You're telling me that a condo on Lake Michigan doesn't have an alarm? How stupid do you think I am?"

She couldn't stop the tears from flowing, the pain was worse than the cold. "I swear, I don't have an alarm. There's never been a need."

He paced to and fro for a few beats. "Fine. You're coming with me, then. You'll just have to distract those cops for me, huh?"

"Why should I? You're just going to kill me anyway."

He put his face into hers. "If you're telling me the truth, I have no reason to kill you. But if you make any kind of commotion, I'll kill your ass and anyone who gets in my way. You hear me?"

Oh, she heard him. Loud and clear. At least she bought herself some time. Time to figure out how she could come out of this alive.

He pulled her out of the cooler and onto the dock, but with her ankles tied together, she could only hop. "You gonna untie me or haul me around looking like a prisoner?"

If he removed her bindings could she jump from the vehicle when he least expected it? It wouldn't kill her, would it? Oh, maybe scrape her up a bit, maybe break a bone or two, but she'd be alive. That was the key element. Staying alive.

He pulled a knife from his pocket and cut her ties. Hallelujah! She rubbed her tender wrists and followed him to his truck. Or someone's truck. The plates were from Wisconsin. He opened the passenger door. "Get in."

She climbed inside. Before she had a chance to get comfortable, he pulled out a set of handcuffs from the glove box and attached one end to her right wrist and the other end to the door handle.

"Just in case you get it in your head to jump out."

So much for that plan.

* * * *

Adam threw his coat on his chair. He hated coming back to the station, but where else could he go? If he went to the condo, Spencer would only want to know what was going on. It was better to keep that ghost in the dark.

And he couldn't go to Zane's. That would be leading Glenn straight to Brina. So he called Zane instead and warned him. Zane said he'd call in some friends to come and help keep watch. There really wasn't anywhere else they could go that would be safer.

A box sat on Celia's desk and a smartphone sat charging on the box. "What's this?"

Celia turned around. "Spencer's phone. I was hoping to find Harper's phone using his, but the battery had died. When you told me you found her phone, I didn't bother putting it away. Seems we don't need it anyway. Benny is looking for the cell towers her phone would have pinged while Glenn had it driving her to wherever he stashed her."

"He's not stupid. I'm sure he didn't use the phone anywhere close to where he stashed her."

"He didn't need to use the phone to ping the cell towers. It just needed to be on."

"And it was," Benny said from the other side of Celia's desk. "I got a hit. Didn't you say you thought she was in a boat?"

"A large cooler," Celia said. "The kind some fishing boats have."

"Don't know about that, but I got a hit near the lake. Come see."

Adam walked around the desk. "Lake Michigan? Really?"

Benny pointed at red dots on his monitor. "These are the cell towers it pinged. You said she was taken at the funeral home. Was it in this area?"

"Yes." Adam pointed to a cross street. "She was here. He abducted her and drove her in her car to wherever he stashed her. Called me on her phone. Then he drove her car back, parked near the funeral home, and took off in a truck."

"Okay. This cell tower was pinged at three. Someone made a call at 5:45. Then it was pinged at 7:38."

Evie had arrived at the funeral home around three. She must have called in the pizza at 5:45. Glenn called him around seven, apparently not at that cell tower. "7:38? Damn I really did just miss him, didn't I?"

Benny continued, "I checked each tower close to the one that was pinged and got a trail."

"But those dots go up and down Lake Michigan," Celia said.

"Yes, but only one of these towers got pinged once. The rest were multiple pings."

"Meaning he stashed her near the one that got one ping and the multiple pings were from the trip there and back?" Adam asked.

"That would be my guess," Benny said.

There was an inlet to Lake Michigan not too far from the tower. Adam gripped the desk. Holy shit. Could he have found her? He turned to Celia. "Send someone out there to start checking all the boats. I'll meet them there."

She grabbed his arm and pulled him away from Benny. "Do you think that's wise? You need to distance yourself from this case."

Adam shrugged free and stalked to his desk. "Like hell I do."

"Adam. Think." She grabbed his shoulder and spun him around. "If Glenn is there and sees you. You." She emphasized that word with a point to the chest. "What do you think he'll do to her?"

"He's not stupid. He wouldn't dare."

"He's desperate. Think about it!"

He didn't want to think about it, yet that was all he could see: Glenn killing Evie. He slumped into his chair. "You're asking me to do nothing."

"I'm asking you to keep her safe. Right now he needs her alive. For leverage." She grabbed her radio and called in the scene. "If she's there, they'll find her. Does she know where your sister is?"

He nodded. "She helped me move them. I warned my friend. He's taking care of them."

Celia paced. "So she can probably guess who abducted her."

"Maybe. If she got past her panic attack. She doesn't do well in close spaces."

"You weren't lying about that?"

"No, I wasn't lying. She freaked out when that elevator went dark." And how dark would it be inside the cooler? At night? Could she be reliving that day? Granted, it wasn't hot outside. It was close to freezing. Oh shit. Why'd he have to think about that?

"And you calmed her down."

"Yeah? So?" He wasn't there to calm her now.

"So maybe she learned something. She's a smart woman. If she believes Glenn took her, she might bargain with him. Especially if he went back to finish her off."

Adam grabbed his head. "Damn it. I should have made the bargain, shouldn't I? We could have caught him—"

"Stop. We can't change the past. We can only move forward. Where might she say Sabrina is being held? I can't imagine she'd tell him the truth."

"No, she wouldn't tell him the truth. She would protect Sabrina and Becca. I'm pretty sure. But I don't know where she might say—"

Spencer's phone lit up and chimed. When it had finally connected to the internet, all the old notifications came through. Most from the doorbell app.

The doorbell app.

In unison, they said, "The condo."

Chapter 24

Evie stared out the window as Glenn drove them to her condo. She still hadn't come up with a plan. Should she push him inside the condo and make a run for it? Would he risk firing his weapon inside? Did she want to take that chance?

Instead of turning down her street, he continued straight. A cop car was parked close to the condo's entrance. Damn. Were they there for her or Glenn?

He pulled over to the side and parked illegally. At this point, he probably didn't care about getting a ticket. "I guess you weren't lying about the cop."

This put a crimp in her plans. What little plans she had. Figured she could have said that Adam moved Sabrina and Becca, so there wasn't a need for a cop. But with a cop there… Damn it. What the hell was she going to do?

Glenn shoved the gun in her side. "Don't even try it."

"Try what? I do want to get out of this alive, you know."

He'd have to eventually uncuff her from the car. To do that, he'd have to put his weapon down. Could she grab it and shoot him?

He turned off the ignition and pocketed the keys. Leaning over, he pulled a small case from under his seat. It contained hypodermic needles and a small aerosol can.

"What's that for?" Was he going to knock her out again? How would she get free?

"For the cop. And you're gonna help me."

"I'm not going to help you kill him."

"How many times do I have to tell you, I don't want to kill anyone." He picked up the can. "This will knock him out briefly, just like it did for you." He shoved the can in his left pocket and picked up a needle. "And this will knock him out for an hour or so, just like it did for you. Probably less, since he weighs more. But if you say anything to him to make him reach for his gun or his radio, I'll shoot him. And that will be on you. Do you understand? And if you make me shoot a cop, there won't be anything to stop me from shooting you, now will there?"

Wow. Was this how he got control of his wife? Always blame her for his misdeeds? Well, it was working on Evie. She'd do anything to keep someone else from being hurt. Or killed. Especially herself.

He stuffed a needle in his right pocket, zipped up the case, and shoved it back under his seat. "You ready?"

"What do you want me to do?"

"I figure he must know you. Just walk up to him and smile. Get him to roll down his window. That's all. Once he does, I'll take it from there."

"You're not afraid someone will see?" Although, it was pretty dark out. The cop wasn't exactly sitting under a street light.

"See what? Someone walking up to a police car? Why would they care?" He got out of the truck and walked around the back.

Her time was running out and she still didn't have a plan. If only she could think faster.

* * * *

Spencer hovered in the foyer. This not knowing stuff was driving him crazy. Evie was taken by some lunatic and he couldn't do a damn thing about it. Would she be okay? Would Fox find her in time?

And then there was Erin. He didn't believe anything she'd said. Just because his murder weapon was inside Marvin's SUV didn't mean Erin had tried to save him. She could have controlled Marie to kill him and stash the weapon away. But why? Why would Erin want him dead? Or rather, why did she want to frame Marie? That seemed the likely scenario. Erin did not like Marie.

Solving his own murder didn't seem to matter anymore. Nothing mattered if Evie died. Nothing.

He popped out onto the sidewalk. When had the police car arrived? Were they expecting Evie to return? He popped inside the cruiser. Oh, the officer was writing up an incident report.

Someone knocked on the officer's window. Spencer turned. Evie?

He floated through the roof. A tall, muscular man stood closely beside her, holding a gun to her back.

Oh shit. That had to be Glenn.

Evie smiled at the officer and indicated he roll down his window. Once the cop obliged, Glenn sprayed the man's face, who then slumped over. Glenn took out a needle and stuck it in the officer's neck.

"You did good. Now let's go get my wife." Glenn looped his arm around Evie's.

Wife? Why would he think… Oh. Evie led him here on purpose. But why? Did she think the doorbell camera would help her? It would if the notification went to anyone important. Damn it! Spencer followed them into the foyer.

"Fuck! You have cameras?"

She looked up. "No. They're fake. I swear. That's why they haven't caught Spencer's killer yet. They don't know who did it. The HOA may get cameras eventually, because of Spencer's murder, but it hasn't happened yet."

She pushed the up button and the doors squeaked open almost automatically.

"What the fuck is wrong with the elevator?" Glenn asked.

"The doors squeak. Nothing's wrong with the elevator. I wouldn't use it if there was." Evie stepped inside and pushed the button to her floor.

"This building is shit. You don't have a code to get in. Your cameras are useless. What kind of place is this?"

"Hey, you shut up about my building." Spencer stared at the panel. If he could disable the elevator car, would that make it better or worse? Probably worse. His luck, he'd cause the car to plummet and that wouldn't be good. But what could he do to stop Glenn? To help Evie get away?

He popped up to his floor. Could he rip up the carpet, cause the guy to trip? Or would Evie trip first? Everything he thought of would hurt Evie more than help her. And it wasn't like he had a lot of time to actually do anything.

The doors squeaked opened. Evie pointed to the right. "My condo is that way. At the end of the hallway."

"Go." Glenn poked the gun into Evie, prodding her to move.

"Don't hurt her!" Spencer screamed. The hallway lights surged. Glenn and Evie both walked as if drunk.

"What the fuck was that?" Glenn said.

"We've been having electric issues," Evie said.

"And they cause the floor to move?"

That couldn't be good. He needed to watch his temper. The last thing he wanted was to cause the building to collapse.

Glenn shoved Evie up against the door and stuck the key into the lock.

Maybe she needed a distraction to get away? Spencer popped into the condo. Bailey was by the window, but hadn't seen Spencer yet. He waited. The door opened.

* * * *

Adam pulled in behind the police car. "Did you call this in?"

"No, just the marina," Celia said. "Figured we were closer and didn't want to pull anyone away in case she's there. We don't know if she's here."

Adam's gut said otherwise. When Spencer's phone started showing all the missed notifications—the last when Evie had left for the funeral home—Adam was sure that Evie would take Glenn to the condo. If Glenn had gone back for her. And why wouldn't he? What else could he do? He was running out of options.

In case Glenn had reached the condo first, Adam brought Spencer's phone with him. So far it had remained quiet. He climbed out of the car and approached the slumped over officer. "What's wrong with him?"

The window was down. The officer wasn't moving. Adam placed two fingers against his neck and found a pulse. "He's alive." Shook the officer. "Hey!"

"He's out cold," Celia said.

Just like Evie had been when Glenn had abducted her. Spencer's phone buzzed. The doorbell app was live. Adam pushed the button. "It's Glenn. And he's got Evie with him."

"I'm calling for backup."

"They won't get here in time." Adam gave the phone to Celia, rushed inside, and just missed the elevator. Damn it. He pounded the up button.

She followed him. "You can't go up there by yourself! We need to wait for backup."

"Like hell I will." He stared at the door for the stairs.

"It'll be quicker to wait for the next elevator than to hike twenty flights," Celia said.

Yeah, but the waiting was torture.

* * * *

Evie practically kissed the door as Glenn pressed her face up against it while he inserted the key into the lock. There was no running away like this. No dashing back to the elevator, or even the stairs. She was going to be shoved inside the condo and then what? Shot to death?

As Glenn opened the door, Bailey squawked, "Spencerrr!"

The entryway was covered in bird poop.

"What the fuck was that?" Glenn shoved her.

She leaned right, forcing him into the worst of it. He went down in a hurry. Turning and hopping, she made a beeline to the elevator, not bothering to see if he'd knocked himself unconscious.

She pushed the button, but the doors didn't open. Damn it, it had already left. The stairs. Hurrying as fast as she could, she'd made it down several flights when the lights went out. She missed her step, twisted her ankle, and landed on her ass in tears.

* * * *

Spencer cheered in glee as Evie made her getaway and Glenn was lying in bird poop. Couldn't have happened to a nicer guy.

Glenn got up and started searching the condo. "Sabrina! You can't hide from me. Come out here!"

It didn't take long for him to realize the place was empty, except for Bailey.

"You lying bitch!" He ran back to the door, where he slipped on the poop again. "God damn it!"

Spencer laughed, but it died quickly as Glenn made a dash for the elevators. The down button was lit, but no sign of Evie. He opened the door to the stairwell. Footsteps echoed in the enclosure. Glenn was headed that way when the elevator doors opened. He dashed inside and pushed the button for the first floor.

Shit. There wasn't much time before Glenn would ambush Evie.

Spencer popped inside Marvin's condo. Erin was sitting watching TV.

"Unless you want me to fry the whole building again, I suggest you join me in the basement. Now." Before he gave her a chance to respond, he popped down to the electrical box in the basement.

It was all brand new. But not secure. Tony hadn't bothered locking the box. Probably thought the door would be good enough. For once, Spencer was glad the guy was incompetent. If the lock was there, they might melt the whole system again, and he really didn't want to do that.

Erin appeared. "What do you—"

"I need to shut the power off to this building. You can do it better than I can."

"That box has energy."

"I know that. But the lever doesn't. Does it?"

"Why?"

"I don't have time. Either you do it now or I will!"

She flicked her wrist. The handle moved down. She'd done it so smoothly. So easily. He'd have mucked it up for sure.

The basement went dark. The emergency lights did not come on. But Tony could easily come down here and turn it back on.

"You want to tell me why I needed to do that?"

"Can you bend the handle so they can't turn it on right away?"

"What do you take me for? Hercules?"

"Can you or not?" If he could burn the whole thing, surely she could bend a little handle.

"Hold on." She closed her eyes in concentration. The handle bent about an inch.

Ahh, success. "Thank you!"

Hopefully that would give Evie enough time to escape through the stairwell.

"Now, tell me why," Erin demanded.

"Crazy man in the elevator. I had to stop him."

"Crazy man?"

He couldn't see Erin in the dark, but somehow he pictured an evil grin on her face.

* * * *

One elevator was on its way up. The other was stopped on the tenth floor. What the hell? Adam was ready to pull out his hair.

"She's getting away." Celia showed him the live feed from Evelyn's condo.

"Where is he? What's he doing?"

"I don't know. There's no sound on this thing!"

The elevator still had a way to go to the twentieth floor. The other was still stopped. "She won't wait for the elevator if she feels threatened." And why wouldn't she feel that way. The guy had kidnapped her. "She'll take the stairs. You wait here. I'm going to meet her."

"Take this." She handed over Spencer's phone. "So you can keep track of Glenn."

Adam took the stairs, two steps at a time. By the fourth floor his legs were feeling it. The live feed showed Glenn running out of the condo. Adam stopped, held his breath as best he could, and listened for a door opening and closing. Only sound filtering down were faint footsteps. Probably Evie's. If he yelled for her, would Glenn hear?

He couldn't take that chance. Onward and upward.

As he reached the fifth floor, the power went out. Thankfully he was gripping the hand rail and kept himself from eating the stairs.

Someone cried out above. He risked calling. "Evie?"

"Adam? Oh God. Adam. Help me."

"I'm on my way." He waited a couple of seconds, but the emergency lights did not come on. Because, of course not. He turned on his flashlight app and semi-cautiously climbed the stairs. He didn't need to miss a step and break his neck. "What floor are you on?"

"I just passed the twelfth floor. I fell and hurt my ankle."

"Hold tight. I'll be there soon."

It felt like forever before he finally met up with her. She sat on the step at the landing between floors, holding her ankle. Looked up and brought her arm up to block the light from his phone.

"It's okay. It's just me." He rushed to her side and hugged her tight as relief flowed through him. "Are you hurt bad?"

"Bad enough. But I feel so much better now that you're here. Glenn's here. Somewhere. And he has a gun. I don't know where he went."

"I didn't hear him come into the stairwell after he left your condo, so I'm guessing he's stuck in the elevator." He held up Spencer's phone. "This kind of came in handy."

She breathed deep. "I'm so glad you found me." She hugged him again. "I didn't think I'd ever see you again."

He'd had the same thought. Couldn't be happier to be wrong. "Let's get out of here, okay?"

"I don't know if I can climb back up to my condo. And he might still be in the hallway. The camera doesn't reach that far."

"Shhh, hold up there. I didn't ask you to go up. Going down will be easier, and help is waiting for us in the lobby. You can stand on one leg, can't you?"

"Yeah. Just don't let me go."

"Don't worry." He caressed her cheek. "I hadn't planned on it."

As they slowly made their way downstairs, he tried calling Celia. Nothing. "Guess the stairwell is as bad as the elevator shaft. I can't get a signal."

"Try the hallway on the next floor. I doubt Glenn would be there."

"Good idea." On the next landing they exited and he was able to get a call through to Celia. "I got her. No signal in the stairwell. She sprained her ankle, so it's slow going. We're on the tenth floor."

"Any sign of Glenn?"

"Unless he has Ninja skills, he's not in the stairwell. I'm thinking he's stuck in the elevator."

"Don't know how long that will last. The building manager went down to the basement to find out what's wrong. It could be something easy to fix."

"It could be." But he doubted it. If Spencer was watching it all unfold, it was highly possible he had melted the electrical box again. And frankly, Adam wouldn't blame the ghost. "See you in a bit."

He disconnected the call and grabbed Evie around the waist. "Let's get out of here, shall we?"

"Sounds good to me."

When they reached the sixth floor, the door opened. "Ah man, it's out in here, too?"

Adam nearly had a heart attack, thinking Glenn had taken the other stairwell and made it down before them. Instead, it was just a tenant, some guy around twenty. "Seems so. No need to evacuate right now unless you have to. It's probably temporary. You'll be contacted if you need to evacuate. Will you let your neighbors know, please?"

"Yeah, sure. This place sucks!"

* * * *

Spencer left Erin and popped into the elevator shaft. Floated upward until he found the elevator car. Glenn was inside, holding his cellphone, the flashlight app turned on. Good. The creep was trapped, giving Evie time to escape.

Voices could be heard through the doors. Glenn placed the cell on the floor with the light up. Using the barrel of his gun, he pried the inner doors open. The outer doors were just above him.

"Hello!" Glenn yelled. "Can someone help me?"

Please don't let anyone answer. Please, please, please.

"Whoa, are you stuck in there?"

Shit. So much for praying.

"Since when did idiots afford a condo along Lake Michigan?" Glenn muttered. "It appears so," he said loudly. "Can you find something to pry the doors open so I can get out?"

"Oh yeah. Sure. Hold on."

Spencer concentrated on the outer doors. Could he keep them closed? Hell, he couldn't even move a stupid lever. What made him think he could hold elevator doors closed?

The door opened a crack. A flashlight sat on the floor and lit up the area. Glenn holstered his gun and helped to make the opening wider. "You need to keep holding this so I can get out."

"Yeah, sure. What about the other door."

"You let me worry about that one, okay?"

"Is this the crazy man?" Erin said. "Seems pretty smart to me."

Spencer jumped at her arrival. "Do you see his gun? He's trying to kill Evie."

"Can't you warn your friend?"

Could he? He popped into the stairwell. Light bounced along the walls going down. He followed the source and found Adam and Evie going down slowly. Evie was basically hopping on one foot. No way Fox could hear him.

He popped back to the elevator where Erin was still watching. "He's not alone. Can't see or hear me."

Glenn picked up his cellphone and squeezed through the opening with help from the man in the hallway. "Thanks. That's quite a power outage. Even the emergency lights didn't come on?"

"They're supposed to. We were promised they were fixed. This place sucks!"

"Can't argue with you there."

"If you're going down, or up, be careful. Lights aren't working in the stairwell, either."

Glenn waited until his helper left, walked to the stairwell door, then turned off his light. The darkness was complete. Spencer couldn't see a thing. Which meant, neither could Glenn. When he opened the door, a faint light appeared. The light from Adam and Evie. Glenn quietly stepped onto the landing and shut the door.

Spencer followed into the stairwell. The light below kept on moving, so Adam must not have heard anything. Figured. He turned to Erin. "Can you control him?"

"No. He feels me."

Glenn slowly worked his way downstairs.

"That figures. I wish… Wait." There was someone who could help. Hopefully.

"Wait, what?" Erin asked.

"I got an idea. Can you distract him with the cold? Slow him down? Anything?"

"Sure, why not? It's not like I can go back to watching my movie, now can I?"

"Thanks." Spencer popped down to the foyer.

At least the foyer had some light from the street, but even that was minimal. Detective Delavau wasn't anywhere to be seen. Where the hell did she go?

As if an answer to his thought, she returned with a flashlight and was headed for the stairwell.

He couldn't have her go up there yet. Not now. He prayed he got her attention in time and that she'd understand his intentions. Spencer ran his hand thorough her shoulder.

The detective stepped back and shined the flashlight his way.

"Yeah, not a person. Just me." At least she stopped. Spencer repeated the process.

She jerked away again, but a moment later looked around. "Spencer?"

Yes! He touched her again.

"Would you stop it?"

"Not likely." He reached out and ran both hands through her.

She flattened against the wall. "Okay, apparently you need to tell me something. Can you touch my right arm for yes and left for no?"

That, he could do. He touched her right arm.

She stared at her right arm. "Wow. Okay, so what's the matter? No, no, no. That's dumb. Yes or no questions, idiot. Is there something I need to know about?"

Yes.

She looked at the door to the stairwell. "Is Adam in danger?"

Yes.

"How? I'm sorry. You can't answer that, can you? It's just… Glenn's in the elevator."

No.

She stared at her left arm. "He's not? Shit. Where is he? I mean…" She hit her head with the heel of her palm. "Is he in the stairwell?"

Yes.

"Behind Adam?"

Yes.

She remained still as if thinking through possible scenarios. Spencer couldn't think of any scenario that wouldn't hurt or kill Evie, but then, that's why he needed Detective Delavau's help.

After the longest moments, she pulled out her weapon and opened the stairwell door. "Adam?"

"We're coming."

"Well, try to hurry it up."

"Yes, ma'am!" Adam chuckled.

She entered the stairwell and closed the door.

Spencer followed, but couldn't see a damn thing except the light Adam carried. What the hell was Detective Delavau doing?

* * * *

Adam had to chuckle. Celia was getting antsy. Hell, he was getting antsy. But he was going as fast as Evie was able and there was no reason to rush since it appeared Glenn was trapped in the elevator. He was tempted to carry her down, but wasn't sure that was the smart way to go, either. His flashlight app only lit up so much.

As he turned on the landing of the fourth floor—according to the door—the light shown upon Celia, who was standing at the next landing down, holding a finger against her lips.

Evie squeaked and Adam covered her mouth. "I got you."

She pulled his hand off her mouth. "Thanks."

Celia pointed up. Adam's heart dropped. So Glenn wasn't in the elevator. Damn it! Adam wasn't going to question how Celia knew

231

the bastard was behind him, because why would she care otherwise? He gave the phone to Evie. "Go with her," he whispered in her ear.

"What?" she whispered back.

"He's here."

Her eyes widened, but she nodded. Lighting the way Adam had done before, she continued downward with Celia this time, hopping a little faster. She still wasn't putting weight on the injured ankle, but if Glenn was in the stairwell—and how, Adam had no idea—she had motivation to move quicker.

He followed them to the third floor landing and waited in the corner away from the door. Surprise was on his side, he only hoped he could pounce on Glenn and not get killed in the process.

The darkness was starting to freak Adam out, so he did as his grandmother taught him all those years ago. He closed his eyes, took a calming breath, and listened.

Soft footsteps sounded on the landing above. If Glenn turned on his flashlight, he'd see Adam crouched in the corner, away from the door, but then the flashlight wouldn't have made him stealthy and that was to Adam's advantage. He counted the footsteps as Glenn descended and waited for the perfect opportunity. As soon as he calculated Glenn was half-way down the set of stairs, Adam tackled Glenn and knocked his gun free.

Glenn grunted. "You'll pay for this."

The stairwell lit up. Celia's flashlight. "Freeze! Or I'll shoot!"

"Like hell." Glenn twisted, punched Adam in the face, and pushed him.

Adam landed hard on a step and slid to the landing. Glenn picked up his gun and pointed it toward Adam. The door to the third floor opened just as Glenn fired and Adam ducked. The echo reverberated in the stairwell. The door had saved him by taking the bullet meant for him. The door opener cussed as they quickly retreated, and Celia fired before Glenn could get another round off. He stumbled against the railing, grabbing wildly for it before falling to his knees and tumbling head first, landing on Adam.

Adam huffed as Glenn's weight knocked the air out of him. He scooted out from under the body, and with shaky hands, felt for a pulse. Nothing. "Holy shit! He's dead."

Celia backed against the wall and dropped her flashlight. "Dead dead?"

"Is there another kind?"

"I've never killed anyone before."

"Oh." Shit, neither had he. "You okay?"

Before she could answer, the stairwell swarmed with police officers.

Chapter 25

If it weren't for her ankle, Evie would have paced the foyer in worry. A gun had gone off as the police had stormed the stairwell. Then a second shot was fired, but no one had come down yet. Not Celia. Not another police officer. Not Adam. God, who got shot?

Tony emerged from the basement. "Was that gunshots?"

"I think so. Cops are in the stairwell. Can you get the power back on? They need lights in there!"

"I tried. Stupid lever is bent and I need a hammer. Why would someone do that?"

Why, indeed. Nothing was making any sense. "How would anyone have been able to turn off the power? Isn't it locked?"

"The door was."

"But not the box?"

Tony lowered his head. "Well...I had planned on locking it today. Honest!"

As Tony headed back toward his condo to find a hammer, an EMT truck arrived out front. She first thought Celia had called in about her ankle, but when they came in with the gurney, they passed Evie and headed toward the stairwell.

No, God, please, not Adam! Where was he?

Finally, Celia emerged, and Evie stumbled over to the woman. Her mouth became dry and she could barely speak. "Where's..."

Celia pointed to the door just as Adam appeared.

Oh thank God! Tears streaming, Evie ran to him to touch him, to hold him, to assure herself he was really all right, but because of her ankle, she nearly face-planted on the floor. He moved in quickly to catch her and she fell sobbing into his arms.

"Thank God! I was so afraid." She hugged him tight. Relished his scent. He was alive. He was really okay. "When I heard that shot…"

"Hey. I'm okay." He pulled away and kissed her lightly. She must have winced or something as he stopped and stared at her face. "What did he do to you?"

She'd forgotten all about being slapped. "It's okay. I barely feel it now. I'm just so glad you're okay."

"Makes me doubly glad the guy is gone. He can't hurt you or Brina anymore."

"He's dead?"

"Dead dead." He smiled and turned to Celia. "You sure you're okay?"

She nodded. "I will be. The guy deserved it. It was you or him. I wasn't going to let him take out my partner. That wouldn't look good on my record."

Except there were two shots. If Celia had shot Glenn, then Glenn had to have shot first.

Evie pulled away. Blood was all over Adam's shirt. "He shot you?"

He took her hands and held them together. "Not my blood. He missed. I'm not shot, okay? Thanks to a door…and Celia."

Celia, who had come to the rescue. Evie could almost kiss the woman. "How did you know Glenn was up there? My doorbell app doesn't reach the stairs."

"Spencer told me."

Adam stiffened.

Evie yanked free. She couldn't have heard Celia correctly. "What?"

Celia's eyes widened. "I mean… It was just a hunch."

Adam shook his head. "You really suck, you know that?"

"I'm sorry."

Evie looked from one to the other. Something was going on and she hated being in the dark. "What is she talking about? Who's Spencer?" And why hadn't she heard of this other Spencer before?

Adam pointed to her foot. "You should have your ankle looked at."

"Forget my ankle. Answer my questions. Who's Spencer and how did he know Glenn was in the stairwell?"

He sighed. "I'll answer your questions, but not out here. Can you make it to the meeting room?"

If it got him to talk, she'd go anywhere. Using Adam as a crutch, she hobbled into the meeting room. What little street light came through the windows and sliding glass doors kept the room from being in total darkness.

He led her to one of the comfy chairs. She sat, but he remained standing.

"Well. Spit it out," she said.

"Sorry. This isn't easy for me."

What could be so difficult? "Why don't you start with telling me who this other Spencer is?"

"Um… Not another Spencer. Your Spencer. Spencer…Elliott."

She shook her head. "Spencer is dead. I saw his body. Didn't I?" Or had someone played a gigantic joke on her?

"Yes, he's dead. But he's still technically here. As a ghost."

"A ghost." Well, hell. Hadn't she suspected Spence was hanging around, especially with the way Bailey acted? Now Adam was confirming her suspicions. "She can see ghosts?"

"No. She can't see them. But she can feel them. Just like you can."

"Me? You mean the cold air?" Adam nodded. But just because she could feel the cold, didn't tell her anything. "How did she know it was Spencer, though?"

He shoved his hands inside his pants pockets. "Because I told her. I'm the one who sees ghosts."

"You? But you said—" Lies. He'd told her lies. "Is he here now?" She stood—which was a mistake as her ankle screamed at her—and looked around as if that would do any good. Not only was the room dark, did she really believe she'd be able to see Spencer?

"Please sit. Your ankle."

"Fuck my ankle! Is he here now?"

"I don't know. Spencer, if you're here, touch her, okay?"

Something cold touched her cheek and brought out goose bumps. She palmed the chilled skin. "Oh my God. You said you can see Spencer. But you can't see him now? How? Why?"

"I can see and hear ghosts when I'm alone."

"Hear? You can talk to them, too?" She plopped back on the chair, her ankle thankful of the move. "All this time… He's been here all this time and you didn't think to tell me?"

Holy shit. Had Spencer been spying on her? Watching her every move? She shivered.

"I couldn't tell you. No one knows."

"Your partner knows."

"Because I had just told her today. It was the only way I could find you. And without her knowledge, we might not have gotten away from Glenn."

"None of this makes sense. I felt the cold air blasts before Spencer died."

"Yeah, well, there's another ghost hanging around this building, too. It's possible you felt her."

Another ghost? Shit. "You should have told me. Especially when I suspected he was still around. Wait a minute. How long have you known Spencer was a ghost?"

"Since the day he died. When we came to your condo, I went off looking for him. To find out who killed him."

Holy shit. Secrets. Damn secrets. "All this time you knew I hadn't killed him and you treated me like a suspect. You interrogated me! You searched my home for the weapon!"

"He doesn't know who killed him. Celia suspected you. I had to go along with it until I could prove otherwise."

"All you had to do was tell me. Then I wouldn't have had to get Keith involved." Her stomach churned and she leaned over. How could she ever trust Adam again? "Oh God."

"I know. I'm sorry. I just wasn't sure how you would react. If you moved and Spencer got mad, I just didn't know what to do."

She looked up. "Spencer didn't have a mean bone in his body."

"While alive, sure. But being a ghost changes a person. And a mad ghost is bad news."

"You didn't trust me." How could she love someone who didn't trust her? It was like Keith all over again.

"I do trust you."

"No, you don't. If you did, you would have told me about Spencer before today."

"Evie… I—"

"I want you to leave."

"What about your ankle?"

"That's none of your concern. Just go. I need to think." Think about if she could ever trust Adam Fox again.

Damn. Now not only did her ankle hurt, her heart did, too.

* * * *

Adam left Evie alone in the meeting room. Man, he'd really screwed things up. But at least she knew now. Would she stay? And how would Spencer take that?

Celia came up to him. "I'm really sorry. I wasn't thinking. But you should have told her. If you're as close as I suspect, you should have told her."

"What was it you said earlier? Stop dwelling on the past. Look to the future. Well, I didn't tell her and now I'm not sure how to fix this." And he wanted to fix it. More than anything.

"You need to give her time. I'm sure she'll come around and see why you didn't tell her. If you have a good enough reason. Do you?"

"Besides the fact I haven't told anyone?" Yeah, that wasn't going to fly. "I guess you could say that technically I was afraid of Spencer and what might happen if she found out he was still hanging around."

"Are you saying he can be dangerous? He didn't seem dangerous. He saved your life."

"Let's get something straight. You saved my life. Thank you, by the way. He saved Evie's life. She's all that matters to him. And now that she knows…"

Celia's eyes widened. "She might not stay here, is that it? You think he'll be mad?"

"You've seen what he can do. He took the power out once. Hell, he probably took it out this time, too. And those building shakes? That was him, too. I need to talk to him. Would you make sure Evie gets her ankle looked at?"

"Where are you going?"

"To the roof. Where I usually talk to him."

Before he reached the stairwell to climb that long trek upstairs, the lights in the foyer came back on. Tony emerged from the basement with his hammer held triumphantly high.

* * * *

Evie wiped her eyes. The power had come back on, which meant she could probably go back up to her apartment and cry up there. Except she should get her ankle examined and make sure she hadn't broken it. Thing was, Spencer's car wasn't here. It was who knew where. Shit. She was just getting accustomed to owning a car and now it seemed she'd lost it.

The door to the meeting room opened and Celia poked her head inside.

"What do you want?" Yeah, that sounded rude, but at this point she really didn't care.

Celia entered and sat on a chair next to Evie. "I came in here to apologize. You didn't need to find out that way."

"You have nothing to apologize for. He decided to keep that information from me, not you." Didn't matter what she'd told Adam before. If he could prove ghosts exist, why couldn't he just convince her? It was like he didn't trust her to keep his secret. What did that say about her? Or rather, him? "I just can't believe he told you first."

"Frankly, I don't think he wanted to. But your life was in danger and he probably felt he had no choice. He did tell me he was going to tell you eventually. I think he just wanted to solve this case first."

"So what made you believe Adam? How were you able to communicate with Spencer?"

"Adam got the ghost to touch me. On command, practically. And later, when the two of you were up in the stairwell, he touched me again. Several times. I figured he had something to say, so I asked yes and no questions." Celia chuckled. "Or I tried. He was kind of freaking me out. But he knew you were in trouble. He knew Glenn was in the stairwell."

Spencer had communicated with Celia but never thought about communicating with her? Hell, she even called out his name and hadn't gotten a response. Why? "Men. I don't think I'll ever understand them."

"They can make things more complicated, can't they?"

"I'll say. So, what about Connor? Did he admit to killing Spencer?"

"No. We don't believe he did it, either. It's possible Marie, your neighbor, might have been possessed—"

"Possessed?" *Holy shit.* "You mean, that other ghost? But why? Do I need to be worried?"

"According to Adam, as long as we feel the cold, she can't...use us. But it seems Marie can't feel spirits. It's just a theory right now, but so far the most likely. I don't know how we're going to close this case. How can we say a ghost was responsible for Spencer's death?" Celia grimaced. "I'm sorry. I shouldn't be dumping all this on you. It's just…"

"Weird?"

She chuckled. "Yeah. Weird. I don't know how Adam was able to keep this secret for so long. I'm so afraid I'm going to say the wrong thing. Again. Please don't be mad at him."

"He accused me of murder and he knew I wasn't responsible. How can I not be mad?"

"Because he was following orders. It was my case. My call. He was doing everything to prove you weren't guilty. And succeeded, didn't he?"

"Why couldn't he have just told me?"

"Because he's a cop first. And he was working a case. A case he didn't want to be pulled off of. And he apparently made a promise to Spencer, too."

"Spencer?"

"Yeah. Adam's afraid Spencer's going to be mad that you know. Because if you know, you'll move out."

That wasn't too far off the mark. Evie was already contemplating packing up and moving to the lake house for a bit. "What could Spencer possibly do as a ghost?"

"Remember when your building shook and I thought it was an earthquake?"

It had actually shaken twice. The second time when Glenn was pushing her in the hallway. "That was Spencer?"

Celia nodded. "I can understand why Adam didn't want to get him mad. Anyway, just think about it. Adam's a good guy. He really is. Now, would you like a ride to the hospital to get your ankle looked at? I can stick around and then take you back to your car. I believe these are yours."

She pulled a set of keys and dangled them in front of Evie.

"My keys!" She grabbed them and held them against her chest. "A ride would be nice. But I don't know where my car is."

"I do. It's just waiting for its owner."

* * * *

The ride up to the top floor was quiet. The climb to the roof even more so. Adam wasn't sure what he was going to say to

Spencer to keep the ghost calm. He'd screwed up more ways than one and his brain hurt trying to think of a way to fix things.

"You got here quicker than I thought. Power must be on, huh?"

"Yeah. I guess you're getting better. Didn't melt anything this time?"

"Well, actually, I had help. Erin can be very accommodating when you threaten to make the power outage permanent. She was able to pull the lever and then bent it so it couldn't be fixed right away."

"What? They didn't lock that thing down?"

"The electrician told Tony that the box had to be locked. The HOA told Tony it had to be locked. But apparently, Tony hadn't gotten around to it yet. Lucky us, right? We probably would've blown the power if it was locked. I know I would have."

Adam shook his head. "Yeah. Lucky. Look, I'm sorry about Evie. I didn't plan for her to find out this way."

"You're sorry? No, I'm sorry. I'm sorry you felt you had to keep your ability a secret. Do you think she'll leave?"

"I don't know. Does it matter? Now that you know she's safe, are you ready to move on?"

"No. I have too much I want to say to her and no way to say it. Would she believe you if you told her?"

"Actually, I think she hates me. I'm not sure she'll listen to anything I say."

"I don't believe that. You hurt her. If she hated you, she wouldn't care. But she probably hates me, and I really want to apologize."

"We both need to apologize. But she needs time." And so did he, to come up with a solution.

"If only I could talk to her like I talk to you. Maybe I could try that possession thing."

"No. That's not the answer." But he could help. Help Spencer. But more importantly, help Evie. It just required being brave for once. "But there is a way you can talk to her."

"There is?"

Adam pulled out his smartphone.

"You're saying I can talk to her on the phone? But I've talked when you were on the phone before and no one seemed to notice me."

"Because you were missing one important element. If I tell you, you can't let Erin know. I mean it. Not a word. I really don't trust her."

"You're not the only one. I try not to talk to that psycho unless absolutely necessary. I think she used Marie to kill me. She says she was trying to save me, but I don't believe her. But I did find the murder weapon. It's stashed in the back of Marvin's SUV."

Of all the things to learn… "What? Why would she move the murder weapon? If she wanted Marie to be caught, why not leave it out in the open?"

"Your guess is as good as mine. But if it has Marie's fingerprints on it, she could be arrested, right?"

Arrested and jailed. Shit. He couldn't let that happen. Not when it appeared Marie was being used. "You let me figure that out, okay?"

This case was just getting more bizarre by the moment. How was he ever going to close it?

Spencer hovered in closer and pointed to the phone. "So, I promise not to tell Erin. What's the important element for me to talk to Evie on the phone?"

"A ghost can be heard over the phone when they're touching a person who can see them."

"What are you talking about? I can't touch anything."

"You can touch me." Adam held out his hand. "Go ahead and see. Just make sure your feet aren't too high off the floor. Or in the floor. It may not matter, but why chance it?"

Spencer's hand shook. He looked down at his feet, which were hovering above the ground about an inch above it. He took Adam's hand and dropped that inch as his feet touched the ground.

Adam tried not to let a grimace take over his face. Not only was Spencer's grip strong, the cold was nearly unbearable.

"Holy shit!" Spencer wrapped his hand around Adam's. "I can smell the air." He touched his face. "I can feel the cold. Damn, it's cold out here! But your hand is warm. Actually warm!"

And it was losing its heat quickly. But Adam smiled at Spencer's childlike behavior.

"Why didn't you ever tell me this before? Nevermind. I get it. Can't really trust a ghost you don't know, right?"

"Something like that. Plus, you're cold."

"Oh, sorry." Spencer released Adam. "Wow. Talk about a letdown. I can see why Erin shouldn't know. Touching could be addicting."

Adam rubbed his hands together. "That it can. But hopefully you won't get too addicted. Once you talk to Evie, you should move on."

"But how I can talk to her when I'm touching you? Wouldn't I just disappear when she came on the line?"

"You'd think that, wouldn't you? But other ghosts have done it. Don't see why you can't do it, too."

"Was this your plan all along?"

"To tell the truth, no. If I could have helped you move on without it, I would have gone that route. But I think Evie needs to hear from you just as much as you need to talk to her. I'm doing this for her. Your moving on is a bonus."

"So what's the plan? Do you have one?"

"Gotta figure out your murder first." But how does one arrest a ghost? Man, this whole thing was giving him a headache. "After that…" There was no way Evie would take a call from him. Not right now. Unless… He pulled out the other smartphone in his pocket.

"That's mine," Spencer said.

"Yep."

Chapter 26

Adam entered Zane's house. He'd called ahead, making sure Brina was still up. News like this was never easy, more so since it involved his sister. Would she break down? Or would she be relieved? Would she blame him or…thank him? At least he could honestly say he hadn't pulled the trigger. Not that he wouldn't have if he'd had the chance.

Brina and Zane were on the couch, watching TV. At least Adam made it here before the eleven o'clock news. Granted, no names were released until Brina was notified, but the incident would be the top story.

Brina smiled when she saw him, then her eyes narrowed. "What happened to your face?"

Adam rubbed the bruise forming on his cheek. "Glenn happened."

Her eyes widened and she stood. "He's here?"

"Don't panic. It's okay."

"How can you tell me not to panic when Glenn is here…hitting you, apparently."

"Should I leave you two alone?" Zane asked.

"No. You can stay. You're gonna find out eventually anyway." Adam sat beside his sister. Took her hand. "Brina…Glenn is dead."

"What?"

He told them about Evie's kidnapping and the showdown in the stairwell.

She covered her mouth. "Oh my God! I never knew he could… Is Evie okay?"

"Yeah. A little mad at me, but okay."

"Mad? Why is she mad?"

"Because I failed to tell her…something." And now he would have to tell Brina. Would she be just as mad?

"You didn't know Glenn would go off the deep end like that, did you?"

"It's not about Glenn. It's about me. There's something I've been keeping from you." He glanced at his friend, whose eyebrows were raised to his hairline. He was never going to live this down, was he? "You were right. I can see ghosts."

"I knew it! And you told me I was imagining things." She looked at Zane. "Wait a minute. You knew?"

Zane smiled. "Yes, dear. But to be fair, I have the same ability. I suspected he had the gift and approached him first. That's the only reason Adam told me."

"No wonder he never mentioned you before." She turned toward Adam. "So you've always seen them?"

"No. Not until after my accident at the lake, when I technically died. That missing boy apparently touched me while my spirit was out of my body. When I was revived, I came back different. Didn't know it until I was alone, though. That's when I started seeing ghosts. And I've been seeing them ever since. But only when I'm alone. I can't see them if a non-seer is with me."

Brina hugged him. "Oh, Adam. All this time…" She pulled back. "Wait. Is that why Evie's mad? Because you told her you could see ghosts?"

"She's mad because she found out from Celia."

"So you finally told your partner," Zane said. "Good for you."

"It's not like I had a choice at the time. It was tell her or lose Evie. I wasn't going to lose Evie."

"Of course not," Brina said. "Why would that make her mad, though?"

"Because I told her I could see her roommate, Spencer, and have since the day he died."

"Ohhh. And Spencer knew she didn't kill him and you accused her anyway?"

"In my defense, Spencer doesn't know who killed him. But…yeah. That."

"I'm sure once she has time to think, she'll see why you didn't tell her. I just don't understand why you couldn't tell me. I'm your sister!"

"I couldn't tell you when we were kids. You would have blabbed it to all your friends."

"No I…" She had the decency to blush. "Okay. Maybe I would have. But you could have told me later."

"Later. Like after you married Glenn? Yeah…no. It wasn't like we communicated all that much after you married him, anyway."

"Is he really dead? Did you see his ghost, too?"

"Not everyone turns into a ghost." Especially the evil. They didn't always have a choice. And it appeared either Glenn didn't have a choice, or he just didn't wish to stick around. Whatever happened, he was gone. For good. "But he is dead. How do you feel about that?"

"Guilty."

"Guilty?"

"Guilty that I'm not feeling sad. That I'm glad he can't hurt us anymore. Hey, does this mean we can go back to your apartment? No offense, Zane. You've been more than kind, but I don't want to put you out anymore."

"Oh, but putting me out is okay?" Adam teased.

"Of course! You're my big brother." She shoved him playfully in the chest. "Becca will be happy to go back. Says she misses her friend George, whoever the heck he is. I thought I brought all her stuffed animals, but maybe I missed one."

"Oh shit." He'd forgotten about George playing with Becca. Would Sabrina get mad about that?

"Oh shit, what? Do you know who George is?"

"George is the ghost in my apartment building."

"What? How would she be able to see ghosts? She never had a near-death experience."

"No, but she's young. Sometimes they notice…more. And George is harmless. He's just waiting for his wife to pass. When he discovered Becca could see him, he's been playing with her. But he can't hurt her. You rethinking about moving back in with me?"

"Well, I really don't want to go back to Springfield. That was Glenn's home, not mine. You say George is harmless?"

"He is. You don't think I'd stay there if he wasn't, do you?"

"Guess I better go pack and wake Becca."

"No, no, no. Don't disturb her. I can move you tomorrow. I may crash here tonight anyway."

She hugged him again. "While I'm not sorry he's dead, I am sorry I brought this all on you."

"It wasn't your fault, Brina. I'm glad you came to me. I'm always here for you. Don't ever forget that."

"I won't." She stifled a yawn. "Now, if you two will excuse me, I think I'm ready for bed now. See you in the morning."

Zane stood while Brina left and climbed the stairs to her room. "Should I get bedding for you?"

"Later. Sit. I need to talk about Erin McCallister. Spencer thinks she possessed someone to kill him. We just can't figure out why she would do it."

Zane took his seat. "Possessed? Like Allie was possessed?"

Zane's late wife could be possessed by a ghost once she was asleep or relaxed enough. She'd come in handy at times whenever a ghost needed help. The only reason Zane ever allowed the possessions was if he or another ghost seer was present. One touch from a ghost seer would jettison the ghost out.

"I don't think so. Spencer told me that Erin can possess someone who doesn't feel her. Make people do things without their knowledge. I have no idea how long she can possess, since she only demonstrated a brief moment to Spencer. But if she used Marie to kill Spencer, then she had to have had control for quite a while."

"Marie?"

"Oh, yeah. Spencer's neighbor. That's who Erin used."

"Wait a minute." Zane left the room briefly and returned with a notebook. "Erin had a sister by the name of Marie."

"Well that can't be a coincidence."

"No, it can't. Marie would be 55 this year."

"The age fits." Adam jerked to his feet. "Shit. I can't pin the murder on Marie. But it seems Erin wants me to. Why?"

"Maybe it's time we go talk to Erin."

He heard the 'we.' Maybe Zane could talk some sense into that ghost. "It's late. Do you want to do it tonight or wait until morning?"

"I'm not tired and ghosts don't sleep."

"Tonight it is, then." He could sleep once this case was solved. If he could solve it.

* * * *

Using her crutches, Evie hobbled to Spencer's car. She couldn't believe how freaking long it took for her to see a doctor, let alone get her ankle wrapped. It was nearly morning. Luckily, she was able to hire an Uber to take her to the car. And luckily it was still there. In one piece.

Then again, who would steal a car in the parking lot of the police station? Attempt? Maybe. But succeed? Probably not. At least it didn't look like anyone attempted to steal her car. It was still in one piece.

Evie pulled the door. Locked. Of course it was locked. D'oh! She leaned against the vehicle and rummaged through her backpack. She missed her purse. It had spots for everything. She knew she should have bought more than one at the time, but noooo. Now she would have to search for another one just as good.

Yeah, good luck with that. She hated purse shopping.

Key in hand, she pushed the fob to unlock the door. As she climbed in and got comfortable behind the steering wheel, she nearly screamed with joy. Her purse! It was in the footwell. And her phone was on the passenger seat. She'd felt lucky to be alive. Having her stuff back was a bonus.

She tossed the crutches to the passenger side. The doctor told her to stay off the foot for a few days, at least. Once she got home, that wouldn't be a problem.

After the noise and bustle at the hospital, peace and quiet were on her radar, and she didn't even bother to turn on the radio. But as she drove home, it turned out that peace and quiet were just a dream. Her brain worked overtime, and the questions wouldn't stop.

What was she going to do about Adam? Was she being unreasonable? Did he have a real reason to not trust her? Damn it. She'd been so sure he was the one. Now? How could she be with someone who didn't trust her?

Maybe she was being unreasonable. Trust took time, right? And they'd barely been together. But he'd declared his love. If you love someone, you trust them. Shouldn't matter how little time had passed. Hell, she'd been in love with Adam since she was seventeen. She kind of hoped he'd felt the same. But apparently he didn't.

She parked in the garage. Getting out of the car took more maneuverability than getting in, especially holding her backpack and purse. But she was one determined person and managed to succeed without too much pain. She hobbled into the foyer just as Adam and Zane entered from the street. Seeing him now didn't seem fair. She was vulnerable and needed more time to think.

"Is it broken?" Adam asked as he pointed to her foot.

"Just a sprain. What are you doing here? I told you I didn't want to see you." Although, her body was super happy to see him. Wanted to run into his arms and kiss him silly. Thank goodness they weren't alone. She might have done just that.

"We're here to talk to…someone." He pushed the up button.

"Awfully early to be talking to anyone, isn't it?" If it weren't for the fact that Zane was with him, she'd assume he was here to talk to Spencer. Or that other ghost. But if Zane was here… "Is Sabrina okay?"

"She's fine. More like relieved. Would you believe she was more worried about you than her late husband?"

The elevator doors squeaked open. She hobbled inside. Before she could get her hand free to push her floor, Adam pushed it and only her floor.

"Are you here to see Marie? Celia mentioned she might be…involved." Damn, she almost blurted out the ghost stuff. She'd be just as guilty as Celia for doing it, too.

"No. Ummm. Erin, actually."

"Who's Erin?" Evie didn't remember a resident by that name.

"That other ghost I told you about."

She looked at Zane. Just how many people knew Adam saw ghosts? And he couldn't share that news with her?

"Yes, I can see and talk to spirits, too," Zane said. "I run an organization called HeSMO. It stands for Helping Spirits Move On."

"Move on? What does that mean?"

"When a spirit is stuck here, it's usually because they have unfinished business. We do our best to finish up that business so they can move on to the next…" He tilted his head. "Level."

"Like Heaven?"

"I can't say. It could be. It could also be a waiting area for you to be reborn. Or to meet up with your soul mate. Or wait for them. It could be anything."

"But what if it's someplace bad?"

"It's not bad. That, I know."

He seemed pretty certain and she wanted to ask more questions, but the elevator doors opened and the men waited for her to exit first. "Is Erin on my floor?"

"No," Adam said. "I'm hoping Spencer can bring her up to the roof."

"Are you helping Spencer move on, too?"

"Yes. But he won't go until he knows you're okay."

"In the meantime, I gotta live with him?" She didn't mean for it to come out accusatory. Like Adam could control what Spencer did. That lake house was sounding so much better, but unfortunately, it was being rented out next week.

"Actually, no. Since he didn't die in the condo, he's not tied to it, so he wanted me to tell you that he'll stay away. Do you need help to your place?"

"No, thanks." Her purse was unruly, but she could manage. She'd managed this far. She headed toward her condo, but stopped and turned around. "Tell him he doesn't need to stick around for me, okay? He can move on, or whatever. I'm fine."

She left them and hobbled to her condo. When she opened the door, she paused. No cold air greeted her. She wasn't sure whether to be relieved or sad. She flipped on the light. The floor was littered with more bird crap on top of the crap she and Glenn had slipped in.

"How the hell did you crap so much? Has someone been feeding you?" Because it certainly wasn't her.

"Bailey hungry," Bailey said on his perch by the window.

He hadn't screeched Spencer's name. If she needed proof, that was it.

She shut the door, tossed her purse and backpack on the couch, and headed for the kitchen. "So am I. Let's go get something to eat, shall we?"

The mess could wait.

* * * *

Adam's heart ached as Evie hobbled to her condo. She'd talked to him, which was more than he'd hoped for. Could he still have a chance? Or was that the last time he'd see her?

Zane clapped Adam on the shoulder. "She'll forgive you."

"You sound so sure." His heart wanted to believe that, but his brain was being skeptical. And for good reason. He'd basically lied to her. Told her he didn't trust her.

"She just needs to get used to the idea. She seemed like she was dealing with it fine in the elevator."

"Yeah, because you were there. She was being polite."

Zane laughed. "Maybe. Maybe. She also seemed interested. Don't give up quite yet."

Hell, he didn't want to give up at all. But he refused to act like Keith O'Hara. If she didn't want him around, he'd stay away.

"Shall we head for the roof?"

"Yeah. I'm surprised Spencer isn't here hanging around. I hope that means he's on the roof. If he isn't..." Adam opened the door to the stairway.

"We'll cross that bridge when we get there." Zane waited for Adam to start climbing and then followed.

"Do you think it's wise that we question Erin here?" Adam asked. "I'd hate to see the building crumble. Especially since we're on top of it."

"If I knew of another way to talk to her, I'd use it. My goal isn't to get her upset."

He pushed the door open to the roof. Even at this late hour, the city lights lit up the area. Spencer was hovering along the edge, staring out at the city.

"Hey, Spencer. I'm glad you're here."

"You told me she was mad, I just didn't realize how mad. She really hates me, doesn't she?" The ghost turned around and his eyes widened. "Wait a minute. If you can see me... He can see me? You can both see me?"

"Yes, we can both see you. This is my friend, Zane. I thought you were eavesdropping in the elevator."

"No. I didn't want her to feel me. So I just popped up to my floor. Saw how mad she was and then came up here. I figured you were here to see Marie."

"Marie can wait until morning. We're here to talk to Erin. Can you bring her here?"

"I'm not sure I can bring her anywhere. That ghost hates it when I disturb her, so I doubt she'll come because I ask her nicely. So what should I tell her to make her want to come up here?"

"Tell her we want to talk to her about her sister," Zane said.

"She has a sister?"

"Just get her, okay?" Adam said.

"Oookaaay." Spencer vanished quietly.

"Don't you think they should come with sound effects?"

Zane raised an eyebrow, but didn't say a word.

"Might as well sit and get comfortable. He might take awhile." And that awhile ended up being about ten minutes.

Spencer appeared with Erin in tow. "Seems I told her the secret code. Who knew?"

She put her hands on her hips. "You better make this quick. The commercials don't last forever."

Zane stood. "Hello, Erin. My name is Zane. I'd like to talk to you about your sister."

"That's what Spencer told me. What about her?"

"She lives in this building. Doesn't she?"

Spencer's eyes widened. "Your sister lives here? Who is she?"

"So what if she does?" Erin said. "It's not like I have control over where she lives."

"You don't like her so much, do you?" Zane asked.

"No."

"Is that because she won't let you go?"

"Wait," Spencer said. "Someone can keep us from moving on?"

Zane nodded. "If the bond is strong, yes, that can happen."

"I hate her!" Erin said. "When her husband died, she had no problem saying goodbye to him. I watched him leave. I tried to follow, but I couldn't. It was like a barrier kept me from going any further. That's when I realized. It was her keeping me here. Every stinkin' year she's out there." She pointed toward the lake. "Crying about my death. Asking for forgiveness. What the hell am I supposed to forgive, huh? Forgive her for having a life? Forgive her for having a family?"

It was starting to make sense to Adam now. "Is that why you're trying to get her arrested for Spencer's death? You think if she leaves, you'll be free?"

"Wait. What?" Spencer turned to Erin. "Marie is your sister?"

"She can't hold on to me if she's not here!"

"I'm sorry, but I'm afraid it doesn't work that way," Zane said. "We should be able to help. That's why we're here."

"Right. Like, where would I go? I'm a murderer, aren't I?"

"So you did kill me?" Spencer asked.

She looked at him. "Not you. I didn't kill you. Neither did Marie. The weapon was there. I made her pick it up and stash it in Marvin's car. I figured eventually someone would find her prints all over it, but apparently I was wrong." She turned toward Adam. "What kind of cops are you?"

Adam had to laugh. "Maybe if you hid it somewhere we could actually find it?"

"Now that would be stupid, wouldn't it? What kind of criminal does that?"

"The same kind who leaves the murder weapon at the scene?" Spencer said. "So, you do know who killed me?"

"If I say, you're just going to leave me, too."

She wasn't too wrong there since that was one of two things that had to happen for Spencer to move on, so Adam went about it a different way. A way that Zane was probably plotting out already, anyway. "Will you tell us if we can get Marie to let you go?"

"Again, where would I go? Murderers don't go to Heaven, do they?"

Zane glanced at Adam, probably thinking the same thing he was: if she was a killer, she would have already been taken.

"Who did you kill, Erin?" Zane asked.

"All those guys on the lake. They all died because of me."

Spencer's eyes widened. "You killed innocent people for some kind of revenge?"

"No, that's just it. I don't mean to kill anyone. But every year, I relive that awful day. Every year, I'm taken out to that lake. And every year, I fight to get away. I just want the nightmare to end." She disappeared without a sound.

Adam felt like he was back to square one. Oh, he could find the murder weapon, but apparently it would have the wrong person's fingerprints on it.

Spencer stared at where Erin had been last. "Holy shit. What now?"

Adam stood. "Well, we apparently have a killer in this building, and if we want to know who it is we need to help Erin move on. Which means...we talk to Marie." And another person would learn of his secret. Shit, this day was just getting worse and worse.

"No," Zane said. "I'll talk to Marie. She doesn't need to know you can see ghosts."

Adam breathed in relief. "Thanks. I appreciate that."

"Do you really think she can help Erin?" Spencer asked.

"I know she can," Zane said. "What you need to do is find Erin and stick by her side. If her door opens up, you'll want to be there."

"I'm not ready to leave yet."

"You misunderstand. Seems like she knows who your killer is. Do you want that information to leave with her?"

"Oh hell no."

"We're getting there, Spencer," Adam said. "But we still need your help so you can say your own goodbye."

Chapter 27

Stifling a yawn, Adam draped his overcoat along the back of his chair and headed to Celia's desk. He had yet to get any sleep. After telling Spencer when they would return, they left the condo. Zane headed home for some rest while Adam headed toward a diner for some much-needed food. And coffee. Rest could wait. He wasn't sure he could sleep all that well, anyway. Too much going on. In his head. In his life. This looked to be one long day.

But would it be a day that ended on a high note—the discovery of Spencer's murderer—or a low one—with Erin not moving on or sharing what she knew?

No, he refused to be pessimistic. The day *would* end on a high note, with the arrest of Spencer's killer. And then he could sleep for the next couple of days. He'd need his rest if he were to convince Evie he was worth a second chance.

Celia was busy at work on her computer. She'd been there awhile, if the four coffee cups were any indication.

"Did you get any sleep last night?"

She chuckled. "Some. My mind was working overtime. Figured I might as well come in and shut it up." She looked up from the monitor. "I could ask you the same thing. You look like you slept in that suit. Back to wearing Wrinkles Are Us again?"

"Well, considering I've been up for nearly twenty-four hours, that would be why it's wrinkled. I haven't even made it back to my apartment yet. But I did get some information." He told her about the meeting with Erin.

"Oh God." Celia rested her head on the desktop. "We're never going to solve this case, are we?"

"Don't be so pessimistic. Zane is going to talk to Marie this morning. Once she realizes what's been happening, she'll let Erin go, Erin will move on, and Spencer will discover his killer. Then it's back in our hands again."

"Glad one of us is optimistic."

"It's gonna work. You'll see. So what are you working on?"

"I'm still looking to see who owns the property maintenance company. Legal was a little bit of help, but I haven't been able to tie it all together yet."

"Well, maybe once we get the name, it'll become clearer."

"You're really gonna believe…your little friend?"

He assumed she meant Erin. "Once she sees her exit, she won't have a reason to lie." He pulled a chair next to Celia and sat. No one was loitering, but he kept his voice soft all the same. "How are you really with all of this?"

"What, that my partner can see…things the rest of us can't?" Her shoulders sagged. "I am sorry about yesterday."

"Will you quit apologizing about that? I was going to tell her eventually."

"Were you? Really?"

"Yes. Really. When you meet the one, and you want to keep the one, you can't have secrets. Right?" If only he'd come to that conclusion earlier.

"You think she's the one for you?"

"I know she is. I just have to convince her that I'm the one for her."

Celia laughed. "Optimistic."

"So, back to my question. How are you really with all of this? Or do I need to find another partner?"

Her face scrunched in confusion. "I thought you liked to work alone."

Another conclusion that had hit him over the head recently. "I thought I did, too. But I was wrong. You've opened my eyes to what a partner really is, and I'm grateful. Will you stay my partner, or is this too much for you?"

"You're under the impression I'll get the promotion. This was all temporary, remember? But relax. Yeah, it still kind of freaks me out, but I'll get over that. You have a gift. I think working with you will become way more interesting now. You trust me to keep my mouth shut, though?"

He patted his stomach. "My gut says I do."

"You and your gut."

"Hasn't failed me yet. So, are you gonna continue your research or just wait for a name?"

"No offense, but…I'll continue. Just in case we need it later. But if you're just waiting for answers, why are you here instead of at home sleeping?"

"I thought I'd look into another one. Remember Michael Watterson?"

"The you-know-what at the funeral home?"

Adam shook his head. "We're really going to have to come up with another name. How about victim? Does that work for you?"

She smiled. "Yeah, that works. Thanks, Adam."

"For what?"

"For trusting me."

* * * *

Spencer popped into Marvin's condo. Erin was perched in front of the TV, her usual spot. Marvin wasn't anywhere around—he probably went to bed—but the TV was on. How Erin managed to do that, Spencer didn't know. Wasn't so sure he wanted to know, either.

He couldn't believe that Marie was Erin's older sister, but that did explain the picture he'd found in Marie's study earlier. He'd gone back after Fox and Zane left, and sure enough, the younger girl was Erin. She and Marie didn't really look all that much alike, but according to Adam and Zane, they had different fathers. No offspring resulted from their mother's third marriage, to the bastard who had molested and killed Erin. At least he went to jail, but even that didn't help Erin any. She was still stuck here.

Guess he didn't need to worry about Evie keeping him here against his will. Hell, she would probably kick him through the door if she could. At least he'd be able to apologize. Provided she answered her phone. That was the one part of Fox's plan that had a huge condition. If she didn't answer… No, he wouldn't think like that. It served no purpose, anyway.

Besides, it was time to do a little convincing. Zane was due to visit Marie any minute now and Spencer wanted to be there. But no way would he leave Erin's side to do that. Which meant…getting her to want to come along.

"Zane is going to talk to your sister."

"Good for him," she said, keeping her focus on the TV. If it was a show, he might have expected that, but a commercial for some cancer drug? Yeah, she didn't make any sense.

"We're to meet him at eight o'clock. I thought you might want to go."

"Uhhh, no."

That answer was not a surprise. "Come on. You're telling me you're not even a little curious?"

She finally looked up at him. "If you want to hear what she has to say, go. I'm not stopping you."

"But you are. If Zane gets Marie to let you go, your opening will appear. And you're the only one who knows who killed me. Since you don't want to tell me *now*, I need to be with you when it happens. If you want me to leave, just tell me who killed me now and I'll leave."

"You believed that drivel?"

"You *don't* know who killed me?" Was she just full of lies, was that it?

"No. That Marie will let me go and my door will appear." She air-quoted door.

"Why wouldn't it? She's what's keeping you here. Right? Or did you lie about that?"

"I didn't lie."

"Then what are you afraid of? The door is going to appear or it's not. If it appears, don't you want to know why?"

"*If* it appears, it could lead to someplace…bad. They still haven't convinced me that I'm not a murderer."

"Well, if you hadn't popped out so abruptly, you might have learned more." And if he knew of a way to keep her in one place, he'd do it. "According to Detective Fox and Zane, if you were destined for Hell or wherever bad people go, you'd be there already. Regardless of your feelings or anyone else's."

"They're just saying that so as not to scare me."

"No, they're not. They've talked to ghosts who have seen it happen. And apparently it's not pleasant. You're still here, therefore the door will only lead to good."

"And if my door doesn't appear, what then?"

"Then you can tell me who killed me, come back down here, and continue to watch TV alone, like you've been doing."

"What makes you think I'll tell you then?"

Apparently barbs still stung even after death. "You're going to hold me here against my will, just like your sister is, is that it? What did I ever do to you?"

She lowered her head. "Nothing. Fine. I'll go."

Nice to know he could guilt her into it. He held out his hand. If he could touch Fox, surely he could touch another ghost. "We'll go together."

"What are you doing?"

He grabbed her hand. It was cold and soft, but solid. He squeezed it gently.

Her eyes widened. "I didn't know we could touch."

Wow, he knew something before her. Score! "I just assumed, and apparently I was right. Shall we?"

Her smile was brief, but it was there. Spencer would swear on it.

They popped in front of Marie's condo, still holding hands. Zane hadn't arrived yet.

"Are you going to continue to hold my hand?"

He was hoping that holding onto her would keep her by his side, but if he said that, she'd probably try leaving, and if he was wrong… "You don't like it?"

"No, that's not it. I'd forgotten what it was like. You hoping I don't disappear on you again?"

"I just miss touching someone. But if you don't like it—" He opened his hand.

"No, it's fine." When she continued to hold on, he closed his hand over hers.

The elevator dinged and the doors squeaked open. Fox poked his head around the corner, saw them, and straightened. "Zane's on his way. I'll see you on the roof when it's over, okay?"

He gave a quick wave and was gone.

"He's pretty confident, isn't he?" Erin said.

"I guess he trusts you. Or the system. Or whatever it is." Spencer wanted to trust her, too, but she wasn't giving him the warm fuzzies.

A few minutes later, the elevator dinged again. This time Zane appeared in the hallway. "Hello, Spencer. Erin, I'm glad you decided to join us."

"Yeah," she said. "Might as well hear what the bitch has to say."

"Hey, is that any way to talk about your sister?" Spencer asked.

"Like you don't talk about your brother like that?"

He was going to argue, but she kind of had a point.

Zane knocked on Marie's door.

Marie opened the door. She pulled her robe together as if the zipper hadn't done its job. "Yes?"

"Hello, Mrs. Diamante. My name is Zane Grey. May I come in and talk to you about your sister, Erin McCallister?"

Marie's eyes widened. "Erin? What about her? She's been dead—"

"Yes, I know. I want to talk to you about her…" He leaned in close. "Ghost."

"Ghost? Is this some kind of prank?"

"Not a prank, I assure you." He pulled out a card, handed it to her, and waited for her to read it. "Please. May I come in? If you want what is best for Erin, we need to talk."

"She's not going to let him in," Erin said. "Who lets a stranger into their home? Especially one talking about ghosts?"

Spencer was about to agree with her when Zane spoke.

"If it'll help, I'm friends with Detective Fox. The detective working on Spencer Elliott's murder. If you need to call him so he can vouch for me, I'll wait."

"Oh, no, that won't be necessary. Detective Fox was very nice." Marie stepped aside and opened the door wider. "Come on in. Can I get you anything to drink? Coffee? Tea?"

"No, thank you. I hope I won't take that much of your time." Zane stepped inside and Marie closed the door.

"Let's go." Spencer pulled Erin inside the condo.

Marie indicated Zane take the couch. She flicked the card. "Is this for real? There's a business that helps spirits move on?"

Spencer glanced at the card once Marie stopped flicking it. HeSMO: Helping Spirits Move On.

"It's very much real," Zane said. "Just not advertised. Most of our members wish to be anonymous."

"Gee, I wonder why?" Erin said. "Probably because everyone would call them nut heads?"

Spencer gave her a stern look. "Stop."

"Why? They can't hear us."

Yeah, but he could. Her negativity was getting on his nerves.

Marie sat on a chair, oblivious to Erin's remark. "You're saying Erin hasn't moved on? She's here as a ghost?"

Zane sat on the couch. "Yes, ma'am."

"How do you know this?"

"I've seen her. Talked to her."

"What?" Marie looked around the room. "Is she here now?"

"She might be, but I can only see the spirits when I'm alone. It's quite inconvenient for me, but I have no control over that. She knows about this visit, though."

"Look at the way she's looking at him," Erin said. "I bet she's rethinking letting him in now."

Spencer couldn't argue the point. He wasn't sure if he would have believed someone could see ghosts before he became one.

Marie's shoulders dropped. "She must hate me."

Zane smiled. "She's frustrated, yes, but she doesn't hate you."

"Don't go telling her lies," Erin said. "I do hate her!"

"I understand you were nineteen when Erin died, but you were thirteen when your mother married Chuck Tomlinson."

Marie wringed her hands. "Yes, I suppose that's correct."

"How did you know he had something to do with Erin's disappearance?"

"I just did. Does it matter?"

"It matters if you feel you could have prevented her death."

Marie covered her face. "I don't see how any of this is relevant."

"Do you think of Erin often?"

"Every day." She played with the armchair cover. "I think of her every day."

"And what do you do every August 18?"

She looked up. "That's her birthday, did you know? She went missing on her birthday. I assume she died on that day, too. So I celebrate her birthday. And tell her I wish it had been me."

"Why did you move into this building? Was it to be closer to her?"

"I do feel…something. I mean, they found her body here, on this land. And it's not far from where Chuck kept his boat. When Don and I married, there was a vacancy. I didn't tell him why I wanted to move here, and he didn't ask."

"What do you do to celebrate her birthday?"

"I bake her a cake. And I go out on the docks and watch the boats. I believe she died out there, on the lake. He took her out fishing that day, like he did most Saturdays, but came home alone. Said she'd run off because he refused to let her date some boy. Told Mom not to worry, that she'd be back. But when a day went by and none of her friends had seen her, they called the police."

"So you relive that day?"

"I guess I do. I need to feel her pain. As my punishment."

"And what punishment is that? You weren't responsible for her death."

"Yes, I was. I knew what that bastard was capable of. And I didn't tell anyone. He told me he would leave her alone if I kept quiet." She broke down and cried.

Erin moved toward Marie. "He raped her, too? No wonder she hated him."

"You didn't hate him?" Spencer asked.

"Not at first. He was great. Always played with me. Took me fishing, just like she said. But then I had a crush on a boy. He refused to let me date. Refused to let me even see him with other friends. But on my birthday, while we were fishing, I told him I was fourteen. I could date if I wanted and there wasn't anything he could do about it. He thought differently. Said I was his, and he raped me to show me. I tried to get away, but he was too strong. Held me under water. He would bring me up in time for me to breathe, but the last time he waited too long. Or I was too weak. I figured he'd just throw my body into the water, but instead he covered me up, came back at night, and buried me at the construction site. I guess he thought they would pour cement over my grave, but work stopped for a bit and when they came back, they needed to dig for the basement. That's when they found my body."

Zane handed Marie a tissue. "I understand how you feel, but you need to let her go."

"How can I let her go? How can I forget her? It's because of me that she's dead."

"It isn't. It's because of you that she's still here. Her killer has been apprehended, which should have been enough for her to move on, but she can't. You won't let her. And because of that, she's been forced to relive that event. Do you really wish for her to continue to relive it until you die?"

"What? No!" Marie shook her head. Tears ran down her face. "Oh, Erin. I'm so sorry."

Erin moved her hand and the framed photo of Marie's late husband fell over on the side table.

"What was that for?" Spencer asked.

"I need to talk to him."

Zane stared at the frame and stood. "Would you please excuse me for a moment? I think someone wants to talk to me."

Marie looked at the frame. "She knocked that over? Erin?"

"That's my guess. Why? Does it fall over often?"

She picked up the photo of her late husband and set it upright once again. "It does."

Erin tugged to release her hand. "Let go."

"Why don't I go with you?" Spencer asked.

Zane exited the condo and headed toward the elevator. Spencer and Erin followed.

"There you are. Was there something you wanted to say to your sister?"

"Tell her it's not her fault. I provoked him."

"No, you just gave him the excuse to make his move," Spencer said.

"Doesn't matter. Marie isn't to blame. Can you tell her that?"

"I can," Zane said. "Anything else?"

"Tell her I understand. I didn't before, but I do now. Tell her...I love her."

"Okay. Be prepared. Your door might appear soon." Zane returned to Marie's condo. Erin didn't make a move to follow.

"You don't want to go back?"

Erin shook her head. "I don't want to watch her cry again. I didn't realize what she'd been through. Why didn't she tell anyone? That was the first thing out of my mouth after he raped me. That I was going to tell."

"And he killed you for it."

"Not before I pushed him." Erin covered her face. "That's how those men died, isn't it? Out on the lake. I pushed them."

"I don't know. They could have just been accidents."

A light shone overhead. Spencer stepped back. "What is that?"

"Oh my God! It's my daddy." Erin hugged him. "Thank you."

So that's what moving on looked like. Damn. It was beautiful. But she was leaving. "Wait." He grabbed her arm as she started floating upward. "You can't go yet. Who killed me?"

"Oh, yeah. Sorry. Almost forgot." She told him one wild story and then she was gone.

* * * *

Adam paced the rooftop. The morning was clear, but chilly, and the breeze cut right through his coat. He should have brought a blanket. Or waited to come outside. Yeah, that would have been the smarter option. He sat on the bench, where the building blocked the wind, and played a game on his smartphone while he waited.

He looked up several times—because ghosts were quiet—and eventually spotted Spencer. He was grinning.

"Did it work?"

He nodded. "It was beautiful."

"Okay. And…"

"She moved on."

Gah! Why did the ghost make it so hard? Did he think it was a game? Probably. "Tell me you got the information we need."

"Oh, yeah. Hugh. Hugh Latimer killed me."

The board member? They must not have checked deep enough into his financials. Adam called Zane. "You're good. She moved on."

Spencer moved in close, most likely to overhear. Adam relented and pulled the phone a bit away from his ear.

"Excellent," Zane said. "Did Spencer get his information?"

"He did. Thanks for your help."

"No. Thank you. This is a wonderful day. Oh, and I got your e-mail about Michael. I'll work on that next. Talk to you later." Zane disconnected the call.

"Who's Michael?" Spencer asked.

Adam pocketed his phone. "The ghost at the funeral home." His research came across the missing person's report, but that was it. Michael's body had never been found. Adam figured Zane would have more time to get the details from the ghost than he did.

"Zane likes helping ghosts, huh?"

"We all do. Did Erin know why you were killed?"

"No, but apparently Tony recorded the whole thing."

"What?" He knew that guy was hiding something. "How?"

"Actually, my question to Erin was how come she was down there in the first place. Seems she knew Marie was out with Marvin's car and was hoping to possess Marie and wreck the car. Thought that would get them to break up, or something. Instead, she stumbled onto my murder and a blackmail scheme.

"Seems good ol' Tony had his own camera recording the foyer. Told Hugh he was tired of always going out and checking strange noises. Whether or not he saw Connor and me fight, Erin didn't know, but he certainly had recorded it. Erin said that Connor scrammed when someone closed a door in the garage. Shortly after, Hugh came into the foyer, saw me slumped over, and then returned to the garage. Erin followed and watched him take the tire iron out of his car. He came back into the foyer and bashed me in the head! Can you believe that? Just like that! I still don't know why."

"We can find out the why later. What happened next?"

"Oh, yeah. So that's when Tony comes storming into the foyer, wanting to know what Hugh was doing. So apparently he was watching, or maybe he watched too late. Who knows? Erin said that Hugh ushered Tony back into the manager's office, and of course, she followed. That's when Hugh told Tony to be quiet. That he'd lose his job if he so much as uttered a word about it. But then she said Tony grew a backbone and basically blackmailed Hugh back. They're both idiots, if you ask me."

Adam couldn't argue that point. "So how was Marie involved?"

"Well… Erin still wanted to 'mess with Marie,' as she said it, and went back to the garage just as Marie pulled in. Decided she would implicate Marie in the murder instead of crash Marvin's car. So she possessed Marie, moved the tire iron from the murder scene, and placed it in the back of Marvin's SUV, thinking Marie's prints would be all over the weapon. But after Erin was booted out of the body, she noticed Marie was wearing gloves. Marie's prints are not on the weapon."

"Holy shit." Adam called Celia right away, just like he promised. He also kept the phone out so Spencer could hear. "Hey, I got our answer. Hugh Latimer. He's our killer."

"Hugh? I knew it!"

"How?"

"I just found out his wife works at the property maintenance company. She's in charge of the money. I didn't see it before because she works under her maiden name."

"Holy shit!" Spencer yelled. "How did I not know that?"

Adam ignored the ghost. "Wow. Good job. Maybe you didn't need my help after all."

"I wouldn't go that far," Celia said. "I don't have proof. Yet."

"Ahhh, but we do. You need to get over here. Now. It's time to talk to the building manager again. I'm sure you can get him to crack. Plus, it's your case. You should have the honor of arresting Hugh."

"You have proof? Actual proof?"

"That's the word. Just get over here. I'll explain when I see you."

"Yeah, yeah. I'll be right over!"

Adam pocketed his phone. "It's almost over, Spencer."

"I hope that bastard rots in jail. But what about Marie? I mean, she could be on that video."

"I'm not so sure she is. Wouldn't Hugh have gone after her if she were?"

"I suppose. But if he knows the tire iron is in Marvin's car, Hugh could implicate her."

"And if she's not on the video, he has no clue where the tire iron ended up. Will you relax? We'll figure it out. Okay?" Adam took a deep breath. Finally, he was in familiar territory. He just had a partner who could help.

He stood up to leave.

"What about you and Evie?"

The pleading in Spencer's voice caused Adam to pause. "Please don't let the status of our relationship keep you from moving on. Evie wouldn't want that."

"But—"

"No buts. I mean it, Spencer. This can't be an issue for you."

"But you're still going to try, aren't you? You're not giving up?"

Was it giving up if he were pushed away? "As long as there's a chance, I'm not giving up. She's the one for me. But it's not my choice. You understand that, right? If she doesn't want me in her life, then I will abide by her wishes. I will not be another Keith O'Hara."

"Even if she's wrong?"

"Even if. I want her happy. That's what you want too, isn't it?"

"Yes. That and safe."

"She'll be safe, regardless of whether I'm in her life or not."

"She loves you."

Yeah, he knew that. But right now she didn't like him. And that could be a problem.

Chapter 28

Adam opened his eyes to a strawberry-stained mouth.

"Unkka Adam!"

"Rebecca Ann, I told you not to wake him." Sabrina pulled the child away and picked her up.

Adam rubbed his eyes. He'd fallen asleep on top of the couch and in his clothes. At least his back wasn't killing him for once—doubly good choice on the couch. His alarm was due to go off at seven, in five minutes. "It's okay. I need to get up anyway."

"You got in late last night."

Yep, it had turned out to be a long day, like he'd predicted. Being awake for over 36 hours did a number on his body and mind. And sleep had occurred quickly. "We finally arrested Spencer's murderer." It had been a rough day, with lots of interrogations, but it all started when Celia had gotten Tony to cave like an old coal mine. That woman had talent. The video sealed the deal. And it appeared Hugh had disconnected the feed when he found the camera. It hadn't captured Marie moving the tire iron. If it had, who knew what Hugh would have done to her? She was one lucky lady.

"You did? Who did it?"

"Hugh Latimer. One of the board members."

"He confessed?"

"Not exactly. But the whole thing was recorded and we have the video. He really doesn't have a case."

"That's wonderful. I'm sure Evie is relieved. But shouldn't you at least be able to go in late today?"

"It doesn't work that way. Do I smell coffee?"

She smiled and put Becca down at the dinette set. "You do. Bedroom and bathroom are free, too."

He wove around the scattered toys and trotted to the bedroom. He really needed to get to work on finding a bigger apartment. Maybe there was an opening in his building. Wouldn't hurt to check it out.

The shower was refreshing, and putting on a clean suit seemed to be the cherry on top. He headed back to the kitchen and poured a cup of coffee. Stuck two slices of bread in the toaster.

"I could have fixed you breakfast."

"That's okay. I need to leave soon." He took a sip of coffee. Damn, he'd never made it this good. Having her for a roommate could be a good thing. "I'm hoping you can do me a favor later today."

"Sure. Anything."

"You don't even know what it is."

"I don't have to. You're my big brother. And I'm pretty sure it's not illegal."

He laughed with her. "No. Not illegal."

He told her his plan. Turned out he didn't have to worry. She was completely on board.

* * * *

Evie closed her laptop and leaned her head back against the couch's armrest. Her foot was propped up on a pillow, short of the other armrest. She'd been working this way for a few hours to keep her foot elevated, but it wasn't comfortable. She'd rather work at her desk, but it would take longer for her ankle to heal and she wanted that sucker healed.

She picked up her cellphone. Just like the other hundred times, no notifications. It had been eerily silent since yesterday, and she didn't even have it on mute.

Why she thought Adam would call, she didn't know. She wasn't even sure if she would take his call. He practically lied to her. When she'd asked him about ghosts he… Well, okay. Maybe lie was a bit harsh. He'd certainly skirted the issue, though. Turned it around to her. And when she'd said ghosts didn't exist, he didn't correct her. But then again, why would he?

Why couldn't he have trusted her to tell her the truth? Had Spencer really threatened to cause harm? Did he really think she'd move out? Like, where would she go? Her bank account wasn't all that flush. She barely lived month-to-month, as it was. She'd relied on Spencer's generosity more than he'll ever know. And more than she would admit.

Or maybe he did know. Why else leave her his estate?

Her cell beeped a notification just as someone knocked on her door. Wow. What timing. She opened the app. A mixture of disappointment and fear ran through her. It wasn't Adam.

"Just a minute." She moved the laptop to the coffee table and grabbed her crutches. She kept the security latch in place and opened the door a crack. "Hello, Connor. What do you want?"

The man in the hoodie looked up. His eyes were just like Spencer's. "You know who I am?"

Celia had left her an e-mail yesterday with news that Connor was no longer a suspect. That they got a break in the case and would make an arrest soon. Claimed she couldn't say more than that. So either the case was solved or they were still investigating. No one had bothered to tell her anything since that e-mail.

"I saw you at the funeral. When you were arrested."

"But they let me go. Can we talk?"

"Are you here to tell me you're contesting the will?"

"What? No." He shook his head. "No…no, I'm not. I just want to talk. I promise, that's all I want to do."

Was Spencer hovering around in the hallway? She didn't feel a blast of cold. Bailey was being quiet, too. Maybe Connor was okay.

"Hold on." She unlatched the security and opened the door all the way. "Come on in."

"Thanks." He shut the door behind him and looked around. "Wow. This is quite the place, isn't it?"

"Did you just come to see where he lived?"

"No. Actually… Have you watched Spencer's video yet?"

The video. Shit. She'd forgotten all about it. The DVD was still in her purse. "No. Haven't gotten around to it yet. Why? Didn't the lawyers give you a copy?"

"Oh, they told me I could come in and get one, or I could watch it in their office, but… I'm sure he has nothing good to say to me, and I thought if you'd seen it already, you could just give me the condensed version. But if you haven't seen it—" He turned toward the door.

"Wait." She had hoped to watch it with Adam. Now she wasn't sure she wanted to do that. "We can watch it together if you want."

"I don't want to intrude. I'm sure he has nice things to say to you."

"You won't be intruding. I'd rather not watch it alone, okay? Have a seat. I'll be right back."

Her purse was in Spencer's office, which was now her office. Seemed it didn't take much to move in, either. Just her laptop and drawing supplies. She'd have to get used to working in there. The view was spectacular and almost distracting.

She grabbed the DVD and returned to the living room.

Connor stood. "You sit. I'll play this."

She pointed to the player and plopped herself on the couch. Grabbed the remote and made sure the tissues were handy.

* * * *

Spencer hovered in the kitchen, trying to stay out of Evie's way—and Bailey's—so she wouldn't suspect he was there. He'd seen Connor walk inside the building and had followed him.

If only there was some way to reach Adam. Oh sure, Connor wasn't guilty of murder, but that didn't mean his brother wasn't dangerous.

Connor was being nice for the moment, but it had to be an act. What was he after? Trying to get on her good side so she'd give him some of the money? Now *that* Spencer could believe.

After inserting the disc in the player, Connor sat on the edge of the chair as if he was ready to bolt.

Evie started the recording. Spencer had decided to record himself behind his desk, wearing his favorite suit. Thought it would look more…legal. Instead, he just looked sterile. Or maybe he'd always looked that way. Why couldn't he have just worn jeans and a T-shirt?

Probably because he didn't own a T-shirt.

"Hey, Evie," his video image said. "By now the will has been read and you're probably in shock wondering why I left everything to you. And why I never told you. I didn't tell you because I knew you'd make me change the will, and I'm not about to do that. Well, unless I get married and have kids, in which case you won't see this video and it won't matter.

"So why did I choose you? After Mom died, you were there for me. You've always been there for me. And I know you hate people taking care of you. God knows I tried several times. But that's how I know that my money won't be wasted."

Connor twitched on the chair. Spencer pointed at his brother. "Yeah, that was aimed at you."

His video self continued, "I bet the first thing you thought about doing was giving it all away. Am I right? That's why I put in stipulations. To force you to take the time to realize that it won't be a burden. It'll be a relief. A relief not to have to worry about your next paycheck. And maybe you won't need my money. You're so talented, I'm sure you'll be making your own millions soon enough."

Evie laughed. "Yeah, right."

"Please keep it. For me. If you're watching this video, then I know I was too stupid to tell you how I really felt about you. I love you, Evie. I always have. But I'm no fool, either. I know you think of me as a brother. And I'm okay with that. I'll take you however I can have you. You and Lee were the family I always yearned for. And I did promise your brother that I would take care of you. So keeping this money will fulfill that purpose, too. See? You're not doing it for me. You're doing it for Lee, too.

"Which leads me to my other secret. My brother. Or rather, half-brother, Connor.

"It's hard to talk about someone who hates who you are for just existing. You and Lee had the perfect relationship, and you welcomed me without question. To burden you with my problems didn't seem fair. So I kept quiet. Made you think I was an only child. Because frankly, I was. Connor didn't want a relationship with me.

"Connor, you were born with a brother, but somehow you didn't want me. I never could figure out what I had done to you. But each time you boasted about how Dad loved you best, I figured he must have said something to make you hate me. So I can imagine the shock you felt when he left his estate to us equally. I was shocked. I'd been so sure he hadn't loved me, either. But I was okay with that. He was gone, and I thought that maybe then you and I could mend fences.

"But no. All you cared about was that you didn't get it all. That you didn't get control of the house so you could sell it. I always knew I didn't matter to you. But I realized then how little Dad mattered to you.

"So, Connor, you got your wish. You no longer have a brother. No one to bail you out of your messes. And Evie, don't let him talk you into doing that, either. He doesn't appreciate it. Never did. He's a no-good piece of shit."

Spencer grimaced, but Connor hadn't moved from his perch on the chair. If he was going to make a scene that would have been the time. Huh.

"Evie, I hope one day you find the right guy. I'm sorry it couldn't have been me, but so glad it wasn't Keith."

Spencer laughed as his likeness widened his eyes. He'd remembered the panic that went through him then.

"Please don't let it be Keith. I really don't like that guy. He's not good enough for you. I don't know if anyone will be. And maybe I made it harder for you to be sure, now that you have all this money. But I'd like to think I made it possible for you to take your time. You don't have to rush into anything anymore. That is the gift I gave you, and I truly hope you'll keep it.

"I love you, Evie. Goodbye."

The screen went dark. Evie wiped her eyes with the tissue.

Connor stood. "I guess it could have been worse."

"Why did you come to see him last week?" she asked.

He shrugged. "Does it matter? He's dead."

"It matters to me. I'd like to understand your relationship."

"Well, as you can see, we didn't have one."

"But you're here. You were here earlier looking for him. Why?"

"I was trying to apologize. To mend those fences he talked about. But I can't even seem to do that right. He assumed I wanted money, I got angry he assumed that, and I shoved him. I'm not proud of that, but I am working on it. I have anger problems. I have money problems. I have…problems." He chuckled. "I can't afford therapy, but I do go to Gamblers Anonymous. I gotta clean up my act if I want to keep a job. And without a job, I'm on the street. They won't let you stay on unemployment forever.

"But I wasn't here asking for a hand-out. I just wish I'd have told him before…" Connor sat down and cried.

Spencer covered his face and nearly cried himself. "Connor, Connor, Connor. Why didn't you just tell me? Damn it."

Connor took a tissue from the box Evie held out to him and blew his nose. "Do they know who killed him?"

"I was told there was a break in the case and should be an arrest soon. That's all I know. Are you going to be okay?"

"I will be. I got a job interview later today."

"Can I have your number? I can call you once I hear anything about Spencer's case."

"That's nice but you don't need to bother. I can't afford a phone."

"I can give you Spencer's." She started to get up. "Oh wait. The police still have it. Once I get it back, I can give it to you. I won't need it."

"I can't afford—"

"I didn't ask for any money. But you need a phone if you're looking for work, right? How else will people get in touch with you? Come by tomorrow. I'm sure I'll have it back by then." She took a piece of paper and wrote something on it. "Here's Spencer's number. Use it for your interview or application since it will be your number starting tomorrow."

Connor wiped his eyes. "Thank you. I don't deserve it, but thank you. I can see why Spencer loved you."

"I'm sure Spencer would have been happy to hear your apology. And to see you turning your life around." She stood with the aid of her crutches. "See you tomorrow afternoon?"

"Yeah, I'll be here. Thanks again." He left.

Spencer followed him out into the hall. If Connor was acting, the façade would break down now. But Connor continued to cry, wiping his eyes several times on his way to the elevator.

He rode down to the foyer and stopped at the mailboxes. "I'm so sorry, brother. I shouldn't have pushed you. It was all my fault. Maybe if I had behaved, you'd still be alive. Truth is, Dad didn't love me best. I was a disappointment to him. Or a mistake. One he never bothered to make again, didn't you notice? I was looking for love from the wrong person. I'm sorry I pushed you away. So sorry."

Connor exited the building. Spencer could only hover and stare. He'd been wrong about his brother and couldn't have been happier.

* * * *

Another detective clapped Adam on his back. Congratulated him on solving another case. Like with all the other congratulators, Adam pointed out that it was Celia's case. That she was responsible. She'd gotten Tony to confess about the video. The video did the rest. But would any of them listen to him?

No.

"You're a team, right? Good job."

Yeah, they were a team. But would it kill them to actually tell Celia those words? It was like she was invisible. "People are idiots," he grumbled.

"It's okay," Celia said. "You did do the heavy lifting."

"No, I didn't. You were figuring it out before I gave you a name. And then you did exactly what I would have done if it were my case. Exactly." Why couldn't people see that?

"We still don't have the murder weapon."

They both knew where the murder weapon was, though. But implicating Marie was not an option, and thankfully Celia agreed.

Adam ran a hand through his hair. "I wish I knew how to get it out of Marvin's car without, you know, asking him."

"But we could."

"What do you mean?"

"I mean, he said Marie forgot to lock his car that night."

Maybe his brain was still sleep deprived. "What does that have to do with anything?"

"Just that Hugh could have easily stashed it there, if he was just looking for an open car."

"Well, hell. You're right. I knew you'd figure it out eventually."

"Yeah, well, you would have too. I'll go set up a team to search the cars in the garage. Starting with Marvin's since we know it was unlocked." She winked. "By the way, Evelyn Harper called me. I told her Hugh and Tony have been arrested. She wanted to know if we were done with Spencer's phone. You still have it, don't you? I can give it to her when I go get the murder weapon."

It hurt that Evie had called Celia and not him. But then, what did he expect? He hadn't bothered talking to her yet. "I do, but it's at home. Tell her someone will bring it by later today."

"Are you gonna do it? 'Cuz you know she's gonna ask me that."

"You can truthfully tell her I will not be delivering the phone. Okay?"

"What are you up to?"

"That's none of your concern. And best if you don't know. She'll get the phone back, okay?"

"Fox! My office," Captain Nevin announced from his door.

Adam stared at Celia. "I won't tell him anything, okay? It's your case—"

"It's okay. We did it together. Go on. Don't keep the man waiting."

He took a deep breath. What had he done now? He shut the door behind him as his captain sat behind his desk.

"Good work on the Elliott case."

"It wasn't just me, you know. Celia did the work."

"Did she? The last time you two were in here, she didn't seem to have a clue what was going on."

"That was my fault. She gave me a job to do and I failed to update her before telling you. This was her case and I messed up. Okay?"

The captain sat back and crossed his arms. "You're saying she did all the work on this case?"

"She solved it, yes, sir. She got the suspect to confess, not me."

"Very well, then. I'll pair her up with someone—"

"Sir? I'm okay with her as a partner."

"You? I thought you hated having a partner. You swore if I gave you another one, you'd quit. Transfer. You may be a pain in my ass, but you get the job done. You make this department look good. So what changed?"

"I guess maybe I just didn't realize how valuable one could be. And Celia and I work well together. I'd like to keep working with her. She said she'd like to remain my partner, too."

Nevin shook his head. "Get out of here."

Adam smiled. "Yes, sir."

"And tell her I want to see her."

"Sure thing." Adam trotted over to Celia's desk.

"What are you grinning about?" she asked.

"It's a secret. Hey, the captain wants to see you."

"What? Now? I was just headed out—"

"Yeah, now. Partner."

She shook her head as she stood. Then froze and looked at him with wide eyes.

"Go on." He shooed her away with his hands.

One more down, one more to go. The most important one. Chills ran down his body. He could do this. He could.
He hoped.

Chapter 29

Adam pulled into the garage of Evie's condo. It was D-Day, or would that be E-Day, or Now-or-Never Day. Whatever day, he couldn't still the nervousness that ran through his body. And it wasn't just because Evie might reject him. A lot of it was toward Spencer. If it went badly, would he take it out on him?

Frankly, it really didn't matter. Life without Evie would be miserable.

"Are you going up with me?" Brina asked.

Adam got out of the car. He had picked up his sister and Becca, dropped Becca off at Zane's, and then came back here to start his plan. A plan he still wasn't sure would work.

"I'll go up with you to the floor, but not her door. Once I point it out, you're on your own. I'll be up on the roof with Spencer."

They walked into the foyer.

"Do you think he's here?" she asked.

When wasn't the ghost around? No one else was in the foyer, so the coast was clear. "Spencer, if you're here, would you do the honor of letting my sister know by touching her arm?"

She shivered and rubbed her arm. "Holy shit!"

"I guess that would be a yes, then." He pushed the elevator button.

"That is so cool. You can't see him?"

"Not while you're with me."

The doors squeaked open.

She squealed in delight. "Oh my God. Did they do that on purpose?"

"Do what on purpose?"

"Make the doors sound like Chewbacca? That's so cool."

He gently nudged her into the elevator. "I don't think it was a planned feature, no."

They rode up to the top floor. He pointed down the hall. "Her place is at the end. You sure you're okay with this?"

"Hey, I tried to hook you two up before I knew you two had hooked up. Of course I'm sure! You think I'm going to pass up on a chance for you to thank me for the rest of your life?"

"How do you figure?"

"Every anniversary of your wedding, you'll have to thank me, because without my help you two wouldn't have gotten married."

"Technically, you're the back-up. I might not even need your help."

She placed her hand on his chest. "If she's as mad as you say, you need my help. Now, go on."

"Don't forget to text me when—"

"Yeah, yeah. I know. Go on."

Adam climbed to the roof. The sun was poking through the clouds and the wind whipped his hair a bit.

"You want to marry her."

Figured Spencer had stuck around to hear that. "If she'll have me, yeah. But I don't plan on proposing today. Is that a problem?"

"No." Spencer grinned. "No problem. You have a nice sister."

"Nice? You call that nice?"

"Yeah, she loves you. You don't think that's nice?"

"I guess it is. But that doesn't mean she's always nice to me."

"She's your sister. It's her job to torment you. At least, that's what Lee always told me about Evie. You two remind me of them together. So is the case closed?"

Adam sat on the bench. "I suppose you want the details, huh?"

"Well…duh!" He laughed. "I just don't understand why Hugh would want me dead."

"His wife works, or rather, worked at the property management company. You know, that company you wanted the books audited? Why didn't you tell me you had requested one?"

"I told you I was interested in buying out the company."

"That's not the same thing, and you know it. Lucky for you, Celia was able to uncover a whole bunch of illegal activity."

"Hugh's wife was embezzling our money?"

"Bingo! And not just yours. They had an elaborate scheme going on, and he didn't want you to uncover it. When he saw your unconscious body, he took advantage. Unfortunately, he didn't realize Tony was recording the whole thing. And once he saw we had the video, he claimed his wife had coerced him."

"That sounds like Hugh. Throwing someone under the bus to save himself. All because of money."

"Money makes some people do crazy things. You of all people know that."

"I saw you got the murder weapon today. Is Marie being implicated too?"

"No. That's the sweet part. Hugh had disconnected the feed when he discovered the camera. Neither one of them had seen Marie. We got really lucky. Hell, Marie got lucky. Who knows what Hugh would have done to her. But she's in the clear."

"Thanks to you."

"No. Thanks to Celia. Couldn't have solved this without her. She got her promotion, by the way."

"So she won't be your partner anymore?"

"No, she's still my partner." His phone dinged.

Spencer stared at the phone. "Oh my God. Is it time? What do I do? What do I say?"

Seemed Spencer was just as nervous as Adam. All for different reasons.

"When you touch me you're going to sit."

"Can't we stand? I feel better standing."

"I'm not going to stand. If your door opens, I'll pass out. I'd rather do that sitting on this semi-comfy bench." And he'd make sure to lean back. Lessons learned.

"Why would you pass out?"

"Believe it or not, I don't have all the answers when it comes to ghosts. I've never seen a ghost move on. Those times when it was just the ghost and me, I passed out. All us seers do. We only know it happens because other ghosts have seen it. Like you saw Erin move on."

"Yes. It was beautiful."

"And that's how we know. You have nothing to be afraid of. Me, on the other hand…" He hadn't meant to say that last part out loud.

"Why are you afraid?"

Why indeed? What did he have to lose by not telling the truth now? "Ghosts can be dangerous when they're solid. You might not mean to hurt me, but if this doesn't go well and you get mad…"

"I can hurt you? How?"

"You'll have unimaginable strength. And if you haven't noticed, no one will come running to my aid if I scream up here."

Spencer blinked several times. "I won't get mad, then."

"That's easier said than done."

"Okay. If I get mad, I'll let you go. I promise. I don't want to hurt you. You're my friend. Whatever happens with Evie is between me and Evie. It has nothing to do with you."

"You don't have to convince me. I'm doing this for Evie. And I'm…trusting you."

"Yeah. You can trust me. I won't disappoint you."

"You'll only disappoint me if you don't move on. Are we clear?"

"Yes. And she'll be able to hear me? On the phone?"

"If she doesn't, then you'll just have to use me to tell her. Okay? But it's worked before. I don't see why it wouldn't work now."

Adam prepared for Spencer's touch. Ice enveloped Adam's shoulder.

"Wow! What a rush." Spencer sat on the bench. "And I can sit. Holy shit, I can sit. I'm not hurting you, am I?"

"No. You're good." Adam brought up Evie's number, placed the phone on his thigh, and hit call. "You're up."

* * * *

Evie pulled a banana from the bowl, peeled it, and placed it on the cutting board.

"Bailey hungry."

"So you've said." About a hundred times. Well, at least he hadn't been wailing Spencer's name. Although, she did kind of miss it, even annoying as it was. She cut the banana and placed it in the dish when someone knocked on the door.

Expecting Spencer's phone, she put the dish on the mat and hobbled over to the door. She'd been afraid that Adam would be the one to return it, even though Celia promised her he wouldn't.

And she hadn't lied. One peek through the peep hole told Evie that. It wasn't him. But it might as well have been.

Evie opened the door. "Hi, Sabrina. What brings you here?"

"I came to talk. Is that okay? Can I come in?"

One look down the hall showed no sign of Adam. No sign of a little one, either. "Where's Becca?"

"She's with Zane. He promised to take her to the zoo today."

Evie held the door open. "So why are you here? I hope you're not here to apologize. You couldn't have controlled Glenn."

Sabrina shook her head. "No, not that. I am sorry for what he did. You are okay, though. Right?" She pointed at Evie's foot. "Did he do that?"

Evie glanced down at her ankle as the crutches dug into her arm pits. "Indirectly. I sprained it running down the stairs."

"I don't know what I ever saw in that guy. But Zane says I need to stay positive. Think about the good things. Like Becca."

"He's not wrong."

"Where's your phone?"

"On the coffee table. Why?"

"Can we sit over there? You look so uncomfortable standing with those things."

Because she was. But she also didn't need this to turn into some kind of chat fest about Adam. Why else would Sabrina be here? "Sure. You want me to get you something to drink, too?"

Sabrina's face turned three shades of red. "Oh my God. I'm so sorry. I'm not doing this very well."

"Listen. I like you, Sabrina, I really do. But I can't talk about Adam. So if that's why you're here—"

"It's not." She gave the Girl Scout's sign. "I swear. Please sit."

Evie took her place on the couch and propped her foot up. The throbbing quieted to a dull ache. "So if you're not here to talk about Adam, why are you here?"

"To make sure you answer your phone." Sabrina picked up the cellphone and held it out.

Evie took the phone. "I don't want to speak to Adam, either."

"I get that you're mad at him. I was a little at first, too. I mean, I'm his sister, and he didn't tell me he could see ghosts. But I kind of understand why he didn't say. Our parents laughed at him when he told them what he saw. Laughed. Can you believe it? I don't think I could ever laugh at anything Becca said to me, unless she was telling a joke or doing something silly on purpose. You know? But that was our parents. So I'm thinking he thinks no one will take him seriously if they knew. It was wrong thinking on his part. Wasn't it?"

"So you're saying he can't trust anyone?"

"No. I'm saying that I think he finally realizes he *can* trust people. People who care about him."

"Your parents must have cared."

"No, they didn't. When they got divorced, they fought over who would get stuck with us. Neither wanted to be bothered. I don't know why they bothered having us in the first place."

As badly as Evie sympathized, she did not want to talk about him. "If Adam's not calling, who is?"

Sabrina was typing on her phone. "Just wait. You'll see."

The phone rang. Spencer's face showed up on her screen. Whoever was calling had Spencer's phone.

Sabrina leaned over. "Cute guy. Please answer it, okay?"

"Why should I?"

"Because you'll break his heart if you don't."

"I told you, I'm not ready to talk to Adam."

"And I told you, it's not him." Sabrina accepted the call. "Better talk quick, before she hangs up on you."

"Hey, Evie?"

The voice sounded like Spencer, but that couldn't be possible. "Who is this?"

"You can hear me! She can hear me! It's me. Spencer."

"Is this some kind of sick joke?" The question was not only directed to the caller, but to Sabrina, too.

But Sabrina remained silent. The caller, on the other hand… "No. I'm able to call you because of Adam. I'm solid when I touch him. Can you believe it? It's me, Evie. Really me."

"Adam, this isn't funny."

"It's not Adam. Wait. I can prove it to you. Where's Bailey?"

"In the kitchen."

"Hold on. Don't hang up!"

She just stared at the phone. What the hell was going on? She was about to hang up anyway when something cold brushed against her.

Even Sabrina rubbed her arm. "Oooh. Not fair. You could have warned me!"

Bailey squawked, "Spencerrr!"

Evie stared in the bird's direction. This couldn't be happening.

Sabrina chuckled. "Cool."

"You still there?" Spencer asked from the phone. "Bailey saw me. Did you feel me?"

Spencer. Was on the phone. Talking to her. "How is this possible?"

"I told you. I'm solid when I touch Adam. I can pick up phones. Talk. Smell. It's wonderful."

"So Adam is there with you?"

"Well, yeah, but he's not calling you. I am. Listen, I saw that Connor visited you yesterday."

"You *were* here. But Bailey didn't—"

"I made sure to stay out of Bailey's sight. And I wouldn't have even been there if it weren't for Connor. I wish I could talk to him, too. I was wrong about him."

That sound in Spencer's voice. Regret. She was sure of it. "You want me to give him the estate? Is that it?"

"What? No! No-no-no. That's yours. You need to keep it. Please keep it. Tell me you'll keep it."

"According to the stipulations, I don't have much choice."

"Evie, you know what I mean. Tell me you'll keep it."

If him knowing she was keeping it would help him move on, she wasn't about to say otherwise. "I won't do anything foolish, okay? But what about Connor? Are you saying I shouldn't help him?"

"You can help him, just not support him. He still needs to work on his demons, and I can see that he's trying, but he needs to help himself first. I love that you're giving him my phone. It's little things like that that will make his life easier, but not prop him up. You get what I'm saying?"

"I think I do, but there isn't much else I can help him with."

"Ahhh, but there is. I was in the process of purchasing the company who maintains the property of our condo. Which, apparently, is the reason I was killed. Anyway, the building manager position is open. Connor might do well there. He's very good with his hands, was always building things. I'd like you to complete the purchase and give him the job. Provided he wants it, and I think he will. It does come with a place to live. If he doesn't do well, if I'm wrong, you can fire him. Let him know that, too. Do you think you can do that?"

"I don't know anything about running a business."

"Sure you do. You run your own. You'll just have employees to do the work."

"I'll have to think about it. Can I think about it?"

"Sure, but don't wait too long. I'm sure you could buy the company at a much lower price now. And the remaining board will definitely be looking for another company, what with the scandal and all. Talk to Aaron. He's been involved from the beginning. He'll be able to help you."

"Okay. I'll talk to Aaron, and I'll seriously consider it. Does this mean you're going to move on now?"

"Not before I say this last thing. Evie…I was wrong not telling you my true feelings. I do love you, but I think deep down I knew I wasn't right for you, either. If I had known what that boy in the picture you drew meant to you, I would have helped you find him. I would have helped you find Adam."

Evie's eyes watered. "Why would you have done that?"

"Because it would have made you happy. I want you to be happy. Life is short. Please don't waste it like I did. Oh wow. Lee."

"What?"

"I see Lee! And Mom. Adam, look. Oh. He was right. He passed out."

"What? Is he okay? What's going on?"

"The pull. I feel the pull. I love you, Ev—"

The line went silent, but they hadn't disconnected.

Evie gripped the edge of the sofa. "Spence? Adam? Someone talk to me!"

Sabrina placed her hand on Evie's knee and disconnected the call. "I think Spencer moved on. Adam told me that when he's alone in the room with a ghost who moves on, he passes out. Nothing serious, he said. But I'll go check on him and bring back Spencer's phone. Okay?"

Sabrina hopped up. "Oh, and you should know. Adam took a big risk letting Spencer touch him. Apparently, the ghost is strong then. Strong enough to kill. But Adam was willing to do anything for you." She rushed out of the condo.

Evie wiped her eyes. Stared at her phone. She'd talked to Spencer. It was like he was alive again and now he was gone. Again. Her heart ached for her friend.

But Adam. He passed out. Was he okay? Really? And would she ever see him again? Did she want to?

* * * *

Someone shook Adam. He opened his eyes. That someone was his sister, and she seemed really tall. Could be because she was standing and he wasn't. "Hey, Brina."

"Hey. You okay?"

He hadn't fallen off the bench, so that was a good sign. And the cold that had permeated through his body where Spencer had touched him was slowly dissipating, not that the outdoor temp was helping any. He sat up and nodded. "I take it he moved on?"

"He said he saw his Mom and…Lee? Then he just cut off. Who's Lee?"

"Evie's brother. Good. That's good. How's she doing?"

"Emotional." She picked Spencer's phone off the ground. "I told her I'd bring this back."

"She's still mad at me, huh?"

"I don't know. She seemed pretty worried when Spencer said you'd passed out."

Worried, huh? Well, it probably didn't last. Adam slowly stood and waited a beat. His world wasn't spinning so he probably wouldn't pass out again. "You go ahead and take that to her. I'll wait for you at the elevator."

"You're not coming?"

"I promised I wouldn't return the phone, and I'm gonna keep that promise."

"But Adam," she whined. "She needs you."

"She doesn't need anyone. And she certainly doesn't want me right now. I'm giving her time."

She mumbled something.

"What was that?"

"Just wondering if you're going to wait another eleven years."

"Hey, that's not fair. I didn't know how to find her then."

"And you could lose her again if she moves. Right? She doesn't need time. She needs you!"

He'd like to believe that, he really would. But until those words came out of Evie's mouth, he wasn't going to get his hopes up. He held the door open. "Just take her the phone."

Brina shook her head as she headed downstairs. He followed her to Evie's floor and stayed by the elevator. She turned the corner and stopped. Backed up a few steps and looked at Adam.

"What?"

"Catch." She tossed the phone and dashed down the stairwell.

He caught the cell before it hit the ground. "Damn it, Brina!" But there was no going after her now. Maybe he could just knock on Evie's door, leave the phone on the floor and skedaddle before she had a chance to see him on the camera or in person. He turned toward her condo and froze after the first step.

Evie was standing in the hallway, balancing on her good foot. "You're okay? Spencer didn't hurt you?"

Everything in him wanted to run to her. Hold her close. But he remained glued to his position. "I'm fine. You?"

She nodded. Then shook her head. Started crying.

Ah, damn it. Instinct had him rushing to her. His brain stopped him before he could hug her, but his heart ached to hold her. "Evie. Spencer's good. He moved on."

She sniffled. "I know. Are you moving on, too? I don't want you to move on."

Hope was a dangerous thing to have. It caused too many broken hearts. But she was saying the words, not someone else. And she wouldn't be that cruel. "I'm not going anywhere you don't want me to. I love you, Evie."

She lurched into his arms. Hugged him. Held him tight. Burrowed her head into his shoulder. "I love you, too. I want you to stay."

Damn it. Sabrina was right. He *would* have to thank her. And he was okay with that if it meant having Evie in his arms whenever he wanted.

Chapter 30

Lying in bed, Evie lifted her cellphone from the nightstand. Over two hours before her alarm would go off and she couldn't sleep. Might as well turn off the alarm, since it seemed she was up for the day.

Adam wrapped an arm around her and snuggled in close. "Time to get up?"

"Not yet. Go back to sleep." Sleeping in the same bed with him every night since Spencer moved on had been heaven. Turned out Adam didn't need to get a larger apartment for him and Sabrina. He'd pretty much given his apartment to her. And Evie was okay with that. Especially if he said yes.

Probably part of the reason for her insomnia. The other part had to do with lawyers. And financials. And contracts. Her head was still swimming with all the details. But at the end of the day she should be a business owner, and then they could celebrate. Celebrate with her asking a huge question.

Oh man, this day couldn't end fast enough.

"What's the matter? You nervous?" he asked.

Nervous. Anxious. Terrified. Yeah, terrified. Not because she was afraid he'd say no. More like she still wasn't sure how to be a business owner. The previous owner was supposed to go over the audit of the books annually, but had trusted Hugh's wife. Mainly because he'd been sleeping with her, *with* Hugh's knowledge. The whole thing was icky to think about, and one of the reasons she hated having money. It made people stupid. She was determined not to be stupid. "Guess I just have to get used to the idea."

"Ah, you'll be great. Just tell yourself that you're doing this to help Spencer's brother."

Connor had been thrilled with her proposition, even knowing it was all probationary. Once she signed everything and made it official, he would be able to move into the manager's residence. But what if he had a relapse in judgment? Could she really fire him? He was Spencer's brother. "I have no idea what I'm doing."

"Stop thinking." He leaned up and kissed her cheek. "You need to relax. I know a way. You know, if it'll help."

She laughed. She knew all about his relaxation techniques.

He kissed her neck. "How much time do we have?"

Already his kisses were heating her up. Especially when he latched onto a nipple. Sleeping in the nude made it easy to find. Well, if she couldn't sleep… "At least two hours."

"Two hours? Hmmm… Maybe I should go back to sleep."

Whether he was teasing or not—and she was fairly certain he was—she pushed him onto his back and straddled his body. "Too late. You revved up my engine."

He tweaked her nipples and she nearly came. "You don't say."

She rubbed up against the object of her desire, eliciting a gasp out of him. She loved the way he reacted to her. Hell, she loved him. And would love him forever, if he let her.

She lowered herself on him. Oh yes. This was what she needed. All her anxiety disappeared. She would just bask in feeling Adam. Life was good. And it would get better. She was sure of it.

As they climaxed together, she collapsed on top of him. She was certainly relaxed now.

He rubbed her back. "Gonna go back to sleep now?"

"No. But I don't mind staying here and snuggling."

"Snuggle all you want. So what's the plan for today?"

"Oh, sign some papers to buy the business. Sign some papers to become the management company for this building. Oh, and sign some papers for Connor's employment." So much for a paper-free society, huh? As long as there were lawyers, there were papers to sign. At least, that's what it seemed like.

He kissed her neck. "You sure you don't need help picking up Connor?"

She shook her head. "If he had a lot to move, I'd take you up on it, but he said he doesn't have much, and what he does have, he doesn't want in his new place. I told him he could have Spencer's bedroom furniture, since I won't be needing it anymore."

She and Adam had moved her stuff into the master bedroom. It had taken some getting used to, but it was her room now. No, their room. She hoped. Spencer would have wanted her to treat it that way, too.

"Let me know when you want to move the furniture and I'll come over."

"Don't you think I could help him move? My ankle is all healed, or didn't you notice when we moved my furniture in here?"

"I noticed. But it's not like you moved it far. Plus, how else am I going to feel like He-Man if I can't help move some furniture?"

"I told him he could have Spencer's clothes, too. If he wants them. And they fit."

Adam shook his head. "That's right. Rub it in. I'm not fat, though."

She almost laughed, remembering his look of mortification when he couldn't button Spencer's suit coat. Spencer might have been as tall as Adam, but in muscle, he was downright skinny. "I didn't say you were. You're my He-Man. And you have very nice muscles."

Ahh, she could lie here all day. That would be bliss. But then they wouldn't have anything to celebrate tonight.

And they would celebrate. She couldn't wait.

* * * *

Adam lay in bed as Evie walked into the bathroom. Naked as the day she was born. Was he the luckiest guy or what?

But while she was getting ready for her appointment, he sprung into action. He didn't need to be at work until nine, so he had plenty of time. Well, not plenty. She had an eight o'clock appointment, so he still needed to hurry.

He took a quick shower in the other bathroom. She was still in the master bath when he returned. Not wasting any time, he dressed, putting on a pressed suit. It still kind of stung that none of Spencer's suits fit him. The people at the station would have been jealous for sure. But maybe it was a good thing. He didn't need to be a walking reminder that she'd lost her best friend. And while she had her good days, there were still moments when it would hit her. He was just glad to be there when those moments occurred.

He patted his pocket—still there—and trotted into the office. Uncovered the bird cage. "Hey, Bailey!"

"Bailey hungry."

"You don't say." Of course, he said that every morning. Probably his way of saying hello back. Adam opened the cage door and gritted his teeth. He'd only done this once before and it hadn't gone well. This time he was prepared. He draped the towel over his arm and held it out. "You ready?"

Bailey hopped onto the extended arm, as if he'd done it all the time.

Adam took the bird to the kitchen and settled him on the perch. His arm survived, poop-free. Whether that was thanks to the towel or Bailey liked him now, Adam didn't know. Or maybe Bailey knew he wouldn't get fed if he crapped on his feeder.

Yeah, that was most likely it.

Adam grabbed one of Bailey's bowls and poured some feed into it. Placed the bowl on the mat like Evie had shown him. Bailey jumped down and proceeded to eat.

Him. With a pet. Who knew he could do that?

He patted his pocket again.

Coffee brewing. Check. Bagel in the toaster. Check. Cream cheese and silverware on the table. Check. Now he waited. But not for long. When she came into the kitchen, he stood. "You look hot."

Who knew he had a thing for smart business women? Okay, one smart business woman. His smart business woman.

She looked down at her business suit. "I was going for professional."

"You are. Professionally hot. To me. Sit down. I'll get your breakfast." He grabbed the toasted bagel and placed it on the plate. Took the plate and the coffee and placed them in front of her.

"You didn't have to go to all this trouble. You even fed Bailey."

"I did. See? I'm not a total slacker."

While she spread cream cheese on her bagel, he sat and pulled out a box from his pocket. "Evie?"

She looked up, saw what he held, and froze. "What's that?"

"I know we haven't been together long, but I feel like I've known you at least eleven years, and I don't want another second to go by without you knowing how much you mean to me." He opened the box displaying a diamond and pearl—her birthstone—engagement ring. "I love you and will love you forever. Will you marry me?"

"Oh Adam." She put the knife down. "You beat me to it."

That wasn't the answer he'd been expecting. "What?"

She climbed onto his lap. "I was going to propose to you tonight. During our celebratory dinner. Because I love you and will love you forever. So, yes. I'll marry you."

He laughed and slipped the ring on her finger. "Ah, Evie. Great minds, huh?"

"The greatest." She kissed him.

From the Author

The last few years have been rough. I can't deny that. All I have to do is look at how long it has taken me to finish this story. I thought maybe the pandemic was to blame. It wasn't. Then I thought it was because I had a person of color as one of the main characters. It wasn't. And while I don't like to THINK my health had anything to do with it, apparently it did. Seemed it took one clear CT scan and the words "remission" to re-awaken my interest in writing. Go figure!

So thanks to all of you who have patiently waited for this book to be released. I hope it meets your expectations. And if you can, please leave a review. It will help this book be seen by more people.

I promise, it won't be another four years for the next book to be published. But it won't be in this series. Or the vampire series. I've tried my hand at something new. If you want to know more, and haven't already subscribed, now would be a good time to sign up for my newsletter. You'll get notified first about all future books. Plus, you'll get a free short story for signing up. Just go to my website, http://stacymckitrick.com, and look for the form on the home page. It's easy!

About the Author

Stacy McKitrick always had stories in her head; she just never knew what to do with them. Then one day she decided to give writing a try and discovered the passion she'd been looking for all her life. She waived goodbye to accounting and now spends her time writing romance featuring vampires, ghosts, and aliens. All with happy endings, of course. Born in California, she currently resides in Ohio with her husband. They have two grown children. You can learn more about Stacy at her website www.stacymckitrick.com.

Books by Stacy McKitrick

Ghostly Encounter series:
Ghostly Liaison
Ghostly Interlude
Ghostly Protector

Bitten by Love series:
My Sunny Vampire
Bite Me, I'm Yours
Blind Temptation
A Vampire Wedding
Biting the Curse
Finding the Perfect Mate

Short Stories in the Following Anthologies:
Home for the Holidays
Love's a Beach